RANDOM
HOUSE

LARGE
PRINT

THE
INVISIBLE
MOUNTAIN

THE

INVISIBLE

MOUNTAIN

CAROLINA DE ROBERTIS

RANDOM HOUSE
LARGE PRINT

Published in the United States of America by Random House Large Print in association with Alfred A. Knopf, New York.
Distributed by Random House, Inc., New York.

Cover art by Marc Yankus
Cover design by Barbara de Wilde

Grateful acknowledgment is made to the following for permission to reprint previously published material: Alfred Publishing Co., Inc. and SADAIC Latin Copyrights, Inc.: Excerpt from "El Dia Que Me Quieras," words by Alfredo Le Pera, music by Carlos Gardel, copyright © 1961 (renewed) by Korn Intersong Ed. MUS (SADAIC). All rights on behalf of Korn Intersong Ed. MUS administered by Rightsong Music, Inc. All rights reserved. Reprinted by permission of Alfred Publishing Co., Inc. and SADAIC Latin Copyrights, Inc. • Pemora Music Publishing Co., Inc.: Excerpt from "Caminito," words by Gabino Coria Peñaloza, music by Juan de Dios Filiberto. Reprinted by permission of Steven Morand, on behalf of Pemora Music Publishing Co., Inc. • Sony/ATV Music Publishing LLC: Excerpt from "I'll Follow the Sun" by John Lennon and Paul McCartney, copyright © 1964 by Sony/ATV Music Publishing LLC. All rights

administered by Sony/ATV Music Publishing LLC,
8 Music Square West, Nashville, Tennessee 37203.
All rights reserved. Reprinted by permission of
Sony/ATV Music Publishing LLC.

The Library of Congress has established a
Cataloging-in-Publication record for this title.

ISBN 978-0-7393-2857-6

www.randomhouse.com/largeprint

FIRST LARGE PRINT EDITION

10 9 8 7 6 5 4 3 2 1

This Large Print edition published in accord with the
standards of the N.A.V.H.

Tonita and Pamela,
this book is for you

But you, why do you return to so much woe? Why do you not climb the delectable mountain, the source and cause of every happiness?

—DANTE ALIGHIERI, **Inferno**

A silence so great that hopelessness is shamed. Mountains so high that hopelessness is shamed.

—CLARICE LISPECTOR, **Soulstorm**

CONTENTS

PAJARITA

Uno The Girl Who Appeared in a Tree 3

Dos Strange Wires and Stolen Sacraments 60

EVA

Tres Voices, Faces, Wineglass, Table, Words 121

Cuatro The Art of Making Oneself Anew 192

Cinco Across Black Water, a Secret Sea 246

SALOMÉ

Seis The World Is Pushed by Many Hands 329

Siete Steel Rabbits and Songs That Melt Snow 379

Ocho Keens, Howls, Hunger for the Sun 451

Nueve Soft Tongues by the Millions 489

Acknowledgments 539

PAJARITA

THE GIRL WHO APPEARED
IN A TREE

When Salomé finally wrote to her daughter—
by then a young woman, a stranger, thousands
of miles away—she said **everything that disappears
is somewhere,** as if physics could turn back time and
save them both. It was a maxim she'd learned in
school: energy is neither lost nor created. Nothing
truly goes away. People are energy too, and when you
cannot see them they've just changed places, or
changed forms, or sometimes both. There is the exception of black holes, which swallow things without leaving even the slightest trace, but Salomé let
her pen keep moving as if they did not exist.

Her skirts were wet and clung to her legs and her
pen moved and moved without her hand seeming to
push it, forming the spires and spikes and loops of
cursive words, sharp **t**'s and **j**'s, **y**'s and **g**'s with knots
at their base as though to tie themselves together, tie
women back together, and as she wrote the loops
grew large, as if more rope were needed to bind what
had blown apart inside her, and not only inside her

but around her, and before her, in her mother's days, her grandmother's days, the hordes of stories Salomé had not lived through but that came to her as stories do—copiously, uninvited, sometimes in an easy sprawl, sometimes with a force that could drown you or spit you up to heaven. Other stories had never come; they went untold. They left hollow silence in their place. But if it was true that everything that disappeared was somewhere, then even those still breathed and glittered, somewhere, in the hidden corners of the world.

The first day of a century is never like other days, and less so in Tacuarembó, Uruguay, a speck of a town, known for starting centuries with some peculiar miracle or another. And so the townspeople were primed that morning, ready, curious, tingling, some drunk, some praying, some drinking more, some stealing gropes under bushes, some leaning into saddles, some filling gourds of **mate,** evading sleep, peering at the slate of a new century.

A century before, in 1800, when Uruguay was not yet a country but just a slice of colonial land, huge baskets of purple berries had appeared at the altar of the church. They came from nowhere, succulent and perfectly ripe, enough to feed the town twice over. An altarboy called Robustiano had watched the priest open the door to find the gift sweltering under Christ's feet. For years Robustiano would describe the priest's face when he saw those berries sweating in the stained-glass sun, three baskets as wide as two men's chests, the fragrance rising to intoxicate God. Robustiano spent the rest of the day, and the rest of his life, describing the way it happened. "He just turned white, white as paper, then he went pink, and his eyes rolled into his head, and—**páfate**—he collapsed onto the ground! I ran over and shook him, calling, **Padre, Padre,** but he was like a rock." Years later, he would add, "It was the smell that was too much for him. You know. Like the smell of a woman who's been satisfied. **El pobre padre.** All those nights alone—he couldn't take it, those berries hot from the sun, in his church, too much for a priest."

Women, gauchos, and children came to feast on the berries. The pews were not accustomed to such a crowd. The berries were small and bulbous, ripe and tart, different from anything that had been seen growing in these lands. As the town lay down for a digestive siesta, an octogenarian stepped up to the altar and told the tale she'd heard in her youth, of the miracles that came to Tacuarembó on the first day of each century. "I'm telling you," she said, "this is our miracle." Her bearded chin was stained with convincing purple juice. Miracles are miracles, she said; they come unannounced and unexplained and have no guarantee of giving you what you want; and yet you take them; they are the hidden bones of ordinary life. She told them the story of New Year's Day one hundred years prior, in 1700, exactly as it had been told to her, and no one had a decent reason to doubt this: on that very day, songs in the old native Tupí-Guaraní language had haunted the air, from one sunrise to the next. Though most **tacuaremboenses** had native blood mixed in their veins, even back then many had lost the tongue. But still, the sounds were unmistakable: the guttural clips, the lilt like a stream shocked by stones. Everyone could hear them but no one could find the singers; the music rode, disembodied, potent, broken, on the wind.

Pajarita heard all these stories as a little girl—the berries, the songs, the purple-skinned woman. She had no idea what Guaraní sounded like. All she heard at home was the Spanish of Tacuarembó, the hum of fire, the staccato of knife through onion, the low rustle of her aunt Tita's skirt, the bright lament of her brother's battered guitar, the crows outside, the hooves of horses, the chickens quibbling, her brother berating the chickens, Tía Tita's constant fold and clean and stir and cut and sweep and pour. Tía Tita barely spoke a word, except when she told stories, and then she was unstoppable, exhaustive, demanding of uncompromised attention. She told them as she cooked. They purled and flowed and rushed from her, spilling everywhere, filling their one-room hut with fluid spectres of the dead.

"You have to know," she'd say, "why your brother is called Artigas," and this was Pajarita's signal to come and cut beef for the stew. She knew the contours of the story just as she knew the knife's shape before she grasped it. She nodded and came and stretched her ears so wide they felt like the openings of wells.

"He's named after your great-grandfather. I know some don't believe it, but José Gervasio Artigas, the great liberator of Uruguay, is my grandfather—it's true. Yes, he led the fight for independence, with gauchos and Indians and freed slaves. Everyone knows he did that and next time I'll tell the story. But he also sowed his seed in the belly of a gaucho's daughter with hair down to her knees. Analidia. She made the best blood sausages this side of the Río Negro. She was fourteen. No one will believe you, but you can't let that matter, you have to be relentless to keep history alive. **Mira,** Pajarita, cut the meat a bit smaller. Like this."

She watched Pajarita until she was satisfied, then bent over the cooking pit and stirred the coals. The raven-haired girl holding blood sausages hovered behind her, translucent, wide-eyed, palms opening and closing on the meat.

"**Pues,** that José Gervasio, he spent one night in 1820 sweating on fresh hides with Analidia, right before he was defeated by the Brazilians. He fled to the Paraguayan forest and was never seen again. Analidia gave birth to a perfect baby girl. Esperanza. My mother. Remember her name? She was stronger than a bull in a stampede. When she grew up she fell in love with El Facón, that crazy gaucho, your grandfather. He was born Ricardo Torres but it didn't take him long to earn his real name. Nobody wields the **facón** knife like he did. I'd like to see the angels try."

Pajarita, chopping, chopping, saw her grandfather, El Facón, as a young gaucho, holding his own **facón** up to the sky, blade glinting, dripping fresh red bull blood to the ground.

"In those early days, before your father and I came along, El Facón was famous for his sweet voice, touchy temper, and deadly aim. He roamed the land freely with his **facón** and his **bolas** and lasso and he chased down cattle and took their flesh and hides south to the ports. He brought home gifts for Esperanza, jewels from India and Rome, fresh from exotic ships, but she didn't care much about them. They piled up in the corner of their hut. She wanted him next to her, more than anything, and so she suffered. When I was born she was alone. She made herself sick reading the leaves of her ombú and ceibo tea, which bore terrible warnings. Obvious warnings. War was everywhere. Every season a new tyrant came through, gathering an army, killing an army off, gaining power, losing it. Young men cut one another up and threw the pieces to the dogs. So much blood was shed the earth should have turned red. Don't make that face, Pajarita. Look, the water's boiling."

Pajarita squatted at the red-hot cooking pit and heaped the beef into the pot. It was flesh from a cow, not youngman flesh. Late sun lacquered the dirt floor, the table, the sleeping hides; soon it would be time to light the lamp.

"So there they were, El Facón and Esperanza, living in a countryside torn apart by fighting. And then the Saravia brothers came. Aparicio and Gumersindo—he was doomed, that Gumersindo—and grew their army here in Tacuarembó. They were hell-bent on independence from the latest tyrant, they were sure that they would win. Your abuelo, El Facón, he believed everything they said. He followed them out of Uruguay, to Brazil, into the battlefields. There are things he saw there that he never uttered, that he swore he wouldn't say even in hell. The devil couldn't stand it, he said. So we don't know. But we do know he buried Gumersindo with bare hands, then watched the enemy dig him up, cut off his head, and parade it everywhere. Well, after that, three years after, El Facón trembled back to Esperanza. They built this **ranchito,** this very one we stand in now, and your father was born here, and so was your brother Artigas. And that's how Artigas got his name."

Tía Tita stirred the stew and fell silent. Pajarita teemed inside (with severed heads and long long hair and gems from overseas) as she cleaned the bowls and knives.

Pajarita's brother, Artigas, remembered exactly when Tía Tita moved in: it was 1899, when Pajarita was born the first time, before the tree, before the miracle.

That year, he had turned four and his mother, La

Roja, had died in childbirth. She left nothing but a sea of blood and a baby with big black eyes. The birth before that had ended in death also, but it had been the baby who had died, and Mamá who stayed to cook and sing another day. This time she stopped moving. The blood soaked the pile of hides the family used for sleep and they were clearly ruined, so Artigas was afraid when he saw his father, Miguel, rubbing them against his face, weeping, staining his skin red. The baby was crying. Miguel ignored her. There was no sleep that night. In the morning Tía Tita came, and looked around the hut. La Roja's cow-skull stool had been taken from its place at the table. Miguel held it with both hands, sitting still, facing the wall. Behind him, Artigas sat on congealed hides, holding a writhing baby. The cooking pit was cold and empty; Tía Tita filled it with wood. She scoured the bloodstains from the walls, made **tortas fritas,** hauled out the ruined hides, and cleaned the clothes. She found a young mother four hillocks over to nurse the unnamed baby. **Esa bebita,** that baby, they called her over the wells of Tacuarembó.

Tía Tita stayed with them, and Artigas was glad; his aunt was like an ombú tree, thick-trunked, alive with silence. He curled into the shade of her. He slept against the warm bark of her body. The seasons churned from cold to heat and back to cold. Miguel grew hard, like beef in smoke. He didn't touch the baby. One night—as the winter wind swept through the cracks in the walls, and outside the treetops arched and swung against clear sky in which the moon looked big enough to spill a calf out of its belly—the baby girl cried in Tita's arms.

"Shut her up, Tita," Miguel said.

"It's the wind. And her teeth are coming in."

"Then kill the little whore!"

Artigas crouched into the shadows. His nameless sister gazed at her father with large eyes.

Tita said, "Miguel."

"Shut up."

"Miguel. Calm down."

"I'm calm. I said kill her."

Tía Tita tightened her arms around the baby and stared at her brother, who stared at the baby, who did not look away. Artigas felt the need to defecate; he couldn't stand the expression on his father's face, a look that could have slashed a man to pieces. The fire ebbed and crackled and his father turned and pushed through the leather curtain at the door. Artigas imagined him standing outside, alone, under a bowl of stars, and heard him slide onto horseback and ride out over flat earth.

The next morning, the baby was gone. Though they all slept on the same hides, the Torres family hadn't felt her leave. A thorough search of land around them yielded absolutely nothing: no crawl-marks, no clues, no miniature corpse. A week after her disappearance, the gossips of Tacuarembó proclaimed her dead—or, as the devout Doña Rosa put it, carried off by angels into heaven. She had died of starvation. She had died of abandonment. She had died under an owl's claws, unnamed, unwanted. Miguel said nothing to this, neither agreed nor disagreed, neither wept nor smiled.

Only Tía Tita kept searching for the baby, with a mare's tireless pace. She looked everywhere: green fields, low hills, thick bushes, tall or deep or shady trees, the sun-drenched slope that led to town, the plaza, the church, the three stone wells, and the homes—**ranchitos** peppered sparsely along the landscape, small cubes with cut-out windows, the women inside ready to cluck their tongues and gesture **no.** At night, Tía Tita brewed a tea of ombú and ceibo leaves. She stared at hot, wet shapes for a sign of the girl's whereabouts, or at least a sign of her death. None came. The search went on.

She took Artigas on some of her quests. One of them changed him indelibly (and he wondered, years later, as an old man toting rifles through the jungle, whether without that day he might have aged uneventfully in Tacuarembó). It happened on a Sunday that began with mass at the town church, a place Artigas hated for reminding him of the last time he'd seen his mother, enshrouded in black cloth and wildflowers. The priest spoke with a passion that edged his mouth with spittle and Artigas' knees got sore. On the way home, his aunt pulled the bridle and changed the course of their ride without warning or explanation. Artigas gazed around him at the grass, the tall eucalyptus, the distant sheep. No sign of his sister. They rode in silence, the sun's hot liquid all around them.

An hour passed. Artigas grew restless. "Tía," he asked, "how much longer will we look?"

She neither answered nor slowed down. Her skirts sang **swish, swish** against the horse's skin. The detour might be for a special sprout or crooked leaf or bitter root for one of her healing teas or balms. She was always gathering and gathering. In town she was notorious for hitching her skirt up to her thighs so she could carry weeds she'd ripped out of someone else's ground. The Gardel boys teased him about it, I saw your tía's legs covered in mud, your tía's crazy to chase dead babies. Artigas had come home scraped and bleeding and victorious.

When Tía Tita finally stopped, she slid off the horse and didn't move. He slunk down behind her.

They stood in an unfamiliar field. There were no cows, no sheep or people, no baby girls falling out of the sky, nothing at all except grass and a couple of ombús. Empty. Empty. Sisters can't be found in empty space. Little girls do not survive the wild. Even if they found her she would be mangled, all white bone and gnawed flesh, like the carcass of an abandoned sheep. Artigas sat down and stared at Tía Tita's back, with that long, dark braid running down its center like a seam. She stood impossibly still. He waited. Nothing happened. The sun bore down. He was hot and he wanted to slap something. This bare, dumb field. This heavy sun. That strange, unmoving back of Tita's. He leaped up. "Tía, what are we doing here?"

"We're listening. To birds."

Artigas opened his mouth to protest this absurdity but nothing could come out because in the time it took to draw his next breath it had occurred, it was too late, the sound of the field flooded his body, birds sang in the sky and in the leaves, his bones were bursting open, there were birds in his bones, singing, small and loud and delicate, hidden in flesh, hidden in foliage, saying the unsayable in keens and croons and cries, almost unbearable; the field, the fierce little throats, the open world, beyond his understanding, and the sound shimmered open and spilled a secret music that could steal him and never bring him back. He filled with terror and something else and had to pee or cry but couldn't, and so he buried his face in musky grass and listened to birds.

They found no baby that day. In fact, on New Year's, it was neither Tía Tita nor Artigas but young Carlita Robles who galloped to the plaza with the news. Artigas saw her walnut braids flying behind her with the exact same hue and gleam as her horse, as if they had been soaked in the same dye. Her timing was perfect. The century was nine hours old. The plaza's cobbles sizzled from the stare of morning sun. Stragglers still clung to the site of the party: snoring drunks, young lovers, stray dogs, Artigas with his worn guitar (with which he strained, against all reason, to enter the hidden lairs of sound). The devout

Doña Rosa still hadn't emerged from church. She'd been there since midnight. She'd been fasting since Christmas so that God would not make their miracle a bad one, like a massacre or cholera or a flood of infidelities (though nobody took her campaign too seriously, as three years earlier, when her son had disappeared with Aparicio Saravia's rebel forces, she'd become obsessed with fasts and prayer and if her husband couldn't find her he simply rode to church, where he'd invariably catch his kneeling wife and bring her home to cook his dinner. Such a patient man, people said. Not an easy lot, to be cuckolded by God).

"I found it—the miracle!" Carlita called. "There's a baby in a tree!"

Artigas stopped strumming, the couples stopped kissing, and Alfonso the shopkeeper lifted his groggy head from the bench.

"Are you sure?"

"Of course I'm sure."

"Let's go see."

They went to the chapel first, to tell Doña Rosa. Stained light eased over their heads and sidled to the pews, down the aisle, over Doña Rosa's pious back. Carlita dipped into holy water and made a rushed sign of the cross. Artigas followed suit for her sake (she was so pretty).

"Doña Rosa," Carlita whispered. "The miracle. There's a baby in a ceibo!"

Doña Rosa looked up from her rosary. "A baby?"

"Yes."

"Ah." She frowned. "What a blessing."

They rode the dirt path toward the eastern edge of Tacuarembó. Artigas settled into the hot equine muscle beneath his legs. The sleepless night had left a veneer of alert exhaustion and he didn't want to rest. He would ride his horse to the edge of town; he would ride his horse to the edge of the world; it was a new century, he would ride and ride, and a baby could be, no it couldn't, impossible, but if it was. How bright the colors were around him, the green and gold of summer grass, the hot blue of morning sky, the darkwood brown of the **ranchitos** out of which more people came to join their travels. Kerchiefed women craned their heads through curtained doorways for the news, then left embers glowing alone in cooking pots. Men drinking **mate** in the sun untied their horses and scooped their children into saddles.

The group doubled, and doubled again, growing the way armies do as they sweep through towns. By the time they arrived at the ceibo tree, the sun had brushed its zenith and begun to slide. The tree towered over the eastern well, and at the very top, thirty meters from solid earth, grasping a slim branch, there perched a girl.

She was not quite a year old. Her skin was two shades lighter than hot chocolate and she had high cheekbones and chaotic hair that spilled to her naked waist. Her eyes were round and moist like birthday cakes. She looked neither afraid nor eager to descend.

Artigas threw his head back. He burned to catch her eye. **Mírame,** he thought.

"She's a witch!" one woman said.

"A **bruja** sent us a **brujita**!"

"Don't be ridiculous," snapped Doña Rosa. "She's an angel. She's here to bless Tacuarembó."

"With what? A rain of baby caca?"

"That's no angel, it's just a child."

"A dirty one."

"Maybe she's one of the Garibaldi kids. They're always climbing trees."

"Only the Garibaldi **boys** climb trees."

"And they only climb ombús."

"That's true. How could anyone get up this trunk?"

The necks of fifty **tacuaremboenses** craned up at the girl. The tree looked impossible to scale. If it had been a native ombú, with its low, inviting branches, there would have been no miracle or legend or ninety years of carrying the story. But here was the tallest ceibo known to Tacuarembó, its lowest branch many meters from the ground. No one could imagine an adult shimmying up with a baby in her arms, let alone a baby's lonely climb.

"Very well. Doña Rosa, you've got your miracle."

"Our miracle."

"Miracles are miracles, what more can we say?"

"Only thanks be to God."

"If you say so."

"I do. I certainly do."

"I meant no harm."

"Hmm."

"Look, everybody, let's not quarrel."

"We've got to find a way to get her down."

"A ladder!"

"Let's shake her out."

"There's no ladder big enough—I know, I made them all."

"I could climb the tree—"

"You can barely climb onto your horse, **hombre**!"

"We should wait for a sign—"

"And what? Leave her up there for another century?"

The infant sat high above the din, impassive, barely moving. Artigas thought: **Mírame.** She turned her head, this way, that way, and their eyes met. You. You. Their gaze had flesh, their gaze had strength, their gaze was a branch between them, invisible, unbreakable, bound to last forever, or so it seemed.

"I know her," he shouted. "She's my sister."

Fifty faces turned toward the boy.

"Your sister?"

"What sister?"

"Ay . . . he means . . ."

"Poor thing."

"Look, Artigas." Carlita Robles knelt beside him. "This can't be her."

"Why not?"

"She's been gone too long."

"She couldn't have survived."

"Little girls can't survive alone."

"But she did," Artigas said.

Carlita and Doña Rosa exchanged a glance.

"Besides," he added, "if it's not her, where did this girl come from?"

Doña Rosa opened her mouth, then closed it. No one spoke. Artigas looked up again at the infant in the treetop. She stared back. She was far away, close close to heaven, yet he could swear he saw the texture of her eyes: dark pools, wide awake, red veins in the whites. He imagined himself soaring up to meet her.

"Wait for me," he called into the foliage.

He mounted his horse and galloped down the hill.

He found Tía Tita outside their hut, plucking a chicken. He dismounted in a rush and told her everything about the morning plaza, the crowd around the ceibo, the child up on the branch. She listened. She tilted her face to the sun. Her lips moved without making any sound. She wiped her wide hands on her apron and untied it. "Let's go."

By the time they arrived at the ceibo, most of the town had formed a ring around it. Women had brought their children, children had brought their great-grandparents, men had brought wives, the stray dogs from the plaza had brought one another. Horses grazed. Doña Rosa had sacrificed the front of her dress to kneel on the ground and pray intensely with her rosary that had been blessed sixteen years earlier by the pope. The shopkeeper's son brandished a wooden flute. Dogs barked and brayed. Several **mate** gourds and baskets of empanadas circulated from hand to hand. Arguments rose and broke and rose again, about the girl, about the pastries, about who drank how much and did what with whom last night in the plaza. The infant stared at them from the high foliage, which held her like an adoptive guardian's arms.

Tía Tita and Artigas slid from their shared saddle. The crowd grew quiet. Tía Tita was not tall, but she was large somehow, hard-jawed, commanding. "Leave us alone," she said, looking at the baby but speaking to the throng. No one wanted to miss the story, break up the party, let someone else fix the problem. But Tía Tita—odd, unfathomable, needed for the cure of old men's creaks and the froth on soldiers' mouths—could not be easily denied. Slowly, grudgingly, the crowd dispersed.

"You too, Artigas."

He did as he was told. Horseflesh moved damply below his thighs. The air was hot and thick and heavy. He joined a cluster that had formed in the shade of an ombú, and turned to watch from his saddle: Tita and that high speck of a girl, still and dark against a ruthless sky. Tita raised her arms and seemed to wait, and then the treetop shook and rushed with leaves and sudden-downward-streaking and her arms closed around a thing that thudded against her chest. Artigas watched his aunt walk from the tree, away from town, returning home on foot. By the time the moon had risen, all of

Tacuarembó knew the story of the fall that turned to flight or flight that turned to fall.

They called her Pajarita. Little Bird.

Not all lives begin that way. Look at Ignazio Firielli. He never disappeared or reappeared or had a village call him miraculous. He did have his day with magic, once he was a grown man far from home, but even then it was for a single day that only served the purpose of forcing him toward love. That's how he told it, anyway, years later, to his grandchildren—especially to Salomé, listening, smiling, fatal secrets tucked away. He would say the sight of a certain woman made magic spring from his hands. It was only as a carnival performer, bumbling through tricks in a gaudy suit. But memory is an expert at sleight-of-hand: it can raise up things that glitter and leave clumsiness and pain to be swallowed by the dark.

Before Ignazio knew a thing about magic, or Uruguay, or women born from trees, he knew Venezia. He held Venezia in his body: the canals, vast, veinlike; the lilting brass of his language; the smells of brine and basil and freshly cut wood in his family home. Above all, he knew gondolas. It was the family business to make gondolas of every size and style. Arcs of wood leaned beside the window; he could trace them with his hands and eyes and know where he belonged. Their shapes could keep a person gliding on the surface of the water, he could not drown, he would not drown, surrounded by planks and prows, gondolas for fishing, for coupling, for heading to the market, and, most of all, gondolas for taking the dead to the tomb-ridden Isle of San Michele.

Gondolas linked Venetians to their dead. Gondolas linked Ignazio to his dead. A history of death and gondolas lived buried in the corners of his home. When Ignazio was eleven, his grandfather revealed the past as they sat alone in the workshop. Nonno Umberto was not usually loquacious. He spent long hours by the window, bony hands at rest, swaying in the rocking chair he'd carved as a boy. He stared out at the houses reflected on the water, at linens on clotheslines, calm, quiet, no matter how loud the shouts got in the kitchen. He was deaf. He pretended to be deaf. Ignazio was never sure which one was true. He came and sat on a low stool at Nonno's feet, in search of calm or at least a pretense of it, and finding, one day, the telling of a story, slippery, secret, as furtive and as heated as confession.

Long ago, said Nonno, the Firielli family made a modest living building simple gondolas. They had done this for centuries, and assumed they would do it for centuries to come. He was born into the business. He grew up. He married. He had seven children, and his family also lived among saline slabs of wood in raw states of formation. It was a bad time for Venezia. Cholera ran rampant; no one had enough to eat; corpse after corpse swelled the cemetery of San Michele. "The Austrians." Nonno Umberto gripped a fistful of the quilt on his lap. If the quilt had been alive, Ignazio thought, it would be choking. "They had blood on their hands. They took from us and let us rot."

Sun streaked the walls and fell on the skeletal boats around them. Nonno stared out the window. Ignazio stared out also, and he saw the old-time Austrians, big men with monstrous faces, wearing crowns, reclining in a gondola and laughing at beggars on bridges and shores. In the kitchen, the shouting continued, his mother, his father, a slap, a fall, more shouting.

Nonno went on: the revolution came. It was 1848. Venetians chased out Austrian rule. Umberto and thousands of others danced on the cathedral steps until the sun came up. The city churned with hope: freedom was theirs, they were independent, Venezia would be restored. For a year that was true, and then the Austrians returned. Cholera flared back up and burned across the city. Within six months, six of Umberto's seven children had died of cholera. Four daughters and two sons. Only Diego survived ("your father, Ignazio; your father was the only one"). On the night that his last sister died, nine-year-old Diego went silent and said nothing for two years and thirty-seven days. On that same night, Umberto sat beside his silent son, empty as a rag that has been wrung over and over. The undertaker arrived, shrouded in black, his face masked in a hood with slits for eyes. He stared at young Diego through the slits.

"Don't look at my son," Umberto said.

"It won't harm him."

"Don't look at him."

The undertaker raised his hands. Umberto punched him and the man reeled back and Umberto punched him again until the hood lay flat and crushed against his head.

"May fever take your house," the undertaker shouted. "May you all rot." He stumbled out without the girl's body.

Later that night, Umberto woke up to a rustle at the foot of his bed and saw an angel ("I swear it," he told Ignazio, "an angel, with wings and all!"). Umberto sat for a minute in the glow of silence. Then he asked the angel how his last son might be spared. The angel said **God hears what crosses the water.** A wing tip brushed Umberto's head, and he fell back asleep. The next morning, he entered his workshop and stayed for three days and three nights without sleeping, and built a funeral gondola that shocked him with its beauty. Four pillars held a ceiling upholstered with lush velvet. He carved his prayers into the wood: ornate crucifixes on each pillar, rolling vines and grapes and fleurs-de-lis, cherubs with their trumpets, a witch tearing her hair out, sylphs engaged in coitus, Hercules weeping on a mountain, and, at the helm, Orpheus with his golden lyre, poised to sing the way to Hades. The day that gondola crossed the water with their last daughter's body, it caught the eye of a duchess and she commissioned one for her husband, who had died of syphilis. After that, Firielli gondolas carried the corpses of Venezia's finest dead.

That's how Nonno Umberto told it. Ignazio listened, surrounded by wood chips, sure that Nonno was a liar. He could not accept his grand-father hammering at a gondola three days straight—when now his arthritic hands barely brought fork to mouth. He could not accept an angel perching anywhere. Nor could he see his own father, Diego, as the small boy mute with pain, when now he was the farthest thing from silent, the farthest thing from small. There always seemed to be too much of him: too much volume, too much hair, too many wine bottles emptying too quickly. Too much laughter at the wrong times (his laugh had claws; it unfurled sharply). He eclipsed everyone—Ignazio himself, his brothers, his sisters, his mother with her broad hips and bull-headed love, and Nonno, with his rocking chair, his window, his corrugated skin, the loosened hold on life that caused him to stop carving, stop trying to shape things, just let them float or sink in their canals.

One summer night, when dinner was over and heat thickened the house, Ignazio reluctantly left childhood behind. It was a Wednesday. He was twelve. From the kitchen came the clanging water-song of his sisters washing pots and pans. His father slid his arms into his coat sleeves. His cheeks were red with wine. Ignazio's older brothers followed suit and waited, hands in pockets. Diego Firielli turned to his youngest son and crooked his finger in the gesture of **come.** The brothers laughed. Ignazio flushed and rushed toward his coat.

Outside, their gondola sat, dispassionate, on the water. Ignazio stepped in last. The wind curled on the surface of the canal, and they glided along the water in silence. Diego turned to look at Ignazio with a strange expression, expectant, mocking. The thick bush of his hair blocked out the city behind him.

It was late, even for Venezia, but the house they went to brimmed with light, noise, and women. Red velvet drapes hung to the floor; wine poured freely; languid chords pushed out of an accordion; the women laughed and swayed and rubbed their bodies against men. Ignazio stood in a corner between a curtain and an ornate oil lamp and tried not to look at anyone. He wished the lamp would darken so he could melt into the wall. He stepped farther from its sphere of light, but his father approached, a girl on each arm. "Here," he said, thrusting one toward Ignazio.

Upstairs, on the stale mattress, Ignazio's hand shook as he touched the girl's knee. It was cool and smooth. Her shoulder preened with freckles. Black ringlets fell around her face. She sat, half reclined, on the thin bed. He was afraid of her, uncertain, humiliated by the fact of his own fear. She drew his hand to the hem of her skirt and he did nothing and she rolled her eyes and reached to unbutton his trousers. Two minutes later, as he pushed into her body, he heard his father's voice through the curtain to his left, grunting rhythmically, and realized that his father could hear him too. What if he made an audible mistake? He groaned in time, his sounds overshadowed by his father, and the girl lay still. She felt like a crushed peach, soft, moist, alarming. His father finished and Ignazio bit the girl's neck to climax in absolute silence.

It began soon after that. The unraveling. When Ignazio turned thirteen, his voice deepened and his father broke his mother's ribs. At fourteen, he went to the kitchen one night and saw a thing that itched his skin: his father, seated at the table, sobbing. He made no sound. His glass was empty. His chin dripped with snot and tears. Ignazio crept out and raced to bed, where he lay in the sea of Nonno's snores, itching, until the sun returned.

Fifteen: Ignazio cut and sanded, carved and built, until his hands grew raw. He rose for work before dawn, and kept on into the night. One night, in his exhaustion, he sawed the tip off his ring finger. Still, the Firielli business teetered on the edge of disrepute. Orders arrived, Diego ignored them, half-made gondolas lay naked and deserted. Funeral dates came and went, their commissioned vessels unfinished. Customers grew wary; the family soups thinned. By the time Ignazio turned sixteen, his brothers and sisters had married, gondola orders had fallen to half, and hunger felt as familiar as the pulse of water under wood.

One night, at the brothel, Diego shattered a chandelier and two wooden chairs. He was thrown from the building and told not to return. The next night, at his father's insistence, Ignazio brought their gondola to dock at the brothel's steps.

"Come with me."

Ignazio shook his head.

His father stepped onto land, drunk, unsteady. He banged the brass ring against the gilded door. He yelled that he would enter. Three guards came out and punched him and then dragged him down the steps. They pushed him into the gondola, which swayed beneath the pressure.

Diego said, "You can't—"

"Shut up," a guard snarled. Ignazio could not see his face; his massive silhouette turned toward Ignazio. "Can't you control your father? For God's sake. For your family name."

Ignazio felt a hot and creeping slime beneath his skin. He longed to leap into the dark canal and swim very far and never come back. He nodded and pushed the gondola out onto the water.

Six months later, on a cold winter night, Diego cracked his wife's skull against the wall and loped outside. The canal growled under the wind. From the window of his room, Ignazio saw his father's shadow teeter on the edge of the canal, then fall as if thrown from an invisible fist.

Ignazio lay silent until he heard his sister-in-law's cry from the kitchen—**dead, dead, Mamma is**

dead. He closed his eyes. His mother flooded across his mind: embracing him at six years old when he'd scraped his knee, her thick breasts covering his ears so that they filled with sounds like the inside of a shell; humming, tenor-low, while kneading dough for gnocchi in the kitchen; watching him as he put his coat on with his brothers, flesh swollen around her eyes. His chest burned. If his father had not thrown himself into the water, Ignazio could have killed him with bare hands. He heard Nonno sit up in the bed across from his. "Eh? What happened?"

Ignazio spent the next five hours cleaning blood from the walls and the body.

Two days later, Diego's body washed up at the front steps of a count whose gondola order had never been completed. He surfaced just in time to make the journey to San Michele with his wife.

The corpses crossed the water, thronged by the living. The sky was pale with shock. A fleet of mourners—sons, daughters, wives and husbands, children, great-aunts, uncles, drenched in black—rode their gondolas in an entourage behind the coffins. San Michele loomed before them, with its township of tombs, soaking in the prayers and wails that ebbed over the water.

Ignazio rowed numbly. The world was not the world but a mere painting of itself; apart; impenetrable; all the grieving people only brushstrokes; he in the midst of it, pretending to be real, wearing a life of someone else's making. Only Nonno Umberto still

seemed viscerally true. His breath labored as they disembarked, audible through the drone of Hail Marys.
He leaned on Ignazio's arm. He smelled of soap and
vinegar and a bitter trace of sweat.

Sepulchral rows, priestly mutterings, aunts weeping, slate moved aside to lower caskets into ground.
Ignazio watched the remains of his parents (man and
wife, he thought, killer and killed) sink slowly, together, into the dark. The stone slab groaned as his
brothers pushed it back into place, shutting in the
dead.

"Ignazio," his grandfather said. "Take me for a
walk."

They escaped the praying crowd and walked the
cobbled path. The tombs of the rich loomed around
them, edifices twice the size of the Firielli kitchen,
wrought with statues. Sylphs and ancient gods and
grieving angels gazed their way. They moved past
them to a row of simple tombs, unadorned boxes
submerged in the ground. Nonno stopped at one of
them. Ignazio read the names etched into marble:
PORZIA FIRIELLI. DONATO FIRIELLI. ARMINO
FIRIELLI. ROSA FIRIELLI. ERACLA FIRIELLI. IS-
ABELLA FIRIELLI. He chanted them, one after the
other, in his mind, **Porzia, Donato, Armino, Rosa,
Eracla, Isabella,** his aunts, his uncles, frozen children, unknown ghosts.

"Your father," Nonno said. He stared at the
ground. "You can't be like him."

"No."

"But you have to accept him."

"He's dead."

"Exactly."

Ignazio kicked a pebble. He nodded blankly.

"Are you going to leave?"

"Leave?"

"You know you can't stay here."

Ignazio felt transparent. He did know. Or he had wondered. His mother was gone; the family business was dead; his older brothers fought like vultures for its remnants; his sisters had married away. The house was a hull of shadows.

Nonno Umberto looked immensely tired. "You should go. Our name is cursed. And soon Italy will be at war again." He bent in closer. Ignazio smelled the tang of his white hair. "Listen. I have a little money in the floorboards, and I'll send you to the New World if you swear you'll build something. Gondolas, maybe, or something else, something useful over there, something worth building. Anything. Swear."

It broke, then, the canvas stretched over the world, and Ignazio was not numb, not in a painting after all: he stood in a raw, unfinished world, surrounded by the dead, exposing a fresh layer of living skin.

"I swear," he said.

As they turned back toward the burial, Ignazio looked across the water at Venezia. The city sprawled in all its dense, corrosive beauty. Gondolas split the water with their motion, with their silence, with their prows that aimed at faraway lands, at long-backed rivers and broad-backed seas that led to God knows where, to something new.

Four days later, Ignazio bought a ticket on a steamship. It was February 1, 1911. The boat was headed to Montevideo, a city he'd never heard of, but he was restless to embark, and in any case, the more anonymous, the better. He boarded and stowed his scanty possessions, then found a sailor and asked what Montevideo was like.

"The whores are cheap. Fishing's good. It's on the Río de la Plata."

Ignazio nodded and tried to smile.

They crossed the vast blue dazzle of the Atlantic. The Italians reeked and retched and bent their hopeful words to sound more Spanish. Babies shrieked and grown men wept like babies. Ignazio would have shriveled from loneliness if it had not been for Pietro, a Florentine shoemaker, the kind of man who could talk a statue into dancing. When they first met, Ignazio watched him roll a cigarette: he flicked the paper just so, as if it had been waiting to bend to his will, then twisted the ends, sealing all escape routes (surrender, tobacco, no fate for you but smoke). He brought it to his lips, the sun setting into the sea behind him as if slowly falling to its knees. Ignazio cleaved to him. He wanted to be like him, light, confident, disdainful of discussions of the past, swaggering across the deck as though the future were a naked woman, waiting, open-limbed.

They spent long afternoons leaning on the rails. They stared at the ocean. They smoked, stared, lit up, and smoked again, until the tobacco ran out and they just stared and gnawed on substitutes—fish scales, shreds of cloth, errant twigs from the homeland. Pietro treated Ignazio like an entertaining little brother (he was ten years older, twenty-seven or so), though he softened once Ignazio beat him at cards. Nights in brothels had made Ignazio a good gambler. Pietro laughed when Ignazio showed him his twelfth winning hand.

"Not bad. You'll need this skill in the New World."

New. World. It sounded fresh and large and daunting. Ignazio shuffled the cards and stole glances at the horizon, thin and blue and pressing at the sky.

Three months later, Ignazio—stinky and exultant—disembarked at the Montevideo port. A strange and satisfying stench assailed his nostrils: a mix of cowhide, sweat, piss, and the brash alkaline wind. The port burst with ships bearing flags from all over the world: England, France, Italy, Spain, the United States, and dozens of unfamiliar design. His fellow travelers poured around him like dazed children. He had thought Pietro was right behind him, but now he turned and turned and saw him nowhere. The air was heavy, humid. Voices rattled and screeched out singsong strings of Spanish words. People bustled everywhere: sailors, vendor women, grimy little children picking at dead fish. A boy looked up at him from the fish bins he was scrubbing. The boy's nose sloped widely to either side, and black eyes looked out of a face more darkly hued than he had ever seen. Pietro had assured him that Uruguay was full of Europeans and their descendants. A civilized place, he'd said. Ignazio's eyes met the boy's. He felt a surge of—what? fear? fascination? shame? It struck him, then—the obvious and unthinkable fact that he was in a strange land, worlds and worlds and long blue worlds away from home. His ribs tightened inside him. He longed for his only friend. He searched, pushing past women's wide baskets and sailors' hard smiles, until he finally found him, smoking a cigarette (how had he found one?) and leaning nonchalantly against a stucco wall. "Don't worry," Pietro said. "We'll get used to it." He laughed. "Here, have a smoke. What do you say we find a place to eat, a woman or two? We can think about jobs and rooms in the morning."

He slapped Ignazio's back, and they began to navigate the brackish din of Montevideo.

Monte. Vide. Eu. I see a mountain, said a Portuguese man, among the first Europeans to sight this terrain from sea.

Monte. Vide. Eu. But Ignazio saw no mountain at all, just flat, cobbled streets.

Monte. Vide. Eu. City of sailors and workers, of

wool and steak, of gray stones and long nights, biting-cold winters and Januaries so humid you could swim through hot air. City of seekers. Port of a hundred flags. Heart and edge of Uruguay.

It was El Cerro they'd been talking about. Those Portuguese. They had glimpsed El Cerro from their ship, and spawned the city's name. **Monte.** What an exaggeration. Ignazio beheld it every day from his work at the port: a mound the shape of a huge fried egg, spread long and low across the other side of the bay. It was absurd, barely a hill, pathetic, and he should know, coming from a nation with true, majestic mountains, the Alps, the Dolomiti, the Apennines, Vesuvius, Presanella, Cornizzolo, real mountains that he himself had never seen but could be trusted to exist, to have weight and height and substance, not like this thing they called El Cerro he stole glances at all day as he worked, aloft on a steel crane, remembering those first fools to have seen Uruguay from sea.

Many things looked different from the top of a crane. Boats. Mountains. Smooth water below. The long, heaving arc of a day's work. Cranes were new to Montevideo; the first ones had arrived the same week as Ignazio. He quickly learned their language, the hoist of pulleys, the lever's growl, the careful gait along their big steel snouts, exposure to damp cold and scorch of sun, the metal muscle of modernity, the thrill in lifting giant crates into the air.

At dusk, Ignazio walked on streets lined with

wrought-iron balconies and ornate doors to Calle
Ejido, where he lived in the shadow of cannons that
had once guarded La Ciudad Vieja when it was not
just the Old City but the whole of the city itself.
Strange, that the first settlers here had built their little town with an armed wall around it. They'd built
a port wide open to the waters, yet closed to surrounding land. What had lurked in the earth around
them? What lay around them now? Just across the
wall, in the newer part of the city, roads turned into
packed earth, lined with huts like humble boxes
made of wood, surrounded by wild and sudden
space. There were strange things about this city.
Amethysts used as doorstops, leather used for everything, a stone wall between Old City and New. An
obsession with the president, a man called Batlle y
Ordóñez, who had promised schools, and workers'
rights, and hospitals (secular ones, scandalously so,
with crucifixes banned from the walls). All the laborers Ignazio worked with—even the immigrants,
of which there were many—spoke of Batlle the way
Italians spoke of the pope. These men were also obsessed with **mate:** a brew of shredded leaves and hot
water, concocted in a hollow gourd, then drunk
through a metal straw called a **bombilla.** They drank
it as if their lives depended on it, and maybe their
lives did, sucking at **bombillas** on their high steel
beams, pouring water while awaiting the next crate,
passing the gourd from hand to calloused hand. The
first time he was offered **mate,** Ignazio was shocked

by the assumption that he should share a cup. He was eighteen, after all, a grown man. He thought of refusing, but didn't want the others to think him afraid of tea. The gourd felt warm against his palm. The wet green mass inside it gleamed. The drink flooded his mouth, bright and green and bitter, the taste, he thought, of Uruguay.

He was able to find morsels of Italy: fresh pasta, good Chianti, the reassuring cadence of his language. El Corriente, the bar downstairs from his dingy rented room, brimmed with the sweethard liquor **grappa miel** and music from an out-of-tune piano and the company of immigrant men. He headed straight there after work. Sometimes, in the middle of the night, he crept downstairs to hear Italian spoken in loud and slurring voices. He needed them. They filled something even whores could not fill.

Pietro worked for a brilliant but arthritic shoemaker. He met Ignazio at El Corriente a few times a week until, three years after their arrival, he married a Sicilian girl with placid eyes and solid bones. Ignazio stood by him at the altar as the organ sang and the silky bride approached. The priest mumbled, made signs in the air, and gave his blessing for a kiss. Outside, on the steps, Ignazio threw raw rice at them and called his congratulations as the couple ran to their carriage. They rode off without looking back.

He saw less of Pietro after that. Some nights, loneliness and exhaustion wound together in a slow noose around Ignazio's neck. He lay on his thin mattress, hour after hour, staring into blackness, forcing canals from his mind. He had food, cash, work, a room, everything he needed to survive, and yet his days felt like mollusk shells with the bodies scraped out—empty, useless, ready for the trash bin. It was not what his grandfather had sent him for. He tried to recall his grandfather's face, painting it on the black canvas of the ceiling. Its details had grown hazy but he could not let it fade. He reconstructed it with his mind, hovering, enormous, sometimes young and angular, sometimes absurdly scarred. The face shifted with the seasons, with the texture of the nights, and Ignazio fell asleep watching it, as a man underwater watches light on the surface of the sea.

One November night, as the rays of his fourth Uruguayan spring swept the chill from the air, Ignazio met a group of men at El Corriente. They were playing a raucous game of poker when he came in. He was struck immediately by their bright clothing and odd appearance: a burly giant with a curled mustache, a man in gold hoop earrings and a red bandanna, two robust, blond identical twins, a hairy Spaniard in ostentatious jewelry, and a shark-eyed midget who stood on his chair to reach the top of the table. The laborers at other tables pretended to ignore them. The midget looked up and caught Ignazio's stare.

"In the mood to gamble?"

Ignazio pulled a chair up. The giant dealt the cards with delicate precision. Ignazio felt the Spaniard's dark eyes resting on him, the way a man sizes up flanks in the market. He did it subtly, but Ignazio noticed. He had learned to notice everything when gambling: the shift of eyes; the drop of temperature around the table as cards were cast against it; the exact tautness of muscle and breath in fellow players. They were his secret weapons, and his thrill. He spread his cards on the table. The giant, having lost the most, grunted peevishly. The others laughed.

"Come on," said Hoop Earrings Man. "Let's play again."

The Spaniard dealt this time. Ignazio won another round. Then another. He felt the shift around him: the rise in heat, air tightening like wire. Less laughter, more glances, more swigs. Ignazio used his winnings to buy a round of drinks. The air eased. Muscles relaxed. He won again.

The midget glanced at Hoop Earrings Man. The Spaniard watched Ignazio more intently. All but Hoop Earrings left the hand. Ignazio raised the stakes; Hoop Earrings stayed. Ignazio spread his hand on the table and met his opponent's eyes. They were dark green, surrounded by laugh lines; the man reminded Ignazio of a pirate, although he'd never seen one. Hoop Earrings put down his hand: a royal flush. All eyes turned on Ignazio.

A moment like this could turn into a brawl from one blink to the next. He'd seen it happen. He bowed toward the winner and pushed the cash toward him. "Congratulations."

Hoop Earrings fingered his new coins. "What's your name?"

"Ignazio. Yours?"

"El Mago. El Mago Milagroso," he added dramatically. "But people also call me Cacho. You Italian?"

"Venetian. From where the gondolas are."

Cacho exchanged a blank look with the giant. Ignazio opened his mouth to explain, but the Spaniard leaned in close. "**Che.** You. Gondola."

Ignazio turned toward him. He smelled the pungence of his beard.

"How about you work for me?"

"Doing what?"

"As a stable boy. These men"—he gestured around the table—"are part of my **carnaval.** We're leaving next week for our summer tour."

"Our stable boy was shot last night in a duel." The midget sneered. "Over love."

The Spaniard smiled, revealing three gold teeth. "I pay well." He fanned the cards on the table. "So?"

Ignazio gazed at the cards, with their red and white backs. He longed to turn one over and crawl into it, searching for himself in stems of spades or diamond slopes. He was greedy, he wanted them all, hearts and clubs and jacks and aces, but life and poker are not like that. You have to choose and follow the road you open. You step on the boat and Venezia fades and the ocean is everywhere, you can't go back. You give up on a flush and keep your mouth shut if the deck gives you the right card a round too late. You weigh your city life against an offer that glitters, rustic, foreign, unassayed, an adventure in the hands of total strangers. It was a gamble. It was always a gamble.

"Bueno," he said.

The Spaniard sealed the deal with a nod.

Six days later, Ignazio set out eastward with Carnaval Calaquita, which consisted of a dozen men, a few of their women and children, and several horse-drawn wagons packed with tarps, poles, circus-style tents, wood planks, awnings, collapsible stages, bright game wheels, weighing scales, twisted mirrors, garish masks, flour, rice, trumpets, smoked beef, coops of pigeons, coops of chickens, coops of rabbits, and trunk upon trunk of costumes. The road thickened with the dust each horse kicked up, so that they clattered through low brown clouds. What a road. Ignazio had lived all his life in the city, and had not known that urban bricks could fall away to reveal such open earth. He had known that it existed but had not been prepared for its lush quiet, its immensity, the soaring urge within him as he rode. They rode and rode, and land unfurled, abundant, immodest, naked, fragrant, endlessly green, peppered with sparse huts, full of heat and thorns and animal sounds.

Their first stop, Pando—a few buildings clustered around a plaza—received them with all the enthusiasm of its early Christmas fervor. The crew slung together a little world of games, mystique, and spectacles. Ignazio sweated and hauled and cleaned up horseshit, and then he stood in a sequined blue suit and watched the **carnavaleros** ply their trade. In that world they could do anything. Make a saint thrill with urges and a sinner drop the burdens of tomorrow. Make grown men beg, at the edge of humble wagons, for them not to pack, not to go, not to disappear as they did along the wide, hot road.

Town after town embraced them. They traveled all over the countryside—west to Paysandú, east past Rocha to the Brazilian Chuy, north toward Artigas. Ignazio loved the way he imagined that he looked in people's eyes: untamed, free, a little dangerous. He felt that way, leaving towns behind, gazing fondly at bright-eyed children, men riding over fields, sturdy women carrying water buckets home. He wondered what home was. He sought it that summer in the horse's back, the wagon's shake, the stars' cacophonous light, **mate** and liquor drunk by the campfire. He made friends with Cacho Cassella, the magician-not-pirate, with his bright bandannas and round laugh. Cacho had descended from gauchos in the east, who ate Brazilian **baurús** and spoke the hybrid border dialect **portuñol.** He and Ignazio shared a penchant for long, firelit nights. Over orange embers, Cacho sang gaucho ballads and taught Ignazio tricks that made a man seem to command esoteric powers. He also taught Ignazio how to gamble the old Uruguayan way, using cow vertebrae, white chunks of bone cast on dark ground. Sometimes they fell **con suerte,** with luck. Sometimes they fell **pa'l culo,** like ass. Sometimes, the two men sat in silence, passing the **mate** gourd, stoking the fire, watching the sky turn from black to velvet blue hemmed by a pink ribbon of dawn.

"These are real gaucho nights," Cacho assured him.

It seemed like magic, to Ignazio, that you could put a culture on like clothing, button it up over your body as if it were sewn for you, as if nobody would notice the disguise.

In the third month of travel, Cacho woke in the afternoon with a hangover so acute he couldn't stand, let alone lead El Mago Milagroso's magic show. It was their first night in Tacuarembó. Scores of townspeople waited in a throng at the door of the tent.

"Damn him!" the Spaniard swore behind the stage curtain. "If we have to cancel I'll—"

"You won't cancel," Consuelo, Cacho's wife, assured him. The pink sequins on her leotard winked as she spoke. "Gondola can take his place."

Ignazio stared at her. "What do I know about magic?"

"What does Cacho? What does anyone? You've watched the show plenty of times. And you'd fit into his clothes." Since she was the resident seamstress, her claim on this was irrefutable. In the tents they called her Mistress of Disguises. She tilted her head to a sensuous angle. "I'll whisper instructions from the coffin while you cut me in half."

"She's right," the Spaniard said. "You're the best we can do. Get into costume. Hurry."

Twenty minutes later, Ignazio parted the velveteen curtain with trembling fingers. Hands applauded; trumpets blared. The stage felt infernally hot, and the reek of sweat and peanuts almost overwhelmed him. The crowd blurred into a sea of color. He raced his way through the opening speech, attempting the jokes and dramatic flourishes he'd seen Cacho use night after night. To his surprise, laughter and shouts rose from the audience. Consuelo joined him onstage and winked in encouragement.

He was halfway through his second trick when the crowd came into focus (he was calmer now, it would be all right): and from that mass of human color, she emerged—a young woman with high cheekbones, steady eyes, and long black braids that ended in green bows. She seemed as if she'd just landed on Earth from a stranger, better planet. She sat alert, attentive, solemn. When he looked away, the imprint of her face floated before him, like a ghost.

His nascent stage presence began to crumble. He stuttered. Three boys snickered in the front row. It was time to solicit a volunteer from the audience. "Who can help me?" Many raised their hands up high, front-row boys included, but he pointed at the girl in the back. "How about **esa morochita** in the corner?"

She came to the stage. Years later he would not re-call the murmurs of surprise, arms crossed in disappointment, the peanut shells that grazed his calves, but only that she came to the stage. He placed a yellow silk scarf in her hand. The trick was simple. He would impress her. The scarf would disappear and he would retrieve it from her ear, and then his sleeve. He waved his arm and the scarf disappeared. The crowd moaned appreciatively; the young woman gazed in a still, unsettling way. She stood so close. Ignazio leaned toward her (oh her smell) and pulled the scarf out from behind her ear. The crowd clapped. The young woman smiled—slightly, a soft tug of the lips, but she smiled. The scarf disappeared again. He drew himself up and said, "Where do you think it is?" His volunteer cocked her head. He grinned victoriously and reached into his sleeve. Nothing there. He reached again, fumbled. Nothing. The spare yellow scarf, hidden in the lining, was gone.

He heard giggles, mutters, he saw bodies leaning forward in expectation. He looked at the young woman in panic. Opening his mouth, he could not speak. She stepped close and reached into his sleeve with fingers that scalded him and left too soon with a yellow scarf captured between them like limp prey.

The room erupted. The crowd laughed at him and praised the girl, called to her by name. Pajarita. The name flew from their mouths, up his empty sleeve, into the middle of his hollow chest. Pajarita. It roosted there for the rest of the show, through the sawing and the rabbit and the pigeons careening from their box. It fluttered as the sea of people finally ambled out. It flapped and furled between his ribs as he lay under the stars, trying to sleep, eyes wide open. Pajarita.

When he drifted off, Ignazio dreamed that he lay by a canal, pulling scarves out from under a woman's skirt, more and more scarves, until they enfolded him and he rocked and rocked and yellow silk was all that he could see.

The next morning, his mouth twitched as he gulped his bread and **mate.** He wandered distract- edly about the camp. He groomed horses that evoked her carnal grace. He hauled ropes that launched his mind toward sleek black braids. He pressed poles into deep sleeves of earth—he had to find her.

This was not difficult; it was a very small town. That afternoon, Ignazio knocked on the crude open- ing of the Torres hut with hat in hand, praying he looked calm and respectable. A woman with a weath- ered face and pendulous breasts emerged to meet him.

"Good afternoon," he said.

She gestured him through the doorway, past the leather curtain, into her home. She gestured again to offer him a seat at the table. He moved to accept, then saw that all the stools around the table were not stools at all, but animal skulls with hard, pale faces and black pits for eyes. Flames shone from a pit in the dirt floor; the skulls leered at him in the flicker- ing light. He didn't sit. He tried not to shudder. The woman eyed him, then crouched down at her cooking fire.

Silence swelled between them. The woman broke it first. "You're here for Pajarita."

"Yes."

"She's at the market."

Ignazio scratched his nails against the rim of his hat. "Will . . . your husband be home at some time? I would like to speak to him about your daughter."

"Her father will come." She threw chopped parsley into boiling water. "You want to marry her."

"Yes."

"Why?"

"She is the most beautiful woman I have ever seen."

The woman looked into his eyes as if they were tubs of dirty linens she could wring dry. "What else?"

"I don't know." A wisp of yellow silk flashed through his mind. "I—I want a wife. Look, Señora, I'm a good man. I come from a good family, back in Venezia. We made gondo—boats, we were boat makers."

Her eyes did not leave his face. "Pajarita will be home at dark. You can wait here."

He sat on a log outside the house and watched the light deepen slowly over the landscape. Chickens everywhere, clacking terribly, pecking the air in his general direction. One hour. Two. Or was it more? He shifted, stood, walked a few steps and came back again. Dust gilded his only pair of patent-leather shoes. He was ridiculous, a man whom boys saw fit to accost with peanut shells. An impostor. A sad and lonely man. It was stupid to wait here, he would leave, any moment he would leave.

He stayed.

She came.

She carried woven baskets at the flanks of her horse. The green bows were gone from her braids, and her dress looked like it had been made to fit a woman twice her size. She swam in it. She swam in the air. She was perfect.

Ignazio stood and removed his hat. All the brilliant things he had thought of saying were gone. She was closer now. An ache rushed through his body as he watched her dismount. He wanted to leap forward and crush her to his hips, but instead he bowed and said, "Good evening, Señorita."

Pajarita stood with the dusk gathering around her like a darker and darker skirt. She looked at the woman, who had appeared in the doorway. "Tía Tita, what's this man doing here?"

Tía Tita, Ignazio thought, must have been born before humans learned to blink. She wiped her hands on her apron. "You bested him at magic, and now he wants to marry you. Maybe you should let him stay for dinner."

Ignazio sat at the crumbling kitchen table, having finally surrendered his backside to a skull. Tía Tita and Pajarita chopped and cleaned and stirred. He folded his hands together, raised them to the table, laid them flat, folded them again and dropped them to his lap. Should he start a conversation? Silence seemed so natural and familiar to these women. They wore it like a cape. He raised one hand, tapped on the table, stopped. Pajarita glanced at him. He smiled. She glanced away.

The father came just before dinner, sat down on his skull, and looked at the stranger in his house.

"Good evening, Señor, my name's Ignazio Firielli."

The man nodded. "Miguel."

Ignazio waited for him to say something more, but he said nothing.

Dinner was served. Ignazio had expected a boisterous country family, bustling with children whose favor could be curried with card tricks. There were none. The four of them ate, their silence punctuated by questions from Tía Tita—what's Montevideo like? how far is Italy? what can you possibly mean, water for streets? Ignazio's answers were simple at first, then grew more embellished, and he was in the midst of a description of the unrivaled pragmatic grace of gondolas that surely would persuade the father to look up and see his guest in a new light, or so it seemed, when the father stood and left.

Ignazio stopped in midsentence. He heard Miguel's horse snort and lope away. The women said nothing. He could have punched the wall, only it looked as though it would break and crash if he did, and then where would his bid for marriage be? He had lost the chance to speak to the father, and yet it had begun to occur to him that this family's rules did not adhere to the standards he'd imagined, or to any standards he had ever fathomed.

The fire in the cooking pit had faded to an ebb. It was time to go. He rose, hat in hand.

"Thank you so much for dinner."

Tía Tita nodded.

"May I call on you tomorrow?"

Tía Tita looked at Pajarita, who cocked her head and stared at him. He felt exposed under her gaze. She nodded.

He left and walked through the grass toward the carnival encampment. He turned back for a last look at the **ranchito,** and glimpsed—he was sure he glimpsed—a face in the doorway, an exquisite face, before it darted back behind the walls.

This, Pajarita thought, is not the world. It is home: over there is the table, and here, to my side, the breaths of family sleeping. There, through the window, the soft slash of the moon. There it falls, making silver light on the ground. This place is home. And it is good. But it is not the world.

The thought surprised her. It felt fresh, an unknown herb against the palate of her mind. The world held many things that were not Tacuarembó, and Pajarita knew this: that Tacuarembó was only part of Uruguay; Uruguay just a sliver of the continent; the continent one of many to be found across those waters called The Seas—and she had always known about The Seas because her abuelo, El Facón, had ridden to their shores and traded for exotic things that came from other lands. She had a bracelet, inlaid with jade, that he had brought for her abuela. She knew, she had been told, that Tacuarembó was a forgotten speck that did not even merit a dot on maps of the world.

And yet, in the rhythmic shapes of days, there was little need to recall this. The world, on a normal day, held the same paths through the same fields and smells and hums and crackles, each season, as a turn of the seasons before, and that was her world, her lived one, the only map she needed.

But today was not a normal day. This man had come to her door. She couldn't sleep. It must be the moon, spilling in light, keeping her up. What a strange feeling: dizzy, thrilling—like those times when, as a child, she had spun and spun until she stopped and looked around at a world that whirled before her eyes. All things danced, nothing stayed still. The man carried another country in his mouth. His Spanish emerged in odd shapes and sounds. He knew about faraway places, like that city riddled with rivers for streets—who could believe it? And his pink skin had gone pinker as Tía Tita launched her questions. But he answered. **For me.**

Men had looked at her before. Of course. In the plaza and at the market, along with the plump hens. Boys vying for manhood tried to carry her basket. And yet, at sixteen, she still had no serious suitors. She was the miracle child, strong enough, as a baby, to survive out in the hills or trees without a family. What would this mean for a husband? No one had tried to find out. The moon was pooling whiter. It looked like fallen milk. Beside Pajarita, Tía Tita shifted in her sleep. Her broad back was turned to Pajarita, her face turned toward Pajarita's father. She always slept between them, a human wall. Tía Tita had not married, and she could carry two large buckets full of water. She could skin a bull in three swift strokes. She could make a tea or balm to cure all ailments, teaching Pajarita as she went. Marriage was not vital. It could even harm. Look at Carlita Robles, worn down by the rough edges of her husband, too broken to come to market anymore. Look at her own mother, dead from giving birth **(to me, to me).** Marriage could mean death; or children; new places; the close flesh of a man. This stranger would not take her to a palace, nor streets of water, nor faraway lands. But maybe he could carry her toward something, toward another little stretch of the world.

No. She longed to throw a blanket over the relentless moon. This was home. She knew things here, and she was known. Life was familiar, like the shape of her teeth against her tongue. She needed teeth. She needed home. She did not want to leave. That was a lie: there was something ravenous inside her that pushed constantly to stare at the horizon and wonder what would happen if she galloped to the edge of her small world and kept going without ever turning back, riding and riding, past fields and hills and rivers that drenched her skirts, tasting the dark intensity of nights that blazed with stars, the way Artigas had done, that bastard, how she missed him. He had always been a force that kept her on the ground. His company formed a sphere, a raw keen humming place, that encompassed them and all their hidden thoughts, so that she had known before he said it that he planned to leave. He loved his music and was restless and the countryside was changing, **estancias** spreading, with their rich owners and long land wrapped in barbed wire. It was harder each day to stay a gaucho. The future here held work under a **patrón** on hemmed-in land, a hemmed-in life, a nightmare for her brother. And they both knew, though neither would say it, that he would be even more constricted by their father's gloom. She couldn't blame him. She accepted it, the loss of him, the way she accepted dry wells in times of drought.

"I know where you're headed," she'd said, handing him wood behind the house.

Artigas swung his ax and cracked a log.

"Brazil."

"Por Dios," he said. "No secret is safe from you."

Pajarita's braids hung like ropes of lead down her chest. "I suppose I can't come with you."

"Ha! It's dangerous on the roads. Outlaws, jaguars, jungles."

"That's exactly why you need me to protect you."

"I think the bandits"—he raised his ax—"need protection"—he swung—"from you."

"Will you send letters?"

"Of course."

"Artí, promise, or I'm coming to the jungle to find you."

He picked a splinter from his hand. Behind him, the land stretched its green and gentle way to the horizon. "Pajarita," he said, and there it was, their sphere, the hum of close exposure, in which they glimpsed the depths of their own minds. "I promise letters will come."

They never did. Two years had passed. He couldn't be dead. Any moment now, a letter would come, strangely stamped, bearing good news. Or Artí himself would arrive at the door, dusty, glowing, telling tales, inviting her to cities full of music. Or he would not and she would lie here, night after night, completely alone, awake on the old family hides. Unless she left—for where? Montevideo? The stranger's home? Montevideo had rock-solid roads and ships at dock from everywhere. A city beyond the Río Negro, which she had never crossed; there were stories of travelers who'd drowned, horse and all, trying to ford its waters. Even now, with a bridge in place, very few **tacuaremboenses** had ventured over it. But this man, this stranger, this fumbling magician, had.

He had looked at her as if she carried sunshine in her body. As if he'd wanted to get under her skin to taste it.

Tía Tita's breath came steady, steady, deep in sleep. Pajarita reached her hand beneath her nightgown. She let her fingers feather along her belly, her thighs, the silky hairs between them. The heat beneath.

The moon poured milk into the room, lush, familiar, and she thought of all the rooms and lands and bodies being washed by the same light.

Ignazio strode, urgent, through the grass. Its fronds brushed sultry heads around his knees. It was his second visit, and tomorrow he had to leave Tacuarembó. My last chance, he thought, and rolled up his sleeves, then remembered propriety and rolled them down again. He arrived at the **ranchito,** knocked, and crossed the leather curtain. Tía Tita and Pajarita squatted at the cooking fire. He removed his hat.

"Pajarita," Tía Tita said, "we need more firewood. Show our guest the woodpile."

He followed her along a foot-worn path, through air still fecund from the heat. She stopped at a pile of cut wood that reached her waist. Don't think about her waist, he thought, stop shaking. He held out his arms. She gave him a log. She gave him branches. More branches. Twigs. It was a gamble. It was always a gamble.

"Pajarita."

She looked up at him. Her face filled with dusky light. **"¿Qué?"**

"Will you, you know, will you marry me?" He wished he could kneel, but his arms were full and he feared that he'd send kindling flying everywhere. "You are so beautiful and perfect and I'm tired of being, well, I want you with me, in Montevideo. Come with me. Be my wife."

He could not read her eyes; they didn't waver. All around them rose the musk of summer grass.

"I don't know."

"Do you love someone else?"

"No."

"Do you love me?"

"I don't know you."

"I love you, Pajarita. Do you believe me?"

She paused so long he thought she might never answer. "Yes."

"Yes—to what?"

"Yes, I believe you."

"Oh." He faltered. "We leave tomorrow. I could save some money, visit in the fall. Maybe then you'd have an answer?"

"Maybe."

He strained for something else to say—something gallant, captivating—but she was already walking back down the path. He followed her, spilling twigs. Dinner sped by, and much too soon it was time to go.

Ignazio slept fitfully that night, and woke up queasy. He could not ingest a thing, not even **mate.**

"**Ay.**" Cacho passed the gourd to Bajo, the midget. "No **mate.** I see it's serious."

They took apart the tents, booths, and stages. It was a rapid process; they were flimsy, makeshift edifices, after all.

The Spaniard slapped his back. "Don't worry, Gondola. There's plenty of other women."

Ignazio said nothing.

"Look," Consuelo called from her wagon, pointing to the western hills.

Ignazio turned and saw two horses on a green crest, one carrying Tía Tita, and one carrying Pajarita, poised amid bags of belongings, looking like a savage angel. They rode up to Ignazio. Pajarita looked down from her saddle. Her eyes were dark waters he could drown in. "The priest is at the church," she said. "If we go now, he can have us married in an hour."

Ignazio glanced at the Spaniard, who nodded his permission. He mounted her horse, his thighs against her hips. They rode together into town, with Tía Tita, Cacho, Consuelo, and Bajo on horseback in their wake. By the time they arrived in the plaza, three dozen **tacuaremboenses** had joined their caravan. In the church, the pews crackled with attention as Ignazio and Pajarita exchanged vows. For better or for worse, the priest intoned, almost melodically. In sickness and in health. Yes, they said. Yes, again. A sigh rippled through the pews. Cacho wiped his tears with leather rope. An infant next to Cacho howled in satisfaction (she had made terrific tooth marks on a Bible). The priest pronounced it done: man and wife.

They rode back to the campsite, where the blond twins blared their trumpets, wreaking havoc among the horses.

"Señora Firielli," the Spaniard pronounced and, carried away by the moment, bowed. "Welcome to

Carnaval Calaquita. We'll escort you to your new life." He reached for her bags. "We've made room for your things."

She moved his hand. "This one stays with me."

"Of course," he said uncertainly, and took the remaining bags.

Ignazio beamed at Tía Tita over his bride's head. "Doña Tita, don't worry. I will treat your niece like a queen."

"You will. You must." Tita reached across the divide between their horses, and pressed Pajarita's palm. She touched the sack her niece had guarded. Ignazio felt his new wife's breathing deepen, and tightened his arms around her. Tía Tita seemed to drink Pajarita with her eyes. Then she pulled her reins and rode up the path and out of sight.

The company rode for many hours that day, all the way to the tranquil shore of the Río Negro. That night, before crossing into the southern half of Uruguay, Carnaval Calaquita camped at the edge of the river. Consuelo, the magician's wife, Mistress of Disguises, found a secluded grove and made a nuptial bed of cowhide, wildflowers, and the blue velveteen that had curtained the stage the night the couple had met.

Ignazio lay down with Pajarita under the round light of the moon. He kissed her shoulders. He untied her braids and shook her hair loose and it poured into his hands, dark, rich, as smooth and dangerous as water. She reached for him. He meant to touch her with slow reverence but urge propelled him into her and she was ready, wide, sighing. Afterward they slept an opulent sleep.

He woke. She was in his arms. It was still night. He listened to the low, wet murmur of the river, and breathed the scents around him: sex, grass, eucalyptus, leather, and, above all, her. His mind roamed to the sack she'd kept with her. It lay a few paces from their bed, plump with whoknowswhat inside it. He crawled out of the hides and carefully opened the bag. Out spilled armfuls of ceibo leaves, ombú fronds, eucalyptus, plants he did not recognize. Rough barks. Black roots. Sharp little kernels. Their acrid smells deluged his nose and imagination. He felt a surge of horror—he had married a stranger; his life was entwined with a stranger's life. The thought struck him like a slap, both harsh and thrilling, like the moment he'd first left Italian land. When he finally fell asleep, Ignazio dreamed of gondolas full of ceibo leaves, gliding down the Río Negro, perturbing the dark waters in their wake.

STRANGE WIRES
AND STOLEN SACRAMENTS

Montevideo was unspun wool, full of rough billows, gray mazes, raw promise.

Monte. Vide. Eu. I see a mountain, one of the first Europeans to sight this land had said. Pajarita had never seen a mountain, but even she could tell there were none here. This city had no slopes. No, that was not true: its ground lay flat, but buildings pushed up everywhere, gathering their height into the sky. If only she could be a bird in more than name: she'd soar above the city and then—what would she see? A mesh of cobbled streets and walls, riddled with people, crushed up against the sea. No, not the sea: it was a river, that long smooth water, fringed with rocks. Argentina lay somewhere on the other side. Perhaps, in her high glide, she would glimpse it winking into view.

Here, in this city, one could think of flying. Here it was easy to forget about the ground. Like, for example, in their new Ciudad Vieja apartment, where everything seemed vertiginously high: the flights of stairs to the door, the brass bed frame that suspended their mattress over air, chairs twice as tall as bull skulls with upright wooden backs, the stove made for cooking standing up instead of squatting. And the window at which she perched to absorb Calle Sarandí, with its stony breath; its men in clean black hats and women with their baskets; the clap of horseshoes and the subtly sighing trees; the sweet press of a far accordion and the hawking voice of the grocer who had told her that the world was at war.

In that first autumn of 1915, Pajarita spent long hours watching the street from her window while Ignazio worked at the docks. At night, every night, she discovered him anew, like terrain whose growth and wind patterns keep changing. Ignazio. Unslakable. He liked everything she fed him. He succumbed on a nightly basis to his appetites. He arrived home after dark, sea-salted, tired, just in time to eat, make love, and sleep. These happened in the same order every time. A rhythm formed between them: the fall of dark, Ignazio's steps home, Pajarita in the kitchen, **milanesas** frying noisily in the pan, their home suffused with the oily scents of living. They came together around a small square table. Dinner sang its crisp and clinking sounds. Ignazio, revived by beef and wine, filled with his other hunger. He turned down the oil lamp and stared at her; she let herself be seen; he reached across the table to touch her. She heard her fork fall to the floor. He carried her, half naked, to the bed, and there she writhed and shook and wept as if the world had broken open, as if knives of intense light punctured the world.

Then, before dawn, she slid from his arms and cleared the table for breakfast. He was gone to work before full morning's light. How strange, thought Pajarita, to live so close to a man and rarely see him in the sun. Daylight was shared only on Sundays, when, after mass—or instead of it—they often strolled along the edge of the river, husband and wife, hand in hand, shoes sinking into sand. Here, the thick feel of Montevideo untied slightly, easing out over gentle waves. Rounded stones and sudden seashells lined the ground. Fishing boats caught long arms of sun. Here it was the easiest to envision flight: a lift of salty breeze and there she was, above the shore in the expansive sky, soaring toward the blue crown of the world.

Part in flight, and part beside him, she listened to Ignazio. He spoke of work. Of dreams. Of Venezia, though not about his family: Ignazio never said a word about his mother or his father or any other relative. The whole territory of Venetian memory seemed devoid of human presence. From his telling, it appeared that Venezia held only gondolas, elegant, unpeopled. These swarmed through the city, cool, carved creatures, water-beings made of wood. He spoke of them with the timbre of obsession.

"I won't always work at the docks, **mi amor.**" He picked up a flat, pale pebble. "Gondolas will make us rich. I can feel it. I'll build them, and we'll sail them, right here on the Río de la Plata."

He scanned the river's surface as if measuring it with his eyes. He threw the pebble; it skipped along the water and then sank. "A peso per ride. People will love that, don't you think?" He clasped Pajarita's hand. "I can just see it now, our little fleet gliding across the water. Our fleet. Our water."

Pajarita felt his eager squeeze around her fingers and squeezed back. She felt the scar on the finger whose tip had been cut off, somewhere, sometime, in a story she did not know. A fishing boat with red peeled paint glided near the shore. A fisherman stood inside it, hauling a net onto deck. It looked almost empty: nothing but a flapping trout or two. Other days, she'd seen nets rise and glisten with a mass of silver bodies. No one knew the rhythms of the deep. On an angry day one hundred red boats could stay empty.

Ignazio put his arm around her shoulder. She felt his calloused palm against her neck.

"Before all that," he said, "I'll build you a house."

And so he did. He borrowed money from his friend Pietro, who now owned a shoe store on a dense little street near the Plaza de Zabala. With this loan, Ignazio bought supplies—planks, bricks, saw, nails, hammers, doorknobs, sheets of glass, mysterious new things called electrical wires, the right to a little patch of land on the outskirts of town, in a rustic area called Punta Carretas that reminded Pajarita of Tacuarembó, with its open air, flat earth, low grass, and small **ranchitos.** Only here, of course, a saline shore breeze swept through her hair as she walked dirt paths. A nearby lighthouse beamed a slow, slow swirl across the night.

"With that **farol** there," Ignazio said, "we'll never get lost in the dark."

Board by board, their house arose. Brick by brick, it strengthened. Ignazio hammered, measured, mortared, hauled; Pajarita sewed and watched him. She watched for when he needed something from her basket—hot **mate,** a spinach **buñuelo,** an empanada she'd stuffed with ham and cheese the night before, a handkerchief to wipe his forehead, extra caresses, extra nails. He worked on it for months. Each nail pierced a dart of hope through wood. Each strange electric vein ran prayers through the walls. Each corner came to being through their wanting, through their sweat. No prior lives had seeped into these spaces: they could leave the past outside and begin their own story, a sprawling narrative encased in four fresh walls, with unknown chapters and generations and twisting turns whose very notion made her long to crane her neck into the unlit reaches of the future.

"This is our palace, **mi reina,**" he called down from the roof. "I can see everything!"

Pajarita, standing on the earth below, called back, "Careful, don't fall."

"These men," a voice behind her said. "They're always climbing a bit too far for their own good."

Pajarita turned. A woman stood a few meters away, holding a large basket. Bloodstains streaked her apron. She stepped closer.

"I'm Coco Descalzo," she said, "from the butcher shop." She pointed down the path at a house with a hand-painted sign. "What's your name?"

"Pajarita."

"Where are you from?"

"Tacuarembó."

"Really! So far north!" Coco squinted up at Ignazio, at work again. "Your husband too?"

"No. He's Italian."

"Ah." Coco moved her basket from one ample hip to the other. "When your house is finished, come get a nice **churrasco** from my shop. A welcome gift."

Pajarita and Ignazio painted their house the color of sand and filled it with a bed, three chairs, a table, and mint-and-lemon wallpaper. They cleaned out their apartment in La Ciudad Vieja and left it for good. They ate **milanesas** and rice in their new kitchen under the lighthouse's pulse. In bed, their rhythm slowed to match the beam gliding over them: a beat of light, then pulling back, a beat of light.

The next morning, Pajarita made her husband breakfast, saw him off, and walked the path to Carnicería Descalzo. The butcher shop had low ceilings and sharp, pungent air. Two women talked at the counter. Coco presided behind it. Pajarita lingered near the door and examined the beef. It was good meat, red and lean and freshly slaughtered. The women were talking about war. The English, apparently, were winning: the woman who was shaped like a soccer ball had heard this. The lady in the huge hat had a son who liked the war because soldiers need uniforms, and Uruguay had wool.

"**¡Por favor!**" Coco said. "That makes it good? Do you know how many boys have died already?"

"I suppose," said Huge Hat Lady. "In Europe. But here we're doing well."

"Hmmph," Coco said. "That's thanks to **batl-lismo,** good schools, good pay, not the war." She pursed her lips. "Pajarita. Come in!"

Pajarita approached the main counter.

"This is our new neighbor. I promised her a **churrasquito.**" She bent to look for one among the thin, lean sheets of meat.

"I'm Sarita," the big woman said, staring at Pajarita with frank curiosity.

Huge Hat Woman squinted at Pajarita. "Well? What do you think?"

She looked uncertainly at the woman. Her eyes were small and mouselike. "About what?"

"About the Great War! Is it good or what?"

She hesitated. These women spoke of things that happened so very far away, as though they saw across great distances and were accustomed to appraising the turning of the world. She thought of Europe, a nebulous place her mind could not bring into focus. She thought of soldiers, like the ones who'd joined the rebels in her grandfather's time, returning to Tacuarembó with missing limbs, howling dreams, twitching mouths.

"It must be 'what.' "

Sarita laughed. The woman in the hat scowled, took her package, and left.

"Don't worry about her." Sarita looked vaguely victorious. She smelled of vanilla perfume. "She loves to complain."

Coco handed Pajarita a neat paper package. "Welcome to Punta Carretas."

Pajarita returned the next day and the next, and within a week she began drinking **mate** upstairs from the **carnicería,** in Coco's home, during siesta time while the butcher shop was closed. Coco's husband, Gregorio, stayed down in the shop, cutting and carving and hanging up meat. Their baby, Begonia, crawled underfoot. In days where work began before dawn and went into the night, the siesta hour at Coco's was a refuge, a raft of time, a stolen sacrament for those who came. The Descalzo living room teemed with knickknacks, bright décor, and an authentic English tea set enshrined at the center of the mantel. Coco was extremely proud of her Anglo cups and saucers, which gathered dust while her **mate** gourd made daily rounds. Above the tea set hung a photograph of José Batlle y Ordóñez, the recent president, who, Pajarita gathered from conversation, had transformed Uruguay into a modern, democratic nation with his thoughts and laws and words. The photograph, framed in silver, showed a large, jowled man gazing gravely to the right of the camera. There was always a large platter of **bizcochos,** whose sweet-pastry layers melted in the mouths of Punta Carretas women. These women. Like Sarita Alfonti, with her inescapable scent of vanilla, her laugh like two copper pots colliding, her hands that cut the air when she spoke. And La Viuda, who had been widowed so long that her original name had been forgotten. She sat in the corner, on the rocking chair, and blessed or dismissed comments with a wave of her hand. And María Chamoun, whose grandparents had come to Uruguay carrying the spices of their native Lebanon. Sometimes she still smelled of them, very faintly, a nuanced aroma that made Pajarita think of summer shadows. María had hair like a prize stallion's, lush and dark. She had perfected the art of making **alfajores al nieve.** The two biscuits were smooth and slender, dulce de leche joining them with calibrated sweetness, powdered sugar pressed on curves with delicate tenacity. María Chamoun oversaw their consumption with the pride of an unrivaled champion. Clarabel Ortiz, La Divorciada, always leaned into sofa cushions, the first woman in Punta Carretas to exercise her legal right to divorce. In Coco's living room, this gave her notoriety and an intangible mystique. Her face was pallid, her lips painted pink. Her body was shaped like a fence post. Clarabel held occasional séances in her newly empty home. Some women joined her. Others scoffed.

"Hmmph! Shaking teacups tonight?"

"They don't always shake, Sarita, and you know it."

"Still. I'd just as soon leave my dead alone. Even if they could be raised, which they can't, why give myself more headaches?"

"Espera. Pero no." La Viuda raised her palm. "Séance or no séance, the dead are there for more than headaches."

Silence hung in the room. Coco took the **mate** from Pajarita's hand. She poured in water and gave it to María Chamoun.

"Did you hear?" María said. "Gloria's granddaughter was found by the lighthouse, pushed up on the rocks under a boy." She dropped her voice. "Her blouse was open."

"¡Esa chica!"

"She's been trouble since her birth."

"I heard she got a good whipping from her father."

"She'll never see the boy again."

"That's all a bit **exagerado.** So what if she has a boyfriend?"

"Clarabel! You have the strangest ideas."

Clarabel also believed that women should have the right to vote, and would soon gain it. She had her friends practice by casting votes on perfumed pink papers that she gathered in a basket and mailed to city hall. They were still discussing the recent election of President Viera.

"I just couldn't put his name down."

"What other choice did we have?"

"Granted, he's not as good as Batlle, but no one can be."

"Phht. He tried to stop the law for eight-hour workdays. Good thing he was too late."

"Well, thanks to Batlle, we have it."

"And education. And pensions."

"And divorce."

"And peace." La Viuda's hand flew up, a bony bird. "Reprieve from coups and bloodshed. The last century was terrible. I remember."

They found Pajarita fascinating, with her darker-than-most-of-them skin, her **campo** origins, her name after an animal. They demanded stories about her gaucho family, and the way she'd lived in Tacuarembó, as if it were all wild and romantic and just a touch unsavory. Pajarita felt a bit like the English tea set, removed and exposed, only not for the fragile glint of china but the leathery musk of **campo** life. She drank in their presence as a way to taste the city, and slowly it occurred to her that through her they perhaps reached for the land. That's how it is, she thought; we carry worlds inside ourselves and long to taste the worlds of others, we stare and prod and sip and can't inhabit. Sometimes she felt their interest as a slight—Oh, look, Pajarita, she is brown, she cannot read, isn't it novel? Coco was not like that. She came in close, bold as a hare. Sometimes, after siesta hour, Pajarita lingered alone with her, helping her clean up, listening to her chatter and confessions. She gave Coco herbs to ease her female cycles, her nerves, her secret impatience with husband and daughter. They were easy to concoct out of the stash she'd brought from Tacuarembó and the wild trees and weeds in the neighborhood. In return for these gifts, Coco helped her write letters home.

" '**Dear Tía Tita,**' " she dictated, as Coco wrote

and eked the last weak flavor from the **mate, " 'How is home? I miss you. Montevideo is colder this winter than the last. It's never as hot as in Tacuarembó. Ignazio is well. He has been promoted at the port. He says business is good these days, there are many exports, because of the—'"**

"War in Europe? No, don't say that. That's not happy news. How about 'because of his hard work'?"

"Ta. **'How is Papá? How is everyone? The town? The family? The chickens? Send everyone my love. Thank you for the wool. And please let me know if you hear from Artigas.** Con cariño, **Pajarita.'"**

The late-siesta sun seeped through the window, grudging and golden, taking its time. The room smelled of mothballs and fresh sausage and soap. Coco finished writing and then laughed, for no good reason, her laugh a warm brass bell.

"Mi reina," Ignazio asked in bed, "are you lonely all day without me?"

Pajarita fingered the curls on his chest. "No."

"Why not? You don't love me?"

"Don't be silly. I just like the neighborhood. I've made friends."

"Men?"

"No."

More grimly, this time, "men."

"Please, Ignazio—no."

The lighthouse swept its beam through the silence. It swept again. Ignazio sat up sharply. His broad silhouette blocked out the window. "I wish you would get pregnant."

Pajarita sat up too. She turned on the lamp beside her and waited until the electric light no longer jarred their eyes. She had been stalling, waiting for the right moment, unable to intimate its shape. "I am."

Ignazio's face went blank, then soft, then (just for an instant) pained, then he kissed her mouth, her cheeks, her body. The light clicked off.

Being pregnant felt like turning into an orange: her skin turned taut and round and she was full of potency. She ripened more each day. The thing inside her made her sick until it made her euphoric, full of tears and heft and motion: the strange being inside her turned and lurched and pelted in the middle of the night, making her ravenous for the future.

Birth came the day that men across the oceans signed a paper to end war. On November 11, 1918, while the streets of Montevideo filled with drums and confetti and loud sweat, Pajarita lay at home in white-hot labor. She survived the birth without injuries, with the small exception of a scolding from the doctor for having squeezed the baby out while he was gone from the room. He had left to confer with Ignazio in the kitchen, when they heard a cry and ran to the bedroom to find Pajarita, red-faced, heavy-breathed, a drenched blue infant wailing between her thighs.

They named him Bruno. Friends filled the house, including Cacho and his wife, Consuelo, who had sewn baby clothes adorned with sequins; Coco and Gregorio Descalzo, with Begonia and their new baby girl and the ribs of a whole cow; the Punta Carretas women with their baskets of hot food; the Spaniard and Bajo the midget, bearing poker chips; and Pietro (tall and sparkly) and his wife and baby. Their little house swelled with noise and laughter. Cacho did magic tricks that made Sarita gape and Clarabel cheer like a sailor. The Spaniard fawned on La Viuda like a fresh young suitor, making the old woman blush for the first time in twenty years. María sang baby Bruno an Arabic lullaby as he drowsed against her prodigious breasts. Bajo, to his delight, beat Pietro several times at cards.

After the last person had left, Pajarita still felt the loud, tender breath of guests. It curled around her as she lay in bed, cradling Bruno, listening to her husband turn off the kitchen light, enter the room, and sink down beside her. He lay completely still. She touched his shoulder.

"What are you thinking about?"

"Being a father."

She stroked his skin. "Are you happy?"

He didn't answer. He turned away. She stared at the outline of his back.

"Ignazio?"

No answer.

She lay still for a minute, then another. Bruno

squirmed and began to whimper. She raised her nightgown and placed him on her breast. Lay silent in the dark while he ate.

That night Ignazio dreamed he swam underwater, in a Venetian canal, looking for the body of a woman. His father's corpse, blue and engorged, floated toward him. Rotting arms pushed forward to enfold his body. He tried to scream, tried to resist, but when he opened his mouth it filled with putrid water.

A prison arose in Punta Carretas. Right there, across from Carnicería Descalzo, the crank and haul of strange machines brought it into being. A vast wall formed, with an arching gate at its center, and behind the gate a huge box of a building was taking shape. It was imposing, castlelike, the most majestic structure Punta Carretas had ever known.

"At least it's pretty," Sarita said, leaning on the sausage counter.

"But it's a prison," Coco said. "It blocks our view of the lighthouse. And what kind of neighbors will we have?"

"There's no stopping it." La Viuda spread her hands in a gesture of doom. "The whole **barrio** is changing. Punta Carretas is pure city now."

This was true. The stone and density of downtown was creeping into Punta Carretas. The city had

claimed the **barrio.** Pajarita's door no longer opened
to a vague dirt path, but onto hard stone sidewalk.
By the time she gave birth to Marco (a solemn baby,
compared to Brunito's restless roving), Punta Carretas
had changed beyond recognition. Houses thronged to
either side of them, pushing wall right up to wall;
cobbles filled a street outside their door; a church
took shape beside the rising prison. The air thickened. The lighthouse stopped reaching its slow beam
into her home. And all of this, the mayor said, the
president said, was progress; the city was larger, mod-
ernized, developed, Montevideo a worthy capital for
this nation, the Switzerland of South America, full
of hope and promise.

Amazing, Pajarita thought, how much the world
could change. How accustomed she could grow to
electricity, high stove, high chairs, high bed. How
land could disappear beneath homes and rock-hard
paving, and how men could turn into husbands who
then turned into—what? What was Ignazio becoming? Someone different from the **joven** she met years
ago; a man she sometimes barely recognized. It began
with the birth of their first son and deepened with
the second. Something inside him—pale and
pained—had swollen to unmanageable size. It
bulged. It never showed its naked face. It sank into
the sea of all the liquor he drank. It kept him far
away from her: in an era of eight-hour workdays, Ignazio came home later and later, drunk, face drawn
tight like reins on an unpredictable horse—or, other

nights, face loud, loose, unfettered. I don't deserve you. You don't love me. How could you. Why wouldn't you. Did you did you yes you did. She tried to answer but there weren't enough words and he never really posed a question. He grew obsessed with the idea that she had a lover. They fought over this phantom man's existence. There were nights when they fought until they collapsed against each other, and only in those hours could she reach for who she was and who he longed to be and open them toward each other, strain to fuse them in a crucible of heat. On other nights she woke to feel Ignazio rustling into place beside her and he reeked so strongly of drink and women's musk that she sent him out to sleep on the living room floor so she could lie alone, free of his scents, and miss his body.

She bore a third son. Tomás. Who looked so much like her brother, Artigas, that it hurt to look at him. Those same lean bones and bright eyes. She went to séances at Clarabel's house and asked about her brother. Nothing came. He couldn't be dead, couldn't be dead, couldn't be alive and not have written.

The pile of pesos Ignazio brought home each week slimmed down. It was too thin, barely stretched to feed the boys. She cornered him on a Sunday morning at the kitchen table.

"Ignazio. You're not bringing home all your pay. You have three sons, **querido.** You have to stop."

She had thought, she could have sworn, that he would fight; that his jaw would tighten, his voice would raise, his fist would crash on the table. Instead he stared at her, then out the window, toward the lighthouse hidden behind the prison-almost-finished. He was quiet. She waited. His profile stood crisp against striped wallpaper.

"Remember," he said, "when we first came to the city? How we walked along the shore of the river? As if it had no end. As if we could walk and walk and find only more waves, more sand, more water. I always wanted to put gondolas on that water. I'm going to do it. A peso per ride. We'll have more than enough for all of us."

Pajarita let her hands rest on her lap. They grasped each other. "How much would it cost to build them?"

Ignazio shrugged. "A sum."

"And where would that sum come from?"

"Leave that to me."

That night he was voracious with her, even more so when she dug her nails into his back and broke the skin.

Three days later, the prison across the street opened to great fanfare. **Montevideanos** from all parts of the city came to see. El Penal de Punta Carretas, it was christened. The mayor appeared on the steps and cleared his throat.

"My fellow **montevideanos,** we are here today to celebrate progress, to celebrate this formidable new building, but above all to celebrate this city." He wiped his forehead, rich with sweat, and adjusted his wool suit. "Montevideo is one of the most beautiful and modern places on the continent. Our climate, our beaches, our literature are unparalleled, and in the past twenty-five years, we have become a world-class city. Immigrants from Italy, Spain, France, and other nations have found a home here. We have established a democratic system inspired by the highest humanitarian ideals—the ideals of **batllismo,** the ideals at the heart of Uruguay." The crowd clapped, and the mayor paused, his chest puffed out like a sparrow's. "Yes, yes, we have accomplished this—while our giant neighbors, Argentina and Brazil, only dream of such stability. We may be small, but we are an exemplar of a nation; we are claiming our place in the world!" He pointed his index finger vigorously at the sky, and held it aloft as applause washed over him. "And so, my dear **montevideanos,** as we mark this day, as we open this state-of-the-art facility here in Punta Carretas, let us also look to the future. With all we have achieved in this century so far, just think of what awaits us in the rest of it. Our children and our children's children will stand on the foundations we have built for them, and carry us forward to our destiny. We are a city of the future. The future belongs to Montevideo!"

He sliced the red ribbon that hung across the gate, dripping sweat, beaming in a deluge of applause. Sarita Alfonti shouted behind Pajarita. She felt the crowd's excitement, its hunger and pride. Champagne corks popped. An accordion pushed out chords. El Penal's cream-colored walls loomed, high, clean, unmoved.

That night, Ignazio did not come home. Pajarita awoke at 4 a.m. in a still-empty bed. She stared at the ceiling until it grew pale with dawn. Then she rose and made breakfast for the children: toast and warm milk and what was left of butter. Today was Ignazio's payday. When he arrived, more butter would come.

But he didn't arrive that day. Or that night. Or the next. Onions—she had onions; she could fry them for dinner and serve them on bread. More bread with mayonnaise for lunch.

He arrived on the sixth night. He looked ashy and haggard and did not meet her eyes. He smelled as if he had just been spit out of a war zone. He slouched in silence at the kitchen table. It took Pajarita two hours of pouring **mate** to coax him and discover what he'd done.

After his last night at home, Ignazio asked his boss for an advance on the next two months of work. He was a faithful employee, and so the request was granted. The loan constituted a third of what he needed for a fleet of gondolas. He took it straight to El Corriente, to triple it at the poker table. It didn't triple. He lost it all.

How smooth the wooden table was between them. Solid, it seemed—and yet one bite of an ax could, at any moment, break it open. Send halves reeling. Pajarita gripped the table's edge as though that act alone were keeping it in place. Gone. Two months of pay. And days yawning in front of them like mouths.

"What will we do?"

No answer.

"Ignazio—"

"Shut up, woman!" Ignazio stood so suddenly that the table knocked from her hands and fell. "Shut your stupid fucking mouth."

Pajarita stood too. "Don't shout at me."

Ignazio tightened backward in an enormous bow and arrow and the force of him flew forward in a fist that crashed against her face so that she fell against the wall, toward the floor; she curled around her burning face—the world was turning turning, full of shouting, full of stars, full of silence. Silence. Pain ebbed slightly. She was alone. No, not quite alone; his sounds came from the living room. She should go to him. She would not. She would stay here, furled on the floor, while he wept. But she was bleeding. She stood and sought a rag to wipe her face. The taste of iron tinged her tongue. She wet the rag and wiped again. Thank god thank god the children were asleep. She lifted the table into place, back onto four legs, and cleaned blood from the floor. Dizzy. She listened for living room sobs. None. She went to look. There he was, her husband, tear-streaked, drunk, fast asleep in the rocking chair. She walked past him to her room, to bed, to sleep.

The next morning, when she woke, the rocking chair was empty. No Ignazio. She used the last of the flour for bread that day. Crackers. There were still crackers. The days went by. No Ignazio. The crackers ran out. Only a quarter jar of mayonnaise left. Her hands (scrubbing, folding, brushing Bruno's hair, opening her blouse for hungry Tomás) shook.

Coco saved her with free meat, and an idea.

"First of all," Coco said, pushing a hefty package into Pajarita's hands, "you're taking this meat. I don't care what you say. I know your husband's gone—the **desgraciado.**" She sat her ample body down at Pajarita's table. Pajarita stared at the gift.

"I have no way to thank you."

Coco continued as if she hadn't heard. "Secondly: your plants. They're strong. You should sell them."

"Sell?"

"To women in the **barrio.** You can start in the store, behind the counter with me. Look, once word spreads about your cures, better than a doctor and cheaper too, you'll be putting food in those boys' bellies."

It had never occurred to her, but she couldn't think of a reason not to try. She took her children and a basket of leaves and roots and barks to the butcher shop. The boys resumed an epic pretend game of gauchos-in-the-**campo,** riding imaginary horses among the chunks of flesh that hung from the ceiling. In one corner of the room, between the chopping block and meat hooks, Pajarita arranged two small wooden stools and sat down on one. Ignazio, she thought, I want to kill you, to kiss you, to carve you like a flank; just wait and see how I'm going to live without you by my side.

Coco served as a living advertisement. Women began to come. Some of them just needed to be heard; they told sprawling, unkempt tales of death in the family, brutal mothers-in-law, financial pressures, wayward husbands, violent husbands, boring husbands, loneliness, crises of faith, visions of Mary, visions of Satan, sexual frigidity, sexual temptation, recurring dreams, fantasies involving saddles or bullwhips or hot coals. She offered them teas for comfort, luck, or protection. Other customers came with physical conditions—pain in their bones, a stitch in their side, numbness in hips, ears that rang, forgetfulness, sore knees, sore backs, sore hearts, sore feet, cut fingers, quivering fingers, wandering fingers, burns, headaches, indigestion, excessive female bleeding, a pregnancy that wouldn't come, a pregnancy that had to end, cracked bones, cracked skin, rashes no doctor could diagnose, aches no doctor could cure. There were housewives, maids, sore-handed seamstresses, sweaty-handed adulteresses, great-grandmothers swaying with canes, young girls swooning with love. Pajarita listened to them all. She sat still as an owl as she listened. Then she handed them a small package and explained what to do with its contents. Word spread. Women came to see her from all corners of the city. She could barely keep up with harvesting from cracks in the sidewalk, nearby parks, and the pots in her own house. To Coco's delight, the seekers often picked up their daily beef along with their cures. Pajarita set no price. Some gave her pesos, others fruit, a basket of bread, a ball or two of handspun wool. Anonymous gifts appeared on the Firielli doorstep—baskets of apples, jars of **yerba mate,** handmade clothes for the children. They had enough.

She had developed a peculiar sort of fame. Her name was whispered through the kitchens and vegetable stands of Montevideo. Pajarita, she cured me, you should go see her too. And when I almost. You saw me then. If it hadn't been for her. Strange, she thought, that all of this should grow from something as familiar as plants, such ordinary things, opening new worlds, drawing the souls and stories of this city to her doorstep, unveiling a startling thing inside her: a reach, a scope, adventures with no road map, forays into the inner realms of strangers where she roved the darkness in search of something that bucked and flashed and disappeared, slippery, evasive, untamable.

One sweltering afternoon, as a hunchbacked woman who smelled of garlic confessed her infatuation with the new priest, Pajarita felt something stir inside her body. Her mind reached in to feel. She was pregnant. A girl. She filled with the memory of conception, that final night, the clawing, Ignazio's torn and hungry skin. And he was gone. She almost imploded from the sadness.

She let the garlic woman finish and offered her sympathy, a package, and instructions. She crossed the curtain.

"Coco."

"Sí."

"I'm stopping for the day. I'll take the children up-stairs for siesta."

"All right, Rita, I'll join you soon."

She returned to the children. Bruno crouched be-hind the chopping block, a soldier in combat, cow-bone gun aimed at his brother Marco.

"¡Paf! You're dead!"

Marco dropped his femur on the floor. "You cheated," he grumbled. Tomás toddled over and picked up one end of the bone. It fell from his hand and made a small crashing sound against the floor. He gurgled with joy.

In the corner, apart from the game, Andrés Descalzo sat drawing a stick of a person, a square of a house. Plenty of green and orange and purple lines everywhere. Finally a son, Coco had shouted when he was born two years ago. People called him El Car-nicerito, The Little Butcher, born to carry on the family store and save it from the fate of sons-in-law. He even looked like a miniature man, with his earnest face, as if he were always cracking the most important code.

"Time for siesta. Put the bones away."

They did as they were told in a burst of noise. An-drés returned his colored pencils to their box. Pajarita pulled an apple and a knife from her basket, and whisked off slices. She gave slices to her sons. Andrés was ready with an outstretched hand, the only son, just as the one she carried now would be the only daughter, and for one instant, as his hand touched hers and took the fruit, she flashed to a story, an old story, of an apple and a woman and a garden.

Eva, she thought, as she followed the children up raucous stairs. That is your name, and who can help it—no matter what you want to choose, the name chooses the child.

The year Eva Dolores Firielli Torres was born, the Rambla's construction began on the shore of El Río de la Plata. The loud growl of machines lined the city. They carved a sidewalk along the beach, a curving path with cream and maroon tiles where **uruguayos** could walk the edge of things, the line between water and city.

Eva was an acutely curious baby. She had pale skin, like her absent father and Marco and like the city women, but her hair was as black as her mother's, thick from the day she pressed out into the world. She loved things that glowed or glittered, like Pajarita's jade bracelet, bright bits of sun on water, the beam of the lighthouse as it slunk along night rocks.

When Eva was almost two, and talking with great enthusiasm, Pajarita received a letter from Ignazio. She ran immediately to Coco's to have it read aloud.

" 'Mi Reina,' " Coco read. "Hmmph! He has some nerve! 'I pray that you are well. I'm sure the family has been better off without me. Until three weeks ago, I have been in an underworld no lady should ever see. Nor should our sons. Here is a bit of money. I'll send more when I can.

" 'I can't think that you'll ever forgive me, nor believe me when I say this is for your protection. When my demons are gone, I will come home. I love you. Ignazio.' "

Over the next few years, his letters continued to come: intermittent, vague, amorous, folded carefully around damp pesos.

The storm came in from the east. Rain shouted against the roof. The sound of thunder woke and scared Eva, who ran from bed to find her mother in the kitchen, washing pots.

"Mamá! Can I stay with you?"

"Bueno."

"Tell me a story."

"Once there was a very friendly storm cloud—"

"I don't believe you."

"Why not?"

"Storm clouds are mean."

"Some are nice."

"No!"

"Why not?"

"They bring dark, and noise, and lots of rain."

"Rain can be a good thing."

Eva looked doubtful.

"It helps the plants grow."

Eva shrugged. "So?"

"**¿Cómo que** so? So—"

Knocking at the door. The roar of rain. More knocking.

They stared at each other.

"Do you think it's a storm cloud?" Eva asked.

"Let's go find out."

They walked, hand in hand, to the door.

"**¿Quién es?**" Pajarita called.

"Ignazio."

Can't be. Can't be. The door pulsed like a great wooden beast, breathing in rhythm with the rain. She opened it and there he stood, umbrella in one hand, a bouquet of roses in the other. Yellow. Ivory. Red.

She let him enter. He stood uncertainly at the lip of the living room. **"Querida."** Drops gathered and fell from his hat's brim.

"Who's that, Mamá?"

Ignazio stared down.

"Eva," Pajarita said, "this is your papá."

Ignazio's eyes widened. Eva's narrowed. He crouched to her level, taking in her face, her set jaw, thick black hair in braids.

"You don't look like my papá."

"What does your papá look like?"

"I don't know."

"Maybe he looks like me."

"Why do you have those flowers?"

"I thought . . . you might like them."

"Why were you out in the rain?"

"I . . . **este** . . ."

"Eva," Pajarita said, "back to bed. It's very late."

Ignazio hovered in the doorway while Pajarita smoothed the blankets over Eva, crooning a lullaby. **Arrorró mi nena, arrorró mi sol.** She felt his stare on them and on the second bed where Tomás slept. **Arrorró pedazos, de mi corazón.** Rain still pounded above them but, for now, no thunder. Eva's muscles softened into rest.

They tiptoed back to the living room.

Ignazio extended his flower-hand. Sheepishly.

Pajarita took the roses from him. Their tissue paper crinkled in her hand. She pictured herself pulling each rose out, stem by stem, and throwing them at this man now dripping rain onto her carpet. She pictured herself winding them tightly around his neck. She pictured herself slipping them down the top of her dress, crushing them against her, thorns and all. Instead she got a vase of water from the kitchen, and placed the flowers on the coffee table. They sat down on two chairs, with the bouquet between them, two people in an ordinary storm.

"You've kept the house so pretty."

Husband, Pajarita thought. This is my husband. "Where have you been?"

"In the old part of town. In a tenement near Calle Sarandí. Living—no, not living." He paused. He examined the arm of her chair. "One night, Cacho found me in an alley. I was unconscious, bleeding from a stab wound. He saved me. He took me in, cleaned me up, found me work and made me take it. Pietro helped me too. I started writing to you. Every day I dreamed of coming home."

"But you didn't."

"I couldn't. I was a monster."

"What are you now?"

"A man. A husband."

"Do you have any idea what it's like to see your children hungry?"

"They won't be hungry anymore."

"No, they won't—whether you stay or not. I work. We have enough."

Ignazio looked surprised, and she could have slapped the expression off his face. She felt strong, hot, alive with triumph. Oh, Ignazio, sad man, sad bastard, you left one woman but you came home to another, little do you know who I've become: I crush leaves by the kilo, my teas have warmed the city, the city has left apples at my door. She felt her own height, her substance, beyond the dimensions of her body. She sat up in her chair, a queen on her throne, gazing at the supplicant before her.

"I want to stay," he said.

"You'll have to change."

"I will."

"It'll take time."

"I'll wait. I'll sleep on the floor."

"Yes. You will."

He drew back. They sat in the dim lamplight. This could be such a wet and heavy world. It could flood a normal night with ruthless rain; could sweep a man away along its currents, and spit him up again on long-lost shores; could seep into your secret soil, even when you wish you wish you wish you could stay dry. The roses had filled the room with a scent you could get drunk on. Petals preened as if forgetting the dark shrivel of tomorrow or the next day or the next. Ignazio leaned forward. He had that look that happened when he hoped—a kind of lifting in the eyes. His hand touched hers and it was warm and it had stroked her sons at birth, had trembled in her body, had built the roof that stretched above them, wet sky kept at bay; she missed the calloused contours of this hand that made a fist (once) and reached for liquor (more than once). One hand so many uses. One hand so much to hold.

"Pajarita."

She longed to curl up to his body, longed to throw him out into the rain. She stood, left, returned with two blankets and a pillow. "You can use these."

He looked bruised. "Thank you."

"Good night, Ignazio."

"Pajarita."

She turned away and left the room without looking at him.

He slept on the floor for a month. Every morning, she woke up thinking he was gone, he could be gone, she'd go out there and see nothing but a twisted blanket. But every morning, he was there, still sleeping in the pale dawn light. She clanged the pots overly loud as she made breakfast, to wake him up. She thought she'd have to fold the blankets herself, but he put them away as soon as he rose. The children never saw his makeshift bed. The boys were thrilled to have their father back, clambering all over him, laughing at all his jokes, fighting one another for his attention, as if he'd just returned from a protracted but perfectly explicable trip. Eva hung back at her mother's skirts at first, eyeing him, unsure. But within two weeks, he'd wooed her with his conspiratorial smile and old Italian songs. He held her on his lap, **My sweet, my only princess,** and Eva glowed with her transformation into royalty. His tenderness was palpable. It enraged Pajarita. She did not touch him. During the day, he went to work at the port and she went to the butcher shop. In the evenings, he played with the children while she did the dinner dishes. He waited until they had been in bed for three hours before spreading his blankets on the floor. Some nights, she shut herself into her bedroom and left him to spend those hours alone. On other nights, he persuaded her to stay.

"Tell me about your work."

"I've already told you."

"Tell me more."

He failed to hide his amazement at the butcher shop, the bundles, the lines of women waiting for her help. He listened avidly, as if the stories held something he had lost. He himself seemed lost. He was a ship with no anchor, in uncharted waters, uncertain how to steer his bulk and weight.

"When are you going to let me back in?"

"You are in."

"You know what I mean."

"Good night, Ignazio."

She didn't have the answer to his question. It might have taken much longer if it hadn't been for the second homecoming. Years afterward, as a gray-haired woman trying to understand her grand-daughter Salomé, holding her thin hand on a rattling bus after fifteen years of fearing for her life, Pajarita would think back to this year, 1930, the year of homecomings, and decide that there must have been a magnet, some cosmic unseen magnet that attracted—instead of pots and nails—the men she loved back home, just as Salomé was coming home now, like some miraculous, emaciated changeling. Such things do happen; all kinds of ore lies buried inside lives, and surely people can't see all the forces that push them, draw them, hold them up. Sometimes you call the forces forward yourself, without knowing that you've done so. In the year of home-comings, in 1930, two weeks before Ignazio came home, Pajarita had knelt before a ceramic statue of San Antonio and prayed on Coco's behalf. **San Antonio, patron saint of lost things, please make Coco's shawl appear. The red one her abuelita made.** She'd lit a candle and dropped coins in the box. **And also please make anything I've lost come back. Hail Mary and amen.** San Antonio flicks his holy wrist. A magnet stirs. And if she could believe in that, the wrist, the coins, the magnet, then she could believe that what washed up at her door could still be hers.

Late one night, a knock sounded at the door. Ignazio had been home a month, and they sat in the living room, listening to the winter rains.

"Are you expecting anyone?"

She shook her head. More knocking.

Ignazio stood, looking wary. "Who is it?"

"Pajarita?"

The voice pushed at her, made her rise and grasp the knob and turn and pull and there he was. Artigas. Drenched and shivering under a too-small umbrella. Overgrown hair clung to his head. He held hands with a little girl, about five years old, a **mulata** with Artigas' hazel eyes. She was also wet. She stared up at Pajarita.

Artigas said, "Are you going to let us in?"

She motioned for them to enter. Her brother dripped onto the rug. She could taste the verdant plains of Tacuarembó, the hot dry wind, the smell of stew from the cooking pit, the crack of firewood under Artigas' ax, his smell, his voice, his shadow in the dark.

"Hermana."

She fell into his arms and he drenched her. Ignazio was on his feet, staring at the handsome man, the child, his damp wife. I'm dreaming, Pajarita thought. Any moment I might fly or wake or turn into a frying pan. "Artigas, this is my husband. Ignazio, this is my brother—"

"And this is Xhana. My daughter." Artigas squeezed the girl's hand. Xhana pressed her cheek against his trouser leg.

"Hola, querida," Pajarita said. "You must be cold."

Xhana nodded.

"Let's dry you off. Both of you. You'll stay the night."

"You don't mind?" Artigas said. "You have room?"

Pajarita raced through the domestic calculation in her mind. Five beds, four of them children's. Xhana could sleep with Eva: one plus one made one. Artigas could take the living room floor (space number six), except that place was taken by her husband. And what would her brother think at the sight of her husband on the floor?

"Of course there's room. If you don't mind the floor."

"I love the floor."

"Ignazio, could you please get the spare blankets?"

In the next few minutes, Pajarita heated **milanesas,** made hot chocolate, and found dry clothes for her guests while Ignazio made the bed on the living room floor. Artigas put his daughter to bed with Eva.

"She's fast asleep," he said when he came out.

The three of them hovered in the living room.

"Ignazio," she said. "I know you're tired. Perhaps you're ready for bed."

Ignazio hesitated. **"Este . . .** to bed?"

She nodded, as if it were quite natural.

"Artigas. If you'll excuse me."

"Of course. Good night."

She watched her husband disappear behind the bedroom door. "More hot chocolate, **hermano**?"

They sat down at the kitchen table. Artigas wore Ignazio's sweater, which was too broad in the shoulders, and musty from five years spent in a drawer.

He watched her pour more hot chocolate into his cup. "Are you angry?"

She put the ladle down. Looking at Artigas was like peering down a well into the past. You can't see the bottom, you balk at the echoes, but you look anyway. You chase shadows. You wait for lost coins to catch the light. "You promised you would write."

"I know. I'm sorry."

He meant it. If she wanted to, she could stay tightly wrapped and keep the knots inside her. But what a storm, what a late night, what a steaming cup of chocolate in her hands. Time to untie, unfurl, open to this kitchen with its jars of herbs, the miracle of children safe in sleep, the man with magic hands who'd called her to a stage so long ago, torn up and resewn and calling silent questions in her bed, Artigas back from the dead and gazing with the same eyes that, legend had it, coaxed a feral baby from a tree. She covered his hand with hers. "I missed you."

"God, I missed you too. I kept thinking I'd write soon, soon, when I was ready to come back. At least to visit. But it didn't go that way."

"Oh. So what way did it go?"

Artigas poured his stories for his sister.

It pierced him, that first ride into the wind. All the chains that had tethered him to Tacuarembó burst open with the pound of his horse's hooves on uncharted earth. The scenery enthralled him—look at that, a eucalyptus never before encountered, a hut surrounded by unknown chickens, a woman at a well who has never seen his face! The hot blue sky stretched wide above him. And the sounds. Not since he was seven had he heard such music. The wind rushed and moaned and rustled gutturally through treetops. His horse stomped, sparrows keened, and ravens rasped their answers. Crickets droned their rapture through the night. The song of the road poured into his ears, an aural intoxicant, full of all the chaos and insistent polyphony of the world. It made his heart ache like a muscle being moved more than ever before. Music. He gave himself to it, bathed himself in it, surrendered in devotion to the mystery of sound.

The road carried him north and eastward, toward Brazil, across the state of Tacuarembó and into Rivera. Along the way, he found people who could offer him a bowl of hot **puchero,** its broth curling out the scent of slow-cooked onions, or fresh **mate,** or a strip of floor for sleep. In exchange, he sang for them. He sang familiar ballads, and families joined in, opening their toothless mouths wide; he also wrote songs for the people he met, chronicling their fictitious adventures, strumming simple chords on his guitar. One family memorized the song—two lines each—so that, among the twelve of them, they could keep it alive. In another town, a tough-skinned widow wept and offered him three loaves of bread and her daughter's hand in marriage (the daughter blushed; Artigas smiled politely). He never stayed more than a night in one place. By the end of breakfast, there were too many questions about his family, how he could have left them, when he'd see them again. He answered vaguely and mounted fast, riding out onto sonorous land.

Just before the border, Artigas met Bicho and Bronco, brothers from the town of Treinta y Tres. Their family had disowned them for cryptic reasons, and Artigas was more than happy not to probe. They rode beside him. They shared lean physiques, quick smiles, and a fascination with Artigas' name, which evoked images of the heroes who had followed the first Artigas in the war for independence.

"We're like those old-time rebels," Bronco said. "Ha. Lead us into battle!"

"Are you leading us into battle?" Bicho eyed Artigas from under his hat's brim. "Or just into Brazil?"

"I'm not leading you anywhere," Artigas said. "We're just headed in the same direction."

Across the border, they found wilder and wilder roads. They traveled along the edge of the rain forest, a terrain so dense and moist and fertile that it seemed, to Artigas, as if inhaling might turn him green. On their eighth morning in Brazil, Artigas woke alone. The brothers were gone. They had taken his horse, his guitar, his meager pesos and parcel of clothes, even the **facón** he kept sheathed in his boot. He would kill those boys. He would die of terror. He had nothing and didn't know this place, he would be attacked by a snake or entrapped by vines, he would drown and die and rot in the bright, aggressive density of the forest.

He pressed on.

He traveled by foot. Song kept him sane. He sang every ballad he knew, one after another, as if they could stave off death, predators, and the maul of hunger. He sang under his breath, alert to sounds around him, the hum of creatures easing through their trees. On the third day, he finally went mute and listened to the forest. The place unfurled its sounds for him: wet. Thick. Exploding with green, relentless life, crying bird and shaking vine, a hymn of jaguarian grace.

He drank from delicate streams. He ate leaves and, soon, the earth itself, bringing worm-filled handfuls to his mouth. The first time, disgust allowed him to take only a small mouthful; the second time, he gave himself to the forest, kneeling in the dirt and scooping clumps, licking his fingers, feeding from the same place as the trees. He prayed that nothing he ate held poison. He prayed for life. He did not know, nor did he care, to whom or what he prayed. Days later, in an open plain, he found salvation: two iron tracks cut the landscape side by side. Train tracks. Artigas knew about trains, had seen their beams laid out in Uruguay, strange new creatures, faster than galloping steeds. He bent to kiss the shiny metal, then lay down beside it and closed his eyes. Time passed. His ears pricked. A train approached: a rumbling from the southwest, heading toward Rio. Clanks and growls grew louder and the long iron thing roared toward him, huge and fast and wormlike, its brown snout emitting a gust of steam, and suddenly the hulking cars of the train blurred past him, tall wheels churning with blinding speed, and No, he thought, I can't do it but I must he held his breath and leaped.

Wind and iron filled his ears. He clung to the side of a freight car, found a railing with his feet. He looked down and wished he hadn't—the ground rushed by. There was a sliding black door about a meter away, cracked open. He shimmied, carefully, slowly, toward it and held his breath as he lunged in.

A powerful stench surrounded him, the stench of shit. The car was piled, three meters high, with crates of manure. The high summer heat made them redolent with a smell that could invade the smallest pore. He thought of running out, but was frozen by the memory of speeding ground. Shit permeated every part of him, skin and under skin. He explored the narrow corridor between crates, but each step stank, there was no use and no escaping it; he slammed the side of a crate in revulsion. Behind the crate, some-one gasped.

He steeled himself. He longed for his **facón,** but would defend himself without it if he had to. He raised his fists and rounded the corner.

A family huddled among the crates: two young children, a compact young man, a woman with a baby in her arms, and an old man with silver hair. **Indios,** by their faces, which were full of fear. He lowered his fists. The boy shut his eyes. The girl stared up at him, eyes wide as moons. The woman glared.

The young man stood and raised his hands into the air, pleading with Artigas in halting Portuguese. "I won't hurt you," Artigas said. "No, no hurt." He kept repeating this phrase to the man, who was still explaining, gesturing urgently at his family. Finally, Artigas said, **"No soy del tren. Yo,"** pointing at his chest, **"no,"** shaking his finger, **"tren,"** gesturing around him.

Relief flooded the man's face. He rattled out fast, unfamiliar sounds. The woman kissed her baby's head, the small boy moaned, and the old man smiled, revealing a toothless mouth.

The man turned back to Artigas. **"Quem são você, então?"**

"Artigas. You?"

"Galtero."

They conversed in a stilted mix of Spanish and Portuguese. Galtero and his family, Artigas learned, were Guaraní people from the south of Brazil who had lived on Indian land for countless generations until last month, when men in strange suits had come from a place called Zaffari Supermarket Company; they claimed to own the land. They had no legal papers and no proof, but the government did not stop them. The men from Zaffari mowed down houses, razed field after field of manioc and corn, and left hundreds of families without home or harvest, scattered to the four winds.

The woman pulled out a **mate** gourd. She filled it with tepid water and offered it to Artigas. The thought of imbibing anything in this place revolted him—and yet, there it was, the reach of **mate,** that old gesture of friendship. His heart could split in pieces at her generosity. He accepted the gourd, held the **bombilla** to his lips, and drank. It tasted like manure smeared over grass.

That night, Artigas lay on the rumbling floor beside the little girl. In her sleep she sidled up to the crook of his arm. Her thick black braids reminded him of Pajarita. Where was his sister now? Loneliness heaved through him and pushed him down toward sleep. He dreamed of great green pastures ripping open and flooding with rivers of shit.

The next day rankled by to the clank and chant of metal. Galtero's story turned in Artigas' mind like an iron wheel. The cruelty of it crushed his thoughts. He told Galtero this.

"But that's not new," Galtero said. "How is it in your country?"

"We don't have such problems."

"Really? Indian land is respected?"

"No. . . . It's just . . ." He started to say **we don't have Indians in Uruguay,** but the sentence felt suddenly shameful. "We just don't think about it."

"That's amazing," Galtero said, "that your tribe doesn't have to think about it."

Artigas opened his mouth to correct the man, then closed it in confusion. At home he was not **indio;** nobody was. Galtero was wrong—or was he? Weren't there echoes of his own skin and hair and nose and shoulders in this man? Echoes could be faint and still reverberate, as they did now, jarring him, making something clatter in his mind, a story rising, the one about the miracle of 1700, exactly two hundred years before his sister appeared in a tree, when Guaraní songs had filled the New Year's air with lost strains he'd never heard before, nor had he heard the story of how such music had been lost, and at what cost. The clatter moved into his blood and ran through him, loud and red and sparkling, pushing something open in his body.

When the train reached Rio de Janeiro, Artigas and Galtero embraced, quickly, fiercely, and left the cargo car in separate directions, Galtero with his family, Artigas alone.

The streets were steep and raucous. He wandered, gaping at his first city, rife with people, ringed with a shock of verdant mountains. Under the blare and talk and hawking he heard music, drum and song that shook and penetrated him. He ran toward it, down the incline, around a corner, and it grew louder, rhythms locking tightly with one another, from many drums at once, dramatic, shattering, another corner, not the right one, he turned again and there they were, his destination, a troupe practicing for Carnaval, shaking the sky with their music, catching darts of sun in sequined costumes, mouths wide with song that surely was composed of divine voices from the strange sharp land itself, and he approached them, arms open, starved to sing.

The crowd parted fast around him. Dancers and drummers backed away in disgust. He stood alone in a sudden clearing.

"You stink," a lanky man said.

"Oh." His skin went hot with shame. "Sorry."

"Go away! Wash off!"

The man pointed and Artigas saw, down the hill, the crowded beach, and beyond that, the ocean. He ran.

The ocean was more vast and blue and marvelous than anything he had ever experienced. He gawked at it. He ogled. He fell to his knees at the lip of a white wave. It surged around his knees and licked his calves and toes, then washed back down as if to pull him in. There were crowds on the sand, clustered half naked in strange clothes and laughing at him, but he ignored them. Somewhere on the beach more drums were pulsing, urging, crying over and over, **Sí, sí.** He crawled into the water, salt spray on his tongue. Clean, cerulean water wrapped his body. He immersed himself completely and the waves rushed, deep-throated, keening, in his ears. He was engulfed, enfolded, an oceanic creature with a shock of salt at his lips. Shit shook out of his skin and clothes, shit shook from his bones, sorrow teemed from his heart and dissolved in saline water as the vast and ciphered body of the ocean held him in its great wet sway. He floated to the surface and let it carry him, basking in the sun, little tongues of water rippling on his body, and though he had no place to sleep, no cash, no friends nearby, no possessions that were not on his back or in his skin, a word washed through his mind and stayed there. Home.

He had two goals: to survive, and to study the drums. The drums had stayed with him, rang in his mind, shook him on the loud streets and in silence. His guitar was lost on the jungle roads. There was no turning back, no bringing his old music to the rich polyrhythms of this city. He longed to stroke the skin of this land's instruments, longed to feel their pulse against his hands.

For his first goal he found a job washing dishes and a rat-ridden room. The second goal led him to João, a tall man with hands that moved like hummingbird wings. João's hut stood on the slope of a lush hill. From its door Artigas saw the city spread below, from the sudden peak of Pão de Açucar to Copacabana's white curve. Twice a week, he climbed the steep path to his teacher's one-room house and sat in a small circle of men beneath hot stars, reaching for complex beats, sounds like bright and nimble fish his fingers longed to catch. He kept quiet while the men and women of the hill shared the adamantine stories of their days. He was different here: not **negro,** not Brazilian, just learning Portuguese and the language of the samba. He was an interloper, and yet each time he came there was a wooden crate somewhere that he could sit on. And drums. And Ana Clara.

Ana Clara was João's only daughter. The first time Artigas saw her, she was stepping from her hut with machete in hand. Her head was wrapped in a scarf the color of dusk. She moved with a tapir's grace toward a sugarcane stalk that leaned against the side of the house. The machete raised into the air. Slice. The hard stalk cracked in half. She laid the pieces on the ground. Slice. The thick husk yielded again, revealing pale inner fibers, waiting to be pressed for juice. Artigas' hands tripped on goatskin and lost the beat. Ana Clara disappeared into the house.

Months passed. Artigas worked and studied. He developed slow, perennial friendships with João and his neighbors, and set out to earn the love of Ana Clara. This enterprise took him four years to accomplish, since Ana Clara took her time. She was a woman who meant what she said and said what she meant, even if it meant saying nothing at all. Her smile could outshine twenty candles, but she only smiled when she was truly happy, a state Artigas bent his world to create. He brought flowers and fresh pineapples, ballads and thatch to repair her father's roof. He listened to her words and to her silence. "There are things," she once said, "that I only tell the ocean. Go home, get out of here, before I tell them to you." He obeyed this order and descended the hill to the rank little room he called home. He lay in the dark and tried not to think of his other home, the family in Tacuarembó, his stiff, defeated father, Tía Tita's steady arms, his sister, Pajarita, sleeping in the hides without him, dreaming, perhaps, of the letter her wayward brother never sent. He hoped that she was furious at him for his silence, rather than hurt or sad, possibilities that shamed him. He had investigated the neighborhood for letter-writers and had found one who could take Spanish dictation, but Artigas never went to him, telling himself he didn't yet have the money, but how could that be when he had money for pineapples and thatch? It wasn't the money; it was something else, an inability to place the right words in the right order to convey how he was doing to a sister whom he couldn't see or smell or hear. He had never dictated a letter, but they seemed terribly formal, each word placed indelibly on the page and then gone on train or horse, beyond your power to adjust them. The more time passed, the more elaborate and perfect it seemed the letter had to be. And also, once he did write, he should be prepared to say he'd visit, as he'd always thought he would, but now that he was here in the city, with its sharp edges that could cut you open and shine in the sun at the same time, he could not imagine trekking home. He would write, of course he would, he just needed more time, he told himself, night after night, year after year.

Within four years, Artigas had secured João's blessings and Ana Clara's acquiescence for his courtship. The more time they spent together—hand in hand along the beach, side by side feeling papayas for their ripeness—the more Artigas lived the song of her name, Ana Clara, Ana Clara, a lissome melody with endless variations. They married. Artigas built a second room on the side of João's hut, where he and Ana Clara made love and slept on a woven mat on the ground. They made love quietly, since her father was just across the wall, so Artigas tuned into other signs of his wife's pleasure: the shake of her thighs, her fingernail brutality, the expression on her face as if she were watching God and all the demons congregate behind her closed eyelids. He came alive at night in his quests for her pleasure, their pleasure, a pleasure that could have burned down their whole neighborhood. When she became pregnant, their sex turned gentle, oceanic, like the touch, Ana Clara said, of Iemanjá, the African mother goddess of the sea. She gave birth on a long hot night that Artigas spent relegated to his father-in-law's room, listening through the wall to his wife's growls and the aunts and female cousins who surrounded her. He lay awake in a steady panic until he heard the baby's voice. They named her Xhana, and in the years that followed, Artigas learned that love—for wife, for child—was an abyss with no bottom, an open space you hurl yourself into, willingly, constantly, ready to give your life, but you don't die because there is no floor to break against, no limit, and so you simply fall and fall and fall.

He had so much in those years: his new family, the drums, enough work to eat at least once a day, the ocean he had come to call Iemanjá. The rumors began to intrude in early spring of 1930. There was an army gathering in the south. The man in charge was called Getúlio Vargas. He planned to overthrow the present government. Soon his soldiers would sweep north.

"The madness of politics," João said, scraping flesh from goatskin. "Two rich white men squabbling with each other."

"But the president is corrupt." Ana Clara cut the goat meat into cubes. Her belly was wide with child again. "Look what happened with the elections."

João shrugged. "They cheated."

"Of course they cheated. Maybe Vargas would have won."

"What does it matter? None of us could vote anyway."

"It shouldn't be that way."

"But it is."

"Things can change, **Pai.** Vargas would improve things."

"How do you know?"

"He wants to help the people."

"Hmmph! He says that because he needs the people's help."

Artigas, slicing slabs of meat from bone, stayed silent. He knew nothing of the politics of Brazil, but he sensed that he'd entered a thick and murky stream of history. The timbre of Ana Clara's voice stayed with him; there were few things she spoke of with such passion. He looked at the fresh meat in his hands, being cut for João's birthday; they had not cooked goat in weeks. If a president raised wages, they might eat meat more often. He thought of Galtero, and the company that had destroyed his tribe's home and crops with the full permission of the government. Perhaps a new leader would protect families like Galtero's, raise workers' pay, and create a school where Xhana could learn to read. If that was what rebellion meant, what Ana Clara hoped for, it must be a good thing, and he should support it, except that the thought of soldiers in their midst, close to his daughter and pregnant wife, filled him with dread.

Three days later, bureaucrats rode up the hill with a decree. Artigas and Ana Clara stood among their neighbors, staring at the men in ornate saddles. One of them opened a scroll and read: Vargas and his army were close to Rio. They threatened the present government of Brazil. All civilians were ordered to take up arms for their country. They were to report to the military base in four hours.

The man rolled up his scroll. The crowd under his horse was silent. He coughed, pulled his reins, and led the small procession down the path, and out of sight.

Voices rose, an angry flood.

"I'm not going to war for them."

"Me neither."

"Why should we risk our necks?"

"If we don't, it could cost us our lives."

"It'll cost us our lives if we do."

"If we have to fight, we should do it on Vargas' side."

A rush of sound concurred. Artigas tightened his arms around his wife.

A boy ran up the hill. "Look! Look!" He pointed down the incline into the city. "The city is turning against the president!"

All eyes turned down toward Rio: it writhed with people, thronged so close that from a distance they looked like a single liquid. The crowd poured down to join them in a blur of running shapes. Ana Clara pulled away. "I'm going too."

"Going? Where?"

"To the streets."

Artigas grabbed her arm. "Don't."

"Don't try to stop me. This is my city. I'm going." She loped out of his reach, down through shaking grass. At the last curve in full view, she looked up at her husband and he drank her in, Ana Clara, obstinate, round-bellied, red and white dress ruffling in the breeze, waving at him against the backdrop of a seething city. "Take care of Xhana," she called. Then she turned behind a rock face and was gone.

Those were her last words to him. Hundreds of thousands swelled the streets that day. Police opened fire; the mob panicked; it shoved and pressed and lurched in terror. Ana Clara fell to the ground, unseen in the stampede until João's second cousin's nephew came across her underfoot. It was too late.

Ana Clara, Ana Clara, Ana Clara.

Grief scraped through Artigas like a knife. It gutted his will to live. He slunk into his bedroom and did not eat or drink or sleep or talk for six days. On the seventh night, an hour before dawn, Ana Clara appeared at the edge of the sleeping mat in her red and white dress. She was not pregnant. She was not smiling.

"Artigas."

"My God. It's you?"

"You promised. You promised you would take care of Xhana."

He reached for her. "But, Ana—"

She was fading, already, into a red and white mist. "You promised . . ."

Artigas rubbed his eyes. He was alone. He crept from his room and found his five-year-old daughter sleeping on her grandfather's mat, curled into his arms. He knelt on the floor to kiss her forehead. Her scalp smelled of melted cocoa butter. Her nose was tiny, sculpted, innocent, emitting little breaths, in time, he imagined, with her dreams. He lay down on the floor, wrapped his hand around hers, and watched her breathe until the room grew pale with light.

It took two weeks for the troops from the south to break the government. The rebel army swarmed Rio; Vargas arrived on a huge dark horse, his uniform blazing with medallions. Masses filled the streets again, this time in celebration. A NEW BRAZIL! one banner read. WELCOME VARGAS, WELCOME FREEDOM, read another.

João and Artigas stayed indoors. João fumbled with Xhana's hair and Artigas watched his hands, those masterful hands, braid and unbraid and braid again, groping for the skills his daughter took with her into death. The sight invaded his mind, the way soldiers invaded the marketplace, the way fear now invaded Rio's streets. There were guns everywhere these days, along with reminders of what he'd lost. Ana Clara in the plantain-curves of beaches hungry for the sea. Ana Clara in the steep cliff-path into the city and back home. Ana Clara in the taste of mangoes and the sound of a machete cutting sugarcane. Everything familiar was unbearable. He wondered what Ana Clara had been seeking in those streets before she fell, what vision she'd held, how much of it had died with her, what it would take for the rest of it to survive. He dreamed, at night, of fires burning throughout the continent as he ran to quash them with bare hands. He dreamed of leaving. He yearned for the open road, an empty slate, a destination free from the weight of memories and armed young men.

One night he awoke to the sound of a ghostly invitation. **Tú. Túuuu.** He rose and went outside. **Tú. Túuuuu.** He hunted for the source in the faint moonlight. "Where are you?" A laugh drew his attention to a treetop. A child sat on a branch: his sister, Pajarita, as she had perched long ago.

"Aren't you coming?"

"Where?"

She cooed her answer, as if the word held its own tune: "Mon-te-vi-de-o."

He burned with questions, but before he could speak, the girl disappeared, an owl in her place the color of pristine sand. **Tú,** it hooted. **Túuuuu.** Artigas stared into its huge, unfathomable eyes. When he returned to bed, he slept more deeply than he had since his wife's death.

A week later, with João's reluctant blessing, Artigas and Xhana boarded a train to Uruguay. They sat on wooden seats in a car that, for all its sweat and chickens, smelled like heaven compared to his last ride. Xhana pressed her nose against the window and stared at the lush mass of rain forest rushing by, immune to the crushing heat and **clack clack clack** of insomniac poultry. Artigas watched her with as much marvel as she had, watching the world. There she was. His lamp of a daughter. The unexpected quarry of his long hunt.

Once in Montevideo, he dove into the city in search of his sister.

Pajarita poured the last ladle of hot chocolate into her brother's cup. "I'm glad you found me."

"It wasn't hard. People know about you at grocery stores in every neighborhood. You're respected—even feared a bit."

Pajarita looked at the potted plants and jars of herbs that filled the kitchen. They whispered to her in a rustled language, messages that pushed up from quiet dirt.

"Look at you. When I left, you were still a girl." He drew closer. "Tell me how you got here."

"Another night. The sun is almost up." She gestured to the window, a square of drizzle tinged with gray.

"Right. Tomorrow?"

Pajarita nodded. "How long will you stay?"

"Depends."

"On what?"

"Well, for example—how long can we stay here?"

"Artí. Don't insult me."

"Thank you." He reached for her hand. His palm was tough from years of drumming. "If it's all right with your husband."

Pajarita thought of Ignazio, a dark shape in her bed. "You let me worry about him."

Once she had watched Artigas go to bed on the

living room floor, Pajarita tiptoed to her bedroom. She changed into her nightgown without turning on the light. Ignazio's elongated breaths came through the darkness.

"Ignazio."

The breathing halted. Sheets stirred. **"Sí."**

The floor was cold against her bare feet. "Artigas is staying until he finds a home."

The rustle of black shadow, sitting up. "Pajarita."

"Yes."

"Do you—are you—coming to bed?"

She swayed slightly. Her linen nightgown stroked her legs and they were strong, her legs, they could still stand, she could stand alone for decades if she had to. But she longed for rest. "Yes."

She heard the swish of sheets drawing open. She slid in. They were warm, his arms, large and solid folding all around her. Tonight, at least, these arms were solid. She felt his heartbeat, then his hand, then the melting of her body toward his, as they glided, together, into the dark unmoored trajectories of sleep.

"Xhana?"

"¿Sí?"

"Are you sleeping?"

"No."

"Are you scared of storms?"

"Sometimes."

"Me too. I always wanted a sister."

"Me too."

"Can we be sisters?"

"Sure."

"You can sleep here, in my bed, anytime."

"All right."

"And we'll be sisters."

"Sí."

"For our whole forever."

"Sí."

He was there. Again. Artigas stared at the field around him—a soccer field in the shape of South America, a huge grass-grown map, the borders between countries marked in chalk along the ground. Fires shot up across the continent, sudden bursts of glaring light. Quick quick he raced back and forth across the field, putting them out with bare hands. He quenched one in Peru, bolted west to save Guyana, then down to Chile, back across to Brazil. Faster and faster the fires arose. He was so small, he was exhausted, he couldn't possibly keep up. He stopped in his tracks, defeated, blazes all around him. He looked to the north. A blinding fire loomed and glowed and ignited the horizon: a massive conflagration, its sparks shooting south, falling on the grassy map and making it burn—

He woke up in a sweat, the sharp imprint of fire before his eyes. **Xhana!** He felt the floor beneath him and remembered where he was. Xhana was safe, sleeping in the other room, with her cousin. Eva. Her name was Eva.

He crept to the bedroom where they slept, opened the door, and peered at them. They faced each other, arms around each other's small shoulders. Early sunlight washed over their skin. They reminded him of how he'd slept, with Pajarita, growing up—cradling each other, warmed by limbs and hides, dreaming their own dreams beneath one blanket. The way these girls now nestled, the dreams seemed calm and good.

"Sleep well, **mijitas,** you've got a lot ahead of you," he whispered, closing the door.

EVA

Tres

VOICES, FACES, WINEGLASS,
TABLE, WORDS

When Eva was very small, her world still lambent and unbroken, she loved to walk past the Punta Carretas prison. She feared it with the vague and hallowed fear of a child, and yet she slowed down as her family passed it on the way to church. Those high, pale walls; that entryway, its lofty arch sealed by iron gates; beyond those gates, a courtyard, and glimpses of the thick-walled thing itself. It was so big. And pretty too, with its castle pattern along the top, the same up-down-up-down shape her brothers made when building a fortress in the sand. Walking past, peering in, Eva thought of the people locked inside. It was a men's prison, but imagination being what it is, the birthplace of rebellion, she always envisioned women there. Bad women who had done wrong things. In her mind's eye, they were gorgeous, with cherry lipstick on angry mouths. Surely they heard everything that happened on the street—the baby crying at the church door, the women talking at the **carnicería,** the proud, flashy automobiles, the sharp foot-song of horses, Eva's own child-size steps. It seemed to her, sometimes, that she could hear the women laugh. No sounds ever came from El Penal, but she could feel them laughing, a shrieking sort of texture to the air. She couldn't imagine why anyone would laugh in prison, unless they were laughing at the people outside. She saw them with dreamlike precision: these reckless women, all in uniform, heads thrown back, making vast and vivid sound. (Four decades later it would amaze Eva that she'd ever looked at the prison and seen that, heard that, when all she could see now was her own daughter, running, running, leaving fresh tomato sauce to scald on the stove.)

They passed it on the way to church, and if, after church, Papá was happy and the sun was out, they went for a stroll along La Rambla. They ambled through a crowd of ambling people, on a cream and maroon sidewalk, gazing at the shore. The water was different every time. Brown, green, calm, chopped. Stretching out to meet the sky. Eva squinted in search of Argentina on the other side of the river, but she saw only an infinitesimal line, sky on one side, water on the other. Yet she knew Argentina was there because she had learned this fact in school. She had also learned that El Río de la Plata was named that because the first Europeans thought it would lead to silver and gold. They were quite disappointed, Señorita Petrillo explained, her eyes roving the room like an eagle's, sprigs of hair escaping her bun. In fact, though the name stuck, it was not true, **no fue cierto. Cierto. Cierto.** Eva rolled that word in her mouth. Something about the sensuous **ssss** against the palate, followed by the dramatic burst of **ier,** ending with a strong, decisive **to,** enticed her, as though the very taste of it made it worth saying. She would walk that Rambla on Sundays and roll that word under her breath, watching the waves spread onto the sand. The River of Silver had promised something, but it was not true, not **cierto,** like **cierre, cielo, cerrado, siempre:** lock, sky, closed, always. She murmured in time with the waves: **Cierre. Cielo. Cerrado. Siempre.** Lock. Sky. Closed. Always.

They were silly, her word games, and she knew it. She didn't tell her parents about them. Papá, especially, said she took words too seriously. "There's more to life than words," he said, and he should know, having built the house they lived in with bare hands. But Eva loved words for the way they bent and danced around her thoughts, as if her thoughts and words could dance a tango, the thoughts warm and sweating, the words bright and graceful, a rhythm pressed between them. Only Tío Artigas would understand her secret game. He was like a bottle and music was the wine—tangos, folk songs, candombe, anything. She liked to be near him when it poured. Once they made up a tune, **The spider has gone fishing, the bird is flying home, I am bigger than an elephant, but smaller than a gnome,** and he played it over and over for her on his guitar. Occasionally, at dawn, after Artí had been performing all night long, he sneaked to Eva's bedside and shook her awake, smelling of cigarettes and that sweet-liquor scent of **grappa miel.** She'd open her eyes to see her uncle's weathered face, and hear him whisper, **"¡Che! ¿Quieres ir a pescar?"** She always said yes—I want to go fishing, I want to watch the sun get strong over water that shivers in sleep, I want to be still with a rod in my hand and not care if anything bites, I want to sit on a rock with you while light fills up the sky.

Once, on those rocks, Eva did catch a fish, and Xhana gutted it right then and there. She sliced the belly open, pulling organs out with slick and nimble fingers. She skinned it as though the flesh had just been waiting, under scales, for her to free it. She was like that, her cousin; she knew how to grasp a knife, did not fear what was hidden in the body of a fish. She knew so much about knives and songs and the grown-up things musicians spoke of. Xhana had read Marx's **Das Kapital** by the time she was seven years old. Eva tried to follow suit, but found the book impenetrable, big words strung together in odd ways. Still, she gathered that it had something to do with freedom, and maybe music, and everyone in the whole world having those two things. Artí and Xhana seemed to have them. They lived in Barrio Sur, closer to downtown, on a street with old carved doors that were splintered at the edges, where the buildings pressed together like very close friends. Sometimes they disappeared for a month or two, without warning, to Brazil or Paraguay or the Andes. They returned with stories, mosquito bites, holes in their clothes, a photograph of Xhana with her abuelo João, painted drums and **quena** flutes and lessons on how to play them.

Such a life could not hope for universal approval. Coco Descalzo, the butcher's wife, clucked her tongue each time she heard news of Artigas' departure. "There he goes," she said and slapped a stack of sausages. "Wandering dangerous roads with that poor girl. She needs a decent home, a stable home. **¡Qué barbaridad!** "

"**Sí,** Coco." Mamá's black braids swung close to the meat. "But he's not going to change."

"Why should he?" Clarabel Ortiz, La Divorciada, stood in the door, hat in hand. The hat was festooned with crumpled paper flowers. Even Eva knew that Clarabel held an unrequited passion for Artigas. "Just think of the adventures they must have. Xhana's lucky to see the world!"

"Yes, yes," Coco said. "**Buenos días** to you too. We all know what you think and how you'd like to"—her face alight, she glanced at Pajarita, then at Eva attentive in the corner—"**este**"—sighing—"travel. Sausage? It's fresh as can be."

"No, thank you." Clarabel plucked a fake petal from her hat. "I've come to consult with Pajarita."

Mamá and Clarabel crossed the leather curtain behind the counter. Eva followed. She agreed; Xhana was lucky. Who cared that their apartment was small? That two of its windows were broken? On the road, the whole world could be their home, the world with all its dust and flutes and secrets. Eva wanted to see the world too, and so she'd become a pirate in her games with Andrés Descalzo. He was older than she was, by three whole years, but they'd played in the back of the butcher shop since her earliest memory. He had a quick and sparkling mind and together they sailed the seas. Long slabs of ribs, hung from meat hooks, became the sails of their ship. They quested and swung their swords and found treasure in holes they dug in the floor with imaginary spades. Their friendship had evolved out of minor exiles: Andrés was not allowed into his older sisters' elite world of dolls and teacups, and Eva could not join her brothers' knee-scraping bouts of soccer. In exacerbation of these matters, Andrés did not do well with soccer, and Eva was bored by serving empty cups of tea. It was far better to board a ship and explore the oceanic wilderness in all its unbridled perils with Andrés, the captain, who wore an eye patch made of brown wrapping paper colored with black pencil ("that thing will give you headaches," his mother said, but each time she tore one up he made another). Eva, the first mate, had an amazing nose, known across the seas for sniffing beneath the smell of cow flesh for the scent of gold and rubies. Andrés navigated. While Eva kept her nose on precious metals, he kept his uncovered eye out for danger. There were plenty of dangers: crocodiles, dragons, waves big as houses, mean ships full of nasty men who wielded long knives, sharp rocks, mad mermaids, sorcerers with moldy teeth. Andrés steered through it all, toward the lands where treasure lay, waiting to be exhumed and brought to light. That was the best part: the sifting, the finding, the poring over extraordinary jewels—a sapphire ring that made you fly; necklaces that heard the whispered secrets of the heart; bracelets made of bright, delicious candy that could be licked and licked and never get spent, never whittle away, because they were made of **Oro Dulce,** Sweet Gold, which, for fearless pirates, was the prize.

Eva watched her mother and Clarabel settle onto stools. Clarabel was crying already. Eva looked up at the red haunches that hung from the ceiling, the bloody chopping block, the ready knives. When she grew up, she'd be a pirate. She would seek strange and fabulous lands, dig up treasure, and bring it all the way home to Punta Carretas. Mami would be laden with more gold than she could wear. And everyone in Montevideo would gather in the plaza and say look! look! see what Eva Firielli has brought home. And there would be a big party with toasts and streamers and Tío Artigas would play and Mamá and Papá would dance and she would wear a huge magnolia behind her ear the whole night long.

Or maybe Papá wouldn't dance. Papá, after all, could not be predicted. He was like a planet, with atmosphere and gravity all its own. Eva knew about planets and gravity and atmosphere from Señorita Petrillo. She knew that every planet has its own kind of air draped around it, and that every planet pulls things close in its own way. Her brothers seemed to understand this too; they orbited her father like three vigorous moons, Bruno, Marco, Tomás, sidling up to the moody air around her father in a cloud of boyish noise until they blended with one another, Brunomarcotomás. Her mamá called them from the street that way. **¡Brunomarcotomás!** Their presence was instinctive, constant, like breathing. They were always there and yet their club was closed to her, along with its coded ways: the sprint behind a soccer ball, trail of sweat behind them, loud ease around the planet of her father. That planet's weather changed often. One day it glistened, moist with rum; the next day your skin could crack from its aridity. On dry days it was best to let him sit, undisturbed, in his rocking chair that creaked back and forth. On the wet days there was banter, the glad gauze of cigar smoke, magic tricks performed for Eva's bright staccato applause, poker games with Brunomarcotomás, played with seashells as their betting chips (no money gambling in the house—this rule Mamá enforced with steely will), or another game that called for throwing cow vertebrae with stones, a real gaucho game because, as Cacho, the magician, once proclaimed, "Your Papi is a real **uruguayo.**" The real **uruguayo** game filled the living room with bellow-laughs on those good nights. The laughter careened into the kitchen, where Mamá washed dishes and Eva dried and stacked. In every corner of the kitchen, plants mixed their sweet-leaf breaths with the air and the calm and the full-bellow laughter. We are rising, they murmured in their green way. We are rising into all this kitchen air.

Mamá had her own way of navigating Papá's planet. When Eva was nine years old, Papá began taking Brunomarcotomás to a place called El Corriente. Mamá drew out all her weapons. First came logic. "**Por Dios,** they're still children! What kind of example does this set?" Then came memory. "Have you forgotten? Have you?" Finally, and most brutally, came silence. Eva watched her mother turn her father into the Incredible Disappearing Husband. Now He's Here, Now He's Not. Now the man of the house does not exist. There—Ta Da!—is a Ghost Eating Toast in the Morning. Mamá boiled water for a phantom's morning **mate,** placed the gourd on a table where no one sat.

"**Querida,**" no one said.

Mamá said nothing, as there was no thing to answer.

"**Por favor . . .**" There was no man here, saying words that dissolved into colluding air.

After nineteen days, the Man That Does Not Exist broke down and sobbed into his gourd. This gave him flesh again. Papá returned to the table, opaque and fully formed, and from then on Brunomarcotomás—to their dismay—stayed home.

One summer night Papá did not come home. Eva sat in the kitchen, subtracting fractions, while Mamá scrubbed every surface and shifted plant pots late into the night. Forty-seven minutes after midnight, Eva ran out of fractions and drew numbers, over and over, pretending to add, to multiply, to make them into more than what they were. The next day, Eva returned from school exhausted and collapsed into her bed. When she awoke, her room was dark. There was no moon. A warm figure sat on the bed beside her.

"Psst. Eva."

"Xhana?"

"**Prima,** I thought you'd never wake up!"

Eva dragged her mind up from the fog of sleep. "Is Papá here?"

"He was. He's out again. My papá and your mamá are in the kitchen talking."

"Oh."

"Did you hear?"

"What?"

"That your father lost his job."

Eva sat up against the pillows. Air pressed humidly against her. "No."

"That's why he's so upset."

Eva's eyes adjusted, a little, to the dark. She saw the barest outlines of Xhana's face—hairline, eyes, a sweep of nose.

"Do you know why it happened?"

"There's a problem with our economy."

"Oh."

"We have an export economy."

Eva had heard the word **export** before, to describe the company her father worked for. She had always thought it meant Very Big Crate. "What's that?"

Xhana switched on the lamp. Eva blinked, eyes gulping in the light. "The thing is," Xhana said, "we have a lot of sheep and cows. Uruguay, I mean. ¿**Ta?**"

"**Ta.**"

"So people export—that means sell things far away. To countries that are richer and who like our wool. And beef. And leather."

Eva nodded. Xhana had two blue ribbons in her hair. They matched her blouse. They looked so pretty.

"But then these rich countries, they woke up one day not so rich. And said, those **uruguayos,** let's not buy their things. And then, after that, **uruguayos** don't have money. And so they tell people not to go to work."

"I see," Eva said slowly, though she didn't. She saw only her papá's face, sad and arid, surrounded by a cloud of sleep she longed to disappear in. "Are you staying the night?"

"I don't know."

"Do you want to?"

"Yes."

Eva lifted the sheet from her bed. Her cousin

sluffed off her shoes and crawled in, blouse and ribbons and all. Sleep rose around them, one dark swath
surrounding their two bodies.

The autumn months unfolded coldly. March.
April. May. It rained hard. A new sort of silence filled
up Eva's home, and it was not a good or pretty silence, not a fishing-morning silence; this one was
sour and sticky and it settled deep between the fibers
of the rugs, in the corners of the house, filmy and
translucent over chairs and forks and napkins. It was
everywhere, silence that could stain your hands and
prick the back of your neck. Noise did not expel it.
Any word or laugh or song just layered over it for a
moment, hovered in the air, then fell apart and
landed in flecks on the big silence. Life happened on
it and around it and within it: Papá's absences, and
his tense arrivals; his bone-dry brooding and slurred
jokes; Brunomarcotomás, banished from soccer by
the weather, peeling apart into Bruno (gambling
madly for shells), Marco (lost in books), and Tomás
(gambling for shells and polishing his father's forgotten shoes); Mamá, pushing forward like a steady
prow, her fist pounding bread crumbs into beef, her
braids tight and dark each morning. Mamá kept filling her basket each day with freshly cut leaves and
roots for the **carnicería.** Women still came for remedies, though they had less to give in return than before. Eva saw this, watching from her pirate ship,
clasping hands with Capitán Andrés of the Invinci-
ble Eye Patch. She watched women sit on that stool

across the seas, faces strained, hands empty, bodies stooped in the shape of a question mark.

In the winter, in the thick of August rains, Eva discovered a trick, a way to leave the house without leaving the house by diving into words. Each thing, after all, had a name; and each name was a word that could imprint the air, becoming larger than the thing itself. The letters rose one by one, a tall-as-the-ceiling presence in the room. Anything could start it: like the slam of the front door and her father lurching in, hat wet with rain, wool sweater dripping.

Mamá at the edge of the hall. "Where have you been?"

"Out."

Eva sat on the rug, next to the rocking chair. Chair, SILLA. The letters were huge and graceful. S—snakelike, slipping, an enormous, coiled blue boa (S is blue, always blue).

"I noticed that. It's been three days."

The drops from Papá's sleeves made two dark spots on the rug. "Leave me alone."

(I, a high stone tower, the kind where maidens languish under spells. The kind with pirate treasure.)

Mamá said, "You're drunk."

Papá said, louder, "Leave me alone."

(LL, two high brown walls with a hiding place ensconced between them. Safe and dark but tricky to climb out of.)

Mamá stepped forward, back straight, arms crossed. She was much shorter than Papá. "How could you? How could you? When we don't have enough for the children."

"Money!" (A is very strong. A, a letter in a class all its own. A, a mountain with its top half steeped in snow.) "That's all you care about, the lack of money."

"No." Mamá's arms uncrossed. (Look at those slopes in A, so steep. They could be unclimbable. Who has scaled them?) "It's the lack of you."

In the silence that followed (sour and sticky), and even once her father had stormed out, Eva looked them over and over, these shapes that filled the room—snake and tower, walls and mountain:

S-I-LL-A.

They shimmered with the mystery of words stripped down to essence, down to parts, without which there could be no names or stories. She crawled inside the letters, scaled their heights, tried to find their center, the hidden core that made them throb with meaning. She never found that core but she kept conjuring letters anyway; they rose up for her over and over again. There were, after all, a million things with names to them—as Eva discovered that winter, as the names of things (**book** and **basil**, **quilt** and **door**, cow **bone** and oil **lamp** and itchy woolen **sock**) came to floor-to-ceiling life.

In the spring, Eva heard her name through her parents' bedroom door. She was walking down the hall to pee. It was two-thirty in the morning. She heard her mother first.

"Eva?" Mami's voice was loud, and Eva stopped as if she had been called.

"Shhhh, Pajarita—**sí.** It's for Eva."

"Ignazio—"

"Now wait a minute, **mi amor.** Just listen. You've asked me to look, I've been looking. Please sit down."

Pause. Shuffling. In the hall, Eva's bare toes curled into the rug, little hooks keeping her in place. She leaned against the wall, thinking, not for the first time, WALL.

"Bueno," Mamá said. "I'm listening."

"Pietro explained it all to me. The work he has is best for someone younger. It's spring: the port might need me again soon. His store is doing well, so he can use extra hands and he can pay us. He knows how much we need it."

Eva's toes were cold. She had to pee. No corner of her pink nightgown (sewn by Mamá) was allowed to rustle.

"But why Eva? She's only ten."

"Probably so the boys can stay in school."

"Eva's in school too."

"Yes. **Pero mi amor.** Marco could become a doctor. Eva, a wife. Think. This could be a good experience."

Silence. The backs of Eva's calves were cold. Arms too. Her pink nightgown was not enough, on this night, in this hall, where she should not be standing.

"Pajarita," Papi said, "don't start. Think what this could do for the family."

"She won't do it."

"She will."

"You can't force her, Ignazio. I won't let you."

More silence.

"At least let me talk to her."

Rustle, rustle, no more muffled words. The bed-springs creaked. Eva had lost the urge to pee; she padded back to bed on quiet toes and lay staring at the ceiling, which hid behind the dark.

The following afternoon, when Brunomarcotomás were outside playing soccer in the tentative sun, and when Mamá had left for the **carnicería,** and Eva sat at the kitchen table dividing fractions, she heard Papá call out her name.

"¿Sí, Papá?"

"Come here."

In the living room, light glazed the bookshelf, the framed photograph on the sill, her father's hair, as if God had picked up the things in the room and dipped them, one by one, in a pot of sun. As she sat down on the sofa next to Papi, she savored a picture of him dangling upside down in the grip of God's enormous fingers, top of the head submerged in liquid light.

"You know, of course, how much we love you." He smiled. The smile was sincere, but a little sad. "Don't you?"

"Sí, Papá."

"When I was your age, I could build a gondola. Tables I did with my eyes closed." He glanced out the window. "With my eyes closed."

Eva waited.

"My friend Pietro has offered you a job. In his shoe store. It's a great . . . how do you say, opportunity, not to be found in Montevideo, just like that. Your mother thinks you won't take it—but I think you will. You know why?"

Eva shook her head. Papá leaned closer. She smelled his semisweet cologne.

"Because you're a smart girl. So you know that learning happens in a lot of places. Not just in school. Just think what you could learn at a job." He put his palm over Eva's hand. "But that's not the biggest reason. You know the biggest reason?"

Eva shook her head. She didn't know.

"You love your family. And you want to help your family. Don't you?"

"Sí."

"Of course! We all do. And here's your chance." Tiny pearls of sweat had formed on his forehead. "But of course it's up to you."

Eva looked at the framed photograph on the sill. Her parents—young, just married, freshly moved into the city—stood side by side in front of a plain backdrop. Her father's smile cocked to one side; her mother's face was clear and serious. When that picture was taken, even her brothers had not been born. Mamá put the picture up when Eva was five and her papi had just come home (she hazily remembered meeting him, a wet man with flowers, stooping down and calling himself Papi). For years, Eva hated that picture; it reminded her of the strange fact that she once did not exist.

"Would I have to leave school?"

Papá nodded. Eva stared at the photograph. She wanted to smash it; she wanted to burn it; she wanted to wrap it in silk and stow it in a high stone tower, under a spell, where no harm could reach it. Her father—not the father in the photo but the real one—ran a hand through graying hair. The light had mellowed. Sun no longer glazed his head.

She said, "I'll go—"

"Eva, that's—"

"If you promise to stop drinking."

"What?"

"Only if you don't drink."

He looked around the room as if it had just appeared around him. "But do you know what you're asking?"

"Do you?"

This opened her father wide—in the mouth, in the eyes. His lips worked around words he did not say. He closed his mouth. He opened it. He made a snorting sound. "**Carajo,** you're like your mother." He shook his head. "**La puta madre.**"

They were silent for minutes that felt like hours. Papá looked out the window. Finally he turned back and reached out and she flinched, but all he did was stroke her hair, hand warm and rough from years of hauling cargo at the port. Eva leaned toward him, let her body melt against his.

"All right," he said.

"Promise?"

Through clothes and skin, she felt the pump and push of blood inside him. "I do."

Late that night, in bed, Eva couldn't stop thinking. She saw her mother, standing over steaming pots, pretending not to wait for her husband. She saw Señorita Petrillo, with her sharp face and tenuous bun, the day her class had taken a trip to the river's edge, and the water had seemed to wear a ruffled brown dress. Another trip was planned for next month but Eva would not be there. **Cierre. Cielo. Cerrado. Siempre.** Lock. Sky. Closed. Always.

She rose quietly, so as not to disturb her brother Tomás' sleep. She stole a stubby candle from the living room, sneaked into the bathroom, closed the door, struck a match, and opened the drawers of her heart. She fingered what she found there. **Tomorrow,** she wrote, **is the end of school.** Words spilled from her pen, one after another, before she could think them, before she could know them, before she could sense their source. **I want to eat up all of life.** The pen kept moving, faster, faster. Her hand rushed to catch up. **Hold on tight. Hold on tight.** It was done. She stroked the page in wonder. It felt smooth and full, like a glass brimming with water. She had poured it there herself. She felt a little lighter; she would be all right; she had this thing—a poem? could she call it that?—a string of words, at least, that could be rolled on the tongue, wrapped in the mind, stashed in drawers she would learn to hide.

She walked to La Ciudad Vieja, past proud old buildings, Spanish balconies, carved stones heavy with history. She paused in front of Cabán's Cigar Shop and breathed in the Old City, with its smell of cars and frying oil. Noise and movement swarmed the street; electric trams moaned past on high-flung lines; men called to one another and tipped their hats while striding, purposefully, somewhere; broad buildings stood like aging sentinels, keeping quiet watch over the city's central veins.

The shoe store was nestled on a narrow street near La Plaza de Zabala, on the first floor of a four-story building. Its roof crawled with stone cherubs. She opened the door with a tentative hand and stepped into a room thick with racks of shoes. Their leathers—black, red, brown, cream, beige—warmed the air with their scent. A sign next to the cash register read: ONLY THE FINEST URUGUAYAN LEATHER, CUT IN THE FINEST ITALIAN STYLES. A scratchy tango played on an unseen phonograph.

Pietro appeared from behind the racks, two pairs of boots in hand. "Eva. Welcome." He gave her a quick greeting kiss (he smelled like spearmint). "I'm just clearing up from the last customer. Make yourself at home."

She sat on a plush chair next to the window and waited as Pietro gathered boots and shut them into boxes. He was a tall man with an easy smile. He whistled off-key, along with the tango. She relaxed a little. Her memory of him had been hazy, though she knew he had a wife, three daughters, and her father's undying loyalty ("That is a good man," he said last night at dinner, **"bueno, pero bueno"**); he was her father's oldest friend, the friend from the Italian steamboat. She harbored an image of Papá and Pietro laughing at the helm of a ship, gripping the rails, wearing long capes that flapped in the wind as they raced across the Atlantic, like superheroes from the **yanqui** comic books her brothers liked to read.

"**Bueno.**" Pietro approached her. "Let me show you around."

That afternoon, Eva learned the basics of the store: the racks of shoes, standing at attention in tidy soldierish formation (boots, buckled loafers, laced-up oxfords, slim-heeled pumps); the cushioned chairs where customers tried on wares (elegant hems at Eva's forehead as she bent to slide shoes on); the storeroom lit by two naked bulbs, with its narrow walkway lined with shelves and shelves of boxes. There was plenty to be done. There were feet to serve shoes to, and questions to answer from people attached to those feet. There were boxes to sort and rearrange, standing on the storeroom stepladder (high high up, like standing on a table, which was forbidden at home). There were floors to be swept at the end of the day, while Pietro counted cash at the desk in the back room, spreading bills beside the crooning phonograph, sipping his evening **mate.** "How did you like your first day?"

"It was good, Señor, thank you."

"Call me Pietro. We'll have fun, I think. You seem like a very special girl." He tilted his head in the direction of the phonograph. "You like the tangos?"

She nodded.

"You know how to dance?"

She shook her head.

"I can teach you. Tomorrow after we close. Would you like that?"

Eva nodded, still sweeping, eyes on the head of the broom.

Throughout dinner that night (how was work?—good, Mamá) and breakfast the next morning (don't forget your cardigan—no, Mamá), Eva thought about the tango, with its sharp, urgent grace. Walking to work through Parque Rodó, on Avenida San Salvador, she heard a phonograph and stopped to listen. The voice of Carlos Gardel, the king of tango, crooned a melody in one long caress, a sound she could feel on her skin. It came from a blood-red door. A brass sign on the stone wall beside it read LA DIABLITA. Eva fingered the engraved letters. She had heard of this place from Tío Artigas. It was a fashionable café where artists and the elite gathered to lounge and laugh and say smart things, to savor pasta and poetry and wine, to bask in music and clouds of pungent cigarette smoke. **You seem like a very spe-**

cial girl. Gardel's voice rose to a wail. The air felt cool and clear around her. She wished she could dissolve her skin and slide into the café, into the smoke, into the howling motion of the song.

Pietro kept his promise that night. He turned up the volume and danced down the aisle, arms stretched around a woman made of air. "Ready?" he said, and clasped her hand. They sailed around the room and her feet followed his smooth steps and the instruction, **BA pa pa pa,** of his voice; the curves of music pressed him closer, a hand caught her back, not like a little girl but like a lady, grown and gorgeous, vital, infused with borrowed grace. The song ended. They stopped, out of breath. Pietro's shirt was dark with sweat. She pulled away.

"You have natural talent," Pietro said.

She didn't know what to say. The air was thick and shimmered strangely.

"Your parents. They wouldn't approve?"

She shook her head.

"But you like it?"

She looked down at her clunky shoes, schoolgirl shoes, not a lady's. "Yes."

He was silent, and she thought about the trouble she'd be in, how Papá would frown while Pietro shrugged his shoulders, how Mamá would listen too and shake her head, and no more tango, no more curves, no more shimmer.

"Don't worry. I won't tell them."

And he didn't. The tango lessons came a few times

each week. There were complex steps, turns to learn, dips so deep she saw the room upside down behind her. Pietro's body signaled when a turn was coming, when a dip approached, when he planned to sweep her to the left, forward, back. When Eva danced, she became more than herself, larger than life, like the women in the posters outside movie theaters who languished in the arms of heroes. It made her ache in a way she could not define—a wide-skinned, bone-deep, rush-hot longing—it made her want to break out of her body. It was thrilling. It was terrible. She felt closer to the ladies she served, who slipped their feet into supple pumps, who turned easily toward the mirror, whose ankles looked so pretty lifted by high heels, and who did not seem to spend hours bent over the kitchen sink or sitting on a crude stool in a butcher shop.

"What did you do at work today, Eva?"

"Oh, the same. Arranged a shelf. Sold some boots. Swept."

Mami paused, more questions in her mouth, then let them go. Papá winked at her across the dinner table. Only water filled his glass. Eva looked down at her plate and pressed her knife into the meat.

December came. Summer sandals crowded the aisles and Eva turned eleven. On her birthday there was cake and candles, song and wishes, a new green dress sewn by Mamá. On the day after her birthday, Pietro offered her a cigarette.

"Don't tell me you haven't wanted to try." A lit

smoke dangled between his lips, and he looked like a sailor, an aging sailor, seasoned by the seven seas. He raised his brows.

Hesitantly, she reached for the thin white column in his hand. She put it in her mouth; he leaned over his desk, lit a match, and brought the fire to its tip.

"Breathe in."

She breathed in. Smoke filled her, thick and bitter. She coughed.

"Too much?"

She shook her head.

"You're quite the young woman now," Pietro said. "Aren't you?"

They stood for a moment, smoking together, smoke rising from two bright orange tips, forming a flimsy pattern in the air. Me, she thought, I am doing it. I can smoke. A new song began on the phonograph: "Caminito," full of long, ardent chords. Pietro turned it up, stubbed out his cigarette, and took and stubbed out hers. **Caminito que el tiempo ha borrado / Que juntos un día nos viste pasar**—he grasped her wrist with one hand, her waist with the other, and they slid across the room. He pressed her tight, he wheeled her through the narrow room pressed up against his body—**una sombra ya pronto serás**—the room was hot, flanked in boxes, reeling all around her—**una sombra lo mismo que yo**—the dance was large now, larger than her, caught as she was in a crooning voice and rhythmic curves and sharp cologne and sweat, his sweat, bitter and damp, and all around the room the song came beating beating, rising toward its climax as his fingers dug into her and he stopped, they stopped, his hands pulled her in—**yo a tu lado quisiera caer**—into a hard thing—**y que el tiempo nos mate a los dos**—the song ended; his grip was strong; she tried to writhe away and he moaned, strangely, pressed even closer, again, again, then let her go. She stepped back. She did not look at him. His breath was ragged. A tango started up and drowned him out. She heard him step toward his desk and light a cigarette.

"You've become quite a dancer."

Shoes. She stared at her shoes.

"Go home."

Eva walked past the boxes, through the door, out into the balmy summer air. Twilight, with its softening edges, had just begun. An electric tram rumbled somewhere on a street out of sight. A boy careened past on a bicycle, almost grazing her side. She smelled the slow roast of an **asado** on a balcony above her head, the muscular red smell of flesh. She felt sick in the pit of her stomach. Before she turned the corner she looked back at the outside of the shoe store, with its clear sheen and brass bell; then she looked at the top of the building, where stone cherubs waved their trumpets among pigeons. Some cherubs grinned; others rolled their eyes heavenward in supplication. One cherub wailed in stone despair. She saw herself soaring up to him, and farther, out of sight.

"Children," Artigas sighed, "are always growing up. Who can stop it?"

Eva took his hand and swung it in time with their steps. Her shoes sang against the warm bricks of La Rambla. She was flanked by family, Artigas on one side, Xhana on the other, the rest of them—Mami, Papi, Brunomarcotomás, and Bruno's new girl-friend—some meters up ahead. To their left, the Río de la Plata lay still and wide. A thousand tiny splinters of light winked on the water, as if, for New Year's Day, the river itself had donned a sequined gown.

"Still," Artí added, "he does look happy."

He was talking about Bruno. There he walked with his arm around Mirna, a honey-and-almonds girl with a mad mane of hair. They leaned their heads toward each other as if listening to a fairy (or flea) between them. Bruno had graduated from high school. He was formally courting. He was a man. Beside him, Papá slid his arm around Mamá. Her body relaxed into the slope of him. Up ahead, Marco and Tomás walked with the kinds of strides they took when arguing over soccer: brisk, emphatic, purposeful. Marco poured **mate** water from a thermos and passed the gourd with a dismissive toss of his head. Other families swarmed around them: a cluster of children ran down asphalt steps to the sand; a widow leaned into her son while listening raptly to another woman's gossip; a couple on a bench unwrapped em-

panadas under the bright sweep of the sun. Montevideo had lifted and tipped and rolled the people to
its edge, and the people, it seemed, had rolled gladly.

Artigas was in one of his expansive, musing
moods. "The New Year makes me think of your
mother. You know, she was a miracle child."

Xhana rolled her eyes for Eva's benefit.

"Thank you, **mija,** for your filial respect."

Xhana giggled, caught in the act.

"As I was saying."

Eva shared a mocking squeeze-of-hand with her
cousin, but she was grateful for Tío's story, with its familiar pulse (La Roja was our mother, it started when
she died), like the slow sturdy push of waves. She felt
more peaceful on this walk than she had in weeks.
The tango lessons had stopped after her birthday.
When she thought of that last dance, a hot black tar
poured through her, from her heels up to her neck
(then she disappeared in the middle of the night).
Up ahead, Papi turned his head to say something,
and Mami laughed. Her back stretched into an arc as
she laughed, and her braids dipped and brushed the
bottom of her hips. They had been taking this walk,
these two, since that odd, unnerving time before Eva
herself was born. The city had changed since then.
The Rambla had paved over jagged rocks, and buildings had shot up against the north side of the road.
She had never known the shore without paving and
houses. But the water—surely it had stayed the same,
old, calm, constant, able to clean things, even kill

things, like the year that had just ended, drowning in the riverflood of time; she saw the old year like a carcass on the water (some say she flew, some say she fell); time itself was being cleaned by all these waves, drowned, washed, eroded, and perhaps the forceful waters would dissolve her sins like corpses, consume them, and make them disappear.

In January she tried to be the perfect worker. Every shoe in place on its wooden rack. Every customer pampered. At closing time, the kettle boiled right when Pietro started to want his **mate.** No dancing. For a time, it seemed to work. Pietro did not turn up the tangos, he sold shoes, he smiled, he hummed as he rolled cigarettes at his desk. February came. The streets filled with the sounds of Carnaval: **murgas,** with their clownish face paint and bright clothes, belting ballads to exult and mock the country's politicians; **comparsas** pounding beats on sixty drums at once; **tangueros,** in their first summer since Carlos Gardel's death, staging homages to showcase their extravagant grief. Music shook and pierced the city.

"Eva." Pietro was behind her at the window. "Do you like these?"

He held a pair of red heels in his hand. They were high, sleek, the most expensive in the store. Last week, a lady had bought three pairs: two for herself, one for her daughter.

"Yes."

He held them out.

"Oh, no—"

"Take them. For your hard work."

She shook her head.

He sighed, a patient man addressing others' ignorance. "You can't keep wearing those schoolgirl shoes. It's bad for business. You have to model our wares." He smiled. "You do want to do your job, don't you?"

She nodded. He held the red shoes out. She reached for them, slowly.

"That's better." He looked genuinely pleased, a child who's won a prize. "Now put them on."

She put them on.

"Walk around for me."

She walked back and forth, wobbling at an unfamiliar height. The pumps felt steep and supple. Outside, she heard a cluster of men strike up a mournful **murga.**

Pietro leaned back into a chair and lit a cigarette. His eyes grew hard and bright and fell toward her ankles. "Keep walking."

Eva walked. Her legs trembled but she did not fall.

"Good." He said it softly. "Good. Practice every day. You'll walk like a real lady in no time."

Weeks passed. Eva's feet ached. Something else ached too, nebulous and nameless, when Pietro looked at her and also much later, when she was alone in bed, too restive, still sticky with the film of his gaze. Heat and fear and hunger and revulsion. She couldn't understand it and it made her want to leave, to disappear, to slide away into a pair of Nice Shoes and be lost. That was it, slide away, curl up against a sole where nobody could find her. Tall shoes were the safest, the kind that hid the ankle or calf in leather tunnels, strong and thick and cured to last forever. Months passed. She worked. She slip-slid out of sight. She followed the soles of customers into the dark shells of shoes they tried on, she crawled into dark leather caves—take me down into the shoe, grind me deep into the heel where I cannot be seen, invisible, unfindable, the magically shrinking girl, curling up where sweat meshes with the hide.

How was work today, Eva?—It was fine, Mamá.

In May, the winter boots arrived—long bodies on the storeroom floor like gunned-down birds. Eva kneeled, arranging them by style. Pietro came in and ran his hand along her neck. Eva had been imagining herself inside a brown ladies' boot.

"Come here."

"Wait. I have to go to the bathroom."

"Too bad," he said, and the voice belonged to a stranger, some harsh man she'd never met before. He pushed her onto the pile of boots, hand at her hem and under it, crawling clammy up her thigh; she struggled and he pressed her, held her down by the hair while his other hand shoved past her panties into her body—sharp and burning breaking into many jagged pieces—"Shut up, **puta,**" the stranger's voice, a hand covered her mouth, and leather caves ripped open as she fell and fell.

She squirmed and then he bucked and then she tore out from under him and crawled, quickly, rose to her feet and ran, to the storeroom door and past it, away from the voice that called her back, out and down the street like girls should never run, kicking off the high heels and running in bare feet, past horses and glossy cars and alarmed stares over endless cobblestones until she broke through the door of her house and landed, out-of-breath barefoot and burning between her legs, in front of Mamá, who lifted her eyebrows and spatula in shock and came toward her. She leaned into her mother's body and left her own.

She was in bed. She felt her mother's hands braiding her hair. She felt nothing from the waist down. Her father stood in the doorway, looking strange, there and not there, as though he were suspended by invisible strings and expected a wind to blow him away at any moment. He looked at Eva. He was pale as ice. "What have you done?"

She would have answered, she meant to answer, but her mouth was empty.

"Ignazio," Mami said, "give us some time."

He hesitated.

"Some time, Ignazio. Alone."

He left.

"**Mijita.**" Mamá looked worn. Eva searched for anger in her face and could not find it. "Tell me what happened."

"Have—have you talked to Pietro?"

"Your papi did."

"What did he say?"

"That you flirted with his customers and stole a pair of shoes."

"That's not true!"

"**Bueno.** What happened?"

Eva stared at her mother's face: slender, solid, framed by two thick braids. She couldn't see any more than the top of them, but she knew they were there, falling dark and long down her back. Of all the things Eva knew in the world, none were more certain than these two black braids. She could not risk losing them. She longed to tell the truth and could not possibly. The truth was worse than Pietro's version: it was tangos danced at closing time, full of close, forbidden moves; a cigarette, accepted, smoked; the way she'd made him press and moan; two red heels, accepted, worn around the store each day; the horrify-ing heat in her own body. She imag-ined saying these things out loud. A devastating story had opened in her life and she was the villain, the travesty, the disgusting girl, her crime had no bounds, it was endlessly evil and hiding it was the only way to keep her mother leaning close with braids and face and glow. Losing Mami would be worse than losing God.

She was silent.

"Evita?"

"Nothing."

"**Hija—**"

"Mami, I can't feel my legs. I can't move them—what's wrong with me?"

Her legs had disappeared—or, rather, she from them. They were empty, uninhabited, unreachable, like the glaciers at the bottom of the continent. As Mami gently prodded, as the sun fell in a distant sky, as night washed her little room with darkness, Eva sent the tendrils of her mind down past her belly and felt nothing. No pain, no warmth, no hint of movement. She fell asleep and dreamed of a torso with head and arms, her own, dragging itself down a hall by the knuckles.

Dr. Zeballos came the next day. His paunch and jovial voice had always reminded her of Santa Claus. "There's nothing wrong with her, as far as I can see. Inexplicable paralysis. The French call it a symptom of rebellion."

There were apparently no cures for this condition. She stayed in bed. Mamá brought meals, changed her bedpan, and kept Papá at bay. On the third day, Pietro came to visit. When Eva saw him, grinning broadly behind a bouquet of pink carnations, the half of her body she still felt filled with a liquid scream.

"Evita. I've been worried about you. Look, I brought carnations—aren't they your favorite?" He paused for her to answer. She didn't. "I'm giving you another chance."

"You're too generous with us, Pietro," her father said, standing against the wall, stiff as a soldier.

"**Por favor,** Gondola, how long have we been friends? Did you think I'd forget?" Tiny hairs dotted his jaw, more gray, Eva saw, than black. "Your daughter is young; she can still learn. I'll wait." Pietro scanned the room, taking in the homemade quilts, the frayed lamp shade, the Worried Mother Hovering in the Doorway, the girl. "Oh, and I brought your shoes. Don't worry about the ones you stole." He smiled kindly, exposing the pale yellow of his teeth. "I have plenty more."

If only, she thought that night, awake in the dark. If only time, that ferocious river, could be turned to flow back where it came from. If only things could be made to unhappen. She watched the moon rest its light on her windowsill. It was pooling whiter. It looked like fallen milk. It had no right to be here, in this room invaded by pink carnations, whose petals made sharp-toothed shadows on the wall, like crocodiles, like the crocodiles she and Capitán Andrés had fought off a thousand years ago, back when she'd believed in stupid things like Sweet Gold, back before Andrés was so busy with school and she with work they hardly saw each other and even when they did she walked off quickly, not knowing what to say, not wanting to hear his questions about life, work, where-have-you-been, how-do-you-spend-your-days—before all this, a fallen moon, shadows of flowers, villaingirls, the burn (yourfaultyourfault) inside her. And the absence. Absence of legs. Absence of light. Absence of words in her throat. Absence was a viscous thing; she let it spread and spread and swallow everything.

Mamá waged a war against the absence. Every morning, every afternoon at three, and every evening when the dishes were done, she boiled a bitter brew that surely could restore ambulation to the dead. They mended Eva's insides, slowly, by force. Mamá sat and watched and made sure each drop was drunk and said, What are you thinking? what are you thinking now? tell me Eva, but even when the absence faltered there was no conquering the yourfaultyourfault underneath. It steamed and curdled and threatened to drown her world. She could not let it leak out even for a moment. She escaped into shoes on the floor by the closet. She curled there while her mother watched her drink. She curled there when her father poked his head in, briefly, as if she had some disease that would flare up again unless he kept his distance. She curled there when her brothers gave her lectures—Bruno on how to behave with men, Tomás on keeping Papá happy, and Marco on the ethics of stealing. Nobody could touch her, nobody would find her, absence sheathed her from them all. But not completely: Mami's teas (and stark looks and soft kneading) conquered Eva's legs. After two weeks, Eva could move her toes again. In three weeks, she could stand. In four, she could walk and had no numbness to excuse her from work.

On her first day back, Pietro greeted her by pointing to the storeroom. At closing time, she did not fight him off.

Days passed. Weeks. Eva learned the inside soles of a thousand shoes. She learned to scrape herself away from the present moment like a snail abandoning its shell, stowing her soft inner parts in caves of leather, leaving the rest behind to its slow death. This was easier at some times than others. At night she dreamed of falling into blackness, cut open by the long incessant heel of a great shoe. Sundays loomed each week, with their dreaded visits to the confessional. Now that she could walk again, she had to kneel and fabricate petty sins, as if she were a normal girl with a normal soul and normal problems. It was a sin, surely cardinal, to keep this secret and still eat the body of Christ, but Padre Robles' penances had been harsh for daydreaming in class and taking more than her share of birthday cake, and so she couldn't imagine what he'd require now. And yet La Viuda had said once in the **carnicería** that God sees all of it anyway. If there's anyone who can take the truth, it's God.

Surely God would help because God loved her mother, didn't he, and surely did not want Mamá to keep looking the way she did, all stern and sad and probing, as if by sheer exhaustive staring she'd cut through her daughter's curtains, one by one, and unearth the rotten things behind them? Surely God was still with, if not Eva, then at least Mamá, and Mamá was still in battle, wasn't she, and wouldn't it be better if, before her mother won and Eva broke and told, she could do penance and become a bit more pure, a bit more clean, at least in the eyes of God, wherever and whatever his eyes were?

It took two months to seek absolution. She chose a Tuesday so she could have the church to herself. It was a groggy afternoon. The confessional tiles were cold against her knees.

"Bless me, Father, for I have sinned."

"Praise be to God," Padre Robles said mechanically through the grating. "Tell me your sins, my child."

"It's about the man I work for. He . . . does things. I think I started it."

"What sorts of things?"

"He touches me. Makes me touch him."

A pause oozed through the grating. "This is very serious. You must tell everything that happened. God must hear each detail."

Eva pursed her mouth. She forced it open. Her stories poured from her, word by word, touch by touch, prompt from the priest by prompt from the priest. Images slid across her memory like slugs. A waist's-eye view. Hard desktop under her face under her grip. Two knees, her own, too far from each other. Then she stopped, did she hear, no it wasn't possible, from the priest's side of the booth, through the grating, his breath, short, heavy, hard, like Pietro's. She froze. Bile rose to the back of her mouth.

"Continue, my child—" but she had already stumbled out of the confessional, forgetting even to cross herself before turning her back on Jesus nailed above the altar. Outside, the sky stretched its limp gray blanket over Punta Carretas. Behind the prison gate, a guard scratched his crotch and squinted up at the vast lack of sun.

Cierre. Cielo. Cerrado. Siempre. Lock. Sky. Closed. Always.

In the days, the months, the year that followed, and in the year that unfurled after that, Eva burrowed deeper and deeper into the dark caves of shoes that she sorted and stocked and sent her mind reeling into, shrinking, curling, again and again.

Something burst inside her when she saw the blood. She stood in the tiny bathroom at work, staring at the middle of her panties. Pietro had not touched her there in at least a week, yet there it was: a stain like a serrated flower. She had heard about this from the women in the butcher shop. It had something to do with being a woman. Just the week before, Eva had turned thirteen, and there had been cake and candles and a new blue sweater. Bruno's wife, Mirna, had baked the cake; Mamá had spun and dyed the wool and knitted the gift with her ceaselessly moving hands. It was cold outside, rain blowing down, and she wore the sweater now. It felt soft and scratchy at the same time, and here she was, thirteen, two years away from public womanhood, two years since she'd been a little girl. She gaped at the stain. Nobody had caused this blood to flow except her—or whatever mysterious force had found the switch within her, had known to flick. (La Viuda had called it God's curse. But Clarabel, La Divorciada, had scoffed and said, Why listen to priests about a lady's **tú sabes qué**? They're hardly experts, she'd remarked, and she was right.)

Gingerly, Eva touched the spot. It was warm—she jerked back rapidly. She looked at herself in the mirror. She couldn't remember the last time she'd truly looked. A face met hers, high-boned, smooth-skinned, dark eyes staring right at her. She was growing. She had formed a flame of blood. She thought of blood and flames and things inside her that she didn't know about, things that might exist and were not pain. It was almost closing time; she had to hurry. As she stuffed toilet paper into her panties, she ran through the day in her mind to weigh his mood. Closing times were dangerous, more so when sales were slow.

He glared when she emerged. "Where've you been? The water boiled—I had to pour it myself."

"I'm sorry."

"Hmmph." He came closer. He'd been drinking. "You look flushed."

She looked straight ahead at the middle of his chest.

"What were you doing in there?"

"Nothing."

"Don't lie." He pushed against her. She stepped backward, one step, two, until the desk reared up behind her and his hard sex pressed into her waist. He turned her around to face the desk.

"Bend over."

She thought of the red stain, the awkward ball of toilet paper. She didn't move.

"I said bend over."

"No."

"What?"

"No."

"Fucking **puta,**" he said, and grabbed her hair, pulled it so her neck arched back and she saw familiar cracks in the ceiling. "You do as I say." He softened his grip, opened his palm against her scalp. "Now. Bend over."

At that moment Eva saw a weapon, a secret weapon, right there in the open. Slowly, arms out, she bent. Pietro's hand, satisfied, relaxed from her. She neared the desk, he was unbuttoning his trousers, she curled her hand around the **mate** thermos and spun and watched the steaming water fly at Pietro and he screamed and the image seared her— Pietro burned and cringing—before she ran, out, out, down the wet street, without unleashing her high-heeled shoes, through sheet after sheet of shouting rain, running until her lungs burned, running on, not home, not this time, running now on Avenida San Salvador, toward that blood-red door, the streets were dark with rain and she was wet and she was at the door, she pulled the handle, she stepped through.

It was dinnertime at La Diablita. A stir of savory scents rose to meet her. Silverware clinked hungrily on plates, percussion for the melodies of voices. A foxtrot flew on jagged wings out of a piano. The clientele wore well-pressed clothes and leaned into clouds of cigarette smoke. Lush young waitresses glided past wood-paneled walls. Eva slunk into a red chair. She sat for a few minutes, catching her breath, looking for poets, until a waitress approached her with mild curiosity.

"Do you want to order something?" Her skin was heavily made up, hair in careful ringlets around her face.

"Ah, no," Eva fumbled. "Actually, are you hiring?"

"We might be." The waitress eyed her more closely. "I'm leaving for Buenos Aires." She beamed. "I'm going to be an actress. You want to talk to the owner?"

Eva nodded. The waitress led her through the room, past the bar, through a threshold hung with beads, behind which the owner lounged with four drunk friends.

"**Che,** Pato. This girl wants to work here."

Pato looked up. He was a stout, balding man. He's always eaten everything he wanted, Eva thought. Ladies. Food. The moon. He examined Eva. She felt foolish in her homemade sweater, wet with rain, and was grateful for her high heels.

"Have you worked before?"

"Yes, Señor. Three years."

"Where?"

"At a **zapatería.**"

"How old are you?"

"Sixteen," she lied.

"And why do you want to work here?"

The table went quiet. A woman in black silk lit a slim cigarette. They stared at her. She felt too small to answer but she could not let them know that, they would only see her mask. She stood taller. "I believe in poetry. In beauty. I want to work in a place where people are beautiful and free." She let herself draw an innocent smile. "This **is** that sort of place, isn't it?"

The black-silked woman laughed. "Well, Pato? Is it?"

Pato looked at the woman's glass, her shoulders, the ample cleavage pushing from her dress. He looked at Eva. "What's your name?"

"Eva Firielli Torres."

"Eva, come back on Saturday at five. We'll find a way to keep you busy." He turned to his companion. The interview was over.

Eva retraced her path out to Avenida San Salvador, tinged with magic in the gathering night. She walked toward home. Rain traced a mottled crown on her head. She strode for almost seven blocks before the dread set in. Her steps slowed to a stop. Her mother was not home—she was out playing canasta at Coco's, or La Viuda's, or maybe it was Clarabel's apartment. Where else could she go? She could turn and head to Parque Rodó, sit by the fountain with nuzzling couples. She could return to La Diablita and wash some dishes in exchange for a Coca-Cola. She could go to La Rambla and walk up and down, up and down the shore. This would do for an hour, maybe even a night, but not for the rest of her life. And the paper between her legs was soaked, she was bleeding, she was tired, she was wet all over. She would have to find something to tell her father.

By the time she arrived at her house, a dozen possible stories jostled in her head. She unlocked the door and entered. Papá sprang up from the sofa. He hulked toward her. An empty bottle of **grappa** leered on the table; its sweet-liquor smell filled the air. They stared at each other. Papá's hands rolled into fists.

"I talked to Pietro."

"It's not what you think."

"Slut."

"He's a liar."

"He's a good man."

"He's not."

"You break my heart."

"Papá—"

"Whore."

She opened her arms to him.

A fist flew at her face. She reeled back, the taste of iron on her tongue. He punched her again and she fell against the wall and braced herself for more blows, and when they came she was ready, covered, limp, far away from the man whose body had so much to say. When he stopped, she waited to make sure that he was done. Silence. She looked out. He was staring at his hand, watching it curl open, close, open again. He looked at her with crumpled eyes. He looked as though he might say something but there was iron in her mouth, sparks in her head, a space between them that was ripping wider, a steep black rift into which she would not fall.

She said, "I will never speak to you again."

She stood shakily and walked down the hall. She heard him call out, but it didn't sound like Spanish and she had never learned Italian. In the bathroom, she changed the blood-swelled paper, and scanned herself in the mirror. A cut at her lip, slightly darkened, no teeth lost.

She lay in bed and railed against the creep of numbness. Her legs were fading, but no, they could not go this time; what would happen to her new job if her legs disappeared? Don't go, don't fall, don't die, you have to stay. Papá was not the world, and though it broke her in two to think of him, her mind had other places to fly, like the luminous thought of Pietro's skin burning with pain, and La Diablita, with its bright warm smells, its bustling noise, its air that crackled, crackled, calling to that nub in her she'd thought would never flower but that waited (dense, explosive) under her skin.

The café's colors reared toward her as in dreams, from brown wood walls, brown hair glistening in candlelight, a brown piano pouring songs, black dresses, black slick keys trembling all night, black kohl emboldening the curves of women's eyes, pale cigarette smoke, pale pearls around pale necks, red chairs, red tables, red lipstick, bright red laughter, dark red wine.

She wanted to swallow every inch of light and glamour. She stole slices of conversation she culled from clientele. She had a covert way of leaning in, just close enough to pick up words along with dirty dishes. A woman with expensive hair praises a poet in slurred speech. Spittle clings to a student's mouth as he expounds on the Russian Revolution. Young lovers argue about the future of theater, their tones passionate, hands clasped tight under the table. Eva absorbed everything. She took strange orders: "Dante Alighieri" beside "martini"; "existentialism" next to "**Chianti chileno**—another round"; a long list of pasta dishes peppered with names of books. When the food and wine had been delivered to their tables, she stuffed the little pages into her brassiere, to use later in her own voracious feasts at the library downtown. The papers were stained with olive oil and liquor, slick and potent between her breasts. They were treasure maps. She used them to navigate the citadel of books, where each text was a plush home; each text had rooms full of finery to touch, feel, taste, shatter, stroke, knead, rub, fall asleep next to and dream. She loved to break and enter them, a secret interloper on the page.

He wanted to know her secrets, that man who was her father. Where she worked. What she was doing.

What was in her mind. On the first night, he'd knocked—"Eva? Evita?"—six separate times on her bedroom door, every hour on the hour until dawn, and she kept thinking he would come in—there was no lock, after all—but he didn't open the door and she didn't either. The second night he made two visits that consisted of pure knocking. On the third night she came home from work at 3 a.m. to a note on her bed, in that handwriting of his that looked like a series of tiny balloons: **I'll be awake. This is your last chance.** She tore it into pieces and flushed it with her urine.

Pride settled on Papá, a cloak that grew stiffer with wear. They glided past each other as though pretending to ignore a ghost. They spoke to everyone in the room except each other.

"Marco, pass the **salsa golf.**"

"Ask Papi—it's right in front of him."

She scowled at her brother. "Marco."

"This is ridiculous! Papá, your daughter wants the **salsa golf.**"

"I have no daughter." Ignazio skewered a boiled potato on his fork. "No **puta** is a daughter of mine."

She didn't care. She didn't. He could think what he liked; she was free.

She told her mother she was a waitress, and not, in fact, a **mujer de la calle,** despite the makeup, the late nights, a new blouse cut lower than ever before.

"It's a restaurant in La Ciudad Vieja. Good pay."

Eva spread a wad of pesos on the counter, as if presenting a winning poker hand. "Here, take it."

Pajarita kept wiping the kitchen sink. She didn't look at the cash. "What happened with your father?"

"Nothing."

Mamá turned that gaze on her, the one that made Eva feel transparent. "**Hija.** You don't have to do this. Other things are possible."

She absorbed her mother's face, her smell, her hands perched on the counter. She saw gray for the first time, just a strand or two invading the long slide of her hair. Rage flashed through Eva. It breached all decency that those braids could change, that any thread of that solid black should fade, that her mother—that any woman—could go gray without ever once in her life having worn a silk dress.

"Like what?"

"You could come to the **carnicería.** I could teach you."

The morning sun was ruthlessly egalitarian: it lit the pesos and the dishrags, the rosemary and sage leaves and the chipped rims of their pots. Outside, the milkman jingled his bell and reined his horse. Eva heard it neigh in gentle resignation. She knew there was another Uruguay, outside this city and under it and even in her house: a Uruguay where women grew up sleeping on cow skins and sitting on skulls and where they never learned to read, learned instead to make bitter teas for dowdy women who gossiped in butcher shops. But Eva could read—and she had read that story about the girl who fell down the rabbit hole and discovered vibrant things; she could be that girl, she had found that place, in an old stone building filled with candles, rubies, poets, imported cigarettes, red wine. The milkman's horse clopped away down the cobblestones. And anyway, it wasn't as if Mami really needed her. She had Mirna now, and if Marco married that stupid, sap-sweet girl from La Blanqueada there'd be more than enough daughters to go around, daughters much nicer and cleaner than she was.

"No. I'm keeping this job."

"Where is the place?"

"I can't tell you."

Her mother studied her. "You're safe there?"

"Very safe. The waitresses are nice. They help me learn."

Eva's fellow waitresses taught her the mysterious arts of serving liquor, rouging cheeks, and smoking as a means of seduction. **"Mira,"** Graciela purred. "You purse your lips like this." Smoke emerged from her red mouth: svelte, white, undulating. "Try it." Eva tried. Her smoke puffed out in random clumps and made Graciela laugh. She would get it. She knew she would. How could she not, with these **chicas** as big sisters and she so eager for corruption? She listened to their jovial analyses of La Diablita's customers. That eminent writer at the corner table was lying to all his girlfriends. These opulent patrons sipping Chardonnay fancied themselves art benefactors

but gave stingy tips. The bohemian students discussing Batlle, Bolívar, and Marx would each give his
right arm for a date with Eva. "Watch how their eyes
trail you, **nena.** It's obvious." But Eva was most
drawn to a circle of poets that gathered every week-
end in the back room, behind the beaded curtain.
Eight of them tonight, all young except the Well-
Known Poet, who presided over them and spoke
slowly so the **joven** with the little blue notebook
could write down what he said. These were poets—
real live ones. She could tell by the lyrical way they
waved their cigarettes. She approached the table and
placed glasses before them, one by one, listening for
snippets to jot down on her covert papers.

A lanky man was talking. "If only Hitler could
hear your 'Ode to Struggle.'" That voice. She looked
closer at his wiry face and it was him, Andrés
Descalzo, talking with poets as if it were the most
natural thing in the world. He seemed to feel her
stare on his skin, and before she could say his name
he turned away. "Especially that line about washing
the enemy's feet. What an incisive image."

Eva filled a wineglass. She understood. In this
room, he was not—had never been—the Little
Butcher. His ironed ivory shirt was plain compared
to his comrades' clothes but finer than anything his
family wore. She slipped back through the beaded
curtain.

She watched the poets' table with new boldness.
Andrés' presence was an infiltration and it gave her

hope that she too might find a way in. She pretended not to know him. She smiled brightly as she served wine. The Well-Known Poet began to smile back.

"A dance, please."

"**¿Perdón?**" she said, thinking that, in the din, she'd misheard the name of a drink.

"I'd like to order a dance. Or, perhaps 'humbly beg for' would be better?"

They were all looking at her. He was not attractive, not to her, with that graying hair, that rolling laugh, those knuckly hands that were so much like Pietro's. But his eyes were kind.

"Yes."

He lit up with complacence.

" 'Humbly beg' is much better."

The Poet flushed. He ignored the snickers. "Well, by all means, then, let me beg."

There was no dance floor. They went to the corner by the piano. Eva had not danced since the storeroom lessons. The music rose; she held her breath; she pressed her cheek against the Poet's. Her body snapped into the angles of the tango, still there, still beating. Jaimecito, the pianist, enthused, let his voice rise to a wail: **Como ríe la vida—Si tus ojos negros me quieren mirar**—she remembered this, could move this way, could spin and dip and careen with precision. The Well-Known Poet led clumsily, but it didn't matter; the grace was in the bone-beat, in the blood, in the song as it waxed warm—**y un rayo misterioso**—and urgent—**hará nido en tu pelo**—

and hands began to clap in time, and mouths whistled, and the Well-Known Poet actually found his stride; their bodies both said Turn at the same time, then said Swoop down, and Jaimecito sought an ambitious climax beyond his vocal range: **florecerá la vida, No existirá el dolor.** The song ended with a boisterous ripple of the keys and applause. She was giddy. She was shy. Graciela yelled from the kitchen door. The Poet glittered. "**¡Qué cosa!** Will you come sit with us?"

"I have to work—"

"Surely you could take a moment?"

"I'm on shift until midnight."

"Aha! Join us after that. I insist."

At midnight Eva crossed the beaded curtain, not to serve, but to sit. The Well-Known Poet introduced her to the others: Joaquín, the eager college student with the faithful notebook; Pepe, a literature student with a crisp collar (surely ironed by his maid); Carlos, a kind young lawyer with enormous ears; Andrés; and Beatriz, a glowing **muchacha** with unlikely red hair.

"We were just discussing Moradetti's new volume," the Well-Known Poet told her. "Have you read him?"

"**Por favor.**" Pepe straightened his cuffs. "Don't torment our poor waitress. She is paid to wait tables, not to analyze trends in poetry."

"Now, now—"

"No, he's right." Eva formed a fist under the table.

"Poets don't pay me to read them. They don't have to. I read Moradetti entirely for free." She smiled. "Why? Did he pay you?"

Pepe coughed. "That's not what I meant."

"Of course not," Eva said.

The next three hours were a gilded blur. The poets talked; they argued; they bantered and drank and talked some more. Moradetti turned to Mussolini, Mussolini to the purpose of art, art's purpose to modernism (controversial) to the charms of French desserts. Glasses emptied. Ashtrays filled. Eva leaned forward to listen, leaned back to think. She was awake, alive, full of ideas like branches in a greenhouse, growing thick and rife against the glass.

On her way home, she felt more than saw Andrés walking in the same direction, on the other side of the street. He crossed the darkness to join her. They didn't speak. They walked out of La Ciudad Vieja, down the house-lined streets of Parque Rodó. An old, wiry woman smoked a cigar on a yellow stoop. Through green curtains, Eva saw a silhouetted couple slow-dancing to a phonograph. The song was muffled and mournful. Eva's and Andrés' steps rang out on the sidewalk, her sharp little heels and his heavier, deep-toned shoes.

"Where do they think you live?" she asked.

"Pocitos."

"Ah."

They turned a corner.

"Have they asked about your family?"

"My father imports French jewelry. My grand-mother's a clingy pain. That's how I keep them from holding readings at my house."

"I see. And poetry?"

"**¿Qué?**"

"Do you write poetry?"

Andrés slowed his steps, and she felt him think-ing, a crackle and hum in the air between them. "I don't know whether I write poetry, or poetry writes me. Sometimes I feel like all of it—the world, my body, each move I make—is turning into a poem. It's excruciating. I can't breathe until I write." His head was bent toward the ground, dark curls against his cheek. "It must sound crazy."

"No. It doesn't."

"Is it that way for you?"

He touched her shoulder. His hand was full of heat that stung her body. She thought back to the one thing she'd written, before, before everything. "Perhaps."

They kept walking. The houses grew plainer: flat-roofed boxes pressed up side by side. "Remember," she said, "when we were children?"

"Of course."

"We were pirates—"

"Yes—"

"Finding treasures in the floor!"

Andrés laughed edgily. "Treasures in a butcher shop. There's a feat of imagination."

In the silver wash of moonlight, he looked ethereal, otherworldly, a man (a boy) who felt the world turn into poems, a butcher's son, born to inherit cleavers, bloody aprons, meat hooks and their meat. She listened to the mingled sounds of their footsteps.

A few doors before Eva's, Andrés kissed her on the cheek. His skin felt like clean linen. "Good night. Keep coming. Don't let snotty Pepe scare you off."

Eva crept through the slumbering house to her bedroom, where she pulled pen and paper from her sock drawer, careful not to wake Tomás in his adjacent bed. She took them to the bathroom and gazed at herself in the mirror. She'd forgotten to remove her makeup before coming home: she looked womanly, mature; she had danced in a roomful of strangers, she had drunk wine at the poets' table, she could maybe, maybe open her life to poetry, whatever that was—she hoped it was something pure, unfathomable, a force her world and body could turn into, a force that perhaps would write her as she wrote and that could never ever wound her or twist her out of shape. Her cheek still tingled from Andrés' kiss. "I am a poet," she whispered into the mirror. She sat down on the toilet, grasped her pen, and began to write.

Months and years would stretch and turn and she always pined for this: these nights; smoky, electric, succulent, ineffable; the feel of the red table under her hand (chipped and glossy, sticky underneath) as the poets dreamed and joked and boasted; the way the air stretched and shimmered after her second glass of wine; the conversations that coiled intricately through war to recent essays to the deepest meaning of life. A light shone through those nights that Eva could not define, that vanished if she sought it too directly, that gilded everything it touched—voices, faces, wineglass, table, words—with numinous honey. She grew to rely on it, trusting its power to ward off all that must be kept away—drabness, boredom, nightmares, the rage of home, the terror inside shoe stores and of Nazis in faraway lands. She was free inside its unseen sphere, and life became more possible. Surely the other poets felt it too: Joaquín, with his meticulous verses, knotted forehead, and arsenal of freshly sharpened pencils; Carlos, who smelled of shoe polish and stole moments at his father's law firm to scrawl odes on legal files; the Well-Known Poet, with his amiable laugh and unkempt gray hair; Pepe, with his pointy chin and fast martinis; Andrés, with his lucid voice, sharp thoughts, sharp smile; and Beatriz, the kind of girl whose laugh poured like molasses, whose poems brimmed with maudlin nubile shepherdesses yearning for their errant gaucho men. Eva could have borne her poems if she did not also sit so close to Andrés.

"We're changing the world, right, Andrés?" Beatriz said, twirling her hair on a slow finger.

"Poetry alone won't change the world," Andrés said. "But without it, where would we be? Stripped of mystery, passion, everything that urges us to stay awake despite the shit and pain of living. In a world full of war, we need it more than ever."

Joaquín and Carlos murmured their agreement. The Well-Known Poet nodded behind his cigarette smoke. Andrés' words mixed with the smoke, swirling around the table, imbibed on each poet's breath. In a world full of war. Eva felt the smoke and bulk of the **Admiral Graf Spee** within those words. It had been only a month since the German battleship had dragged its huge hard broken body into the port, seeking refuge, trailing fire and smoke and the toxic scent of battle. Uruguay was neutral. Uruguay was far from Europe. Uruguay had not been invaded the way Poland had last spring. But the **Graf Spee** came anyway, and so did the British ships that set it on fire. War's fingers were very long and they stretched over the Atlantic and shook up her city the way a ghost's cold fingers reach through a window and shudder you awake in your own bed. That's how it was when Eva woke to Papá in the hall telling Tomás about the **Graf Spee: the smoke was thick like—well, like—a big black blanket, all over the port, and up on the crane we were coughing like crazy, and I saw the Nazis standing on deck rigid like fucking toothpicks, like everything was fine, like they were breathing air from the fucking Alps.** After the German captain gave up and sank his battleship to the bottom of the river, Eva dreamed of dead wet Nazis smashing her windows and crawling into her bed, cold and dripping, cutting her with shards of glass and ship and with their fingernails.

Andrés had written a sonnet called "**Graf Spee**'s Ghost" and it occurred to her that he might understand. She tapped his foot with hers. He smiled without looking at her.

"The things you say," she told him later on their walk home. "The way you say them. Everybody listens."

"It's just talk."

The heart of things, you touch it when you speak; somehow you shake and shift the flesh reality is made of. "It's more than that."

They walked home together every night, but never all the way to the door. They did not want to be discovered. Eva came to dread buying the family meat, because of the way Coco pinned her with doleful eyes. "What happened to that son of mine? You, Eva, tell me! He barely even lives here anymore."

We are told, Andrés wrote, **that the world is made of burlap: / Coarse, enduring—when really it is gauze, / Layer upon layer, fine, fragile, infinite, / We can see our fingers through it in the light.** And he himself was a light, a beacon, though not like the lighthouse at Punta Carretas, not that slow, predictable ray. He was feverish and erratic. His beam was a bright knife; his words and thoughts could cut open the night. She wanted to get close, be pierced, approach the wick inside him that was hidden from the world, that surely sprang from pain, that held secrets as dark and delicate (she imagined) as her own. He emboldened her. Sitting on the toilet at 5 a.m., she soared, risked, wrote, scripted line after line of words that sprang from a source at once unknown and intimate. Words about freedom; fury; her many hungers; words that gnashed their teeth and bit one another on the page.

A second year passed. Poetry leaked onto her waitress tablet, the skin of her arm, scraps of paper she found later in her socks. That spring, her brother Marco married Raquel, the girl from La Blanqueada, who, Eva had to admit, was genuine in her sweetness, and wanted to make a sister out of Eva, an enterprise she quickly crushed by neglecting to return calls. **You will never understand me,** Eva could have, but did not, say. The following year, she finally recited a poem out loud. She stood in Pepe's living room, opulent with imported rugs and fresh-cut lilies. She should never have looked at the lilies. She lost her nerve and lost her voice.

"Go on, Eva," Carlos urged, leaning forward in support. He had a tomato-sauce stain on his collar, and this gave her courage. Still, she couldn't muster more than a hoarse whisper; the poets mistook this for dramatic flair, and responded with genuine applause.

"Not bad," Pepe said reluctantly. He turned and spoke to the audience, rather than to her. "The lighthouse as metaphor for freedom during war. And a clever allusion to that **inglesa** Woolf."

Eva had not thought of the war when writing that poem (although she should have—the United States had joined the fray, Jews in Europe wore yellow stars, droves and droves were dying) and she'd forgotten all about Virginia Woolf. "Yes, thank you."

"This would be great for the next edition of **Expresión,**" Joaquín said. He frowned earnestly; Joaquín had recently become a communist, a good place for him, thought Eva, considering all his years of dutiful notes. From what she'd gathered, it seemed that communists wrote a lot of declarations, read a lot of books, and discussed the global proletariat over cold beers. "You should submit."

When her poem came out in **Expresión,** a journal published in a poet's basement, Eva clipped two copies: one to keep under her pillow, and one for the dark place between her breasts. It grew damp with sweat each day. By winter the paper had smudged and thinned. She carried it anyway, tucked into place like a little weapon.

In Eva's fifth year at La Diablita, her youngest brother became a man by marrying María Chamoun's daughter, the bright-as-a-flame Carlota. Tomás stood by the altar, dwarfed by his own stiff suit, gaping at the cloud of tulle and silk on its way toward him. In the pews, Eva sat with Bruno, Marco, and Mamá. The bride reached the altar. Padre Robles made the sign of the cross (his fingers were still fat) and leaped into his script. Carlota beamed through her veil. Tomás grinned like a comic-book character. The wooden pew was hard, and Eva crossed and recrossed her legs, picturing herself spitting on the giant crucifix behind the altar.

At the reception—half the neighborhood cramped into the Chamouns' living room—Eva served plates with her sister-in-law Mirna.

"So, Eva." Mirna cocked her head slyly. "When will we do this for you?"

She didn't answer. She looked around for some reprieve. Across the room, Xhana leaned her head toward the boy who had been courting her. César. They had met at the university, where they were both studying to become schoolteachers. César had the kind of eyes an angel might: fresh, wide, midnight-black, lit up by something Xhana was now saying. Eva still hadn't met him; she avoided family gatherings by reflex, to avoid awkward moments with Papá. But she missed her cousin. They were almost strangers. Maybe she could go over there, smile, say hello like a normal girl.

Her father's voice rose behind her. "So, Pietro—how's the store?"

"Wonderful. Wonderful."

Mirna handed Eva a plate. She almost dropped it. "Your daughter works there?"

"Sí."

"I hope she gives you less trouble than mine did."

Pietro laughed amiably. "**Ay,** Gondola," he said.

Eva gripped the knife from the **pascualina** platter. It was long and flecked with spinach—she could raise it right now, slash both of their throats, stop their laughing. Heat rushed through her at the thought. She swung the blade against the platter once, twice, three times, and on the third it tipped and spilled the rest of the pie onto the floor.

Mirna stared.

"I need air," Eva said, loping out.

That night she dreamed she was a bride walking down an aisle. **I never thought this could happen to me.** She held dozens of carnations. She had to crane her neck above them to see where she was going. **Who's the groom?** The dim air crashed with organ music. As she got closer to the altar she heard a terrible cackle, getting louder and louder. She dropped the flowers. In front of her, a giant slice of **pascualina** pie stood on stick legs, a bow tie slapped onto its pastry shell. It was laughing. It smelled like rotting eggs. She screamed, and it laughed louder. She screamed and screamed and woke up sweating. Dawn light seeped through the curtains. She sat up and pulled them back. The sky looked ashen. She wanted to fly out of the window, become a bird, a buoyant speck of grime, anything that might lift off and disappear into the night. The little house felt like a trap, tight, dark, inescapable, cluttered with unsaid words. Her body too. She was eighteen. At her age her mother had been married for two years, and not that she wanted her mother's life or even cared, but who would marry her? And who would she want to live so close to in one corner of the raucous world? Only one person. She didn't deserve him, she never would, but perhaps she had to try.

She waited too long. A week later she was still mustering up courage, searching for the words, when she marched out of the La Diablita kitchen to wipe the sweat from tables and saw Andrés and Beatriz, against the wall, by the piano, kissing. Two mouths locked together. Hands in each other's hair.

She would not drop her tray, with all its dirty dishes, though it was heavy, too heavy, an impossible load. She bolted to the kitchen and disappeared behind its door.

Eva turned nineteen without a hint of marriage. She watched Andrés and Beatriz sit close together, and it turned her stomach, the proprietary way she stroked his neck. She tried to ignore them but they imprinted themselves on her vision as if she had glanced at the sun.

In her last year at La Diablita, Eva worked as many hours as she could and stashed extra cash beneath her mattress, just in case the world ever opened an escape hatch and she had to sling together her own raft.

The World War ended and turned Montevideo into an early Carnaval. Eva woke to the roar of drum and song and shouting from the street. The neighbor's radio blared ecstatically through the wall: "Peace at last—Germany's surrender—no more war . . ." She dressed quickly and ran to the kitchen, where her mother stood still as a hawk, wet rag suspended in her hand, staring at the wall as if boring through its surface to reveal a hidden fissure. Eva felt, against her will, the wide and fickle arms of hope. The world could change. It was changing: this kitchen was not just a kitchen, but a box at the edge of a human river, streaming past their door, celebrating the eruption of peace. She approached her mother and hugged her from behind.

"Mamá."

Pajarita leaned into her daughter. A single wet trail ran down her cheek, as if a snail or tear had crept there. It was not a wetness Eva wanted to see, not an embrace she could withstand. She stepped away, toward the door. Mamá looked at her in a manner that sealed her mission to escape.

"I'm going out."

On the street, Eva opened her veins and bones and senses to loud, fresh peace, swirling around her, thickening the crowd and carrying her past the prison's sunlit walls and past the long church steps all the way to the wide central artery of Avenida 18 de Julio. People swarmed and cheered and howled and shook around her. Men in shiny **murga** costumes belted out last season's ballads; a boy, high on his father's shoulders, chewed a Uruguayan flag; a young couple danced a fervent tango, bumping against the crowd; Champagne bottles popped frothily at each turn; music moved in random eddies, candombe drums here, accordions there, chants and clapping, sounds she could move to, dance to, swept up in the explosion of her city. Peace! someone shouted. Peace! she shouted back, jostling against those close to her. An unknown hand passed her a cup of Champagne. She toasted with the sky—here's to a new world— and drank. The crowd pressed closer, bodies and more bodies, warm and pungent, keen and dense, and she pressed back gladly until one body pressed too hard at her bottom. She froze. Pietro (his hands, his breath, the push of him) shot through her like cold lightning. The stranger's erection dug into her. Pietro leered—she smelled him again, she heard his voice, she had to scream or run, she stood still as the man's hands groped her body. Nausea rose when he lifted her skirt.

"¡Che!" yelled the man in front of her.

She stared blearily at the vomit on his coat, his disgusted face. Hands and penis melted away and left a gap in the throng behind her. She raced into it, away from the man she'd soiled, from the scene of the crime, far away far away from the scene of her crime. She ran. She pushed through the revelry toward emptier streets, until a stitch in her side forced her to slow to a walk. Where was she going? The day's flush now tasted like pure bile. She stumbled into an unfamiliar alley, a damp and narrow shaft lined with brick walls. She belonged in the heel of a shoe. She belonged nowhere, she should pour down the gutter, drain through the ground and be gone. Who would miss her? She was ridiculous, almost twenty, almost un-weddable, a waitress and third-rate poet whose own father thought she was a whore and whose countrymen, on freedom's day, could shove into her dress. Vomit soured her mouth. She had to rinse. She was close to the fountain at Parque Rodó. She turned the corner and walked to the park, to the plaza nestled at the center, and strode to the fountain. She did not care (did **not** care) about the strangers staring from their benches as she scooped water onto her dress.

"Eva?"

She turned around. Andrés Descalzo stood in front of her, looking at her wet chest and then away.

"I . . . spilled Champagne."

"I see. **¿Estás bien?**"

"**Claro. Claro.** I'm fine."

"Are you happy about the surrender?"

"What?"

"You know. Of Germany."

"Oh, right, Germany." Eva stared down at her feet. The tiles beneath them burst with dragons, painted fish, a pomegranate yawning wide with seeds. "Great. Of course. Couldn't be better."

"Things are going to change now."

"**Sí.**"

"You sure you're all right."

"**Sí, sí.**"

"You seem different."

"I'm tired."

"Of what?"

"Of—everything—of my family, of stupid poets, of Montevideo, and every single man in this damn country!"

Andrés laughed. The sun caught on his teeth as he laughed. "Me too."

They sat down together at the rim of the fountain. Blue tiles cool against her skirt.

"How's Beatriz?"

"She broke up with me."

"Oh."

"She's with Pepe now."

"I'm sorry."

Andrés shrugged. "It wasn't working anyway." He looked at her frankly and her face went hot. "She's not like you, Eva. Not someone I can really talk to."

Eva broke the gaze. He was so close. The air she was breathing had been inside his body.

"I need to tell you something."

She held her breath.

"I'm leaving."

"What?"

Andrés nodded. Eva crushed a handful of her skirt.

"I've got to get out of Uruguay." He stared out at impassive trees. "My father wants to retire. If I stay, I'll have to take over the **carnicería.** Who ever heard of a poet who smelled like cow blood? The war's over. It's a sign. It's time to do it."

"Where to?"

"Buenos Aires."

In Eva's mind, Buenos Aires was a dancer, with flashy moves and a scandalous scent beneath her clothes, who danced as Montevideo—her smaller, drabber sister—never would.

"Buenos Aires," she repeated.

"Things are going well there, with the social revolution." His hands locked together, then unlaced. "There are other reasons."

"Like what?"

Andrés studied her face. To her right, beyond the trees, Eva heard a baby crying. Andrés shrugged. "Well, for writers, it's the next best thing to Paris, **¿no?** Paris before the bombs."

Eva said nothing. Obviously it was the next best thing to Paris. "How will you get there?"

"I have just enough money for the ferry, and the first week or so after that. I'll find work. I'm willing to do anything at first."

"When are you leaving?"

"Tomorrow morning."

"No." Eva grasped his wrist. It was smooth under her fingers; perhaps she would leave marks. "You can't do that."

His arm relaxed in her clasp, a supple prey.

"I'll miss you."

"I'll miss you too. You're my closest friend." He stared at the ground; at the tiles; at the fantastic pictures painted on those tiles. "I love you, **chiquilina.** But don't worry, I'll write. I'll send you my address."

That night, Eva breaded **milanesas** in silence by her mother's side. She set the table, fork by fork, each motion a minuscule act of release. At dinner, she ate slowly, floating far away from her brothers' uproar over the German surrender, their wives' interjections, her father's constant reaching for the wine. Later, in bed, she lay thinking and feeling, feeling and thinking, picturing Buenos Aires and picturing Montevideo without Andrés, hearing his words, **chiquilina, I love you.** She did not sleep. Before dawn could bleach the darkness from her room, she reached under the mattress and drew out her stack of pesos. She slid it into a tapestry bag, along with clothes, jewelry, notepads, books. She dressed. She wrote a note to her mother. It was 4:55 a.m.

She crept to the kitchen and placed the note by the sink, where Mamá would be the first to see it. She could almost taste her mother's presence in this kitchen, with its cluttered green cheer, its jars of dark dry plants whose uses Eva had never learned. It would be many years before she stood in this kitchen again, and more years still before the night when she would stand here, in the dark, scraping burned tomato sauce into the trash with desperate gestures, unable to feel the pot in her hands, unable to smell the black ruins, unable to think anything but **No, Salomé, no, no.** Now, in this moment, preparing to escape across the river, she thought only of Mamá. Perhaps, if she breathed deeply enough, she could fill her lungs up with her mother's essence and take it with her. She tried it but her lungs were tight and she felt nothing, so she slipped out of the kitchen into the night.

It was dark outside, and the prison walls formed broad shadows on the street. She could barely make out the castle pattern in the bricks along the top, the shape that had enchanted her as a child. She crossed the cobblestones, passed the prison, and approached the steps of the church. They felt cool and smooth against her legs as she sat down, her back to the chapel, facing Carnicería Descalzo. She settled in to wait.

The street was perfectly still. Only her breath seemed to move. Light leaked over the houses on the east end of the street. Any time now. She could see the door of the butcher shop more clearly with each minute, a dark green rectangle in the wall. She would not miss his exit—unless he'd already left. Anxiety tugged at her nerves; at least it would keep her awake. She hoped her mother had not gotten up to pee. Weak light crawled higher into the sky. The houses of Punta Carretas pressed together, side by side, little boxes in a row. Any moment now, her parents would wake up and find her gone. She pictured them bustling toward her in their nightclothes. She shifted to a lower step.

The Descalzo door opened and a tall silhouette stepped out. She rushed to meet it.

"Psst. Andrés."

His spine tensed. "Eva, what are you—"

"I'm coming with you. You have to take me." She hoped she sounded firm and irrefutable.

"I can't."

"Why not? I want to break away, just like you."

He shook his head, but he was listening.

"I've got money of my own. I'll help you. I want Buenos Aires, I want to be a poet, and I want to be with you. Don't you love me? Didn't you say that?"

The pause between them thickened. She tried another approach. "Look, in any case, I'm after the same thing you are."

He bit his lip. "Which is?"

"Piracy."

He let out a short laugh; it was almost a bark. Then he was serious. He met her eyes. "God." He looked away, toward the prison. "Have you packed your things?"

"What I really need."

"You sure about this?"

"Completely."

He stared at her as if she were a missive he'd just come to understand. "The ferry leaves soon. We'd better head right to the dock."

Just before they rounded the corner, Eva took one last look at her childhood street: the church door's arc, the long prison wall, the road of inlaid stones, the oaks rising out of the sidewalk, the sand-colored house where her family slept. It was more than she could curl her tired mind around. She turned and walked away, toward the river.

THE ART OF MAKING ONESELF ANEW

This city. Buenos Aires. It gleamed like a land of lucent giants. It roared and stretched and shot up from the ground in planes of stone. Eva stood at the lip of Avenida Nueve de Julio and stared. The widest street, her new landlady had boasted, in the world. She lifted her sagging chin as she said it. And there was no reason to believe that the world held anything, anywhere, vaster than this road, loud with automobiles and the bustle of a thousand people's shoes. A proud late-autumn sky vaulted above it. The obelisk towered in the middle of the street, piercing the heart of the city, a long white finger pointing toward heaven, tall, sleek, effulgent with authority and promise. The people seemed that way to her too: smooth and sleek like stone. Slender women with exquisite purses, men in sharp Parisian suits. They poured everywhere and did not relent. Eva turned onto Avenida Corrientes. At the corner newsstand, a leathery man mumbled highlights of his wares—Perón defends new labor plan! Cigarettes! Magazines!

Gum!—between puffs of his cigar. Earlier in the day he might have hollered, but it was 3 a.m. and some territory, only some, had to be ceded to the night. She passed him without slowing, passed the couple kissing against a lamppost; the men just burst from a bar, slick-haired, smelling of liquor and cologne; the dance-hall doors throbbing with tangos; the crowded café where a woman sat alone at a small table, scrawling mournfully on delicate pink paper. The city was too much, crushing against her. Eva stopped and leaned against the window of a closed boutique. She stood still until she sensed the hum, low and constant, beneath the surface of the city. She felt it in her bones—it lit her up, unnerved her, showed the way, filled each sequin and bulb and alley, from dense downtown to her crumbling San Telmo tenement, where paint can be bright as it peels, where **tangueros** danced at bars with cracking walls, where fire escapes were balconies on which to sway to stolen music, taking reprieve from small damp rooms. Even in her own bedroom, Eva was in the hum, and she felt it when she sat completely still. Never mind the roaches that teemed across the floor, the stains on the bedsheets, the way she held her breath to avoid the stink in the bathroom down the hall. Never mind the paper-thin walls through which she heard the prostitute next door conducting business, night and day, man after man with his own pace and push and vocal gait; the families of five, six, nine in single rooms; the knife fights in the alley around the corner. She was home there, still, in the glow of the city, and anyway she'd moved her bed to the other wall, the one adjacent to Andrés' room.

Eva tapped the glass of the boutique window with her fingertips three times and kept on walking. She had done it. It hadn't been so bad. Her eleventh interview; she should be glad. He would pay well, that Don Rufino, with his linen tablecloths and shiny silver knives. His questions had been easy to answer, with the small exception of the way he looked at her breasts with his one good eye while his glass eye wandered toward the wall. "Learn the ropes from the other girls," he said. "You'll do fine."

And she would. She certainly would. In the meantime, here she was at Librería Libertad, where Andrés waited in the poetry aisle. When she walked in, her fingers filled with sparks. Surely every book ever written in Latin America (and France and Spain) could be found on these towering shelves. The city forsook sleep to rove them. She walked past the displays of new literature, through the long philosophy aisle, all the way to the back, where Andrés was perched on a stool, bent over a book. She watched his lips purse and slacken, purse and slacken as he read.

"Andrés."

He looked up.

"I got the job."

"Ah. Terrific."

"How was the cabaret tonight?"

"Fine. Work. One of these days I might actually afford one of these."

"What have you found?"

"Well. For example." Andrés gestured for her to approach. "This **boliviano** here: masterful verses on love."

"Really?" They were so close now, she bent over the book, her hair brushed his shoulder. Lightning could travel on less contact than this.

"Here." He traced a line with his finger. The page was coarse and cream-colored, his finger long and slim. "This line. 'To drink you in a thousand tiny gulps.' What do you think?"

"Yes."

"What?"

"Yes—I like it."

"Me too." He shook his head. "And his war poems—wait, where was—" He fumbled with the pages.

"If you don't find it, don't worry."

"You're right. There's so much here to read."

She settled on the floor at his feet, and dove in.

Dear Mamá,

I am writing, as promised. I'm in Buenos Aires—my address is below. I am very well here. I work in a fancy restaurant. I live in a building that is painted a pretty green. It's a beautiful city. I've written some new poems, which are also enclosed. I hope you like them. Please don't show them to anyone else

(except Coco, of course, so she can read them to you). I love you. Please don't be angry. Please don't worry. I will write again soon.

Love, Eva.

Three weeks later, she received a package. Inside, she found a bundle wrapped in coarse cloth, and a letter:

Dear Eva,

Thank you for writing. I am glad to hear that you are well. But you have no right to tell me not to worry. Say that again and I'll be angry. Until you're a mother, you can't understand.

Coco is here, writing this letter down for me. She says I should be grateful that I know my child is alive. She says to tell you that Andrés disappeared the same night you did and you cannot imagine how she suffers. Do you know anything about this, if you do, I beg you to tell me of his whereabouts. This is me, Coco, speaking.

Pajarita again. Make a tea with what I sent you. Twice daily. You can also put it in your mate. I will send more next month.

Please write again.

Mami

Eva unwrapped the cloth. It was full of dry leaves and black roots. They smelled smoky and sour.

Mamá—slim fingers wrapped around a jar, gilded by kitchen sun. She wrapped them back up and stashed them between her mattress and the wall, and from the next room she heard a groan, then low-down grunting, must be an older man.

She didn't need bundles like this, not anymore. She lived in one of the most cosmopolitan cities in the world. She went to poetry readings where nobody, nobody, knew she was a waitress, a laborer's daughter, a girl who once cowered in a stack of leather boots and lost her legs and drank strange teas to get them back. She could re-create herself, just like that radio actress—the one who shared her own name and had become the mistress of the man who was vice president and secretary of war. Eva Duarte. She'd cut her picture out of the newspaper. She kept it in a drawer beneath her bras. She studied the clipping as if it were a blueprint: the blond gloss of hair, the gems at her neck, the working girl smiling in triumph. She wore diamonds but still spoke out for the poor. Behind the wall, the older man climaxed and went quiet. Then began the shuffling with pants, belt, cash. Eva thought of the photo, the way its ink smeared her skin. She would arrange her own dark hair in a tall sweep. She would pluck and pencil her eyebrows. She would study herself in the mirror, and marvel at the art of making oneself anew.

There was quiet magic too, waking up in Andrés' room. Not the first waking that hauled her out of bed—she did that alone. Andrés' room held the next part, the slow road to alertness that uncoils over rounds of **mate.** They sat side by side on Andrés' bed, his hair askew, his eyelids puffed from sleep. Weak light crawled through a dusty window. She poured water through a gentle silence.

"More, Andrés?"

"Of course."

She passed him the gourd. "The **yerba** is so bitter here."

"I like it."

"Are you going to the reading at Libertad tonight?"

"I've got to work."

"Oh."

"You go, Eva. Don't wait for me."

Eva nodded. She would not go. The last time she'd attended a reading alone, a man with a handlebar mustache (a painter, he claimed) had cornered her in conversation. **I want to hear your poems.** She'd glistened for a moment. **I want to paint you nude.** For the first time, that night, she'd missed La Diablita. Even the thought of Pepe's posturing stirred some warmth.

"Maybe next time."

Andrés brought the **bombilla** to his lips. "Next time."

The tip of the metal straw disappeared into his mouth. She wanted to follow it. She wanted his hands to wrap around her wrists and pin her to the wall, roam all over her and tear off layers of clothing, clasp each other as he begged her to come to bed, begged for her legs and everything above them and between them. She would see how much he needed her. And then she would unfold herself, open for him the way the sea opened for Moses, wide, vital, miraculous. They would be this to each other, sea and supplicant, sinner and salvation. They would be together after that, his wanting would be clear. Now it was still murky; he was polite, a gentleman. He respected her. She would need to be more bold. But not yet, she thought, week after week, as winter spread its wetness through the streets. Not until they found more solid ground.

One October afternoon, she asked, "Have you thought of writing home?"

Rain drummed against the window. Drops leaked from the ceiling into a bucket. "No," Andrés said.

"Why not?"

What happened to his face surprised her. It fell; something covering it fell; she glimpsed the raw darkness underneath. He looked down at his hands. Brown drops fell from the ceiling.

Eva thought of the letters in her drawer, full of Coco's small invasions. "Your mother's worried."

Andrés turned away. Eva stared at the back of his head, the dark little waves that clung to their scalp, the cockroach weaving like a drunkard on the wall behind him. Don't go, her mind railed at him.

When he turned toward her it was over, he was back, the subject of Coco gone as if she'd never raised it.

"Can you believe Perón was arrested?"

Eva dropped the subject too. Anything to keep the ease between them. Because she could not be alone in this vast city; because she could, in fact, believe that Perón was behind bars, that the unions he spoke out for were enraged, that Eva Duarte's radio voice demanded that the people rise in protest ("Perón loves you, workers; how else could he love me?"); and because, when the masses marched and spread a vast human blanket through the boulevards, an electric crowd, rife with banners, chanting, **Freedom for the worker, freedom for Perón,** Eva shouted along from her window but didn't dare descend, didn't roam those streets, couldn't be alone in a sea of strangers, needed Andrés to recall that she was safe, not-whore, in a city that held, in its mazes, a corner of home.

Perón was released. Spring descended on the city with its ample, humid arms. Customers swarmed Don Rufino's linen tables, shaking off the winter chill, hungry for Chianti and hot **churrasco.** Eva worked further and further into the night, swigging gin in the back room to wash down Don Rufino. Every other waitress did it too. They laughed at his jokes, smiled when he groped them in the kitchen, country girls clawing their way into city life. She could handle him. She'd mastered the art of coasting by, quickly, agreeably, too hard a worker to slow down for his hands. Still. He'd started to seem impatient and she wasn't sure how much longer she would last. And how much longer did she want to last? She wondered this, standing under a tower of dry goods, emptying a gin flask into her mouth. Four months into her Buenos Aires life and not a poem published, not a word of love professed. What had she come here for? To scrape together rent and fight off another boss while the man she wanted did God knows what at a cabaret where women—not just any women but Buenos Aires women, **porteñas,** gorgeous, flashy—enjoyed his wit and face and body? While she, stupid girl that she was, waited for his move like she was some kind of white lily, like she thought she had a place in some bouquet. She barely even wrote anymore. She pulled the gin bottle from the shelf and refilled her flask. The cooks' broad voices rose down the hall. One last swig, back to work, tonight she would stop waiting.

The moon had set by the time she arrived in San Telmo. The street lamps shone brightly. She wove past the prostitutes with their bare throats, the men lounging on fire escapes, the accordion player who bent his instrument with scarred hands. The stairs creaked as she climbed them. Light crept under Andrés' door. When he opened it, she smelled the detritus of his night, faint perfume and cigarettes and sweat.

"Can I come in?"

"But of course. Have a seat on the chaise longue." He gestured toward his rusty bed. He looked tired. "How was work tonight?"

"Long. You?"

"About the same."

"Demanding customers, these **argentinos** make."

"Indeed."

"And demanding bosses."

He nodded. He picked up two black shoes and began to polish them with a rag. His fingers moved deftly over their curves, and she was sure that they were warm.

"Have you found any nice **porteñas** out there?"

"They think they own the world. The rich ones. Others are nice."

"No. What I mean is have you met anyone?"

"Me? No. Have you?"

"No."

"Not found a nice **porteña,** then, but maybe a nice **porteño**?"

She laughed. Andrés flicked his rag along two heels.

"I know what you meant, **¡bandido!** But no, there's no **argentino** catching my eye." She leaned forward. "Come on. You know it's long been caught."

"That so?"

"Yes. By a certain **uruguayo**."

He kept his eyes on the shoes as he put them down and sat beside her on the bed. He searched her, dug through her, trying to exhume an answer to who knew what question, and she was closer now, on her way into his darkness, close enough to sense the wick of him, pure, charred, exquisite. She wrapped her hand around his. His face strained as though about to weep. She brought his fingers to her face, ran them along it, trailing heat and shoe polish on her skin.

"Eva," he whispered. "You're insanely beautiful."

Their lips brushed, pressed, opened. His mouth was moist and musky, wetness pulsing slowly into hers. His hand plumbed her hair. Her hands were on his buttons, slid under his shirt, his skin was taut and hot and soft and she was greedy for it.

"Eva."

"Andrés."

"Wait."

His fingers left her scalp. He pried her hands from him and held them like bruised birds. "I—" he said, and stopped. "Let's not do anything we'll regret."

"I won't regret this."

He stared at their hands. "What's done can't be undone."

"So what? I've already done it." She realized how this sounded, and shame rushed into her. "With my heart, I mean." Andrés didn't move. She withdrew her hands. "You don't want to?"

"No, that's not what I—"

"Then why—"

"Come here."

He pulled her into his arms, toward his heart, so that she felt it pump against her ear. She stiffened, wondering what he meant and what was happening, but then the pure embrace of him surrounded her, she wanted to resist but her body melted into him, traitorous body, hungry for this place, greedily surrendering to this place; and she saw her father's face; his hands, calloused and open, gathering her in, a little girl who'd just said yes to a shoe store; something rose against her will, broke through her throat, heaved her back and forth with a force she couldn't stop or shape or keep from turning into sobs that grew more violent when she realized, to her horror, that she was leaving trails of snot on Andres' chest.

"There, there," Andrés said. **"Ya, ya."**

She cried until she had no moisture left for tears. She leaned against his sweaty skin and gave herself to sleep.

She awoke in her own bed, to the sound of the couple downstairs yelling, fighting, throwing a lamp or chair or child against a wall. Pain pierced her head. She sat up groggily. Through the wall to her right, more sounds, a customer who groaned like a crow. **Mate,** she needed **mate** for this hangover. Perhaps Andrés would already have hot water; Andrés; last night rushed into her mind.

She rose. An envelope lay at the threshold of her door. She opened it, and found sixty pesos and a note.

Querida **Eva,**
   You're the best friend I've ever had. Here is a little money to help you along the way. I'm

sorry this is so sudden. For any pain I've ever caused you, I am sorry.

Be good to yourself, chiquilina.

Yours,

Andrés

The words knocked and knocked at her mind's obdurate door. She ran from her room into Andrés', stood there, an empty woman in an empty room, nothing there, tear the sheets off the bed, nothing there, yank the drawer open, nothing, yank another drawer, find it empty, slam it shut so hard that the whole dresser bangs back against the wall. The sound startled her. She stared at the dresser, from its chipped top to its stubby legs. A copper-colored vial peered out from underneath. Lipstick. She picked it up. She knew that men had women—her father did, and so, for that matter, did Andrés' father—but even so, to be lied to. To be left. She opened the lipstick. It was bloodred. She dropped it on the floor and watched it clatter and roll away. It was cold inside her, brittle and cold, brittle enough to break.

Everything could roll away: warm **mate** on wet mornings; forgotten lipstick; her only friend; the girl who thought herself a lily; the fragile tether that keeps a person in this world.

Sola. Alone.

She sank down to the floor.

She'd just sink, sink, roll away, far from the sting of cold and this city pushing at her from all sides.

Sinking is easy when you have, when you are, noth-ing. Deeper, deep down to that dark leather cave, where damp walls hold you, where all things can be swallowed. It was still there. She knew exactly what to do. Just curl up curl up curl against the sole, watch the faces form around her, glowing with slow fever: her father first, rearing up, blood vessels strained as if shouting, though no sound came from his mouth; then Pietro, leering over her too, leering laughing fusing with her father's face and floating apart again, floating fusing leering floating on.

Time's cord stretched beyond recognition.

Pietro, Papá, Pietro, they turned into each other, they turned into Andrés, who pressed her into the heel of her shoe-cave with knuckles the size of her head, bearing down, over and over. Beatriz laughed, far away, she was laughing in the warmth of La Dia-blita; Eva heard the poets' voices in a great big rope of sound, arguing, crooning, roaring with laughter, roaring without her, roaring without end, until, slowly, their roars turned into terror as Nazi bombs rained on them, their voices blearing into a riot of laughs and shrieks, dig deep dig deep into the toe of this place because the sounds were a violent river that could tear her up and carry her away in pieces.

A voice cut the darkness.

"Señorita. Did you hear me? This is not your room."

She sat up. Night had fallen long ago. She squinted to adjust her eyes and saw her landlady, a distortion of powdered wrinkles and eagle eyes.

"I'm sorry." Two roaches tickled their way across her arms.

"Really? Well, some of us have work to do. Get out of this room before I throw you out of your own."

Eva pulled herself up from the floor. She stumbled to her room. Her head throbbed. She looked at her clock: it was almost midnight. She was four hours late for work. She changed her blouse as fast as she could, and ran out.

Don Rufino greeted her with a puff of cigar smoke.

"If it isn't Princess Eva."

"Señor, I'm so sorry—"

"Sorry? For leaving me shorthanded on our busiest night?"

"I had an emergency. It won't happen again."

"It certainly won't. You're fired." Don Rufino leaned closer. His glass eye scanned the floor. Its pupil was red, because he was half devil, he liked to say. His thick stomach pushed into hers. "Of course, there's one way for you to make amends."

Eva held her breath to keep his smell at bay. **"¿Sí?"**

"I tell you what. Come back tomorrow afternoon. Meet me in the storeroom." He touched her the way a shopper tests the wares he's haggling over. "We'll see what we can arrange."

Back at home, Eva sat down on her bed. The rooms to both sides of hers were quiet. She didn't want to think, didn't want to let tomorrow into her mind. She lay down and let sleep crush in.

When she woke up, it was morning. She tried to sit up but could only prop her torso on her elbows. She poked her thigh. Nothing. Her legs had frozen. She could not feel them: they were empty, uninhabited, unreachable. There would be no storeroom today, no red glass eye, no white-linen tables or cash in her hand. She would not rise. The heave of the world could stay where it was, hanging just above her bed, waiting for her to lift up and yoke into it. She would not rise. She was paralyzed, she could not move, it had already been decided. It was easy: she would let it be easy, she would just close down, take-me-deep-inside-you-deep-black-boot-closing-down, shutting out the noise of Buenos Aires, the chain of failures, the vacant room next door, the red glass eye; lying numb like this, she could just wait, she would simply wait to die.

Time swung, shape-shifted, crept and raced and crept again.

Sun slanting through the window grew rich and sank to night.

Night hung feverish and electric until dawn.

Dawn brought light that stretched slow limbs and slowly, slowly collapsed down into night.

Eva ebbed from her body. She was not a young woman in a rusty bed, but a soft, diffuse haze in the air. She rose in translucence, cold didn't matter, and neither did fire—only this, the good forgetting, the extraordinary lightness of being-this-nothing-at-last. Higher now. Through the ceiling, into the sky, buoyed by air. Air permeated everywhere, air pale and swirling, air dark and still, shimmering open a fissure of light through which she could dive to meet whatever could be met there—God perhaps; she didn't care—she dove.

"Eva."

A shake, a rustle, there was a tree: perched in the tree, Pajarita, with dark braids and dark eyes. "Why are you here?"

Feel to her more than speaking: **I'm dying, Mami. Almost there.**

"Why?"

Too. Much.

"Mija." Pajarita's face soared forward, out of the branches. "Don't be stupid. I won't let you in."

Can't. Do it. Alone.

"Alone?" Her mother laughed. "You have the strangest ideas."

A rustle, a shake, and the face of Pajarita shimmers away. A tree dissolves. A fissure closes in a line of light. Then air is falling; air is fallen through; nothing and everything fall toward each other and turn into something solid and throbbing again.

She opened her eyes. The quiet light of morning coated the walls. Sensation flooded back to her: sore neck and arms, parched throat, hunger, headache like a block of lead. She shook her head and fingertips to make sure she still could. Below her waist, she still felt nothing—but above her waist she hurt, she hungered, she was alive.

"Socorro." She sounded like a frog. She willed her throat to open, tried again.

"Por favor . . . help . . ."

Finally, a tentative knock on the door.

"¡Che! You all right?"

"Please . . . come in."

The door opened. The prostitute from next door stood in the threshold, pink towel and toothbrush in her hand. A wiry, compact woman, puffed skin beneath blue eyes. "I thought—what the hell happened to you?"

"Can't move."

"I'll call the hospital."

She left to find a telephone. Eva turned to face the wall. While she waited, she saw more than remembered herself stashing something between wall and mattress, that bundle of leaves and roots. She pulled it out and held it at the cusp of missing legs.

The room they took her to was white and bare and the hospital loomed beyond it, a sterile wilderness, unmapped, enormous. On the second day she woke to the sound of footsteps clapping down the hall. A group of marching feet approached her room.

"This one's an unusual case," a doctor said outside the door. "Partial paralysis, numbness, fever, dehydration, malnutrition, various aches, hysteria, delusions. No stable diagnosis yet. Let's enter."

They trooped in, a flock of white birds in their laboratory coats. Teacher at the front, student doctors flapping all around him. Eva felt their eyes on her chaotic hair, the unbathed sweat of her, the mess of half-written poems on the steel table suspended over her lap. She drew herself up against the pillows.

"Buenas tardes," she said.

The students shuffled. Her body railed for water.

"As we examine her, take care to notice any subtle abnormalities," the doctor said. He was a balding man with canine jowls. "Are there any questions?"

They shook their heads.

"Doctor?" Eva said.

"Well then, let's start." The doctor pulled back Eva's sheets. He placed his stethoscope against her chest, then prodded her neck, arms, palms, waist, commenting to the students as he went. He pressed her thigh. "Can you feel this, Señorita?"

"No."

"Lift your right leg, please."

She tried; the limb stayed limp against the mattress.

"Left leg."

Nothing.

"Interesting." He made notes in her chart. "Well. This will be of interest to Dr. Santos, who will examine the patient this afternoon."

A student murmured. Pens stirred the air and scrawled against clipboards.

"Let's go," their teacher said, and the flock dispersed.

"Doctor," Eva called.

The doctor turned. "Yes?"

"I need some water."

"Ah. **Bueno.** A nurse will be here soon." He smiled nervously, and was gone.

Eva lay back against a starched white pillow. She should be grateful for this place, this clean room, detestable though it was, a sanitized box with too many eyes peering in. She was at their mercy. They asked little about her life and she didn't want to tell them. They didn't need to know about the shatter, Andrés' desertion, the snot on his chest, a mother in a fissure and a father in a boot. They might think she was crazy but she knew what she was—alive, still breathing, and that was a marvel. She'd walk again. Perhaps she would. And if she did, she'd stride to her own future, forward forward never back; she didn't know where she was headed but she knew what she was tired of, roaches, betrayals, dwelling in the bottom of a shoe; she would stride away from all that, toward some new shore, courting miracles with gritted teeth. The world spread out around her in a naked landscape that overwhelmed her when she closed her eyes. She turned to poetry. Words shot from her like sparks. She couldn't stop. Line after line they burned onto the pages that a kindly nurse had brought her. Pen touched paper and she saw flashes that barely seemed possible. They were all she had, these poems, and Mamá's dried plants to slip into her **mate** when the nurses weren't looking.

She picked up her pen and wrote: **You, my fire, are all I have. Naked I still come to you.**

Thirsty. Footsteps moved brusquely back and forth in the hall. **Lick my every part, blue tongue. Hungry I will come to you.**

She tore the page from the notebook, let it fall to the floor. New paper. **I have searched the wildest woods / Wells of terror, mapless roads / For Desire's secret name—**

The light from the small window was deepening to gold. New paper again. **Everywhere everywhere there is hope / If there is still poetry.**

Outside her door, a woman laughed. She sounded like a witch. **Poems like needles pricking you out of dreams, / Poems carry women through holes in the sky**

A knock on the door. The nurse came in, pushing a wheelchair. "We're going to see Dr. Santos," she said, as if announcing tea with the pope.

First there was water to drink, then a sponge bath, and then the nurse trundled Eva into the wheelchair and down narrow halls. Each passage teemed with people: nurses, men in lab coats, a patient with bandaged torso and haunted eyes, a patient who wept and sang very softly to the intravenous device in her arm. They pushed through gray double doors. Another flock of students in white coats filled the room. In their midst stood a man in his thirties with a large nose, a potbelly, and an unmistakable air of authority.

"Dr. Santos? The patient has arrived."

Dr. Santos looked up from his clipboard, meeting Eva's eyes with cool detachment.

"Señorita Firielli." His voice was gently calibrated. "How are you doing?"

"Not so great."

He nodded, slowly, knowingly. "It is hard to be ill."

"It is hard to be in this hospital."

White coats rustled, like low alarms. Dr. Santos stared down at her. "Is that so?"

She had said too much. She flushed. "Yes."

"May I ask why?"

"The doctors. They're disrespectful."

His face remained composed, but she thought she saw a twitch at the corner of his mouth. "Well, Señorita, my apologies. Let's hope our reputation can be redeemed." He looked down at his chart. "You came in with complaints of paralysis, fever, aches, and acute headaches—is that correct?"

She nodded.

"I will examine you now."

He began to touch her, the students in a silent arc around them. He felt her collarbone, tapped her arms, gently pressed her back. His fingertips were warm and unobtrusive. They tiptoed down her spine as though it were a familiar staircase in the dark.

Dr. Santos nodded to himself and wrote notes in her chart. The students followed him into a side room, where they closed the door to confer. When they emerged, he held a small vial of pills. "Please leave me alone with the patient."

The students left. The doctor brought a stool to her wheelchair and sat down. "Eva." His nose was like a beak. A great white bird now close and crooning. "I want nothing more than to help you." He showed her the vial of small pink pills. "These pills reflect the best advances of modern medicine. They are potent interventions for conditions exactly like your own. If you take them regularly, you will get well. And you do want to get well, don't you?"

His eyes were so probing, his coat so starched and white. She nodded.

"I want you to begin your treatment." He gestured for her hand and placed three pills in her palm. They weighed almost nothing. "Take them. Your recovery will begin."

Eva rolled the pills in her hand. She was not crazy, she was not lost, she would find her way. She held the doctor's eyes as she put the pills in her mouth. Cure me, she thought, and swallowed them. A sign had come. Her recovery was beginning. She would be well.

At the core of his mind, Dr. Roberto Santos had filed his upcoming marriage in a drawer labeled Right Things to Do. A perfectly reasonable place to keep a marriage. It was sure to bring some happiness, not only to Cristina Caracanes, who had imported miles of Venetian lace he was not allowed to see, but to his mother and father as well. It would elevate the family name, rather than mar it. Marring the family name was a Santos tradition his parents had spent their lives trying to undo. His mother, Estela, had always been obsessed with "breaking the spell"—and said it just that way, as if their lives were locked in dragon-guarded castles, as if she'd been Sleeping Beauty when Reynaldo Santos found her, fanning herself next to unfinished railroad tracks in the Pampas. She was the daughter of the man who owned the New World Railroad Company; he was a construction engineer, employed by New World to oversee the laying of track. He was struck immediately by the way thin hairs escaped her bun to whip the wind. He was an educated, but not landed, man. His family came from some of the bluest blood of old Spain, traceable back to the second cousin of King Ferdinand of Aragon, but all of this had been tainted by Reynaldo's father, known as Llanto, the last living member of the Mazorca. Llanto had joined up in 1848, when dictator Juan Manuel de Rosas expanded his circle of assassins to keep up with the need for terror. The Mazorca had so many missions then that they recruited new members from among their own sons. Llanto was sixteen when he joined. He quickly learned the art of slitting the throats of a dozen kneeling people in one long blow. He learned ways to force the violinist to keep playing while the blood flowed. He perfected the art of skewering heads on spears so they'd gawk for a week in the Plaza de Mayo. By his twentieth birthday, Llanto had killed over two hundred men and women and eighty-seven children. Then the dictator was deposed and Llanto withdrew in shame to a shack in the plains outside Rosario. At the age of sixty he returned to Buenos Aires in search of a respectable wife. He found Talita, a twenty-two-year-old widow, and sired his first legitimate child, Reynaldo, the construction engineer. Reynaldo grew up tainted by family legacy, determined to change it with the arc of his own life, as if a family name could be scrubbed clean of blood and shame, and the actions of its progeny were the scrub brush. So he'd married the purest girl whom he could find, who fanned herself in silence next to tracks no train had wheeled on. In her fresh-limbed love, she didn't feel the weight of the Santos stain until the honeymoon in Rio de Janeiro had passed.

Roberto Santos had always known the stain. He was raised to continue his father's mission. "**Mira, Roberto,**" his father would say, "there are only three events in life that matter. You know what they are?"

"Yes," Roberto would answer, waiting for the next part.

"Birth. Marriage. Death. That's it. And think— what do you have control over? Only marriage. You'd better choose well."

For years, Roberto had not chosen at all. It seemed too looming a decision, a train whose turn would pull the cars of a hundred years behind it. All that steely history hitched to his back. Instead, he'd poured himself into his studies, throughout school and beyond it, rising from great student to great doctor to a premier researcher in medicine. The Santos name became a source of national pride among scientists, intellectuals, and more recently among the Peronista elite. It was not enough. His parents wanted a marriage; he was their only son.

And now he was so close, having chosen Cristina Caracanes, with her perfectly waved hair, her tight society smile, her high teas and charity balls for orphans with shaved heads and tin begging bowls. Her lineage was impeccable, as were the pleats in her dresses. It had been his father's suggestion, and, Roberto thought, a good one. It even appeared— from his visits to her parlor, where they sipped English tea in the afternoon light—that she liked him. Or liked, at least, the columns in the society pages that lauded their engagement. She was the youngest of three sisters and, at twenty-four, restless to marry. She looked like a horse and laughed like a sparrow. She was proper and right and crisp and boring, the opposite of this **uruguaya** who had invaded his world on a wheelchair, casting out poems like minute explosives.

Fate, he thought, had a ghastly sense of humor, the sort unwelcome at any genteel party, to send this strange patient to his ward. To bring the perfect subject for his studies in the form of this woman, sharp and shiny as cut glass, just as tempting and as hazardous to touch.

He was reckless with her in a way he had not been for years, and he should stop, should not administer to her three times a day and give her pills from his own hand. It was more than he had ever done for a patient. It was her skin. No, her mouth. No. The way she moved, making the drabbest hospital gown seem like satin (the nerve, the gall). Perhaps it was her fragility. Or her tongue. He counted the minutes until he could touch her wet warm tongue.

"Your pills, Señorita." He waited for her to look up from her scribbling.

She smiled and opened her mouth.

Dr. Roberto Santos' fingers itched and burned as they placed three little pills on the soft dampness and paused, then withdrew reluctantly while she pulled her tongue back into that mouth and tilted her head to drink water, exposing her bare neck.

"Gracias," she murmured. "You're very kind."

She wrote ferociously, and sometimes he watched her from the doorway. Propped on pillows, notebook on tray, brow pressed in tense inspiration. What a fascinating specimen. He discerned no particular pattern to these bouts. Eva was like a feral cat: sleek, restless, changeable—and intelligent too, more so than Cristina, with her banal gossip. He could never imagine Cristina surrounded by poems of her own writing. But he also couldn't imagine her in a wheelchair, surrounded by the sickest, poorest people in the city.

It was unsettling to consider where Eva had come from. He tended not to think too much about his patients' world outside the hospital, the dross and tangle of their daily lives. Even now, with this woman, he preferred to keep her in the present tense, to think of her like a fish—spit up from the maw of the sea—and this hospital a dry shore where she glimmered and flapped in need of help without him having to taste the salt of drowning. Worlds like theirs were not meant to mix. Not ever. Which is why **argentinos** of his class—and, even more so, of Cristina's class—had been horrified last week when Perón married Eva Duarte. It was one thing to let such a woman become a mistress. But a wife, and, should he win the election, a first lady?

"What," Cristina had moaned, clinking a porcelain teacup into its saucer, "is happening to our country?"

Roberto Santos had nodded as Cristina griped on. I wonder. Has Eva ever been a mistress?

That, he thought—pacing the hospital hallway, poring over charts, resting his right hand on a grieving woman's back—must be the answer. What he felt must be pure carnal response. If he could make her his mistress, if he only had the luck and balls, he could free himself from this fever. He tried thinking of Eva at Flor de Oro, tried choosing girls who looked somewhat like her, pretended it was her splayed beneath him in the upstairs rooms, but it was no use. He still woke up in the morning with the thought of her in that dreary bed, half paralyzed (God help him) yet so bright, urging him to eat her in one long, slow bite. No: he was fooling himself; he wanted more than he could get with any Flor de Oro substitute. He wanted to **know** Eva. Know— what?—not her past, perhaps, but the shape of her sleeping breaths, the precise curl at the edges of her thoughts. Something inexplicable, internal, made her the strange woman that she was. Her words were flecks of it. He wanted to see more. He wanted, desperately, to see each poem that filled those little scraps of paper. He had the nurses collect them while Eva was asleep, then slip them back before she woke. For his research, he said. (Reckless again: nurses had a way of seeing through things, and what if they suspected? what if they talked? Buenos Aires might be big, but not too big for gossip, especially something like this, a society engagement, a pretty young patient, a doctor scrubbing clean a family name.) He diligently copied the papers' contents into her chart. They enthralled him. He couldn't stop. Each page was dated at the top right corner, in thin little numbers, even if they held only one word, like

Absolute—

or
  (shoelace)

or

sing sing sing

Others held longer fragments, such as

Burning burning as I climb
Take me up and take me down

Or, most bizarrely,

Get out of my ribcage
You pirate butcher fool—

And this one melted his knees,

Falling from the world's edge
Then I was sent Santos;

His neck grew hot; he loosened his collar. Luck and balls, that's what I need. It was a quiet morning in the ward. He had the airy doctors' lounge to himself. Still, he stood in the supply closet, reading Eva's fragments by the light of a weak bulb. He felt silly, lurking this way, taking an absurd yet necessary precaution.

Footsteps approached the lounge. Instinctively, Roberto pulled the door closed. Ridiculous, that's what he was, hiding under shelves of surgical masks. There was no acceptable explanation.

"Just a swig of coffee, then we'll head over." It was Dr. Vásquez. Two sets of feet headed to the far counter. Roberto heard the muffled clink of mugs. "So, what do you think of that poet girl?"

"Bizarre, Doctor." Must be a student. Such wonder in the voice. "I've never seen anything like it."

"It certainly corroborates Santos' hypothesis."

"Will she ever be told?"

"No."

Coffee pouring. The clink of spoons. "It's crazy, Doctor—"

"I know. I know. But you can't divulge placebos to a patient. Anyway, she's a harmless sort of crazy."

"What else can be done for such cases?"

"Nothing. But they help us test the edge of modern medicine." Roberto could hear the smirk in the doctor's voice. The closet air was tight and stale and he could—to his surprise—have punched Dr. Vásquez's stubby nose. He heard two mugs clang in the steel sink, and they were gone.

Roberto opened the closet and took a deep breath. There was the lounge, with its modern chairs, its coffee pot, the ficus tree, whose leaves were tipped with brown. Everything in its place. Everything in good order. Clean, reasonable, empty. Soon.

Eva was not surprised when Dr. Santos made his offer. In her three weeks at the hospital, there had been time to think, to comb and scour the back rooms of her mind, and she knew some things—that she'd come apart, that she could have died, that she had no destination planned beyond these walls. That she'd been stupid with Andrés. Like a child. And now her legs could move again, and under doctor's orders she paced the room six times a day, strolling to the window and back. They would release her, she'd be free to go, and then where to? She could ride these legs back to San Telmo, pick up where she left off, scramble up another rat-and-roaches room and another Don Rufino. Or go home, to Montevideo, with empty hands and worn, defeated shoes, confronting Mamá's sorrow, her brothers' nice lives, the look on Papá's face. She would rather drown in the Río de la Plata. Just below her stood an emptiness, a deep, abysmal darkness she could fall into and never stop, never return, and she would rather die than sink there. If she was to stay afloat, she could not be the same girl she had been.

She also knew some things about Dr. Santos. She knew that a reverent hush gathered around him in crowded rooms, that he was engaged (to a Caracanes, the nurse had whispered), that his fingers shook when they placed pills on her tongue. She knew his visits were a clock by which she could measure time; he slept in a house full of fine things; his gaze lingered like a hungry dog's. He was not a bad man, she knew this too: it was easy to tell a bad man from a hungry one. She thought for days about his gaze, his hunger. She thought of her own tongue, a wet soft muscle in her mouth that made him shake. For all his fame and eminence, she made him shake.

On the last day—after watching her tongue jut from her mouth, placing his pink pill in silence, leaving that trace of salt from two thick fingers—he said, "This is your last dose."

She swallowed without water and watched him rifle through her chart.

"Everything has stabilized. You've recovered all your ambulatory capacities. You'll be released tomorrow morning." He gestured toward the window. "You can return to your normal life."

Eva looked at the window, which had not changed. "I see."

"Are you glad?"

It was too small, the window, and too square. "Why wouldn't I be?"

"Well—Eva." He leaned across the bed, and she smelled his soapy aftershave. "I must ask you. Do you have a home to return to?"

She laced her hands together as if in prayer. "In a way."

"I presume—if I may be so bold—that it isn't much?"

"Perhaps not."

"Well. I have a suggestion. A proposal, you might say."

She stared at her hands and waited.

"I'll arrange an apartment for you."

"I had no idea your hospital had such programs!"

"Ah, no, Eva. I'm not speaking for the hospital."
He coughed. "I, personally, would arrange it."

All silences, Eva knew, were not alike. Some were
empty, some were not. This one hung between them,
writhed with unsaid things. Dr. Santos adjusted his
collar. He glanced at the door, which was still closed,
then back at her. She spoke slowly, as if piecing together a puzzle with each word. "Are you asking me
to compromise my virtue?"

He blinked. "Of course not. I simply . . . appreci-
ate you, as a patient. Your welfare is of the utmost
concern to me."

"I see."

"Let me help you, Eva." His voice dropped. "I
would simply, should you not mind it, come to visit,
to see you, make sure all is well." He paused. "I want
you to be well."

His face was naked. She smiled. "I want to be well
too."

Dr. Santos studied her eyes, her mouth, her neck, her
hair, her eyes again. He closed her chart. "All right." His
lab coat rustled as he stood. "Consider it arranged."

The next morning, Eva's final breakfast tray held a
white envelope. Inside, she found a key, two hundred pesos, and an unsigned note:

**657 Avenida Magenta #10. Take a taxi. See you
tomorrow.**

She felt like a newly minted princess as she packed
her bag (two dresses, Mamá's bundle, panties, lip-

stick, one brassiere, a crush of pages), stepped out to call a taxi, and pressed her nose against the car window as glossy streets sped by. The driver stopped in front of a bronze-colored building. She glided past the gold-buttoned guard in the lobby, terrified that he would shout at her, *Where do you think you're going?* He merely smiled. In the elevator, she wondered what she'd do if the key did not fit. She imagined herself wandering the streets with her bags, a lost woman, abandoned, breakable, with no man or coat to keep her from the cold.

The key fit the lock. The door opened without resistance. The apartment reared up to meet her: wallpaper full of mauve roses and golden lattice, a burgundy sofa, the smooth feel of mahogany under her palm, cream-colored sheets drawn over a wide mattress in the bedroom. She loved the smell of this place, like lavender soap on freshly cut wood, and the sienna-tiled kitchenette, with one cabinet, two, well stocked with tumblers, teacups, delicate plates. Everything accounted for, everything in its place. No roaches, no thin walls, no holes in the ceiling. A little balcony beckoned to her from the bedroom, just large enough for one person (or two, if pressed together). She stepped out, taking in the tall sky, the polished cars, the sculpted laughter of high-society women, the stone pillars and carved angels on the mansion across the street. Its door opened, vaultlike, and a widow stepped out, her veiled hat at a slant. She formed a tight black line against the pavement. At the end of the block stood a bakery, its sign hanging from a carved wooden pole. LA PARISIENNE. She'd have croissants for dinner tonight. Croissants and wine and cigarettes, here in this new lair. She thought of Dr. Santos, with his serious brow, his salt-tipped fingers, his swarm of protégés. Dr. Santos with his blue-blooded fiancée and his secret key. He had given her the sleek side of the city. He had given her a home with many cups. He had given her his word that, tomorrow, he would come. She had these things today but for tomorrow she had nothing if he tired of her. Mistresses get dropped into gutters and no one ever hears of them again. Only wives can keep their silky rooms. She had known too many gutters, and, Andrés, wherever you are, out in this broad city I am scanning from this height, this balcony, looking toward the south side where we used to crawl, you can go to hell and burn up over and over. You can shrivel into a charred husk of yourself and I would step and crush you into dust. I won't think of you. I'm not going to collapse, I'm going to climb and climb, just wait, just watch, I'm going to unfold what I really am. A phonograph struck up on a nearby balcony. **Alma mía, ¿con quién soñas?** She swayed her hips, lightly, in time to the tango. **He venido a turbar tu paz.** A car pulled up in front of the widow's doorstep. The chauffeur walked around the car to open the back door. The widow looked up and Eva felt the stranger's glare through the black net of her veil. A beam of accusation. Eva stopped swaying. Then she started again, swinging farther than before, holding the widow's concealed eyes. **La noche**

porteña te quiere besar. The widow stood frozen, a straight-backed thing in fine dark fabric. Then she brushed her hat, as if swatting a fly, and bent to the car's interior. Eva watched as the car sealed its doors, growled awake, and rumbled down the avenue, out of sight.

He arrived for his first visit at three o'clock, right at the start of siesta. He placed a discreet envelope on the end table by the door. He held his hat with both hands; one thumb fidgeted with the rim.

"Please, Dr. Santos, won't you sit?"

They sat together on the wine-colored sofa. He seemed emptied of things to say. She had not seen him this way before, outside the hospital halls, unsure, nervous, a boy on unfamiliar hunting grounds.

"**Este.** You like the apartment?"

"It's wonderful. Thank you again."

"You are finding everything you need?"

"Yes. Only I'm exhausted."

"Ah. Exhausted."

"**Claro.** It's just my second day out. Quite a transition."

"**Sí, claro.** Well." Sweat glazed his hairline. "Should I leave you to rest?"

She was vivid; more than vivid; she was given substance by his gaze. He was ready to eat her, clothes and all. She pretended not to notice. "Thank you, Dr. Santos. If you don't mind."

He was silent.

"I'm sure I'll feel differently soon."

"Of course."

They sat without moving. He reached for his hat.

She walked him to the door. "Please come tomorrow. Won't you?"

He studied her. His face was pleasant, in a bookish, beakish kind of way. "Of course."

The following afternoon, Eva was ready, armed with a silver tray, teacups, saucers, steeping pot, cream and sugar, and confections from La Parisienne. She wore a new dress, bought with the contents of yesterday's envelope: blue, with ivory dots and matching belt.

"Ah! Looking lovely."

"You're too kind."

"Feeling better?"

Eva lifted the tray. "Much."

"Delicious."

"I hope you'll like them. Shall we sit?"

Eva poured her guest a cup of tea. The liquid fell in a dark curve. They listened to its quiet splash.

"Sugar?"

"Please."

"Cream?"

"Yes."

He watched her pour his cream and stir his tea. It was a hot and humid afternoon, ill suited to this refreshment. She handed him his drink. Steam rose from their cups, a gauzy wall between them. "How was your morning?"

"Busy. Extremely busy."

"Tell me what you did. I'm dying to know."

He sipped some tea. He reached for a chocolate éclair, and began to talk about his day. He told her about the patient who had died with his nine daughters saying rosaries in a circle around his bed. His eyelids had closed under Dr. Santos' fingers, like soft butter. Eva stayed rapt, so Dr. Santos told her more: about the daughters' nine skirts cut from the same coarse purple cloth. The quiet way they pressed against the wall as the nurse drew a white sheet over the body. The halls had been packed this morning, several patients admitted at once. By lunchtime, his feet had grown sore from marching halls and standing over bedsides. At lunch, an argument broke out among four students over the best approach to dosages on painkillers. Dr. Santos, sought as judge in this discussion, had not been able to finish his salami sandwich. He kept talking. The light deepened slowly around him. He told her about his students, the earnest ones and the lazy ones, the ones like mechanized robots trying to memorize every rule (not accepting, to his chagrin, that medicine was also an **art**), the ones made obsequious by raw ambition. How he fantasized about being alone, no doctors, no nurses, no patients at all, just him inside a great white empty hospital. Eva leaned forward, chin on hand, listening and nodding. By the time his stories slowed to a trickle, two hours had passed. He stared at his watch.

"I should go back."

"So soon?"

"I've wasted this time."

"Not at all. It's been fascinating."

"You're fascinated?"

"Isn't everyone?"

Dr. Santos scanned the pastry plate, reduced to crumbs and a single strawberry tart. "No."

"Hard to imagine."

He reached for her thigh. She rose as his hand brushed her, a touch neither acknowledged nor denied.

"What a lovely afternoon. I'm sorry you have to go."

He got up, uncertain on his feet, like a man who'd drunk more gin than he'd meant to. They walked to the door and stood at the threshold, Eva holding the tray of crumbs between them.

"Tomorrow, then?"

"Tomorrow."

On his third visit, he entered with more resolve. Tea poured, steamed, grew pale with cream. "Good to see you, Dr. Santos."

He sat closer today. "And you."

"How was your morning?"

"I'm not thinking of my morning."

"No?"

"I'm thinking of you."

"How ki—"

His mouth landed on hers, big hands on her, wet

pushing; the tea-cup splattered as she fumbled it to the table and hot liquid hit her arm; a hand roved her body, a tongue explored her teeth, she was pressed against the sofa and the hand was at her breast, rubbing, starved, then quick and greedy at the hem of her skirt.

"Roberto."

"Yes."

She made a slice of space between them. "I can't."

"What?"

His face was close. His breath had weight against her cheek.

"Please understand. I'm deeply in your debt—and I wish we could"—she paused—"I do. But I'm a virtuous woman. You know that, don't you?"

He blinked. His lips moved but he said nothing.

"You're surprised." She looked down, as if hurt. "I'm waiting for the man I'll marry."

Roberto's hand pulled on its captured swath of skirt.

"Things are different here, in Argentina. I should have known."

"Eva." His voice was throaty. "I meant no disrespect. But you must know how I want you."

He could have burned a hole in her, just looking. Relief washed through her. He would not use force. She would lose the battle and the war if he used force. But no, he was a good man, addicted to propriety. He wanted her to open, to offer herself in gratitude or debt. She was supposed to do this, the next step of the proper dance. "My dear doctor." She traced his jaw with her hand. "I wish we could. But it's impossible."

A tragedy, perfect in its thwarted longing. A moment when the strings would swell in a romantic film. Eva heard no strings, just the moan of a car and a groomed dog barking on the street. Roberto closed his eyes. His trousers bulged below the waist. Eva cupped his face in her hand. They stayed that way, his hand on thigh, her hand on cheek, close enough to breathe the same charged air.

"Thank you."

"For what?"

"For respecting me."

Roberto lay silent.

"I wrote you a poem."

His eyes stayed closed.

"Would you like to hear it?"

He nodded. She gave him words. His face relaxed, a boy beneath a lullaby. She stroked his hair. It was not Andrés' hair, not curving tightly from the scalp and back again. It did not spring from her fingers in tense, energetic curls. This hair was straight and fine, the morning's pomade had lost some of its hold, she could make it all point in the same direction with just a few caresses. She wondered what the years would be like beside this man, if she won the war and took him as her spoils. How he would hold and see and touch her, and who she would become inside his house. The boy in him was so close to the surface, hungry, delicate, alone. She ran out of po-

etry and fell silent, stroking gently, bringing order to
the doctor's fragile scalp.

He came every weekday. She shaped her days around
his arrival. In the mornings she wrote, smoked, and
idled on the balcony, pretending not to scan for the
widow, who was never there, and pretending not to
gaze over buildings to the south of Buenos Aires. At
midday she strolled to La Parisienne and bought
a sandwich for her lunch and confections from
the gleaming case for Roberto's visit. Back home, she
boiled water and prepared the tea tray under the
kitchen window, where light fell copiously and
seemed to wash her hands. She looked forward to his
knock, which was always the same: staccato, taut, devoid of any flourish. She held court in that apartment as though she owned it, as though his entry
were dependent on her good graces. She gave him
slivers of herself: a lap to rest in, supple words, listening ears, a thigh to brush or lips to kiss on his way
out. She felt the coil of power in her body, between
her hips, a long and steady lasso she cast toward him,
the way a man in gaucho country lassoes cattle, or
maybe the way cattle lasso a man. It thrilled her.
Each visit was a victory over laws as old as gravity, as
constant as the laws of fang and prey: the law of man
and whore, and she was breaking it, wasn't she, turning it upside down and letting all the pieces shake
like false snow in a globe.

"Have another tart."

"I couldn't."

She nudged him playfully. "You could." She held the platter up. He raised hands of surrender and took a glazed pear tart. Eva watched him bite, cleanly, with his front teeth. "How's your fiancée?"

He stopped chewing. His fingers squeezed the pastry crust, creating tiny cracks.

"Of course I know."

"She's fine."

"She must be very beautiful."

"My parents like her." His eyes were so pale. "I have a duty."

"To her?"

He shrugged.

"To your parents?"

Roberto clasped her hand with both of his. Sweet pear and butter crust broke in her palm. "Eva. I want you. You're always in my mind."

"Roberto—"

"But I can't."

"Can't what?"

"Marry you."

They stared at each other. Deep afternoon light edged the furni-ture with gold. She would keep it all, the furniture, the north-side sun, the man. She shook her head, slowly, sadly. "**Querido.** What will we do?"

He leaned toward her. His breath smelled of black tea. "Stay here. Be together. You'll have what you need." He kissed her. His mouth was lush and damp and sweet with glaze. She fell back against the sofa. He was on top of her, already stiff.

"Roberto."

"Mm."

"We can't."

His voice came like a child's. "Why not?"

"You know why not." His sex was firm and so were her hands around his jaws. "We're not married."

He clawed at her, her blouse opened, her legs opened to the push of his knees, and she almost relented—why not, why not, he had waited so long—but when she closed her eyes she saw a dirty alley, fast rats, her own throat bared in the cold. She pushed at him. He did not stop. She pushed harder, and his weight jerked back. He crouched beside the sofa, and made a low sound.

"Roberto?"

He did not look at her. The walls framed him with ornate wilderness: hordes of mauve roses in a lattice cage.

"Roberto."

"I have to go."

He lunged for the front door and disappeared.

The next three hours went by in a haze. Eva drank a whole bottle of wine and watched light fade from her beautiful home. It was not her home. She had lost. He'd had enough. There would be no more discreet envelopes, no more dreams in satin sheets, no more afternoons of subtle glances and slow lassoes and sugar in English tea. Night fell; the room grew dark, tinged with low light from the street lamp outside her window. She should have settled for his offer, stayed his woman-on-the-side, kept what she had and let him satisfy himself, instead of placing all her chips back on the table. If he gave her another chance, she'd take it, but it was probably too late. She'd have to pack her bag. There was little to pack and she had nowhere to go. Buenos Aires loomed around her in all its brutal grandeur, hissing with triumph, you don't belong, you never will, you're nothing. She saw her father in the dark corner of the room, glistening, translucent. Whore, he called her. Stupid whore. She bared her teeth at him and he faltered like a reflection in water disturbed by stones. Her head hurt. She couldn't think. She longed to stop the eddies in her mind. She closed her eyes.

She woke up to a staccato knock and stumbled through the dark room. Roberto stood in the hall.

"I left my hat."

"Come in."

He stepped into the darkness.

"I'm sorry. I'll turn on a light."

"No. Don't." His silhouette approached her. He smelled of cigarettes. She'd never seen him smoke. "Eva."

She braced herself.

"It's all right. We'll get married."

She didn't breathe.

"Say yes."

"Yes."

They held each other in silence. Outside the window, a car gunned by, on its way to a lavish party or lonely bar. Roberto sank both hands into Eva's hair.

Eva breathed into his starched collar. His mouth fell against her cheek, jaw, neck.

"When?"

"Soon," he said, low enough that the corners of the room would not have heard him. "Very soon."

The next day, Roberto broke off his other engagement and reserved the church for a Saturday two weeks away. He handed Eva a list of boutiques. "They're expecting you tomorrow."

She didn't ask how it went with Cristina, but she sifted through the possibilities in her mind. Cristina had raged, thrown precious vases against the wall, cursed Roberto and all his future offspring. She had fallen on her knees, wept maiden-tears, implored him, with her hands over her heart, to reconsider. No. She had smiled a tight, noble smile, said stiff little words (a poor girl, ah, how nice for you), and dismissed Roberto with a nod of the head. She braced herself for Cristina Caracanes to appear at her door, face red, hands fisted, but no such thing occurred. Even the society pages kept their talk of the Santos scandal to two brief paragraphs, having devoted most of their space to the Peróns. Juan Perón had just won the presidency. Evita would be his first lady. It was necessary to speculate endlessly on the future, to herald a new era, to dissect rumors of Evita's inauguration gown. Still. Two paragraphs are enough to hide a knife in. **Srta. Caracanes has been replaced by an**

unknown girl, suspected to be of dubious origin.
Eva sat on the floor in the morning light and read
the sentence thirty-seven times. She tore the article
out and broke it into pieces, smaller and smaller,
until it almost looked like dust. She took it to the
balcony and threw it toward the mansion across the
street. The shreds fell in slow, haphazard clusters.
She went inside and took out a blank page.

> **Dear Mami,**
> **I am sorry I haven't written, but today I**
> **have wonderful news: I'm getting married.**
> **His name is Dr. Roberto Santos, and he's a**
> **highly respected man. Also, he is reliable and**
> **kind.**

The pen paused a moment, then resumed.

> **Our engagement is in the society pages, near**
> **photos of Evita! The wedding is in twelve**
> **days. There is much to be done, as you can**
> **imagine. Roberto wants me to have a whole**
> **new wardrobe. He's very generous. I have this**
> **address until the wedding: 657 Avenida Ma-**
> **genta #10. The apartment has gilded wallpa-**
> **per and beautiful teacups (you'd love them,**
> **Coco). These pesos are a gift from us.**
> **I love you, Eva.**

She immersed herself in preparation. She spent
long mornings in svelte boutiques sheathed in glass

that had once seemed impenetrable. She could love the way the lamps glowed in those places, lending radiance to silks and stones and pearls. She wanted to gleam like gemstones, to flow like a gossamer scarf, to rustle with the dignity of finely crafted petticoats. She was taken seriously by the women who measured and folded and pinned at her ankles (she remembered, acutely, that hem's-eye view of the world). She could finger a satin gown and make it hers with a mere nod. She was asked, in cool, courteous tones, whether she preferred her diamond set in gold or platinum. Gold, she affirmed. Gold in all its boldness. She needed it against her skin for her first dinner with Roberto's parents.

The Santos family home was a place of chandeliers and echoing halls and plush drapes that hid the windows. They ate in a taut silence, broken only by the clink of terse knives on white china. Señora Santos, with her rod of a back and high lace collar, eyed Eva with frank skepticism. Señor Santos slumped over his soup, shaking his head between bites as if to a tragic opera he alone could hear. Eva punctuated the meal with pleasantries.

"What a beautiful home."

Clink, clink.

"That portrait is lovely."

Clink.

"The soup was exquisite, thank you."

Roberto, to her right, bent his head over his plate like a man in prayer or penance. No one spoke. The maid cleared bowls and refilled wineglasses without a word. Halfway through the main course (herbed potatoes, **boeuf au vin**), Eva resigned herself to quiet eating. The sauce was delicious, piquant, rich; she washed it down with long gulps of wine. She would have mopped it with her bread if it hadn't seemed undainty. Her wineglass seemed to fill of its own accord (the maid was skilled, unobtrusive—she looked a bit like Mamá had in old photos, the hair, the glow-black eyes). Eva felt Señora Santos' eyes on the red pour as it landed in her glass. She sat up straighter. The silence was palpable, it almost had flesh, it stretched along the table like a muscle, flexing, issuing its challenge. The chocolate mousse arrived in crystal goblets. She lifted a silver spoon. She would make it through dessert. She had faced many challenges in her life; surely she could survive a chocolate mousse. The thought made her laugh—a short, sharp cackle. Ha-ha-ha! The three of them—his father, his mother, Roberto himself—stared at Eva. Roberto flushed; his mother pursed her lips; his father's mouth hung open. She waited for shame to heave its mantle over her, but she felt only the weight of the gold necklace at her throat. She held her head high (necklace sparkling, she imagined, in the candlelight), and smiled.

"I love chocolate. Don't you?"

She took a bite of mousse (so sweet, so heavy). Señora Santos sent back her own dessert.

"Don't worry," she said to Roberto on the car ride home. "They'll come to accept me." She leaned against his arm. They would because they had to. Roberto took her hand and curled their fingers into a knot.

Their marriage plans were simple: a wedding at the chapel, attended by Roberto's immediate family and a single friend, Dr. Caribe, and his wife. Antonio Caribe had been Roberto's mentor in medical school, and now, as colleagues, they still discussed their work in unrelenting detail. He was the kind of man you could imagine cupping a wounded sparrow with both hands. Priest and veil, vows and rings and the kissing of the bride. No reception. They would head directly to a honeymoon cottage south of Mar del Plata.

The day before her wedding, Eva received a package that held a gift wrapped in tissue, and a letter.

Dear Eva,

Congratulations. I want to meet him. I want your marriage to be very happy.

Please send photographs. Everybody wants to see. Artigas asks about you often. He is in good health, drumming every day, often with César, Xhana's fiancé, who is a wonderful drummer—you remember him of course? They are getting married next month. Xhana is teaching history. And she's one of the best dancers in all of Carnaval. You really should see.

More news: Mirna has had another boy—

you're an aunt, again. And Coco's grand-daughters are growing up to be fine girls. Ay, you should see them, Eva, almost muchachitas **and so pretty—can you believe I am such a lucky grandmother? It's just too bad their good-for-nothing uncle Andrés is still not writing home. If you see my son (you** must **know something!) tell him he's broken our hearts and he should come back where he belongs.**

Back to your Mami.

I never had a wedding dress, hija, **so I can't send you mine to wear. Take this instead. Something old. Something blue. I made it from the curtain that was my wedding bed. The first time I ever saw your father, he was walking out from behind this curtain on a ridiculous little stage. Well. You are missed.** Cuidate.

Love,
Mami

Eva unwrapped the tissue and found a garter of blue velveteen and ivory lace. It was well stitched, but garish compared to the silks and linens of her new life. She brought the garter to her nose: it smelled like camphor and cinnamon; it smelled like Uruguay. The lace tickled her cheek, softly, an echo of lost touch. She pictured Roberto's mother meeting Mamá, a dark-skinned woman called Pajarita, sewer of garters, brewer of bark, bride who spent her wedding night out in the open air, on the banks of the Río Negro, surrounded by horses and trunks of costumes. She could see Señora Santos with perfect clarity, the look on her face, the arch of her wringable neck. Eva would wear the garter. No one would know. She would smuggle it under the vast cloud of her gown. It would rub between her thighs as she walked down the aisle, the friction of memory and lost worlds. Life was full of lost worlds. You could travel miles of twisting roads and think you're far away from all you know and suddenly stumble on the scrap of one. Thirty years ago, a girl lay down in a place that smelled of grass and horses and the dark-wet river. They were all gone now—the years, the girl, the horses. Eva stroked the garter with her fingers. Maybe it would susurrate—though nobody would hear it—under the noise of Venetian lace, the sigh of petticoats, the silence of white roses held in front of her like weapons.

Cinco

ACROSS BLACK WATER,
A SECRET SEA

Fine things filled her life: a house in La Recoleta with an entrance flanked by pillars and a perfect hedge, four-course meals from a cook trained in Toulouse, five boxes of jewelry, warm legs beside her own at night, damask drapes, silver platters, Louis XIV chairs, enough ingredients—surely more than enough—for brewing happiness.

Eva retreated into the house as though it were a huge cocoon. There would be time for the world, but first she sank into the luxury of avoiding it. While her husband spent long days at the hospital, she spent languorous afternoons in the study, suffused in dusty sunlight and the orgiastic scent of old books. She fell into epics, novels, history, reading greedily until the light had drained entirely from the sky. When Roberto arrived, they ate at the long dining table. He talked about his day. She nodded at his stories, smiled at his triumphs, ruffled her forehead sympathetically at his complaints. Later, upstairs, he unwrapped her clothing like a present. Pinned beneath him she would feel as if no wind could sweep her away, no storm disturb the rocking anchor of his weight.

Eventually, she ventured out, a refined lady now in silk and gold. She spent hours composing poems alone in chic cafés. She bought books by the armful. She attended parties where guests sipped Veuve Clicquot and engaged in calculated banter. She quickly learned to ply her wit with politicians, intellectuals, aristocratic women with sleek hair. Some were stiffer with her than others but she held her head up high and kept on beaming. After all, what could they do? It was a new era, when even the first lady could come from poverty, be called a whore behind affluent hands, yet step into the limelight with ferocity. No apologies from Evita Perón. At home, Eva listened to her speeches on the radio. **Perón is everything, the soul, the nerve, the hope of** argentinos. **I am only a simple woman who lives to serve Perón.** The lavish chairs and carpets could catch fire from the sheer heat of that voice. Eva could almost see the spreading flames. **One cannot accomplish anything without fanaticism! It is well worth burning up our lives!** Photos filled the papers: Evita at her office, where droves of Argentina's poor came knocking, every day, asking for help, receiving money, dentures, meals, smiles, shoes, sewing machines, toys, imported rugs, imported curtains, promises of more help to come; Evita in opulent Parisian gowns, dripping with diamonds, laughing toward the camera;

Evita at the microphone, face wrenched with speech, hand high as if about to wave or slap. Eva cut out pictures and kept them tucked in folded under-clothes, hidden from Roberto. Roberto did not like the Peróns.

"They're fascists," he said, straightening his tie in the morning.

Eva nodded blankly.

"They control more each day."

She smoothed his collar.

"We have to be careful. Stay on their good side."

"Certainly, **mi amor.**"

Sometimes, deep in the night, she dreamed she was Evita and a throng of children pressed into her bedroom. They were barefoot. The women followed close behind. She shook Roberto, in bed beside her, but he wouldn't wake. The women and the children put their arms out, open-palmed, demanding, and then Mami was among them with scissors in her hand, she didn't look at Eva, she began to slice the satin bedclothes, and Eva tried to gather sheets around her, tried to scream, but the children had grown bigger, were suddenly young men, tearing at bedclothes with hungry hands. On good nights she woke up before they reached her.

After two years of marriage, Eva gave birth to a son. Roberto. Robertito. His first cries pierced the air and seemed to shatter it. She longed to quiet him with her body, fill him with her milk, but Roberto had made other arrangements. Her son was whisked into the next room, where a wet nurse waited.

"Don't worry," the delivering doctor said. "Just rest."

For months Eva ached for her baby. She lingered fiercely at his cradle while he slept. The wet nurse was called María: a ripe young woman, maddeningly sweet, offering a softness those tiny hands now recognized, pouring what Eva had let dry. Her breasts were wastelands. She was a lady now, had a role to play, a part with no room for babies sucking at her body. Her son grew larger. She barely knew him. She saved his shoes. She couldn't help it, the urge was primal, subterranean, and anyway she did it secretly, there was no one to mind. She played her part impeccably. Señora Santos, Doctor's Wife, Charming Lady, Really a Delightful Poetess. Did You See Her Recent Verse in **La Nueva Palabra**? Quite enchanting. Elite salons opened their doors to her. Even her poems had to fit into her role: she was not, after all, some anonymous girl, some immigrant waitress no one cared about. She mattered; she was seen; her words could lift or stain her husband's career. She corralled her poems into good-wife themes—domestic joys, devoted love, the sweetest slices of motherhood. She also combed each line for anything that could be construed as anti-Peronist. There were writers and editors who'd gone into exile. **If I have to apply five turns to the screw each day for the happiness of Argentina,** Evita shouted, **I will do it.** Eva's poems grew as sculpted as the hedges around her house.

She didn't mind. It was her duty. When she was

tempted to write with too much heat, she took cold baths to drain the poems out of her.

I chose this life, she thought, naked, gritting her teeth against the cold. So I will live it.

Hard white tiles gleamed at her from all sides.

Eva's second child arrived on a day that seemed to rip her into two. The girl shot out red and screaming; Eva was screaming; their voices formed a jagged fugue. The nurse swaddled the baby in a blanket and took her away. Eva calmed her breath. She waited until the room was almost empty. Only she and a single medical student remained.

"Psst."

He approached her.

"Bring me my baby."

He scanned the empty room.

"Please."

"It's against the rules."

"I know."

"It might take a while."

"Fine."

The young man studied her. His face was stocky, earnest, in need of a shave. He left the room. Eva waited. The ceiling tiles weren't moving anymore. She watched them do nothing in their perfect rows. The student returned, darting in quickly, a jewel thief with loot wrapped in a blanket. He laid the baby on Eva's chest, a tiny face, so clean now, strange and wizened, alien, delicate, eyes shut, skin pink, fingers squirming in the unfamiliar texture of the air.

The student was also staring at the baby. "Have you chosen her name?"

"Yes," Eva said, having prepared for a girl one month prior, in the library with a play by Oscar Wilde. **I am athirst for thy beauty,** the heroine had said. **Neither the floods nor the great waters can quench my passion,** and that line had rushed into her, had seemed to redeem the horror that came next. "Salomé."

"Salomé?" He frowned. "Isn't she the one who beheaded John the Baptist?"

"Yes."

"You know the story?"

"Yes."

He cocked his head and stared at her with new intensity. Footsteps rang out in the hall, then faded. He looked at the baby again. He was quite handsome. Eva wondered whether this was his first birth.

"Salomé," he said slowly, as if tasting the word. "What will she do?"

Eva adjusted her daughter's frail weight on her breasts. "Do?"

"With her life. Isn't that strange, the pure potential of one life?"

Eva said nothing. The student closed his eyes and laid a hand on the tiny head. Salomé leaned into his palm with total trust. "You can do anything, Salomé.

Change the world, the course of history. It's all possible."

Eva was exhausted and rapt and vaguely embarrassed, as if she'd stumbled into someone else's private ceremony. She wanted to swallow Salomé back into her body. She wanted to shout at this **joven** to stop interfering, to leave them alone, to stay near them always. The intimacy he'd struck up was unbearable. Salomé's face crunched, she whimpered, and Eva peeled off her hospital gown and pulled the baby to her nipple. The small mouth groped for her.

"It may take a while," he said, "for milk to come."

The baby-mouth found the nipple. Nothing came out. Salomé began to cry.

"If I may," the student said, and reached for Eva's breast. Adjustment, pinching, baby-soothing, **there, there,** and then the mouth arrived again and it began, the smallest trickle, stinging from Eva's body. The young man looked away at the wall.

"What's your name?"

"Ernesto."

"Your last name?"

"Guevara."

"Señor Gue—"

"Just call me Ernesto."

"Ernesto. Thank you."

He nodded. "I should take her. Once she's done."

"Of course."

They waited until Salomé's mouth softened its grip. Eva pried her away and handed her to Ernesto.

His hand was on her baby's head again, holding it up, a necessary touch, but Eva felt the urge to call out, **Stop, you thief.**

"Shall I turn off the light?"

"Please." She pulled her gown back up and watched them leave.

She leaned back into her pillow. Outside, the sun was rising with its entourage of pinks and mauves. In the glare of modern fluorescent lights, she had not noticed. She felt empty. She closed her eyes and turned to the left, then to the right, chasing sleep. When she found it, when she dreamed, he was there too, the student, standing on a rooftop with her daughter in his arms, and he said, **It's all possible,** he said, **anything,** he roared like a lion, he was a lion now, his paws were going to rip her daughter to shreds, she shouted and ran toward them but he threw the baby up toward the sun, a baby growing wings and rising, baby flying, she would get lost or she would burn, a baby Icarus, her baby, **No,** Eva shouted, **no** and **no,** she ran she flapped her elbows like a stupid hen but couldn't fly, couldn't fly; **Don't worry,** the lion said, **it's possible.**

Eight weeks after Salomé was born, one week before the exile, Eva entered the Presidential Palace with a tingle in her breasts. The night felt thick, steeped with not-yet-fallen rain. La Casa Rosada stood beneath it, with its indestructible walls, its scores of lamp-lit windows, its tall entrance guarded by bare-breasted nymphs whose carved faces flickered with hunger or amusement. Eva held her breath as she passed beneath them. Around her, fellow guests pressed forward in a clash of fine perfumes. The tingle sharpened; she tightened her hold on her husband's arm.

In the coat room, Eva removed her fox fur, unveiling her gown, red as the rubies hanging from her ears. A bold color to choose, but this was a night for boldness, her first social engagement since the birth of Salomé. Time to fit back into her slim, boned gown—but it was tight, terribly tight against her breasts, pushing up on swollen milk that should not be there. A proper lady would have run dry weeks ago. She turned to Roberto, who stood absentmindedly by her side, and smiled. "Shall we?"

Roberto nodded. He looked tired. She studied the sag of skin beneath his eyes, the droop and crease of ambitious, unending work. Tonight, back at home, she should approach him with her arsenal of comforts. Rub his feet; recite poems (all poetry, for him, was soporific); change into that black negligée. The negligée, though, had failed the last few times. She wondered what she had done to slacken his interest. Borne a child. Grown too round. She'd expected that while pregnant, but now he still stayed away, working long nights and taking his dinners away from home, for work, he'd say, and she would say for work, yes, naturally. Eva reached up and straightened her husband's bow tie. He smiled, a kind of crumpling at the edges of his eyes, and she missed the hulking softness of his body. They linked arms and walked to the ballroom.

The great hall opened its vast and lavish arms. Everything glittered: gem-encrusted women, medal-encrusted military men, hors d'oeuvre trays, the polished cello weeping lustily. The ceiling dripped with chandeliers and with the echoes of two hundred murmurs. Nearby, a colleague of Roberto's told an anecdote that held five listeners in sway. Roberto headed toward them, and Eva followed. Halfway there, her nipples prickled fiercely; she placed a hand on her waist to steady herself.

"Roberto. I have to powder my nose. I'll come back soon."

In the bathroom, crystal vases held their lilies twice: once on the marble and once in the mirror in which a woman struggled to pull her breasts out from the top of a strapless gown. Two streams shot from her body and spattered onto the mirror. A lady gazed back at her between streaks of white milk. Still a lady. Of course she was. Even if she had two breasts that stole suckles when the wet nurse wasn't there. She had failed to surrender the animal pull of Salomé's mouth, the feel of liquid pulsing from large body into small. Eva removed the cloth she had stuffed into the front of her dress to catch the errant leakings of her crime. She bound it around her chest like a bandage and pulled it tight. Tighter. She thought of her daughter in her cradle—or perhaps, right now, at María's breast. The milky mess on the mirror dribbled down to the marble counter. She wiped it away. The toilet flushed the evidence into dark and unseen pipes. The air smelled of milk and sweat and lilies. She readjusted the front of her gown, checked her hair, and headed back to the party.

The crowd had grown thicker. Starched tuxedos mingled with generals' uniforms and gowns of every color: coral, lilac, emerald, cream. Murmurs; laughter; some kind of sonata on the strings. Roberto was speaking with another prominent scientist, a balding parrot of a man. She joined them and stood at her husband's edge, smiling pleasantly, scanning for people to talk to. Champagne flutes approached on a silver tray. She curled her fingers around one, drank, and saw Lucio Bermiazani, the publisher, across the room. She had never met him but she knew his face—fleshy, with a sharp little smile—from **Democracia**'s literary section; last year, for the debut of Soledad Del Valle, he had been the star of those pages. His limelight had been magnified by the lack of photos of the poet herself, a woman steeped in mystery and journalistic speculation, a blind **paisana** writing verses in the wheat fields of the pampas, reclusive, plebeian, infamous, enchanting the literary elite without ever setting foot in the big city. And the poems. Quiet passion almost shaking off the page. Eva savored them, late at night, long after they had put her husband to sleep.

Her husband was nodding now, while his inter-
locutor praised Perón's Soviet policy. She murmured,
"If you'll excuse me," and launched across the room.

The way a soiree could open and she'd sway
through—after all this time it still seemed like pure
magic. She became acutely aware of her own body, its
motion, the dark gleam of her hair, the perfume
glowing softly from her body. Elegance was a sphere
of power around her. Men stepped back to make way
for her passing, women stood up straighter, eyes lingered, chins nodded or shook from side to side. She
was so much more than a woman scrambling to wipe
her milk from marble: she was noticed, she had
weight, she had incisive things to say.

Mr. Bermiazani was talking with General Penaloza. "Ah!" the general said. "Señora Santos! How
are you tonight?"

"Resplendently well, General."

"And resplendent you look," the huge man
replied, baring crooked teeth. "Lucio. Have you met
Señora Santos?"

"Why, no." Lucio's body stretched at his tuxedo.

"Señora, this is Lucio Bermiazani. And this is
Señora Eva Santos, wife of Dr. Roberto Santos. I am
sure you're aware of his work."

"Of course." Lucio raised his eyebrows. "Your husband has done much for Argentina."

"Thank you." Eva raised her Champagne flute.
"As have you. Your collections are marvelous."

Lucio preened; she could almost see the peacock

plumes fanning out behind him. "Ah. You read poetry?"

"I adore poetry."

"Really? Why?"

General Penaloza wandered off, having spied Juan
Perón across the room.

Eva swirled her Champagne in its glass; its edges
frothed. "Why?" She felt the party, the night, the sea
of jewels and gowns reduce to this instant, this
spot, this beam of attention from a fleshy little man.
" 'Why breathe? Why love? / Why seek the morning?
/ Poems are just wings that grow / In every human's
mind.' "

The publisher rustled his lush, invisible feathers.
"Soledad Del Valle."

"A true inspiration."

"Wait a moment. Eva Santos. I've seen your pieces
in **La Nueva Palabra.**"

"They've published a few."

"If I remember correctly, they are quite nice."

"You're too kind."

"So you like women poets."

"Among others."

"There seem to be more and more of them these
days."

"Indeed."

"Have you published a collection?"

"No." She smiled. "But I do have a home over-
flowing with poems! It makes for interesting house-
keeping."

"Well, I hope that rather than let the broom get to them, you'll send some to me." He reached into his tuxedo jacket and pulled out a business card. "I would like to peruse your manuscript."

"**Ay,** Señor—thank you."

"Señora, it is my pleasure." He bowed. "And now, my dear, excuse me."

Lucio waddled away, and she stood for a moment in the thrill of her victory. She longed to tell Roberto. She turned to make her way back toward him.

She stopped after her third step. Evita stood in full view, glistening like a diamond in a lush satin gown. She was laughing at something someone had just said, mouth a wide red arc, hair a golden crown. She looked gaunt, yes—the rumors of illness must be true; but ill or not, she shone, here she was shining, jewel of the nation, saint, wife, mouthpiece of the people, glue binding the nation to Perón. The Bridge of Love, she was called, and surely the name was apt, surely crossings were made bearable by her presence. Now Evita stood alone against the backs of black tuxedos, surprisingly small, but while she stood, while her mouth arced, Eva could believe what she wanted to believe: that the promises were true; Perón an almost-God; the poor could have glamour, houses, fine brocade; the government loved its people without end; immigrant waitresses could keep their precious stones and publish books of poems. Don't die, Eva thought to her. Don't ever die. Evita turned her head and their eyes met and for a moment Eva shouted her whole soul into her gaze, but Evita just nodded vacuously, smiling the same smile that graced portraits across the nation, and then her eyes scanned on and it was over.

Eva didn't have the chance to tell Roberto her news until hours later, in their car. Outside, rain had finally released itself from the sky. It fell heavily. Eva reached for her husband's hand. "Lucio Bermiazani wants to see my work. I think he's going to publish me."

Roberto kissed her forehead. "All right."

It wasn't the response she'd hoped for. Her husband was a good man. He had done so much for her. He had undone his life and rebuilt it in a new shape just to be with her. They both knew about this debt, too large to be repaid. She squeezed his hand and looked out the window at Buenos Aires cloaked in rain. Ornate doors swung open for well-dressed patrons seeking warmth. Young lovers huddled close under one umbrella, in an alley, laughing. Proud iron streetlamps cast hazy globes of light. She imagined her book in sumptuous detail: its spine, its creamy pages, the gala celebration that would mark its release. There would be Champagne, brilliant flowers, a flood of people. Perhaps even Soledad Del Valle would come. EVA SANTOS, the papers would read, THE POET WHO LURED DEL VALLE OUT OF HIDING. Buenos Aires would toast and shine and wrap its arms around her. Outside their car, the streets were changing, unfolding the large houses of La

Recoleta. The downpour pummeled the metal roof above their heads.

It rained for two days. Wetness surged, eased, pattered, surged again. It was surging hard, the third night, at one-fifteen in the morning, when Dr. Caribe arrived at their door. They were both surprised when María, the wet nurse, knocked at their bedroom door to say the bell had rung. They had just retired. Eva was kneeling on the floor, loosening the laces of her husband's second shoe. She stared up at him in the dim light.

"Expecting anyone?"

"Of course not."

Shoes relaced, collars straightened, a married couple descended broad red stairs (what a fight that had been, for red carpet; Roberto had wanted a dull, unassailable beige, but Eva had held firm and won her red—Diablita Red, she called it to herself, like the chairs where she had first become a poet). Eva stood on the last stair and watched her husband cross the foyer.

"Who is it?"

"Antonio."

Roberto opened the door. Dr. Caribe stood beneath a black umbrella. He gripped the handle as though it were the only thing anchoring him to the ground.

"Please, come in."

Dr. Caribe entered, snapping his umbrella closed. "I'm sorry for the intrusion."

"Nonsense. You're always welcome. But is everything all right?"

"No."

"Your wife . . . ?"

"She's fine. The children are fine. I couldn't sleep. I didn't know where else to go."

Roberto took his friend's coat and hat and handed them to Eva, who hung them on the coat stand. "Would you like a drink?"

In the drawing room, Eva poured Cognac into three curved glasses and sat on the sofa beside her husband. Dr. Caribe faced them on the loveseat, hair damp, eyes glassy. She'd last seen him four months ago, at his sixtieth birthday. The toasts had been emotive and profuse and made Dr. Caribe blush over and over. Tonight his face was pale; he looked old, worn, haunted. A subtle ache crept into her breasts.

"We missed you at La Casa Rosada the other night," Roberto said.

Dr. Caribe did not answer.

Silence returned, enormous, awkward. On the coffee table between them, a vase of white roses stood, impassive. Eva looked at the wallpaper, with its greens and violets, its French peasants dancing under golden trees. Rain roared against the window.

"Have you been reading the **Democracia**?" Dr. Caribe said.

"Sometimes."

Dr. Caribe looked at Eva.

"Yes."

"So you've seen this." He pulled a clipping from his pocket. The picture showed a young man, slim-faced and grave, staring out from beneath a headline: EVIL PLOT AGAINST PERÓN FOILED! POLICE ARREST TRAITOR IN SHOOTOUT. There was a photo of the traitor, a student who'd been conspiring with the U.S. Embassy to bring down Perón. Eva had read the story a few days ago, pulled in by the traitor's name. Ernesto Bravo. She'd reread it to make sure it wasn't the one she'd met, the medical student, but no, it was someone else.

Roberto nodded. "I heard about it. The police arrested a young man for treason."

"That's what it says. But it's a lie." Dr. Caribe stared into his drink. His mouth pursed as if shutting in a toxic word. He swirled his Cognac, once, twice.

"Dr. Caribe," Eva said gently, "what happened?"

He drained his glass. "The police called me five weeks ago. I treat their prisoners. Thieves, murderers, prostitutes. So I thought I had some idea of what to expect. Well. When I got to the station, I was shown to the Federal Police Unit. Special Section. I'd never been there before."

He paused. "They led me into a dark room. A thin **joven** lay on the cement floor. Unconscious. Blood all over him, a deep gash in his head. His face was so bruised that, I swear to you, his own mother would not have known him. I examined him, and two of his fingers and one of his ribs were broken. He had lost a lot of blood.

"I was told to clean him up and get him well—without transporting him to a hospital. That's impossible, I said. He's in critical condition; he needs a hospital. The officer looked at me with a kind of snarl. Just fix him up, he said. A second officer took me aside. Look, he said, it's like this. The beating was unauthorized. Necessary, of course, but not something we can broadcast. He has to stay here until he's, you know, presentable. That's your job. I protested, a little. What if I don't do it? The officer got impatient. He said, Then maybe no one will." Dr. Caribe's bottom lip shook.

Roberto looked away, delicately. Eva's breasts tingled, full of milk; she saw herself pulling the doctor across the coffee table, past the roses, into her chest, as she might a child who'd scraped his knee on the pavement. "Doctor, it's all right."

"No, it's not at all." He stared down at his hands. "I'm ashamed to tell you that I stayed. But the boy needed five doctors. If I left, he'd have none. So I started to clean his body. It took all night. Halfway, I heard the officers outside the door. The first one wanted to kill the **joven** and call it a traffic accident. The second one was undecided. They spoke as if he were an old rag to dispose of. I thought I might be sick, right on the concrete floor.

"At that point, of course, I should have left. I should have refused to come back, ever. But instead I thought, What will they do to me? What will they do to the boy? God, I was such a coward." Dr. Caribe stared over Eva's shoulder as though the concrete-and-iron room were just behind her. "The boy became my life. All my waking hours were with him. When I slept, he filled my dreams. In my dreams he'd turn, sometimes, into my son—they're roughly the same age. Well. In four days he regained consciousness. The officers bandaged his eyes so he couldn't see me. They gave me a pseudonym to use in his presence. They wanted to move him from the prison, but he was still too fragile. It took five more days to stabilize him for transport.

"We took him to a suburban house. A secret place used by the police to . . . do whatever things they do. They set it up for his convalescence. As his face healed, he reminded me more and more of my son. He never spoke to me, except to ask for food or water or help shifting positions on the bed he was hand-cuffed to. He had been warned not to talk, of course, by the police. We both had. But still, I was tortured by the thought that he despised me. That he saw me as one of them. I wanted to explain myself, I wanted to run. Instead I did as I was told.

"Three weeks passed. Finally, an order was issued for his release. It was over. I thought I'd saved him, and saved myself. I was going to put it all behind me. I went home and slept for twenty-two hours.

"The next morning, I saw the **Democracia** and almost dropped my **mate** on the floor. That's how I learned the boy's name." He held up the clipping. "Ernesto Bravo."

Eva's breasts hurt, they were too full, they raged against their compress. "I don't understand."

Dr. Caribe shook the cut page. "Bravo couldn't have attacked the police. He was under my care. He was framed."

Eva leaned against the sofa, trying not to swallow anything—not spit, not air, not what filled the space between them. The French peasants were ridiculous on their wallpaper, prancing as if there were nothing wrong with their golden tree. Ridiculous, yet she longed to be like them, to keep on dancing, hold on to what was bright and polished and well worth burning up one's life for. But something else, a lesion, had opened in her home. A doctor crumbles beside white roses; a young man is brutalized beyond recognition; peasants dance around a painted tree whose real trunk, trapped inside, is dying.

"I'm sorry," she said.

His voice was small, the knee-scraped boy. "I don't know what to do."

"Antonio." Roberto leaned forward. "Put it behind you."

"I can't. I've betrayed everything—my profession, my conscience. Even my wife, who wonders why I never sleep. If I don't do something to right this wrong, this could destroy me."

Eva took in his haggard face and believed him.

Roberto looked wary. "What would you do?"

"I've got to tell people. Besides you. I need advice on how to do it."

"No." Roberto's body almost raised from the sofa cushions. "You'd endanger your job, your family—everything."

"I know."

Eva burned for her guest, for his sorrow, for the young Ernesto Bravo, for the mouth of her baby, sleeping upstairs in a pink crib. "What if you wrote a letter and let it land in the right places?"

"Eva—" Roberto said, a hint of iron in his voice.

"Anonymously," she added. Roberto stared in open warning. She pretended not to notice.

"I can't," Dr. Caribe said. "I tried. I couldn't find words. It's as if there's a boulder in my way." He smiled at Eva, a tired smile, his first of the evening. "Not all of us have your gifts."

"It's just as well," Roberto said. "You could write tomes about this and still not change what happened." His hands pressed together tightly; Eva felt the low emanation of his fear. "The last thing Argentina needs is another good man in exile."

"Maybe you're right."

"By the way." Roberto swept the air with his hand, wiping it clean. "I read your paper on leprosy. It's fascinating."

The conversation moved, changed, grew fraught with medical terms Eva did not understand. She shifted restlessly; time to unwrap; time to go to Salomé.

"Excuse me," she said, and headed to the stairs.

Salomé Ernestina Santos slept in her crib, her

hand a tiny fist, pacifier covering her mouth. Eva pulled the pacifier out and Salomé opened her eyes, cried, and reached toward her mother. She bared her breasts. The little mouth was warm and fierce. Her fist loosened and grasped her mother's skin. There it was, the hotsweet pulling, her power to pour something that was needed. She tried not to think of Ernesto Bravo, twice broken, or of the woman who'd once fed him with her body; she tried not to think of the Peróns, with their pink palace, their shine shine shine over the radio, their dispensations of hope, their printed lies, the intricate equation of their existence, complex, indecipherable, Einsteinian in its paradoxes; she tried not to think of herself, tomorrow and the next day and the next, moving through her life with this secret in her gut, a respectable woman, safe and tidy, with her jewels and crystal cups and damask drapes, letting other people bleed on concrete floors. She disgusted herself already. She tightened her grip on Salomé; the baby writhed and sucked. She could have told her daughter many things, was readying herself to say them, **this is who I really am, breast bared, feeding you, longing to be brave, large, angry, to believe the man who said it's all possible,** but baby and mother opened their mouths at the same time, and Salomé released the nipple, smacking her lips. Eva nestled her daughter back in the crib, settling for a lullaby, **"arrorró mi niña, arrorró mi sol,"** and the baby slept.

She returned to the drawing room. The men were on their feet.

"You're leaving already?" Eva spread her palms to show her disappointment.

"It's not exactly tea time."

"But still! Let me at least accompany you to the door. Roberto." She touched her husband's arm. "You must be exhausted. Why don't you head to bed?"

He did, and minutes later, just as the doctor stepped out into the rain, Eva whispered, "Come back in the morning, when Roberto's at work. I'll help you."

Dr. Caribe squinted at her. Rain beat at his umbrella. "How?"

She leaned forward and drops caught in the edges of her hair. "With the words."

It didn't take long. In three days Roberto burst into the drawing room.

"Eva!"

She looked up from her notebook, where she'd just written, **You burn and.** His face was close to hers, mouth hard, brow pressed, a hunted animal.

"What's wrong?"

"You tell me, Eva. What you did with Antonio."

"I don't know what you mean."

"That night. The things he told us. There's a mimeograph circulating among politicians. Today it was leaked to the press."

Eva set her notebook on the coffee table. "What makes you think I had anything to do with it?"

Roberto glared. "Look me in the eyes and tell me you didn't."

"Surely it was anonymous."

"You have no idea what they're capable of." His eyes were wild, the eyes of a caged jaguar. **You're almost an old man,** she thought. "I got a mysterious call today, suggesting we leave the country. Now tell me, dear wife, why would I get a call like that?"

His eyes bored into her. She willed herself not to look away, not to ask how that could be, how they could know.

"You helped him, Eva. Against my will."

She stood. "Yours is not the only will I follow."

It happened quickly—hands at her shoulders, a rough shake in her skull, and suddenly she was pushed against French wallpaper and a man who was her husband shouted—"What—have—you—done?"—and his hands were at her neck, she couldn't breathe, she couldn't breathe, she didn't need to breathe because she floated from herself, out into the air and if she could only find that fissure—

He let her go. She leaned against the wall. Pain throbbed in a necklace around her throat. Roberto stood a few paces away, his back to her. She could read in the slouch of his shoulders that he was sorry. The living room framed him with its antique table, velvet curtains, plush rug hand-woven in Persia. **He loves me.** She recited the words to herself.

"We're leaving," he said. "Tomorrow. Get the children ready. Eva. You know . . ."

"I do."

He stood still for a moment, then left without looking back.

The next night, at 2 a.m., Eva gazed out of the car window at the waters of the Río de la Plata. Dark. Still. Yielding to the curved bellies of boats at dock. Behind her, she heard the scuffle of men at their trunk, pulling out suitcases full of clothes, cash, photographs, reams of unpublished poems, her covert box of baby shoes (outgrown, essential, relics she could not leave or throw away). Salomé lay dreaming in her arms. Robertito leaned sleepily against her, clutching his stuffed bunny, Papa-gonia. She filled herself with his delicate scent: sweet talcum and tart hair oil. If only she could keep him this way, soft and three and fragrant, somehow defy the speeding laws of time. His intelligence amazed her; today, he had launched inexhaustible questions about where they were going ("to the country I came from") and for how long ("oh, you'll see"). Her husband sat at the other end of the backseat, staring out at his city. He had spent the whole drive in silence. Just as well. Eva adjusted the scarf at her neck to ensure that the bruises stayed hidden.

She wondered how and when people would discover their departure: Roberto's students at the hospital; his parents, with their prim but ample love; María of the breasts that gave and gave. One night, the story would go, in the year of 1951, the whole family simply disappeared. It didn't look like rain.

The clouds had lifted, as if sated by the recent downpour, with no signs of return, at least not tonight
when clear skies meant so much to them. No use wor-
rying about what the sky would do tomorrow.

A boat pulled up to the port. The car door opened
and a hooded man hustled her onto the boat. She set
a foot gingerly inside. Water glimmered darkly all
around her. **Cierre. Cielo. Cerrado. Siempre.** Lock.
Sky. Closed. Always.

The hooded boatmen launched them onto the
quiet river. Nothing but water could be seen ahead,
but Eva knew there would be land because she'd lived
there, she had walked and breathed it, six years ago
it had been home. Montevideo. City of echoes. City
of too many shoes. City of corner butcher shops,
green herbs crowding the kitchen, the simple heat of
Mami's stews. Gliding back, encased in night, for the
first time in fifteen years she prayed: for her son,
Roberto, and for Salomé; for her marriage, laden
with new and unnamed weight; for Dr. Caribe and
his family, somewhere also crossing into exile; for
Ernesto Bravo and his mother and for Evita and Juan
Perón and the Argentina that loved and feared them,
Argentina so enchanted and haunted and severe; she
prayed for Uruguay, for Mamá, her brothers, their
children and wives, all the poets at La Diablita, Coco
with her letters and her missing son, Andrés; she
prayed for the waves to keep chanting at La Rambla
and for Uruguayan wool to keep spinning on its
wheels; for her father, yes, she prayed for her father

and even for Pietro, **sí,** oh God who art in heaven or wherever you may hide, for Pietro too, since this was the only place where she could do it, here between shores, between homes, on this river that ran between worlds.

Hours later, through the darkness, across the long black water, the apricot lights of Montevideo began to glow.

Monte. Vide. Eu. I see a mountain, a captain said four centuries ago, spying a low hill from his boat, approaching a river that would not have any silver. City of misnomers. City of small things. City redolent of leather, fresh wool, saline evening breeze.

Returning was like traveling back in time. All those memories caught in every stone and step and smell. On the first day, the fountain at Parque Rodó almost felled her. Out of its waters reared a spectre of herself, at the end of the war, bending over to wash vomit from her blouse. It leaped at her, soiled and clawing. She stumbled backward, toward the trees and street beyond.

Things weren't the same, returning. The city hadn't changed; it was she who had to adjust her eyes—adjust all senses—to a different light, get used to spectres, get used to things so small and calm. No giant boulevards, no mad blare at the core of Montevideo. Even the cars sounded less tense. Their new apartment was in La Ciudad Vieja, right on Avenida

San Salvador. The wrought-iron balcony gazed over ornate buildings, a cobbled lane, old trees swaying their leaves, and La Diablita. Six years ago, before Buenos Aires, living in this neighborhood would have seemed the height of glamour. Inside, the bed was sturdy, if not lush; the carpets clean, if not red; the curtains quaint, if not fine. She would creep from bed (gently, so as not to rustle Roberto's sleep) and tiptoe to the balcony in slippers and a fur coat. In that safe roost, she'd smoke and sit and stare at the red door as it swung open and closed for customers. The door itself remembered, throbbed and called her; surely if she crossed the street and touched it all the nights of work and longing would rush back to her and show her who she was. That throb kept her awake for hours, cigarette after cigarette burning its slow ash toward her hand.

Returning wouldn't be returning until she went to Punta Carretas. She couldn't go to the house where she'd grown up. She could not see Papá. She thought about it, tried to picture it, tried to drum up things that she could say, but her pictures always ended up at Tomás' wedding, his laugh with Pietro, a **pascualina** pie dropped to the floor. That **pascualina** pie was thick and rotten and could easily infiltrate her body. She feared she might not rise from bed, not kiss her children, not keep from killing someone if she swallowed it again. A stalemate was a stalemate and was better than a war. But Mamá. She had to see Mamá.

She sought her out at Carnicería Descalzo. The air inside was pungent and evoked a pirate girl and boy slaying a dragon, laughing raucously, no longer there. The shop looked just the same, and so did Coco: the same round face, yellow kerchief, and bend toward sausages as she rearranged them.

Robertito squirmed against Eva's skirt. He'd been moody since the move, and would need a siesta soon. Eva waited for Coco, suddenly shy. She too would have liked to squirm against huge skirts. Two flies lazed through the meaty air, perhaps the progeny of the very flies who'd been here when Eva left. The glass case shut and Coco emerged to see her customer, an affluent stranger flanked by a baby carriage and a three-year-old boy.

"What can I do for you, Señora?"

"I've come to see my mother."

Coco blinked. She scanned Eva, up, down, up again. "Eva?" Slowly, as if revving a long-stalled engine. "Eva Firielli?"

The curtain behind the counter opened. Pajarita swept through. She stood in her wool dress, hair half silver, eyes wide. Eva felt a shell crack inside her. "Mamá—" and before she could bolt or sink to her knees for forgiveness, she was gripped by two arms, the scratch of wool, the scent of shredded basil and bitter roots.

"It's been so long," Mamá said.

She let her body melt, a little, toward her mother. She was so small but pressed so fiercely; Eva could barely breathe. Pajarita's shoulders began to shake. Eva resisted the urge to pull away.

Roberto tugged at her skirt. "Mamá."

Pajarita drew back and squatted beside the boy. **"Hola, precioso."**

"Roberto. Say hello to your abuela."

"Hello, Abuela," he mimed politely. He studied the woman before him, with her wet eyes and plain dress. She touched his arm, his hair, his face.

Eva gestured toward the baby carriage. "And this is Salomé."

Pajarita looked into the carriage. Salomé stirred, as if the gaze had broken the thin film of her sleep. Pajarita lifted the infant and saddled her against her waist. The baby grasped a black and silver braid as if it were a rope thrown out for rescue. She pulled hard. Pajarita did not seem to mind, did not seem as though she'd mind if Salomé tore the braid out by the root.

"She's strong," Eva said apologetically.

"They look just like you, Pajarita," Coco said from the counter. She had recovered from her shock, and examined Eva with subtle suspicion. "Look at you. Fresh from Buenos Aires." She emphasized the last two words in a tone tinged with awe, or perhaps distaste. "I wouldn't have recognized you."

Eva smiled, uncertainly. She felt like a child, caught playing dress-up in an aunt's fancy clothes. It was stifling now, this butcher shop with its blood-iron smell, its memories, its proprietress with folded arms. Coco, for all her warmth, did not easily drop a grudge, and Eva was a suspect in the crimes of escaping with her son and causing her best friend pain. Eva imagined Coco and Mamá in the upstairs parlor, over the years, drinking tea steeped with the taste of each other's grief.

"Where is your husband?" Coco asked.

"At work."

"At work! On his holiday?"

"We're not here for a holiday." Eva watched her son wander toward a case of beef. "We're here to stay."

Pajarita faced her, or tried to, her head still bent toward Salomé's fist. "To stay?"

"Yes. We," had to leave, in the dark, on a boat with hooded men, "decided suddenly. That's why I didn't write."

Roberto's nose was pressed against the glass. He was sure to leave a smudge.

"I see." Pajarita stared at her. "When will you come for dinner?"

It was the question Eva dreaded. She would not have, could not allow, the welcome-home party crammed with family, endless empanadas, the noise of two dozen voices, the crawl of nephews everywhere, wine, **bizcochos,** Papá. "Oh, who knows," she answered, too lightly. "The evenings are so full." A shameful excuse. "But I'll come back here and see you."

Pajarita's eyes were gentle but did not bend. "What should I tell your father?"

Eva shifted from her left foot to her right, then back to left again. Roberto tapped the glass two times, **tak, tak.** Naturally Mamá would reach for her, as if the family were a loom and Eva a wayward thread; as if she thought her hands could weave and knot her daughter into place, and the cloth would form a whole, and the whole could drape together, soft, contented, as if there were no goddamn scissors in the world. "I don't know."

Pajarita raised her head, which had been freed from Salomé's grip. "I see."

There was silence. Coco coughed. Roberto tapped the glass case with his fingernails: **tak tak tak tak tak tak tak tak tak—**

"Stop, **querido.**" Eva pulled him away from the glass and up to her hip. He was getting so big. It took all her strength to hold him. "I should take him home for a siesta."

"Come back soon," her mother said.

Eva nodded. "Tomorrow."

Coco grasped Eva's arm on her way out. "Look. About Andrés. There must be something, anything, you can tell me."

Eva studied Coco's liver-spotted hand. "We left together. He was with me in Buenos Aires for about four months. Then he disappeared, and I haven't heard from him since."

Coco's eyes narrowed. "Did he leave you in trouble?"

"No. He was chivalrous. He didn't . . . we didn't."

Coco looked doubtful. The smell of raw beef thickened in the air.

"I'm sorry."

"Just to know he's still alive."

Eva imagined Andrés, bleeding to death in a San Telmo alley, or succumbing alone to pneumonia, or wandering Paris and laughing at them both. "Of course."

"You're different, you know. It's not just the clothes."

So many layers to returning, she thought that night, smoking on the balcony. It's a plunge into the past, simple, myriad, impossible. A plunge into the darkness. The air tonight was thick and damp; stars hid behind low clouds. Down the street, the red door to La Diablita opened, and a girl strutted in. Waitress? Aspiring poet? Eva would not go over there. There had already been enough homecomings. She put her cigarette out on the balcony rail. A man in a long black coat lingered on the street below. A low fedora hid his face. She had the distinct sense that he was waiting for something; someone to arrive, or some quest to be fulfilled. She lit another cigarette and waited for the quest, the harlot, the secret deal. The cigarette burned slowly to its end. Nothing happened.

She stood and walked into her bedroom. Roberto snored softly on his back, jaw slack. He had found a job so easily; the hospitals had vied for him, asked nothing about his reasons for the move. In the dark, she glanced at her neck in the mirror above her dresser. The bruises seemed gone. She leaned in closer, turned to catch the streetlight's beam. Yes, gone. And the silence between her and Roberto was giving way to pleasantries, a Good Morning and a Let Me Take Your Coat at the top and bottom of each day. But it was just a brittle surface. Neither of them had forgiven the other, or, perhaps, themselves, not for mimeographs or exile or moments spent not breathing against the wall.

Eva picked up a notebook and pen. She wrote. In the dark, her letters fell swaying and unruly on the page, but it didn't matter. She wrote nakedly, rapidly, tearing off pages as she filled them, until she had wrung herself free of all saturation. Then she opened a drawer, gathered the pages, and pressed them into a morass of unfinished poems.

Three years passed. Quiet years. On some days, Eva missed the noise and scope of Buenos Aires, but Montevideo, to her surprise, unfolded in new ways, offering its own quotidian lyricism. In the butcher shop, for example, on days when it grew thick with women's sweat and sweet oils and confessions. The same women still came to buy meat and trade gossip, though now they embroidered their talk with boasts about grandchildren. Even La Viuda still came. She had to be older than God. Sometimes she claimed a stool by the door and accosted all who entered with her apocalyptic advice. The women chatted with Eva, wanting to know all about the intervening years, about Perón, there were so many Argentinian exiles here, more each year, they said, and was Perón really as repressive as they said in the leftist papers? Eva answered and the women clucked their tongues: what kind of populist does that to his own people, nothing like our Batlle, may he rest in peace. Small crowds built up in patient wait for Pajarita's services. Some crossed the burlap curtain stoic and came back weeping; a few went in weeping and emerged beatific. Eva watched the children, wrapped meat, wiped a counter here or there. She let her mind dip its toe into her mother's world.

Occasionally, she stole her mother to La Rambla, where they strolled and watched the afternoon sun spark on the river. A loose-limbed quiet accompanied them. Difficult things could be said across that quiet.

"Mami?"

"Mmm."

"I hope you're not angry that, you know, I don't come home."

Eva listened to the wet push of the waves. Her mother looked out to the thumb of land where the lighthouse stood. When their house was built, she'd once told Eva, that lighthouse's beams came through the windows, clear in from the shore.

"You haven't changed your mind?"

"No."

"I can't change it?"

"No."

They kept walking. Mamá looked sad. Her profile moved against the backdrop of clear sky. "Better to have a bit of you than none of you at all."

She saw the rest of her family in piecemeal: Tomás and Carlota visited her at the butcher shop. Bruno and Mirna invited her to dinner, needling her for tales of Argentina over **buñuelos** and boiled potatoes, the children pushing wooden trains across the floor. Marco, now a pharmacist in Buceo, took **mate** breaks to share a park bench with his sister and nag about their father. "You should see him," he'd urge. "You're both too stubborn." Eva would smile and watch the breeze make mischief with his curls.

Xhana's kitchen was her refuge. Xhana lived in Barrio Sur, with her husband and father, a block from César's parents, two blocks from the river, surrounded by Montevideo's small black community. In the kitchen, the square table wore its gingham like a dress. Plates and forks and cups appeared for everyone who came. Their living room often filled with drummers and their music. Eva brought thick packages of Coco's meat—to wrap in empanadas, to fry as **milanesas,** to season for **churrasco.** She watched Xhana rule her kitchen, laugh heartily, cook like a generous demon, explicate the nuances of a new law or a factory strike to friends. She could see Xhana the girl, still there, the one who had gutted fish and devoured Marx without fear. When they had the kitchen to themselves, talking late into the night, girlhood lurked so close that Eva looked at her own hands to reassure herself that they were woman-size.

"It's good to have you back." Xhana poured another glass of wine. "You were gone too long."

Eva exhaled smoke. "Good thing I got exiled."

"Not just Argentina, **prima.** You were gone a long time before that."

Eva fingered the ashtray, with its mound of felled cigarettes. "I know."

"You were my only sister. I missed you."

From the living room, Eva heard Tío Artigas crooning an old gaucho ballad. She remembered it from childhood. César's **repique** fed a candombe rhythm below it, slow and supple. Eva put her cigarette out and lit another. She waited for the question that she didn't want to answer. It didn't come. "I'm here now," she said.

After visiting Xhana, Eva often stayed up through sunrise and wrote. Poems came for their own sake: copious, private, raw. Her secret stash filled three drawers, words caught in musty dark, each word a tiny prism that refracted some small beam of Eva's world. Hunger. Dawn. A city on the shore. Two miraculous children who insisted, despite all maternal longing, on growing and running and becoming little people of their own. The funeral Salomé and Xhana gave a dead swallow in Parque Rodó (so sensitive, her Salomé: she wept as if she'd loved that bird for years). The joy of curling her body around

Roberto's on a rainy night (the young one, not the old, Roberto the young and grave and clever). She wrote about Montevideo's sleepy beauties and its daily return into her skin, about the way a small thing—El Río de la Plata's curving motion, a woman weeping against a balcony rail, the red aroma of beef roasting **a las brazas** at the corner bar—could blow right through her so she shook in sudden winds that woke her to the world and her tenuous place within it. And she wrote and did not write about the haunted nights, when demons seemed to push her through her dreams until she woke up, clammy, gulping air, alone in a haunted city beside a doc-tor deep in sleep. She did not write about the doctor, the stranger in her bed, the film of pleasantry that shielded them from each other. She didn't know, any longer, where these words were going, why she wrote them, what they meant. It was enough to let her pen rove the paper, chasing its edge, giving shape to the unshapable. Chasing home.

"Roberto must miss home," Señora Caribe said, over tea. "I know we do."

Eva sipped from a dainty cup. It had been days since Roberto had arrived before midnight. "Yes, he does."

Señora Caribe looked at her ceiling, where a stained-glass fan stirred heavy air. "Sometimes the papers give me hope Perón won't last. He's gotten reckless. A fourteen-year-old girl? What kind of president makes a mistress of a fourteen-year-old girl?"

Eva shook her head, lips pressed in disapproval. Evita must be turning in her grave, she thought, except, of course, she didn't have one. Turning in her tart embalming fluids.

"Most of all, I want to see my sister before she dies. I just hope her health can outlast Perón. Sometimes I dream she's dead and shouting for me across the river. I can hear her but I can't shout back. I wake up sweating—it must sound crazy."

"No. Not at all."

Señora Caribe smiled gratefully. "Do you ever have bad dreams?"

Eva crossed her legs, uncrossed them. "Yes."

"Ah. Do I have a cure for you." She looked over her shoulder, as if the china cabinet might hold spies. "Who washes your hair?"

It was not what Eva had expected. "I do."

"Who else?"

"My hairdresser."

"Namely?"

"A gentleman in Pocitos."

"Bah! You've got to go to mine. She's the best in the city. She washes hair like that sweet soap of hers could clean away your cares."

Eva smiled at her hostess.

"I'm telling you, it's true. I sleep better afterward. And look how well she cuts." She stroked her gray curls. "I'll give you her number."

That night, after putting her children to bed and washing the din-ner dishes, Eva stood on the balcony and opened Señora Caribe's note. She strained to de-cipher the writing in the lamplight. **Zolá Zapateada, 35-53-99.**

He was here, again, on the street: the man in the dark fedora. Hat pushed low, swathed in his long coat, as if it weren't the humid height of summer. As if the street held something that he'd lost. What drove a man to haunt a street for three years running? He could be a tortured artist; a lover with a broken heart; a criminal on the prowl; a madman with no other place to go. Or just a drifter in a world that sends souls drifting, that unmoors the soul without warning or reason or so much as a match to light the darkness. She returned to her bedroom, with its bare, husbandless bed. She slid under the covers and closed her eyes. Zolá Zapateada, she fell asleep thinking, what kind of name is that?

She made an appointment for the following week. Zolá lived in a stylish high-rise, where the elevator operator's uniform gleamed with freshly polished buttons. She stepped off on the fifteenth floor and knocked on door 1555.

"Just a minute," a creamy voice called from the other side.

A tall, sleek woman opened the door. "Buenas—" She froze.

"Zolá?"

"Yes. Do come in."

Eva entered and scanned the room, the marble

counters, ivory walls, a crystal vase alive with flowers. Zolá wore pearls and violet silk and dark red lipstick. She was staring at Eva with an intensity bordering on rudeness.

"What a nice apartment."

"Eva. Don't you remember me?"

"Remember?"

There was something familiar about her features. Sharp, pleasing. She could not place it. She searched her memory, searched the face, hair, eyes. Eyes. Her throat cinched closed; she couldn't speak. They stared at each other.

A long moment passed. Not possible. Eva's face and hands grew hot. Her hostess was the first to look away.

"Shall I make some **mate**?"

Eva didn't move.

"Please, make yourself at home."

Eva sat on the crushed-velvet sofa while Zolá disappeared to boil water in the kitchen. The room was large and airy, with floor-to-ceiling windows, gold-framed paintings, exuberant potted plants. To her right, the hairdresser's chair faced an oval mirror; to her left, the view stretched over the tops of buildings to the river. She pictured herself falling, out of the window, out of her reality, all the way down to a twisted underwater world. Zolá entered, bearing a tray of **bizcochos** and **mate.**

Eva wanted to laugh, to weep, to shout. "I can't believe this."

Zolá offered her the tray without looking at her.

Eva took a pastry and stared at it. It looked perfectly normal. "How long have you been cutting hair?"

"Seven years. I studied in Buenos Aires, after the Change. It's competitive there, so I came back." She handed Eva the **mate.** "I'm one of the best in Uruguay."

Eva drank from the gourd. The bitter liquid filled her mouth. "And this is what you left me for?"

"Cutting hair?"

"You know what I mean."

"I'm sorry. I do. I entered the hospital soon after we parted. I didn't want to leave you, but nobody could know."

"What did they—I mean—"

Zolá smoothed his (her his her his) skirt. "There's an operation. It was all very new. In Berlin there was a painter who was the first to have it done. That was back in '31. I heard about it from the boys at La Diablita. You can imagine they weren't singing its praises. But it told me that it could be done, so I went to Argentina. You know Buenos Aires. Always trying to be on the cutting edge."

Eva nodded. The next question caught in her throat.

"Go ahead. Whatever it is."

"Why do such a thing?"

Zolá said nothing, and Eva feared she'd offended her. She searched for something she could say to fill the silence. Everything she thought of seemed unsayable.

"To be true."

Light poured copiously, in this high home, glinting on crystal vases, shaking the dust off memories, rearranging the known world. She passed the gourd back to Zolá. She watched her (her!) pour water into the leaves, and place red lips where Eva's had just been.

"And all this time I thought you'd run off with another woman."

"Really?"

"Of course. I found a tube of lipstick under your dresser."

"Whose do you think that was?"

Eva stared.

"I worked in a cabaret. Remember?"

"Oh."

"But it's a sleazy business. I'm better suited to this profession."

Eva thought of the first walk they'd taken home from La Diablita, how ethereal Andrés had looked to her in the moonlight, like a creature from another world, ill matched to the butcher's block. "You have no idea how much I've missed you."

"Clearly," Zolá said, "the converse is also true."

They looked each other in the eye. The gaze was intensely foreign and familiar.

"You look good."

"So do you."

Eva looked away. "Are you afraid of being recognized?"

Zolá smiled, a little proudly. "You didn't recognize me, did you? But I stay out of Punta Carretas. Most people I knew in Montevideo don't come to hair-dressers like me. My clients are mostly—well—"

"Like me?"

"Yes, Señora Santos." She added ironic emphasis to the name. "Like you. So tell me. Who have you become?"

"I can't answer that."

"Why not?"

"I have no clue."

"Tell me what's happened, then."

Eva recounted her story, methodically at first, then urgently, telling of her paralysis at Andrés' departure, the sanitized hospital, the special attentions and small pink pills of Dr. Roberto Santos, the apartment of mauve roses and seduction, the white-pillared house, the birth of her son and daughter, her scat-tered publications, the appearance of a rain-wet doc-tor in the middle of the night, the mimeographed words that sent them into exile, her current balcony from which she watched La Diablita's door, her nights at Xhana's and days at Coco's, her distant hus-band and vivid children and stuffed-in-a-drawer poems. The act of speaking shook the kaleidoscope of memory. Words fell from her lips in splintered col-ors, and the woman in front of her took in every-thing she said. She finally trailed into silence.

"So are you happy?"

"I don't know. Are you?"

Zolá raised an eyebrow. "Yes. But there have been some terrible losses."

"Like what?"

"Like my mother."

An imprint of Coco thickened the room—blood-and-soap hands, a brassy laugh, hips like fortress walls.

"And you."

Eva looked across the room at the mirror. Inside it she could see the clouded sky.

Zolá stared at the coffee table as if it fascinated her. "Are you disgusted?"

Eva gazed out the window. The light was growing golden; shards of it had fallen on the river. The river glistened, long and wide, the same river as always. She had wanted to ride its back for years before she crossed it. She could almost see herself, down on the water, in a boat at dawn, twenty years old, with her best friend, longing for his body, longing for much more, sure of what she longed for, sure of nothing. Perhaps that girl, the ghost of her, still wandered the low waves. A gull soared over rooftops and out of sight. "No."

Zolá looked, for an instant, relieved like a child.

"But. I have one more question."

"Well?"

"Did you give up poetry?"

"No. I have a pseudonym. A poetess persona."

"Ah."

"She's a country girl, from the pampas."

"No."

"And she's blind."

"Zolá, wait. You're not Soledad Del Valle."

"You know me?"

"I can't believe it."

"Just think. A hermit, demure, blind, in the country—how could she ever make a city appearance?"

Eva took a **bizcocho** from the plate, but didn't eat it. She peeled the layers of pastry, exposing soft, pale insides.

"What are you thinking, Eva?"

"That the world is a joke."

"Are you laughing?"

"Who knows."

Zolá smiled. Behind her, the sky seemed to gather like a mantle. "Shall I wash your hair?"

It became her secret treasure, that ride up to the fifteenth floor. Up up toward heaven, toward Zolá's aerie, where there was so much to love: broad streams of light; star-gazer lilies yawning with fragrance; smooth marble and mirrors; tufts of hair, her own, black and slender, falling to the floor. Every time she came it was a different kind of falling. Zolá's hands returned again and again to Eva's hair.

"Eva?"

"Mmmmm?"

"How does that feel?"

"Perfect. The best hair wash in the world."

"I call it a scalp massage."

"Call it what you want. I call it heaven." She sank into her chair and let her head relax further into warm, soft water that smelled of rose and almonds. Skilled fingers sifted through her hair as if in search of specks of gold.

"No wonder women can't get enough of this. You've got to let me pay."

"I won't hear of it."

"But your business?"

"Some things are more important. Sshhhh . . . relax . . ."

She closed her eyes and Zolá engulfed her head with gentle hands and water soft with nut-and-blossom foam. She was a blossom, an animal kind, a sea anemone, slick, unfurling, undulating, full of slippery urges. "**Ay.** Thank you."

"For what?"

"For . . . making me feel like a mermaid."

Zolá laughed. "Perhaps you'll grow a tail."

These hands were the same as they'd always been, even though the nails could now dig red tips into skin. She had seen them sift imaginary gold, turn pages, fill pages, stroke tears from her cheek. She knew these hands, and they knew her—better, it sometimes seemed, than she knew herself: they felt past the string of pearls, the earrings, even the curls, to glide along the hidden, naked contours of her scalp. It felt excruciating to let those fingers know such pale and private skin: as if all the armor she had ever formed could dissolve in a basin of fragrant water; as if nothing could stay concealed from such fingers or would want to. On some days, she did not care about exposure and plunged freely, hungry to be stroked, sculpted, washed, reborn, rebaptized in a secret sea.

When Zolá took to cutting, Eva felt a different self take shape. She entered as an unfinished woman, strong but blurry at the edges, like a photograph taken with a softened lens. Zolá's cuts deepened her definition and sharpened her edges. Anything superfluous, she realized, could be shed. Snip, a layer of weight eased away. Snip, and she was incrementally freer than before. Snip, snip, the scissors sang in brisk, low moans as they danced at the curve of her neck.

After the first cut, Eva walked the Rambla as if her feet stepped on pure gold. After the second, she went home and wept for seven hours. Quietly, so the children wouldn't hear her from their rooms, or from the table where they ate under the half-watchful, half-petulant care of Señora Hidalgo from downstairs. Once an hour, Señora Hidalgo knocked on Eva's bedroom door.

"Doña Eva? You'll still be needing me?"

"If you don't mind."

"You sure you're fine?"

"Yes, Señora. Thank you."

She heard the widow's slow creak away from the door. More tears.

After the third cut, Eva came home and exhumed every poem she could find. They emerged from drawers, socks, purses, the dark under the bed, the hulls of neglected shoes. She spread them on her bed and started sorting, in search of patterns in the chaos.

She took them to Zolá.

"Read me another. Go on."

"Zolá, I have to go." Reluctantly. "I'm late for my babysitter."

"Of course." Zolá seemed reluctant too. She curled on the sofa with her chin on her arms. "They're lovely. Why on earth did we become poets?"

"Because we were reckless."

"Because we love life?"

"Because we couldn't help it."

"That must be it." She gestured at the papers strewn across the table. "Can I keep them for a while?"

"All right."

Autumn approached, with its cool winds and early showers. The season seemed enchanted. Eva could walk down the street—one child-hand in each of hers—and be struck by a fierce and sudden gale of happiness. It made her want to skip and run and kick up puddle water and pursue the sensuous crunch of brown leaves beneath her boots. So much opulent sensation on one sidewalk. "Salomé, you get that one!" Small galoshes crushed a leaf, another, and two giggles (a three-year-old's, her mother's) mixed with the crackling sound. "Roberto? How about you?" A head shook, a wool cap (made by his abuelita) swung its pom-pom. How did he get so very tall? and how so solemn? Many splashed puddles it took to make him smile, but it was worth it for the dawn-break way it came.

Untethered joy rarely goes unnoticed.

"What's going on?" Xhana folded her arms across her apron.

"What do you mean?"

"Please, **prima.** Just look at you."

Eva took a healthy bite of her empanada. Steam unfurled from its pastry shell.

"Papá, isn't she different?"

Tío Artigas played a drum roll on the tablecloth. "If I didn't know better . . . I'd say . . . she's fallen in love!"

Xhana raised her chin in triumph.

"That's scandalous," Eva said.

Artigas said, "Is it?"

Eva looked around, hands spread out, an innocent facing her accusers. She scanned the room for saviors. Oil sizzled in a pan on the stove; a woman rose from the sea in a picture on the wall, stars falling from her hands, the script above her reading **Iemanjá;** drummer and daughter stared at her. No reprieve. She hung her head in mock defeat.

"You're right. I'm in love . . . with my wonderful children."

Shouts railed at her from both sides.

"That's all right," Xhana said. "You don't have to tell. Not even your own family."

"Sure." Artigas leaned toward her. "But we have eyes in our heads."

She wanted to say more; it was impossible. There were new realms in her life that she had no words for. Astonishing how many realms existed in one city, even a quiet city where you could not find a mountain. There were so many Montevideos, behind the myriad doors. Perhaps women were like cities, full of darkened rooms, able to find new worlds down hidden hallways.

"Eva." Zolá's voice slid through the water. "I have a confession."

Eva pulled herself back from reverie.

"I gave your poems to Señora Sosoma."

"The publisher's wife?"

Zolá looked penitent and amused. A drop of water had made a small, dark circle at the breast of her lime-colored blouse. "She's a regular. She loved your work. They both did. I'm afraid they want to publish you."

Eva had never met the Sosomas, but she knew of their collections, elegant volumes published out of Montevideo, with a focus, in their own words, on lifting the voices of women. "You're serious?"

Zolá nodded. "Am I forgiven?"

"Just this once. But I'll have to watch out. You're too good at keeping secrets."

"True. But I'm good at sharing them too." Zolá's face grew indecipherable. "Now, dear, if you would please lean back . . ."

She sank her head into Zolá's hands. Her tresses were sea kelp; the fingers sought pearls between them. She brimmed with pearls. She overflowed. There was so much to be found.

Eva heard the news of Perón's fall on September 20, 1955, over the radio. The announcer's voice, drunk with history, spilled into her kitchen, over the tiles, over everything. **In Buenos Aires, a new military junta announced that Perón has resigned . . . whereabouts unknown . . . Here in Montevideo, some exiles are already packing their luggage, ready to head home.** The voice was euphoric, and Eva felt herself rise from her seat as if on a sudden wind, aloft with hope for Argentina, until the words sank in, **new military junta.** She saw the Caribes in her mind, pressing shirts and combs and teacups into bags, tearing photographs and paintings from the walls. She saw Roberto, standing over a sick child, head full of news and visions of return. She slapped the radio off. The children were at school. The home was hollow with silence. Salomé's favorite puzzle lay on the coffee table: a tiger, grinning amiably, its head and paws unfinished.

That afternoon, at Zolá's, Eva perched before the oval mirror and watched the scissors snip at her wet hair. Zolá stood over her, lips pursed, focused, hair in a high, crisp bun. They were both quiet.

"Shorter, Zolá."

"You sure?"

Eva nodded, wanting lightness, wanting to be shorn.

"All right. But don't move your head." The scissors rasped. "How's it going with the book?"

"Great. It's exciting." That was true—the publisher was immensely kind, and she was almost ready, up late at night arranging her poems into mosaic after mosaic—but today the words were forced.

"Good."

"You heard the news today?"

"Yes. Fall in wool prices. More jobs lost."

"And Perón."

The scissors did not break their flow. "And Perón."

In the mirror, pineapple light spread in through the windows, over the sofa, the mantel, Zolá's pink dress, her string of pearls, her body as it arched to get the perfect angle at Eva's hair.

"What has Roberto said?"

"I haven't seen him yet."

"I'm sure he'll be glad to go home."

"Home? He never comes home." Eva hadn't meant to shout. "He's cheating on me, you know."

"Are you sure?"

"Of course!"

"Don't move your head." Their eyes met in the mirror: a wet-haired angry woman, and another woman close behind her, sweaty, blades aloft.

Zolá resumed her cutting.

"I'm not jealous."

"No?"

"No. At least not of her, whoever she is. I'm jealous of him."

"Because?"

"Because he does whatever he wants."

"And you don't."

"No."

"Why not?"

"It's different for women, Zolá."

Zolá's reflection stayed intent on her work. "Is that what stops you?"

"Part of it."

"What's the other part?"

"Something else." The scissors' blades were at her neck now, cool against her skin. Her skin was hot. "What about you?"

"What **about** me?"

"Are you doing what you want?"

Zolá looked into the mirror. "Part of it."

Their eyes locked. Eva could not breathe. Silence fell over them, and stayed after they broke the gaze, for the rest of cutting, drying, styling. Finally Eva rose to leave. She looked at her hair in the mirror. "It's beautiful."

Zolá was arranging her bottles of sweet oils and soaps. She moved a green bottle forward, back again. "If you leave. You'll say good-bye?"

"Por favor." Eva reached for her coat. She kept her eyes on its buttons as she slid them into holes. "You'll see me again."

On her walk home, Eva took a detour past the Plaza de Zabala, turning on a tall and narrow street.

It was still there. Of course.

The same stone cherubs lined its roof, mottled with pigeon droppings. The same balconies flanked the door with its brass bell. In the windows, rows and rows of shoes showed off their leather—black, red, brown, cream. She hovered at the corner, poised to bolt. Nothing moved. No need to go any closer and no need to run away. The chill of dusk was falling. A streetcar rattled by behind her; soles clapped brusquely against the sidewalk; Montevideo was heading home. She had changed. She was thirty years old, not a girl any longer. She had slight lines at the corners of her eyes; two children; a marriage based on fantasies and masks and earnest trying; a book of poems on the way; a cousin and a mother and three brothers; hands that touched her scalp under lush water; and she had something inside her skin—something dark and slippery and steady, like a rock in the middle of the sea.

A body moved in the store window. Eva shot around the corner, out of sight. She had done it. In every last corner of this city she could stand, breathe air, be true. She wanted, more than anything, to be true.

Roberto's key turned in the door at half past one. Eva listened to him shuffle out of his coat, hang it up, cough, and approach the bedroom. He sat down on the bed. The duvet creased beneath the heft of him. Eva took in his bent back, fleshy chin, the lean beak of his nose. Almost half his hair was gray. When had that happened?

"Good evening." He waited. It was her turn, her moment to say, How was your day? and kneel to unlace his oxfords. She did neither. Roberto looked up in faint annoyance. "I'm sure you've heard the news."

"About Perón?"

"Of course." Roberto hesitated, then reached to remove his shoes. "At work, they gave me a bottle of Champagne." The lace pulled out of each eyelet with almost surgical precision. It was not how Eva did it; she tended to pull too hard. "Have you told the children?"

"Told them what?"

"That we're going home."

"Roberto." She sat down beside him. "I need to tell you something."

His face grew guarded.

"I'd like to stay."

"What?"

"I don't want to go to Argentina."

"Of course we're going back."

"Let me just say this."

"No. Don't say it," he said, too loudly.

She reached out with a soft coolant of a hand. "Just listen for a—"

"No, Eva, you listen, you." He sprang to his feet. "You don't want to go to Argentina. You don't want to. Perhaps you've forgotten why we left. Or where I married you. Where I made you everything you are."

He was red-faced, pointing at her with a pale and fleshy finger. "I give you everything. And in return? This. Exile and now this. A wife who doesn't feel like going back."

Eva rose. It was a relief, this rage, out in the air, palpable. "I've let you down."

"What do you think?"

"What's her name?"

"Whose name?"

"Your mistress."

He drew back.

"Or have there been too many to remember?"

Roberto's face grew expressionless. Eva stepped closer. She smelled the bite of his cologne, quick, pleasant. "Perhaps I'm a bad wife but I was faithful, at least, I never touched another man." Or woman. Or. "At least I can say that."

He turned to the curtains, and then she knew: this room of theirs was far more fragile than she'd realized. Walls buckled at the slightest weight. The air was sharp; it pricked her skin.

A knock on the bedroom door. Eva opened it. Salomé stood, clam-eyed, braids falling against her lavender nightgown. Her face was delicate and small for four years old. Eva knelt.

"**Hija,** what are you doing out of bed?"

"I heard something."

"Everything's fine." She tried her best to sound reassuring.

"I got scared."

"I see. But everything's fine."

"Can I sleep with you?"

"Not tonight."

"Please?"

"Next time. I promise." Eva stroked her daughter's cheek. "Go back to bed."

Salomé nodded, unconvinced. Eva watched her walk back to her room, and closed the door.

Roberto looked weary. "You really don't want to go."

"No."

He nodded, as if she'd spoken the obvious answer. He opened the closet and threw a pair of slacks on the bed. Reached for another.

"What are you doing?"

"Leaving."

"Sshhhhh. The children."

"I'm leaving." He spoke more softly but kept his stride back and forth from the closet.

"Tonight?"

"Yes."

"Where are you going?"

"Does it matter?"

"To her house."

"What if I am?"

"Are you coming back?"

"Why should I?"

She rocked slightly. "The children."

"I won't forget them."

The pile on the bed had mushroomed into a heap

of wool and belts and well-pressed cotton. At this moment a different woman might plead, cajole, fall to her knees, sidle up just so, do anything to keep him here and change his mind. But—the thought shot through her like hard liquor—she didn't want to. Of course she didn't. She was too drunk, she wanted more, she longed to follow her intoxication wherever it led her, however steep the ledges, however far the fall.

She watched Roberto pull the suitcase from its shelf and drop it open on the bed. He worked methodically, her husband, even in the heat of high emotion. A subtle fondness moved through her at the thought. At that moment she could have kissed him (not to keep him) but the gesture seemed ill timed. Instead, she went to the balcony to breathe unfettered air. Avenida San Salvador stretched below her, wide awake. An old tango record crooned through a nearby window; couples strolled, unrushed, hands gliding through each other's hair; on the sidewalk outside La Diablita, people clustered at small tables, braving the cold. She lit a cigarette and watched the ember crackle toward her mouth. The man in the fedora had arrived at his lamppost, coat pulled tight and hat pulled low as always. Sad. Absurd. If he was a tortured artist he should go home and make art. If he was a broken lover he should look for a new love. If he was a madman—well—couldn't he find a better use for madness somewhere else? She was full of the strange liquor of this night. "Señor," she called, "who are you? What the hell are you look-ing for?"

The man stiffened. A young couple, on their way from La Diablita, stopped in curiosity.

"Eva," he said. "Hello."

Eva's cigarette almost singed her fingers. She knew that voice. The man removed his hat. His hair shone gray in the lamp glow, a shade lighter than the old stone edifice behind him. He smiled nervously. His hands chewed on the fedora. From this angle he looked small, a figurine of a father. "I . . . **este . . .** didn't mean to bother you."

Eva crushed her cigarette and tossed it into the street. She wanted to laugh, but she opened her mouth and the sound didn't come. "That was you, all this time?"

Ignazio shrugged his admission. The young couple had stopped walking, and watched in barely veiled fascination. Ignazio glanced at them. They looked away. "Do you think we might, maybe, go some-where? For a drink?"

"No," Eva said. "I'm in the middle of something." Now she did laugh, and it came easily, a madwoman's loose laugh. Her father, at his iron lamppost, stared. "Maybe tomorrow? Five o'clock?"

"Well, then." He replaced his hat. "See you to-morrow."

"**Adiós,** Papá."

In the bedroom, Roberto stood with two pairs of socks in hand. "That," he said incredulously, "was your father?"

Eva thought of Roberto's own father, who would never spend his nights combing the streets like a commoner. Not for a daughter or for anyone in the world. Only the most strange or sick or ardent men would think of such a thing. "Yes," she said, "that's him."

The next morning, Eva woke alone in an empty bed. Light's long fingers curled around the edges of the curtains. The room felt stuffy, crowded by old breaths and hovering words. Light and breath and unsaid things and she alone between the sheets, hollow, euphoric, afraid. She reached for pen and paper and began a poem. In the poem, a woman lost her legs and set out to find them, gritting her teeth, dragging herself along by the knuckles. Dust filled the woman's mouth, and Eva stopped writing, tore off the page, and began another poem, where a woman rode a river in the middle of the night from a shore called Lies to a shore called Truth. She described Truth, its wild vines and flame-colored birds, and continued even when she heard the light feet of her children at the door; she should get up and make them breakfast, but her pen coiled and pushed across the paper and her hand had no choice but to follow. The feet were gone and then sounds from the kitchen and more steps came and then a voice was at the door, saying, "Mami."

Salomé stared up at her, dwarfed by the tray she was holding, concentrating intensely on her balance.

The tray held **mate,** a thermos of hot water, and a plate of toast. How had they done it by themselves? What if they had gotten burned?

"Good morning," Salomé said, uncertainly.

Eva sat up in bed. **"Ay, hija."** Salomé came closer, and Eva took the tray from her and settled it on the bed. She looked at her daughter and remembered her face the night before, trusting and infinitely fragile. A girl who sensed every shift in the wind, who felt everything keenly but was helpless to shield herself, needed someone else to be the mantle. It terrified Eva, the thought of what mothering required, the thought of failing. She felt her face start to crumble. Salomé looked worried, and Eva quickly smiled. "How nice. This is so nice."

Salomé relaxed, a little.

"Are you hungry?"

Salomé nodded, and Eva lifted the covers to let her crawl in. Salomé burrowed against her like a snouted underground creature. How did her own body form this strange and perfect child?

"Where's your brother?"

Salomé shrugged.

Eva called for him, once, twice, and Roberto arrived, half-eaten toast in hand, looking wary and hopeful in his Donald Duck pajamas. They would rise together, make a new life, the three of them a newly fashioned trinity, and who cared how the world shook its head and pursed its lips, it was her life, not the world's.

"Come in, come in," she said.

She broke toast into uneven pieces, and they pressed into her side of the bed, all three of them, close, quiet, feet entangled, eating torn toast, reckless with the crumbs.

That afternoon, Eva entered La Diablita for the first time in ten years. Memories flooded her, from red chairs and bright music and dark walls. She saw herself, thirteen years old, arriving out of breath on tottering heels, that hinge of a day when she'd last spoken to this man, her father, now at her side.

They sat down close to the piano. The waitress who took their order had hair like raven wings, folded in close to the body. Ignazio looked around him. His face had creases she'd never seen. "This is where you worked?"

Eva nodded. She took out a cigarette; Ignazio lit it for her, then lit his own. Their smoke made slow swirls in the air between them. She waited for him to speak, but he just sat there, smoking and tapping fingertips against his thumb. Behind him, a woman with bleached hair bent greedily toward her friend. **Tell me the secret,** her eyes said.

"All that time," said Ignazio.

Eva tipped ash into the ashtray.

"Your apartment looks very nice. From the outside."

"Seems like you know that part quite well."

"I didn't mean to alarm you. Really." He spread his palms. "I can't explain it. I'd be out at night, walking, and then I'd be on your block."

"You never thought to knock?"

"I never thought you'd open."

She wondered whether she would have. The wine arrived, poured into glasses. They drank without toasting. The room was full of murmurs, the keen of a jazz record, someone's too-sharp laugh, someone else's sharp perfume.

Ignazio fingered the stem of his glass. "You never came back." It was not a question, and she would not have had an answer if it had been. "There's a hole in the family."

Eva smoked. Behind him, the woman with bleached hair was gorging on her friend's confessions, elbows on the table, patent-leather foot wagging beneath it.

"Do you hate me?" He said it to the crimson tabletop.

She swirled her wine. She sipped. It warmed her throat. "No."

He struck another match. In its brief light he looked hopeful in an almost boyish way. Once, she thought, he had actually been a boy, somewhere in Italy and then at a steamboat's rail, smoking cigarettes like this one, on his ride to Uruguay, alight, alone, leagues away from home. "I'm going to die," he said.

"Papá. You're sick?"

"No. Just old."

"Not so very old."

"Older than my father ever got."

The mention of his father shocked her. She knew absolutely nothing about him. "Old and dead are two different things."

He shrugged. "I want you to forgive me."

"For what?"

He fingered the stem of his wineglass. "For all of it. For never hearing your side of the story."

Her cigarette was down to the filter. She stamped it out.

"I could hear it now?"

She touched the underside of the table. It was cold; it was sticky; it would soil her hands. "No."

"Or we could leave it in the past."

"Better."

Ignazio stared at the ashtray as if it held a ciphered mystery. "Will you come to the house?"

She busied herself lighting a cigarette. The sharp laugh cut the air again, then stopped, caught in a spiderweb of voices. "Yes."

"And forgive me?"

She blew out smoke, inhaled again. "Why not."

He coughed. He marveled at her fingers, with their carefully lacquered nails. "You look very nice. **Este . . .** how are things with your family?"

Eva laughed. She was light, she was drunk, it was not the wine. "Oh, fine. My husband left."

"Left where?"

"Left me."

"What?"

Eva smiled, absurdly. The woman with bleached hair was gone; her chair held nothing but a crumpled napkin.

"Come live with us."

"I'll be fine," she said, a bit too quickly.

"But still. If you need anything. Food. Money. A place to stay."

Eva thought of the sand-colored house, with its cluttered rooms, its warmth and bustle, the table heavy with plates, forsaken corners she recalled in minute detail. "Thank you."

He shrugged again. "More wine?"

Eva rose to the fifteenth floor. Zolá opened the door. "What a surprise."

"Are you free?"

"Absolutely."

Eva entered. Zolá closed the door. She wore a lilac blouse and she looked lovely, a hothouse blossom, rare, hybrid, labyrinthine.

"Roberto's left for Buenos Aires."

"Already?"

"Without me."

"Oh. I'm sorry."

"Don't be. That's not what I came for."

"You'd like a wash?"

"Zolá." Eva stepped closer. She wasn't sure how to start. She touched Zolá's face, and Zolá's eyes widened with a response that looked like pain. The air roared, and then nothing mattered, they were already inside, they kissed and two mouths moved into each other, damp, pressing, Zolá pressing against her, Zolá's hands in her hair, warm, firm, seeking, more hungry than she'd known, and then she did it, let her hands rove, let them loose on Zolá's body like two beasts rooting for food.

"Can this be?" Zolá said. "Can this really be?"

"Yes," Eva said. "Oh yes it can."

Heaven, she thought, is not in the sky but in skin and skin and skin—

They lay next to each other in the dark, having made love in the dark, to the dark, with the dark holding them like a great cupped hand. Eva thought, I never want to leave, I want to inhabit this place suffused with the scents we have created, with the imprint of what our bodies and voices have done. I want to stay, forever, in this body blended with another body, discovering our cries and pores and lost hollows where longing furls, has furled for years, hungry to release its secret colors.

"I want to stay forever," she said.

"Then stay."

"I mean, I'll go. The children. But leave myself here in a film of sweat between your sheets."

"Mm."

"And never leave you."

"Mmm."

"Your body, Zolá—"

"Shhh."

"It's a miracle."

"Eva."

"It is."

"Eva."

"Never leave me."

"Never."

"Are you crying?"

"Never. Never."

She launched a new life, gently, from the catapult of her own hands. She found a job in a café three blocks from home. The pay was low but her fellow waitresses had mouths full of laughter, and her boss, a generous septuagenarian, sent her home each day with paper boxes of croissants or guava tarts or empanadas for the children. They ate these little gifts for breakfast or lunch or dinner, sometimes right from the box, its white walls stained with spheres of oil. The three of them sat around the kitchen table and ate the pastries with their fingers. Roberto always took his apart methodically, as if he needed to investigate the contents before tasting. Salomé closed her eyes before she bit, as though tasting the filling might require an act of faith. They often ate in silence. They had become taciturn since their father left. At first, Roberto asked daily where his father was, and the answers—still in Buenos Aires; no, not coming back; it would be the three of them now—were not sufficient to keep the questions from returning. But soon the repetition seemed to bore him, and the questions fell away, leaving the quiet sounds of teeth and spoons.

They did not always eat at home. She began to take them to her parents' house in Punta Carretas. The first time they went, she stood in the living room while her father embraced her children, thinking, I am not nineteen, not eleven, not a child at war, not running away in the middle of the night. Her children's bodies fit so easily against their Abuelo Ignazio, as if they had been basking in his affection all their lives. Five minutes and he was already making them laugh, already promising magic tricks after dinner. As long as you eat all your carrots, he said, winking. Roberto nodded earnestly, Salomé shone. At the dinner table, Eva watched her children eat their vegetables first, a phenomenon she'd never seen before. Afterward, she helped her mother in the kitchen while Ignazio and the children retired to the living room for the show.

"They love him," Eva said, trying to sound neutral.

Pajarita smiled. "He's ten times more excited than they are."

They washed the dishes, Pajarita scrubbing, Eva

drying and putting things away. The cups and forks and pots still inhabited the same shelves of the same cupboards as always; they were home, they had a place, they belonged. The counters were still crowded with potted plants and jars of dried leaves and roots and barks that could make a housewife sigh with relief or a daughter find her legs. Eva didn't know what to say to her mother, but it didn't seem to matter; a gentle silence hung between them, interwoven with the sound of running water, clinking plates, and young laughter rising down the hall.

On other nights, they went to Xhana's house, where Artigas and César played with the children. They wrote songs that cast Salomé and Roberto as the heroes, a princess saved by gauchos from tall towers, a prince saving villages from kings. If they didn't like the story, they could change it, but it meant they had to sing. The children glowed in the warmth of Xhana's home, the noise of it, the beat of drums and swell of voices. The family crammed around the gingham table for dinner, arms touching, while Tía Xhana cut Salomé's meat and told stories that chronicled the history of Uruguay: a revolution fought by **indios** and freed slaves, a president who built schools for everybody, factories where people stopped working because they were not happy, brave people who, as she told it, had stood up for their country, for Uruguay, and made it so that they could have this table and food and nice family.

"Let them eat, **querida,**" César said.

"They can hear a little history while they eat. Right, **chicos**?"

Roberto peered into his mashed potatoes. Eva nudged him.

"Yes," he said.

"Yes," Salomé said. She looked rapt, swept up by Xhana's stories. Eva was swept up too; she thought of Argentina, with its long succession of dictators; in comparison, Uruguay had a unique story, a remarkable story, one that proved that a robust democracy—with literacy, labor rights, health care—could exist in Latin America, could be created again in other countries. She said this once, and drew skepticism from the table.

"I wish you were right, **prima,**" Xhana said, "but it's not that simple. All that could become a thing of the past."

"If it hasn't already," Artigas said.

Eva put her fork down. "How can that be?"

"Look what's happened since the end of the Korean War. The United States no longer needs our wool to clothe their soldiers, our beef to feed them."

"Right."

"And so today we have inflation, the fall of salaries, the rising costs. We can't export anything, but we're still forced to import."

"We never should have based our economy on war," César said, so passionately that even Roberto looked up from his plate.

"**Sí, querido,** but what choice did we have? A

small nation like ours? How could we survive without selling to the giants?"

"That's exactly the question to ask now," Artigas said. "We have to find a better way than this. Look at all the unrest this year, the strikes, the arrest of union leaders. The government is not on the workers' side, not anymore."

"They can't be; they're too fractured."

"They're corrupt."

"It has to change."

"It won't."

"Then the people will," said Xhana.

Salomé was listening so intently that the meat had fallen off her fork; she held it absently, spearing the empty air. Eva felt a dual urge to plunge into the conversation—to say this couldn't be, Uruguay was not so fragile, hard times had come and gone before and would surely pass again—and to move it in a wholly new direction, away from anything that could sound to young ears like danger, like a cause for leaving home, as they had done once before. She admired Xhana, with her communist committee meetings, her flyers for labor strikes, her unrelenting analysis of social issues, but she was torn between the instinct to join in and the instinct to protect her family. It was just her now with the children, and they had so much less than before, and yes, true, no one was getting exiled from Uruguay, and surely no one would be, but still, if, if, where would they go? Better to support the struggle in the ways she could, from a distance, in the realm of poetry, and poetry, after all, did matter; words did matter; her weapons were her words.

When they stayed over late, the children fell asleep in Tío Artigas' bed, and Eva and Xhana would spend time alone in the kitchen.

"Have another, Eva."

"Thanks, Xhana. I really am full."

"Any news from Roberto?"

"A letter. He's landed, he's settled in. I suppose he's doing fine."

"Are you getting a divorce?"

"We can't."

"Why not?"

"It's illegal in Argentina."

"So you can't remarry."

"Not that I was going to."

"But in the future, Eva?"

She hesitated for a long time, surely too long. "My future is with my children."

"You could still meet another man."

She didn't mean to laugh, and tried to suppress it, so the sound came out twisted into a witch's cackle. "Let's not count on it."

There was no thought of marriage, no thought of any lover but Zolá, whom she saw several times a week, after work, or before work, or during hair appointments, while her children were under their grandparents' watchful care. She wanted to grow old with Zolá, wanted to know how her touch would feel on wrinkled skin, what age would do to their two naked bodies. She wanted to dig deep into Zolá and curl up at her center, make a nest there, never leave. She wanted Zolá to fill her, again, again, to walk the streets full of her lover's fingers, baptized by her tongue. All their moments were stolen and there were never enough. **Tell me more. Tell me your heart, the whole of it. I was born to touch you, my life for this, my hand along your skin.** Once, years ago, she had wanted to die; now she raged that there was not enough life, that they did not have a thousand years to spend, that one day their pockets would be emptied of days. They had only little coins of time and they spent and spent and spent them, polished them with their pleasure, made them gleam. So this is what joy does to a woman, she thought: it makes you hungry, makes you long to live and live, makes you guard the secret at any cost, wakes the animal inside and makes her growl to break the heavens into pieces.

Fall came and draped the streets with leaves begging to be crushed underfoot. Eva felt them crack against her soles; sometimes she broke them lovingly, a slow, heavy caress, and other times she brought force into her step, imagining they were her husband's face. Roberto had been forgetting to send money. That's what he said when she called him: I've forgotten, yes, yes, I'll send it soon. His voice was tense

and he rushed to hang up, the woman who'd answered the phone surely tapping her foot in the background. And Eva believed him, that he'd meant to
send the money, that it had slipped his mind, that
Montevideo was simply drifting farther and farther
from the scope of his thoughts. It was a small sum to
him, after all; a trifle. Eva kicked a little pile of leaves
as she walked through it. Rent was due in four days,
and she did not have enough.

She confided in Xhana, in her kitchen at 2 a.m.

"Call him."

"I already have."

"Call him every day."

"The woman clearly doesn't like me."

"Who cares? This is his responsibility."

"I'm not a charity case."

"Of course not. They're his children."

Eva lit a cigarette. "They're mine."

Xhana watched the smoke rise into the air in curls.
"I can lend you the rent."

"Thank you."

They sat in silence while Eva smoked.

"I just don't want to need him."

"You could leave your apartment."

"Where would I go?"

"You're welcome here, but there's more room at
your parents' house."

"I can't do that."

"Why not?"

Eva shrugged.

"You see your father a lot now, don't you?"

"Yes."

"And things are fine?"

"Overall."

"Except?"

"I keep waiting for things to sour."

"Maybe they won't."

"Maybe."

Xhana watched her put out her cigarette. "How is the book?"

The knot in Eva loosened, began to glow. "Almost ready."

It was coming out in three weeks. **The Widest River in the World.** A slim volume, a simple jacket with a line drawing of a naked woman silhouetted against a shore. Between the covers, poems sang of hunger and dawn and beloved cities, milk-filled breasts and haunted nights, passions without names and beauty without reason, a young man bleeding in a Buenos Aires cell, Marxists dreaming over a gingham table. The first time she held a copy in her hands, she thought of the girl who dropped out of school at the age of ten, and wished she could reach back through time and open the book before her eyes. That girl breathed between these pages, as did all the girls and women she had been; they stalked the lines of words like phantoms; she half expected the pages to feel humid from their constant exhalations. Two people could read this book, or two thousand—it didn't matter. It existed, she existed, she had sung.

Xhana and Pajarita organized a party to celebrate the publication, at the house in Punta Carretas. They cooked for days, filled the house with fresh-cut flowers, and shooed Eva from the kitchen when she tried to help. She felt a bit like a bride, the bride she would have been if she had married at home, as was the custom. She stood in front of the mirror, applying her lipstick, and imagined herself a bride, tonight, at thirty, in her red silk dress, only who would she be preparing to marry? The woman in the mirror stared and did not blush.

The guests filled the house to bursting, from people she knew well—Bruno, Marco, Tomás, Xhana, Artigas, Coco, Cacho, all the women from the neighborhood, all their families—to poets she'd recently met, and poets whom she hadn't seen in years: Beatriz, Joaquín, and the Well-Known Poet arrived together and bellowed with joy as they embraced her. Beatriz, in particular, seemed hungry to talk. She had changed; her hair was a natural brown, she'd married Joaquín, she'd founded a women poets' collective, would Eva like to join?

"I'd love to," Eva said.

"Wonderful. I can't wait to read your book."

"Thank you."

"Tell me something." Beatriz lowered her voice. "Did you really run away with Andrés?"

Eva fingered her wineglass. "In a fashion."

"I thought so. I really did. Where is he now?"

"That's anyone's guess."

"I see," Beatriz said, and Eva felt the sting of disappointment in her voice.

"Some say he started a new life in Paris."

"Paris!"

Eva smiled. She couldn't help it. "Who knows?"

Later in the evening, at the insistence of the crowd, she read some poems out loud. She stood in front of the living room window, framed by the cool prison walls, and almost wept at the force of the applause, it shook her open, she'd had too much wine, the sound filled her body like a hot sweet drink. After the reading, someone turned the music up, and the crowd began to dance; first she danced with her father, then with Artigas, then with Xhana, then in a circle of fellow poets, and finally alone, among couples, moving her body so the silk of her dress caressed her, red silk, she thought, closing her eyes, what a color for a bride, what a night for an elopement—I could vow inside right now as music moves my hips and nobody would know; why not, who cares if it's impossible, the possible with all its lies and walls can go to hell; the beat is good and raw, my eyes are closed, and you, you, poetry, what kind of groom are you, alluring, unfathomable, after all these years I still don't know what you promise or what you are, but I do know you've never left me; you're the only one that stayed close against my skin, my hands, my sex, my mind, my nights, when I had nothing and was nothing you were with me; rocked me; filled me; come closer, my groom, the heat of my skin and the

push of my breath and the salt of my days I am giving them to you, for better or worse, they are yours,
I am yours, I do. I do. She opened her eyes. The
room was packed. She looked for Zolá, though of
course she hadn't come, as she could not risk recognition; Eva felt her absence like a tear in her own
dress, but she held on to what Zolá had said the
night before, surprising Eva with a candlelit bedroom
crowded with fresh roses, **I'll be there, I'm with you
always.** She scanned for the children. Roberto was
eating empanadas with his cousins Félix and Raúl.
He looked so serious in his shirt and tie, like a miniature man. She looked on, for her daughter, but
couldn't find her. Salomé. Salomé. The house was full
of good adults and this was not a shoe store, there
was no reason for panic, but it came anyway, gutted
her with its instinctive maul, and she pressed through
her guests to the kitchen, where Pajarita stood frying **buñuelos** and did not know where Salomé had
gone, rushed down the hall and into every room
until she opened the door of her old bedroom and
found her daughter sleeping in the dark.

She perched at the edge of the bed, and let her eyes
adjust until she saw the curl of Salomé's body, the
dark splay of her braids, the crush of her ruffled party
dress. Her breath calmed, and she almost laughed at
her own flush of terror, but she didn't want to break
the quiet.

We'll be fine. All of us. The thought swept over
her with its plush comfort. We can move into this

house and we'll be fine. There was a delicate grace to this night, in which it all seemed possible, all the thirst and also all its quenching; the world itself felt different, vaster, dazzling, an ocean of a world where men and women pushed their lives forward like waves; perhaps no surge (no written word no broken night no steam-in-the-dark secret) went unwasted; perhaps they fed the swell of life to come. She could crush this little girl against her, show her viscerally that she'd be safe and free, two things she herself was not in the years she slept in this same bed; safe and free and loved with such ferocity that nothing could keep her from the bright crests of her destiny. But she didn't want to wake her, so instead, Eva etched the promise in her mind.

Salomé slept through all of it, far away on a raft of dreams.

SALOMÉ

THE WORLD IS PUSHED
BY MANY HANDS

Some questions were not for asking. For example, the question of how Papá could be across the river when beyond the river you saw nothing but the sky. Questions about sky and fathers and many other things, they were just for turning on the great wheel of your breath; you inhale without knowing, you exhale the same. Gathered up inside, questions keep their intensity, circulating through you, gusts of their own. Better not to ask too much, better not to make Mamá sad, to chase away her laugh that broke the air to sharp and golden shreds, her smell of flowers and sweat and almonds, her presence itself, smoking, leaning, writing, composing secret messages to strangers or to God. And so Salomé did not ask why they were moving. In any case, she didn't mind; she liked her grandparents' house, with its ivory prison outside and the sleek wind in the oaks, its smells inside of onions frying, rosemary drying, Abuelo's cologne as he gripped her in a tight embrace. Abuela always piled food high on white plates that had tiny pink flowers. Abuelo Ignazio told them stories while they ate: about his adventurous youth in the **campo;** the ride and shine and gamble of it all; the water-streets of Italy, the boats he used to build, and how his heart was stolen by a beautiful woman adept at sleight of hand.

"She stole it, I swear—right out of my sleeve! I never got it back." He pointed at Abuela Pajarita with his thumb. "This one here. She leaped out of the crowd like that Wonder Woman lady."

Abuela smiled. She looked small and old. Salomé pictured her in Wonder Woman's bright bikini, lasso in hand.

"Eat, Salomé!" Abuelo said. "You're growing."

After dinner, Abuelo played with the enthusiasm of a fellow child. He showed them many things: how to play poker, how to bet with cow bones, the card tricks he'd once done on a stage. He shuffled extravagantly, cards flying through the air in a blurred arc. He spread the deck on the table with scarred hands. **Pick one.** She looked and picked. Then back it went, and shuffle shuffle, while his mouth told a tale or riddle. The cards spread out. He told her to pick another, and she obeyed. He knew—amazing!—exactly what card it was. He grinned at her expression, and leaned in close, wine sweetsharp on his breath.

"Do you want to know the secret?"

Salomé nodded.

"Promise not to tell?"

"Promise."

"The trick is to keep their attention on one hand, and work your magic with the other."

Salomé let the trick sink into her, never guessing how, when she was older, stroking guns in a dim room, it would resurface like a buoy in her mind.

As she packed, Mamá would stop in the middle of a gesture to stare out into space, book or dish or box flap in hand, as if something had entered the room that only she could see. She would stay that way, frozen, even if Roberto or Salomé called her name. The morning of the move, the two of them got up early, and toasted bread together for their mother, without discussing it, there was no need to say **she's far away and so let us make toast.** The living room towered with boxes, piled everywhere, marked in pen. Salomé was five now, old enough to put the bread on the griddle, though not to take it off, and old enough to dab cold water into the **mate** though Roberto still did the hot. They brought the tray to Mamá's room. They found her standing on the balcony, in her nightgown, her back to them.

"Mamá," Roberto said.

She turned quickly. She was beautiful, even with that faraway look of hers that revealed nothing. They raised the breakfast tray toward her, a hopeful offering.

"Oh. Thank you so much. Good morning."

Mamá's brothers helped carry and unload boxes.

They arrived at the Punta Carretas house in a flurry
of motion. Her grandparents were waiting for them
with fresh lemonade. Tío Marco approached Eva
with a big unlabeled box. "What's this?"

"Nothing."

"Damn heavy for nothing."

"It goes in my closet," Mamá said quickly.

Salomé wondered what the box contained. She
followed Tío Marco and watched him stow it in the
closet, on a shelf too high to reach. She carried a box
of toys to her new room. She looked around. It was
the same room Mami had grown up in, with its long
window over the bed, overlooking a single tree, and
its frayed lamp and creaky drawers. She tried to
imagine Mami, in that bed, as a child, but she could
only see her mother, all grown up but smaller, smoking a cigarette between the sheets.

"Wonderful," Abuelo said that night. "The house
is full again. I don't like to see it empty."

It seemed, to Salomé, a strange thing to say. The
house was always full. Some nights, it swelled with
tíos—Bruno, Marco, Tomás—and tías—Mirna,
Raquel, Carlota—and cousins: Elena and Carlos and
Raúl and Javier and Aquiles and Paula and Félix and
Mario and Carmencita and Pilar. Abuela Pajarita
worked a magic of her own: the table stretched, the
walls pulled back, room appeared for every member
of the family. The house roared with banter, gossip,
quibbles, toasting glasses, shocks of laughter, squeals
from boys. Mounds of food were reduced to crumbs.

Card games extended late into the night. People sprawled everywhere. Salomé watched her uncles' games of poker, played gauchos with her cousins (Aquiles the bull-skinner, Carmencita the wound-healer, Félix the villainous **estanciero**), and sometimes, when quiet called her, retreated to the kitchen and drew pictures to the sound of washing dishes.

"Look at Salomé," Tía Mirna said. "Such a good girl. So quiet and still."

"It's true," Mamá said, sounding perplexed. "She's very good."

She spent many hours alone, submerged in private games. The buttons from Abuela's sewing basket kept her rapt for days. She sorted them by size, color, texture, shape. They had parades. They formed families. They were a village of small round things, full of dramas and adventures. Metallic buttons were all merchants—grocers, butchers, spinners of wool. Green ones were clever. Pink ones were prone to fall in love. Little buttons tended to get picked on, and the biggest button, a velour veteran from an old coat, often came to their rescue. Every button had a story; every button could belong. The epic loves and struggles were invisible to the rest of the family; they saw only a good girl, unobtrusive, shifting little discs around in silence.

She and Roberto had a hallowed place for silence: a swamp at the edge of town, the last stop of the bus. They went there sometimes with sandwiches and coins for the ride home—to get a little air, as Mamá

put it. The air out there was wide and cool and redolent. She drew pictures. She stared out at the gliding
ducks, the breezy reeds, the opulent trajectories of
bugs. Roberto caught frogs and poked them, released
them back into the mud, and scrawled in his notebook.

"What are you doing?"

"Research."

She looked out across the swamp and wondered
what he'd find. Roberto was going to be a famous
scientist, like Papá. "Your brother is a genius," her
teacher had said on her very first day of school. "Let's
see how you measure up." Salomé didn't know what
"Measure Up" meant, but she knew she longed to do
it. She paid attention in class, did all her homework,
recited the alphabet on her walks to and from school,
a letter for each step. When she got to the end, she
took three **Z** steps, for good luck. She wrote her
name in big block letters. She cut out hearts and dec-
orated them carefully with dry pasta, felt, and shells
from the river's edge. She learned how to put numbers together to make new numbers, and, toward the
end of her first year, began to read. Black lines and
curves became sounds in her mind. She wanted to
be able to read everything: street signs, schoolwork,
her mother's book with poems in it she herself had
written, now alive on shelves throughout the city. In
the afternoons, she studied beside her brother in the
kitchen, until it was time to set the table.

"You two study so much!" Abuelo said. "Roberto,

don't you ever want to go play soccer? Stir up some trouble?"

Roberto looked ruffled.

"Papá," Mamá said sharply.

"I'm just saying, Eva, that he could have a little fun."

"He does have fun."

"He needs a man, Eva, to show him—"

"That's enough," Mamá said. Quiet stretched over the table, covering the serving bowls, the plates, the forks going about their business, clink, clink. Mamá put her knife down, slowly.

"Roberto," Abuela Pajarita said, "do you like to study?"

"Yes."

"And you, Salomé?"

"Yes."

"Then what's the problem?"

Mamá looked gratefully at her mother. "Their grades are perfect. They're going to go to university, and become whatever they want. Both of them."

Abuelo Ignazio stared into his wineglass. "Of course."

Salomé swirled spaghetti on her fork. University. It was years and years away but still it loomed like a castle on the horizon. She would enter it one day and become something, whatever she wanted, and surely there were great things to become.

One day, Mamá came home sad because her boss had cut her hours at work. He had done it because it was a difficult time, he said, there was less money in everybody's pockets, and Salomé imagined coats and pants and shirt fronts from which coins and paper bills mysteriously disappeared, throughout the city, and people shook their heads, bewildered: where did all the pesos go?

A week later, when Salomé and Roberto came home from school, she was waiting for them in the kitchen.

"Before you start your homework, we need to talk."

They sat down.

"You know that swamp you go to?"

They nodded.

"You can't ever go back."

Roberto looked devastated. "Why not?"

"Because it's dangerous."

Salomé thought of vicious ducks, mud turned extra-slippery.

"Dangerous, how?" Roberto said.

"It's become a **cantegril.**"

A new word for Salomé, **cantegril. Cante,** like **cantar,** to sing: a place, perhaps, with too much singing. "What's that?"

Mamá hesitated. She wore a white shirt with pearly buttons down the front. The sewing basket had three such buttons, dreamy spinsters all in love with Big Velour. "It's a new kind of place. Where people live. But not . . . a good place."

"So why do they live there?"

"Because they have nowhere else to go."

Roberto puzzled over this. "But—"

"Roberto. No more questions." She folded her arms across her chest. "No more swamp."

That night in bed, Salomé tried to imagine a **cantegril.** Not a Good Place to Live. She saw men crying on doorsteps, families sulking over their **churrasco,** children losing soccer balls on the street, women hanging laundry as they sang maudlin songs. She looked out the window at a stubborn slice of moon. It peered between the branches of the oak. Surely it saw everything, that moon: her mother's tears, the **cantegril,** the streets, the river hungry to reflect the light. She wanted to see everything. She wanted to understand. It was bad to break a rule, but if she didn't she would never see or know. She couldn't sleep. She turned back and forth, back and forth, until the sky framed by her window turned to sapphire blue. As she turned, her quilt rustled softly against her body. The quilt was made of triangles of blue and green cloth, and it crinkled, as if someone—Abuelita Pajarita, she was the one who'd sewn it—had been cooking and spilled spices between the seams. She imagined the accident, her abuela in the kitchen, trying to cook and sew at the same time, ladle in one hand, needle in the other, spices tipping into cloth from one of her glass jars, seeds and roots and crumbled leaves, and now she felt them raining on her, forming a long blanket, and she finally slept.

Two days later, she took the bus, alone, toward the swamp. The bus emptied as it approached the city's edge. It was a clear day, and Monte-video looked so pretty with its cobbled streets, its flat-roofed houses topped with laundry lines, its grocers with their wooden crates of fruit. By the time the bus approached her stop, she was the only passenger left, and the bus driver stared at her in his rearview mirror, a seven-year-old girl sitting alone.

"**Che, chica,** where do you think you're going?"

"To the next stop."

"I'm not letting you off there."

"Why not?"

"It's dangerous."

"But people live there."

"Exactly. Does your mother know you're here?"

Heat rushed through her. "Please, Señor, if you could stop? I'll just look through the window."

The driver's eyebrows, thick as black thumbs, pressed together. He pulled up to the stop without opening the door. Salomé looked out.

She had imagined people crying at doorsteps but there were no doorsteps to cry at, no houses built, no cobbled streets on which to lose your soccer ball. The swamp was still raw and unrazed; shacks stood on top of it. The walls were made of cardboard and corrugated metal (I'll huff and I'll puff, she thought). They were everywhere. Between the shacks, reeds hung their heads in pools of pee and caca. The smell reared up at her through a crack in the window. People swarmed: a girl with bare feet and a tattered skirt piled newspapers for a fire, a naked baby crawled over a pile of rotting rinds, a shirtless man fed straw to a scruffy horse and stared hard at the bus. At her. She looked away, but she had already seen his ribs, and the horse's too. She felt the heave of vomit in her throat. The low moan of the engine rose to a growl, and they drove away.

Back at home, Salomé could not concentrate on her homework. The numbers on the page kept turning into people—emaciated 7, barefoot 4, a whole family crushed into a cardboard 3. She was restless. She was voracious. She had broken a rule, and perhaps the sky would fall, but to her amazement it hadn't fallen yet, and her world was different for the breaking. She felt a thrill of heat and shame and victory. She wanted to cry for the people she had seen. She wanted to lay bare the secrets in her reach.

Mamá was out getting her hair done; she had a little time.

She slipped into her mother's room, and went to the closet. She stood on a chair. The unmarked box was high and heavy, but she took her time, inching it forward, little by little, until the bulk of its weight was in her arms. It was too heavy for her to carry to the floor without crashing. She pushed it, incrementally, back into place.

She was not strong enough. Not yet.

———

The news from Cuba came on New Year's Day, 1959. Cuba, a small, dense word, full of energy, tight coil shooting into flight, exploding from the radio, **Cuba, Cuba,** darting from drunk people's mouths. Salomé didn't know what the word meant, but she heard pure power in the radio voices, the crackling declarations from a city called Havana, the crowd in Tía Xhana's kitchen. After almost all the guests had left, and even Xhana and César had gone to bed, Mamá and Tío Artigas stayed up listening to the radio. Morning light filled the apartment. Salomé was supposed to be asleep in Tío Artigas' bed, but she woke to a sharp laugh from the kitchen, her mother's laugh. She rose, cracked open the bedroom door, knelt down, and strained for voices from the kitchen.

"I still can't believe it."

"Believe it, Eva." Tío Artigas sounded like a man on a high ledge. "This is the first of many revolutions."

"You think so?"

"You'll see." A liquid poured into glasses. "It'll sweep the continent. Just think about it. Why are wages falling? Why are unions striking?"

"The economy."

"What shapes the economy?"

Salomé shifted her weight from the ball of one foot to the other, quietly, curling low against her knees.

"The market."

"The **yanquis.**"

"Oh, I don't know—"

"Come on. Of course it's true. They turn down our wool, and—**¡páfate!**—farmers are out of work. They lend us money and what happens? They tell our government what it can and can't do for its people. You think Eisenhower cares about **cantegriles**?"

"Things aren't as desperate here as in Cuba. We haven't had a dictator in almost sixty years. There's no comparison."

"Of course there is. You just can't see it because you still believe the dream of **batllismo**."

"**Ay,** Tío, that's not fair."

A man shouted on the radio, but Salomé could not make out his words, only the fierce, bright static that surrounded them.

"He sounds like an **argentino**."

"He is. Ernesto Guevara is his real name."

Mamá laughed. "Are you joking?"

"No."

"I met him once. When Salomé was born."

Salomé felt her hands grow hot.

"Che left to be of use. Same as I'm doing now."

"What?"

"I'm leaving."

"Where to?"

"Cuba."

"When?"

"Very soon."

Mami's silence bloomed like an angry flower.

"Eva. Think about it. No one needs me here."

"Xhana—"

"Loves me, but doesn't need me. And I've been waiting for this for many years." His voice grew teasing. "You could come."

Salomé saw a ship, and herself on it, with Tío and Mamá, sailing toward a far-off destination. It was a white ship, freshly painted, solid against the seas.

Mamá was terse. "I'm needed here."

"Of course. I know. The children." A teasing edge, again. "Or your hairdresser."

"Tío—"

"Yes?"

Silence in the kitchen.

"Eva, I don't judge you. Really."

More silence. Salomé's legs grew sore, but she didn't move.

"What do you plan to do there?"

"Whatever they need. Build, work. I'll go south into the island if they want. I've survived in the jungle before."

"That was ages ago. You're sixty-three."

"Well, then, a perfect age to retire in the Caribbean. Come on, Eva, don't be sad."

Mami sighed. Salomé felt that sigh as if her lungs had made it. "I'll miss you terribly. You'd better write to us."

It happened quickly. Tío Artí took one night to pack, and two days to find a ship that would carry him to Cuba. The night he left, Salomé stood in a throng of family at the Montevideo port, waving a handkerchief at Tío Artí on the deck. He got smaller and smaller as he waved back. It was a humid summer night, and sweat glistened on everybody's forehead. Later, the thick heat wouldn't let her sleep. She lay in bed and thought of the stories Tía Xhana had always told, of brave people who had stood up for their country, people Salomé had always imagined standing in a big circle around her, ghostly, shimmering, watching, standing up, sitting down, standing up again, over and over, for their country, to make history, in a slow and soundless dance. They rose up, now, from the dark. She saw them clearly, saw them reach out glowing hands. Where will you go? they said, and she said, Cuba. They grasped her hands and whisked her, whisked her through the air until she landed in a forest. Che was there, smiling, covered in sweat and mud. I've been waiting for you, he said, since you were born. He handed her a gourd of **mate.** She drank. The forest was wet and rich and dark. Tío Artigas emerged from the foliage, also muddy, a rifle slung over his shoulder. He saw her and said, Salomé, are you ready to rise up? She nodded. He handed her the gun. She hung it from her shoulder and suddenly she too was covered in mud, perfectly radiant, perfectly fearless, perfectly strong. Then Che grinned, bent to kiss her forehead like a father, and said, Let's go.

That summer, Mamá took them to the beach. Salomé and Roberto packed towels and books and the three strolled down La Rambla, all the way to the stone steps that led to the shore. The descent was the best part: when all the supple crush of sand spread out before you, waiting for the baring of your feet, urging you to slide your sandals off, sink toes into the grains, fine, pale, hot from summer sun, stretching all the way to sparkling foam. They read quietly on towels until heat forced them all into the water, where they splashed one another in small, chaotic wars.

Cuba sent ripples through the city: whispers, loud praise, discussions on the radio, Cuban flags and LONG LIVE THE REVOLUTION banners pasted into windows. Mamá was different too. She wrote fiercely. Poems poured out of her, carpeting the floor, pages and pages of fresh verse.

"What on earth are you writing about?" Abuelo Ignazio said.

"Everything. Politics, change, the way things could be."

"What for?"

"For?"

"Why write it down?"

"Writing is essential."

"Hmmph. You can't eat a poem."

School began. Salomé learned to read whole lines of text. She learned to split oranges into halves and thirds that could be added and subtracted from one another. One day in June, Tía Xhana swept in from the cold. She peeled off her coat and scarf and hat. Through the window, Salomé saw the oaks slash their branches against the prison walls.

"He wrote." Xhana held up an envelope. She looked bright, freshly polished. "Papá wrote."

They gathered around the kitchen table. Abuela Pajarita pulled empanadas from the oven. Abuelo had been reading **El País** at the table. Beside him, Roberto pored over algebra. Abuelita stood still, holding an empty baking sheet. Xhana read aloud.

> **Dear** Familia,
> **Hello hello I miss you so much you can't imagine. When I landed here I was in one piece and I still am. I sweat a lot and do not sleep and I am happy. There is so much work to do. Mostly I've been helping turn casinos into schools, private companies into national factories. What belonged to the rich now belongs to the people. The U.S.A. is not happy—we will see how long they buy our sugar. They want their companies back. Nothing is certain, it all depends on hope. And work, of course, always that. I am studying the music of Havana. Such music. African rhythms, similar and different to our candombe. Everything is different and similar.**
> **Everybody please take care of everybody—**
> **Kisses and more,**
> **Artigas**

"Thank God," said Abuela. "The man has finally learned to write home." She brought empanadas to the table. Hands attacked the platter from all sides.

"Sounds like he's doing well," Mamá said.

"Well?" Abuelo said. "He's going to break his back. And what for?"

"To build a better country," Mamá snapped.

Abuelo drew himself up, but Xhana raised a hand to stop him. "First of all, Pajarita, the empanadas are delicious." There were murmurs of agreement. "So that's unanimous. Tío, think of it this way. Think of Uruguay. How much have pensions been cut?"

"Too much."

"Not much left for the elderly."

"No."

"A bag of potatoes, perhaps."

Abuelo ceded the point with a nod.

"Why do you think that's happened?"

Abuelo reached for another empanada. Beside him, Roberto resumed his equations. "Times are hard. Our industries are struggling."

"And what else?"

Ignazio shrugged.

"Debt to the **yanquis,** Tío."

"That's right." Mamá leaned forward, casting a shadow over Roberto's page. He put his pencil down, too hard. "We're taking from our own people to give to those who have the most."

"Debts should be paid off," Abuelo said.

"Not at the expense of workers," said Mamá.

"Hmmph."

"What do you mean, 'hmmph'?"

"That's just what communists say."

Mamá tightened.

"Of course," Xhana said. "I'm a communist."

Abuelo Ignazio looked at Eva. "Are you, **hija**?"

"I'm not sure yet."

Abuelo sighed. "Whatever happened to old-fashioned **batllismo**?"

"Our leaders sold it," Xhana said, "to the highest bidder."

Abuelo Ignazio turned to his wife. "Pajarita, did you know your niece was a communist?"

"Of course."

"What do you think of that?"

"I hope she stays for dinner."

"And what about your own daughter?"

"I hope she stays for dinner too."

Mami laughed. Abuelo Ignazio slunk his shoulders in an exaggerated gesture of defeat.

"I'd love to," Xhana said.

She was eleven years old, a good girl, a plain girl, with two braids that hung limp and thin against her collar, despite Mamá's attempts to enrich her hair, the salves, washes, fragrant shampoos, olive oil soaks that left her smelling like a salad. Nothing worked; she stayed plain. The years that lay in wait mystified and terrified and thrilled her. She wanted to shoot up into new skin, the way Roberto had, fourteen now, separate from her, almost a man, taking a blade to his face in the mornings. They did not cleave to each other anymore. She was alone. She wasn't good at making friends, though there were girls at school who asked her over when they needed help with homework, and in their homes she saw their mothers, aprons tied around broad waists, hair pulled back brusquely as if they didn't care, as if they had more important things to think about than hairstyles. They baked and cleaned and waited for their husbands and did not write poems or seem to have secrets tucked in their closets or clothes or morning errands. She didn't go often. She read constantly. In some stories, very old ones, there were girls who weren't really girls but sprites belonging to the forest, at home inside a tree trunk or reed or river, and she looked, sometimes, on city streets, in her city that was growing a ring of **cantegriles**—far from where she was, but she had seen one, knew its sad, crowded shacks, kept seeing them in dreams—for fairies or ghosts or witches who might open sudden doors in the thin air.

She won a scholarship to a private school. So did Roberto. She didn't know about the application until Mamá showed her the acceptance letter.

"You're happy, aren't you?"

Salomé nodded. She thought of Crandon, a big white building crawling with ivy. She had seen it only through iron gates.

"Come here, **hija.**"

She let her mother hold her. Her hair smelled like sweet almonds. They both pretended she was not too big to be gathered on a lap.

"When I was your age, I left school. Did you know?"

She hadn't known.

"I worked in a store."

She tried to imagine this, young Mamá, selling carrots or blouses or toys while lessons went unattended.

"But you. You can be anything."

Her hand traced slow arcs along Salomé's scalp.

On her first day at Crandon, Salomé woke to an old tango, sung in her mother's tawny voice. She got out of bed and followed the strains. She peered into the living room and was stunned by what she saw: Mami was ironing. Meticulously. At five-thirty in the morning. She wore the same blue dress as the night before. **Y un rayo misterioso,** she sang, **hará nido en tu pelo.** She danced the iron forward, across the crisp white blouse of the new uniform. **Florecerá la vida.** She smoothed the collar and the cuffs and sleeves and now the narrow spaces between buttons. **No existirá el dolor.** Salomé sensed a deeply private conversation between woman, iron, cloth. She retreated quietly and curled back into bed. The sky outside was the color of a very old woman's hair.

She and Roberto rode the bus across town. Her pleated skirt scratched at her knees. Inside the iron gates, slick-haired boys and pearly girls swarmed over a perfect lawn. The classrooms had the artificial lemon-smell of a place that's been scrubbed clean. The windows made polished boxes out of the sky. She had an English teacher now, who did not wear a sweater made of wool she'd spun and knit herself, but a tailored jacket and matching skirt. She spoke English with slow effulgence.

"You will learn . . . to speak . . . like a citizen of . . . the United States. What is the United States? Class?"

Homework piled on. There was absolutely no talking out of turn in class. The halls echoed her footsteps and the footsteps of the slick-haired boys and pearly girls.

"Well?" Mamá asked that night. "How was it?"

"Great," said Roberto.

"Fine," said Salomé.

"Lots of studying to do?"

"Yes."

She studied a whole new language, angular new words for the same familiar things. She studied the United States, the country to the north of the north itself, memorizing its states, fifty of them, from Alabama to Wyoming, gargantuan states, many of them larger than the whole of Uruguay. She studied dollars, how to turn them into cents, their bulk compared to pesos. She learned the capitals of European nations. She learned that there were foreign companies that might hire Uruguayan girls if they were smart, tidy, and adept at typing and English. She learned biology, geometry, and all about the World Wars. At home, she learned how to iron skirt pleats, and how to speak in English for Mamá, saying **please** and **of course** and **what a lovely pair of shoes, Mother.** Mamá cheered and clapped each time.

"I thought you wouldn't like English," Salomé said.

"Why on earth not?"

"It's the language of the **yanquis**."

"So?"

"It's against revolutions."

"That's silly," Mamá said quickly. "A language can't be against anything."

They stood still, looking at each other. It was late afternoon; glyphs of light hung low along the walls.

"Anyway, you have to understand. It's the language of opportunity."

Roberto made a friend, Edgar, a freckled boy obsessed with chemistry. He came home sometimes for dinner, cleared his plate no matter how many times Abuela filled it, and politely answered all of Abuelo's questions. Yes, my father's a lawyer; no, we live in Malvín; I guess I'm okay at soccer; of course Peñarol is my team. Salomé wondered what it might be like to bring a friend home. Most of the girls at school were nothing like her. Their hair was perfectly in place; they had swimming pools in their backyards; they wore a different gold necklace each day; their giggles were delicately calibrated. To her relief, they tended to ignore her. They also ignored Leona Volkova. Leona always sat with her knees together, but not crossed. She never smiled in class. She was the only Jewish girl, soft-spoken and courteous— until the day she shot up to say that Trotsky had not been a madman.

The air in the classroom tightened like a bridle. All eyes turned to Leona, who stood with her hands clasped in front of her.

Miss Magariños looked like she'd just been given a suppository. "Excuse me?"

"He wasn't a madman," Leona repeated.

"Young lady, you weren't called on."

"Yes, Miss Magariños. But still. Thanks to him my family got out of Russia alive." She stared at her teacher, who stared at the wall. She sat down clumsily.

Miss Magariños coughed and resumed her lesson. Students bent back over their notebooks. The air stayed taut and heavy until the bell rang.

After class, Salomé fell into step beside Leona in the hall.

"That was brave."

Leona didn't look at her. Her dark curls seemed about to burst from the rubber band at the nape of her neck. "You think so?"

"Of course."

"That's nothing. Not compared to other people."

"Like Trotsky?"

"Yes. Like Leon Trotsky."

They walked out to the lawn, freshly mowed and fragrant. Leon. Leona. "Were you named after him?"

The sun reflected in Leona's glasses, obfuscating her expression. "How did you know?"

Salomé shrugged. She adjusted her books in the cradle of her arms. "My middle name is Ernestina. My mother says she gave it to me after Che."

"How can that be?"

"She says she met him in Buenos Aires, in '51, when I was born."

Leona laughed. She looked different when she laughed, almost pretty (and years later, fearing for her life, Salomé would remember Leona this way, a grinning child with sun caught in her glasses).

"Do you believe your mother?"

"On some days. Do you believe yours?"

"Yes." She was serious again. She lowered her voice. "You know Che's coming to speak at the university."

"Of course."

"My sister, Anna, studies there. We're going to see him speak."

Leona's eyes were wide, her stance was straight, she smelled of tangerines and toothpaste. Standing there, at the lawn's edge, in a starched and pleated uniform under the heavy sun, Salomé could think of no better fate than friendship with this girl.

Leona glanced around her at the flock of white blouses. "Do you want to come?"

"Of course." The blouses headed down toward the lawn, where they glared in the high-noon light. "But I'll have to ask."

When Salomé asked, her mother's comb sliced hard against her scalp.

"Of course you can't."

Her hands took half of Salomé's hair, divided it in three, and braided briskly.

"But, Mami, why not? We've gone to lectures—"

"This is not an ordinary lecture. It's controversial."

"So?"

"So!" Her fingers tugged the braid tight. They were quick; they were nimble; they knew this weave so well. "There will be police, and a lot of—feeling." A rubber band closed over the braid. Mamá dropped it and started on the left side.

Salomé wanted to shake the two hands out of her hair. "Are you going?"

"No. It's Tía Carlota's card night."

The final rubber band tightened its noose.

On the night of Che's lecture, they ate dinner without Mamá. Abuelo told them stories over the meal, old, familiar stories, embroidered in new places. A man gambles his way into a carnival magic act. A girl reappears from death at the top of a tree. It seemed unreal, absurd, larger than life. But then, Salomé thought, what is gained from smallness? Surely resonance—or the yearning for it, the pull to shout your soul in all its voluble explosions—was no crime. And perhaps Abuelo's tales weren't larger than life at all. Perhaps, during the century, the world itself had changed, its scope diminished, its proportions shrunk, its fantastic edges pulled in at the horizon.

She was clearing the table when Tía Carlota called.

"Where's your mami, Salomé?"

"Out."

"Out where?"

She hesitated. "Playing cards."

"What? With who? Who serves better **picadillos** at their game nights?"

"No one, Tía, I'm su—"

"That's right, **pues nadie.** You really don't know where she is?"

"No idea," Salomé lied.

"Well, tell her to call me."

"Claro."

She hung up and stood in the corridor with the long-moaning telephone pressed against her ear. She had gone. She must have gone. This moment, her mother was in a vaulted room with Che, while Salomé heard only the drone of this empty line. She listened to the drone until it began to sound aggressive. She went to the kitchen. Abuela Pajarita was washing a cast-iron pan. Her silver-and-raven braid swung ever so slightly, as if its tip were brushing her waist clean. Salomé dried plates, drawing moisture from their curves, clinking them into the cupboard. It seemed so easy: wash, then dry, then stack into place. No trace of what's been done.

When she was finished, she crept into her mother's room and closed the door. She did not turn on the light. The moon reached through the window with silver arms. She was tall enough now, and strong enough, and she was not afraid of transgression— or if she was, she would not let that fear command her. All she needed was a chair, like this, dragged up to the closet, to the box that was still there, so she could move it forward, patiently, on tiptoes. It was still heavy; it filled her arms; she brought it to the floor. She smelled eucalyptus when she opened the first flap. Another flap, another, and there they were, exposed in the pale moonlight. Shoes. Children's shoes. Her strappy school shoes and Roberto's oxfords, the ones they had outgrown last year. Each stratum held smaller shoes than the last, until, at the bottom, tiny baby shoes emerged, some with flowered designs, some boyish and plain, and every shoe of every size contained three eucalyptus leaves—no more, no less. She wanted to dive into the shoes, swim through their darkness for a clue to Mamá's mind, for a clue to eucalyptus, or for a clue to anything at all. She brought a leaf to her nose and smelled it, then rubbed it between her fingers as though it were the first leaf she'd ever really felt, as though there were a secret code in the fine veins of its surface, but she pressed too hard, it broke in half, and she recoiled from her own act of destruction. She put the leaf back in its shoe and put the shoes back in their places, the flaps back with one another and the box back on its shelf, the chair against the wall again, no one saw this, no one did this, no one knows.

That night, as she fell asleep, she thought of boxes, doors, lecture halls, the mouths of shoes, and of how much—how very much—she longed to know.

Che's lecture ended in violence. They heard it on the radio at breakfast the next morning. Someone fired a shot, a riot erupted, dozens were wounded by the end of the night. Abuelo complained about socialists becoming too unruly, stirring trouble. Mamá drank her **mate** without looking up.

Leona didn't come to school for two days. Salomé pictured her with broken bones, lacerated skin, welts, bruises. But when she came, she was in one piece, and even smiling. She passed Salomé a note in English class: **Let's talk.** At lunch, they sequestered themselves beneath a eucalyptus tree at the corner of the lawn. Salomé was so greedy for the story that she couldn't eat her sandwich.

"It was incredible." Leona took off her glasses and cleaned them with the edge of her skirt. Her eyes were bright and naked. "He said so many things. That the struggle in Cuba is all of our struggle, that it's something spiritual, beyond borders, that will spread wherever people are hungry. He was wearing a black beret, and his arms danced the whole time he was speaking, and even from far away you could tell he's more handsome in real life." Leona paused as three older girls walked by, hands cupped over their mouths in mid-gossip. "He said we shouldn't hate the imperialists, because then we become like them, and instead we can stay strong, he said, and keep our eyes on victory—**¡Victoria!** Like that he said it: **¡Hasta la Victoria!** And when he said that, the whole auditorium broke into applause."

Salomé longed for that applause—to be inside it, carried by it. "So when was the fighting?"

"Soon after that, but listen, the newspapers lied. Che didn't cause it. We were on our feet, cheering, and then we heard a shot, a bullet flew toward Che. The crowd panicked, the police came in, as if breaking up a fight—but nobody was fighting except them. They beat people who were trying to get out. They broke my sister's arm. I only got a few bruises." She rolled up her sleeve and showed Salomé a round, sallow, half-purple mark. "A small price to pay."

Salomé nodded, turning Che's words in her mind, committing them to memory, cryptic, immediate, oracular. The fading bruise seemed to glow like a medallion.

Leona and Salomé spent long hours beneath that tree. They ate their lunch, watching students cluster on the lawn, or set up camp to study after school. Sometimes they closed their textbooks and discussed books they'd been reading, not the ones assigned in class, but the ones Leona borrowed from Anna's shelf. Anna had Marx's **Das Capital,** Trotsky's **My Life,** various histories of Latin America, books and essays by Bolívar, Artigas, Batlle, Bakunin, Lenin, Castro, Che. Salomé wrapped the books in paper from the butcher shop, so teachers would not see their titles and intervene. The texts were dense; she was grateful for Anna's ink marks, which indicated where the words were so important they should be underlined, or starred, or—strongest of all—underlined and starred with **"¡Sí!"** scrawled in the margin. At first, she tried to bring Mamá's poetry, but Leona read it only out of politeness.

"Poetry," she finally said, "isn't utilitarian."

Salomé fingered her mother's book (hearing Abuelo's voice, **you cannot eat a poem**) and returned it to her satchel. She met with more success when she brought Tío Artigas' letters: every time a new one arrived, Leona pressed Salomé about its contents, until finally she took to copying the letters, word for word, when the family wasn't looking. Such letters. You could almost smell the sweat and shorn-down sugarcane, the muscle and the hunger of his days. After thirty-three years a widower, Tío Artí had found love again, with Constanza, an octogenarian from Matanzas who could make pans and saucers move with her mind. The first time they kissed, he claimed, the kitchen table veered toward them and pinned their bodies to a bright yellow wall. They agreed to spend the rest of their lives together. He spent some days in Havana, others out on the land, always wielding something—schoolbooks, machetes, rifles, medical gauze. The government was strict, he said, but there were reasons for it. Leona read each word voraciously. Salomé loved her for her hunger. This was friendship, true and sparkling, able to meet her longing with full force, to sense where it bent in concave hollows, where it swelled in search of meaning, how it pressed and scratched and burned against the inside of her skin. Leona's longings bent and swelled and scratched right along with her. Words were not necessary to know this. She knew this as they sat, quiet, shoulder to shoulder, watching the branches' shadows creep along the grass.

Salomé turned thirteen. Uruguay was changing: jobs were lost, factories closed, pensions slashed. Montevideo opened its arms to an onslaught of strikes. Butchers, farmers, cobblers, phone workers, oil workers, wool workers clogged the streets. Salomé did not see them, but she saw the photos in **El País,** crowds with shouting mouths and high-held banners. The government set curfews, censored the press, beat strikers, opened fire, made arrests. On the radio, President Giannattasio called his actions Prompt Security Measures. Flyers littered the university in support of the strikes. Roberto, newly enrolled there, complained at the dinner table.

"They're everywhere. On the floor, on desks, taped to the wall. It's a nuisance."

"But the strikes are for good reason," Mamá said. "The Measures steal our civil rights."

"Isn't that what Castro's doing too?"

"It's different there."

"Why?"

"It's for the Revolution."

Roberto said nothing; he heaped more rice onto his plate.

"The boy is right." Abuelo Ignazio lifted his fork

as though it were a scepter. "The university should only be for studies."

Mamá frowned. Her hair was swept into a stylish beehive, which Salomé, with her own drab strands, could not imagine carrying on her head. It was strange that Mamá indulged in fancy hairstyles when money was so tight. It seemed rather bourgeois of her. She'd tried to ask once, but Mamá shot back, **I get a discount, she's an old friend,** and dropped the subject. "Perhaps the current world is worthy of study too."

In the spring, in the time when the Beatles first sang over the radio, Leona called, breathless and urgent.

"Salomé."

"Yes," she said, her mind crowding with reasons for such a call: a tragic death, a sudden boyfriend, Leona's first period (it had happened last year to Salomé; she would tell her it wasn't so bad).

"We've broken ties with Cuba."

"What?"

"The government. It's broken diplomatic ties."

"Oh."

"It's serious. U.S. officials told them to do it. Our government owes them money, so they did as they were told." The line rang with static. "Cowards." The sound of shuffling. "Wait. I'll read it to you."

"Of course I'll wait."

"Okay. This is what the United States said: 'Your government is condoning the intolerable presence of communism on this continent.' Can you believe it? Hang on."

Salomé heard Anna's voice in the background.

"Look, I'm going out. I'll talk to you later, **¿sí?**"

"Sure."

"See you tomorrow."

She hung up before Salomé could say good-bye.

A protest swelled in the Plaza de Independencia. Salomé listened to the radio and pictured it, the shouting, nightsticks, shots, arrests, Leona and her sister on those streets, risking their lives. It occurred to her to sneak away and join them, but it was impossible—Mamá watched her keenly and would not leave the living room. She pretended to do her homework. Two hours later, Roberto burst in, face flushed. He looked old, not like a boy at all.

Mamá said, "You're not in class?"

"I couldn't go. It's occupied."

"What is?"

"The university." They stared at him. Roberto raised his hands. "There are hundreds of them—students, and I think professors too—they've taken over all the buildings. They've got banners, they're shouting. It's this thing with Cuba."

Mamá blinked. "And the police?"

"They've surrounded the buildings."

"They have guns?"

"Obviously."

Mamá rose slowly, and she looked pale, red-lipped, black-haired, Snow White after the poisoned apple.

"That's it. You two aren't going out until this whole thing is over. Salomé, no school."

"But—"

"You heard me. You're staying home."

Salomé bent her head over her books. No school meant no Leona, no updates, no time under the tree receiving stories from the streets. The algebraic formulas stared back at her, stubborn little hieroglyphs with no relevance to this night. From the kitchen, she heard Abuela slicing carrots, or potatoes; she smelled onions frying on the stove. Outside these walls, the world was turning, spinning, whirling on its axis pushed by many hands, fueled by all the cries and chants and marching feet and crowded rooms and burning dreams—and she would not be part of it. She wondered what it tasted like out there.

Montevideo shook and surged for days. Salomé followed the action closely on the radio. The university occupation kept on. On the third day, the Cuban ambassadors dragged their hasty luggage to the Carrasco Airport. A crowd gathered to show their solidarity and wave good-bye. Salomé heard about the violence on the radio: the police used clubs, did not stop when people fell, there was blood on the street, there was blood on the polished glass doors of the airport. Leona still hadn't called. Perhaps she was at the airport, perhaps her blood now streaked the windows. Perhaps revolution was arriving in Uruguay, circling lower and lower like an enormous hawk, something spiritual, without borders, casting a long shadow as it sought a place to land, and history would remember those who cleared space for it. She wanted to clear space. She wanted to be brave. She wanted to experience the axis of the world. Today I can't, she thought, I've been forbidden, I can't find a way to escape. But you, long shadow, circling thing, I promise I will give myself to you. When I am remembered, if I am remembered, it will be for helping the change. If I hold my breath for thirty seconds now, that seals the promise. She looked at the clock. She held her breath.

The phone rang in the hallway. Abuela picked up.

"¿**Hola?** What? César, yes. Oh. Of course . . . I'm sorry. Is she—? Of course."

Mamá's voice. "What is it?"

"Xhana's at the hospital."

"Is she all right?"

"Fractured ribs. Cuts to her head."

Mamá made a low, guttural sound.

"They were at the airport."

"I've got to see her."

"Go—I'll watch the children."

Salomé thought of Tía Xhana, bones cracked, head bleeding, slammed onto the asphalt by an officer's club. She hoped, absurdly, for Mamá to come in and invite her to go. Of course it didn't happen. Restless, churning, trapped inside the house, she listened to her mother grasp her keys and hurry out.

———

Xhana spent five days in the hospital, and once the university reopened and classes resumed, Salomé was allowed to visit. Tío César sat beside the bed, looking more tired than she'd ever seen him. Xhana lay propped up on pillows, and lit up when she saw the carnations in Salomé's hands.

"How nice," she said, smiling, and Salomé saw she'd lost two of her teeth.

Throughout the following year—while she studied chemistry and Hemingway and art, while she whispered with Leona in the eucalyptus shade, through bustling days and nights in the Punta Carretas house—Salomé listened to all the conversations she could find. She was a spy now, surreptitious, urgent, determined to trace the shadows to their source, to see the world in all its tangles and pry herself a space amid the chaos. There were many conversations, hushed, loud, worried, furtive, brash, contemplative, excitable, didactic. She pricked her ears and made herself invisible. In Crandon halls, out on the street, at Coco's butcher shop, in Xhana's kitchen, in Abuela's kitchen, behind Mamá's closed door, at the bus stop, on the bus, she gathered words and pieced them together like a jigsaw:

Everything's changed.

It's temporary.

It's disastrous.

This is practically a dictatorship.

Oh, come on.

You come on. Look at the police.

True.

See?

Our economy is a disaster.

We've always bounced back.

This is different.

We're a tenacious nation. A stable nation.

The Switzerland of South America.

That's in the past.

The past never dies.

You're out of touch.

The unions are strong.

So is poverty.

So is police violence.

Honestly, I can't believe their violence.

It's not Uruguayan.

It is now.

We'll rise up in protest, like the rest of the world.

Look at Cuba.

Look at Europe, China, Vietnam.

Look at Mississippi.

Look at the Tupamaros.

Tupamaros? Who the hell are they?

I'm not sure, but they left flyers around the university.

I think they set off a bomb the other day.

Yeah, in front of the U.S. Navy building.

Hm. What nice men.

I heard they wrote **gringos piratas** on the wall of the building.

I heard they're named after Túpac Amaru.
I heard they rob banks.
I heard they have guns.
I heard they're saving up for the revolution.
I heard they give spoils to the poor.
I heard they're an arm of the Socialist party.
They're lawless.
They're heroes.
Our lawmakers are lawless, so really, who cares?
You're exaggerating.
You're naïve.
They're beating up strikers.
Well, they **are** getting too wild.
Too wild for whom?
Reporters are getting fired.
So? Everybody's getting fired.
We need a revolution.
Of course we don't.
We're on the brink of dictatorship.
Come on—we're not that kind of country.
It's already started.
It can't happen.
Sure it can.
It won't.
I'm telling you, it's happening.
If people are just patient, things will turn around.
But if they don't?
Then . . .
Then what?

Fifteen seemed to race up at her, girls are supposed to keel and scheme and bate their breath for the day of their **quinceañera,** savoring unbearable suspense, but Salomé had to be reminded of it by her mother and Abuela, who rallied for the date months in advance, who sewed the dress during late nights, the living room a garish ocean of white ruffles, asking do you like this? and this? more layers here, what do you think? and Salomé would bob or shake her head yes or no and let them pin, stitch, twirl her slowly, analyze, claim she looked so pretty. She felt gangly in the end result. She was still angular, long-limbed, a sketch of womanhood. And anyway, it seemed to her that the rewards of becoming a woman, the solemn gifts bestowed on her, were disappointing: her first lipstick, pink and sticky on her mouth; high heels on which she lost her balance; long white gloves to match her ruffled dress. Surely there was more to it, more incentive to accept the inscrutable burdens of adulthood.

The party itself dizzied her with its heat and droves and noises, its spread of enough **bizcochos,** empanadas, **alfajores, pascualina,** and **churrascos** to feed all of Montevideo. The cake seemed to yield a thousand slices. One by one the guests told her how beautiful she looked, which made her sheepish and also a bit suspicious. Nevertheless, once she drank two glasses of Champagne and dancing began in earnest, she succumbed to electric undercurrents of pleasure. Joy lurked in her bones after all, hot and thick and streaming, and she saw it in the guests too, as they danced: Tía Xhana and Tío César dipped and reeled their way through a smoldering tango; Coco's and Gregorio's gray hairs mingled as they pressed together; Abuelo twirled Mamá and Mamá laughed and his eyes widened with a kind of baffled awe; even Roberto took to the dance floor, shaking abashedly to the Beatles, **do you want to know a secret,** with Flor—his girlfriend, Edgar's cousin, her loose hair the color of acorns, her body serpentine, her face calm and aglow. Salomé would never be like Flor, so attuned to the filigrees of desire, able to command them and draw them into her sphere without uttering a sound. No matter. She didn't want to be Flor, glossy, vacuous, while the world broke apart and transmuted around her. She kept smiling for the crowd. Leona was not there. She missed her friend, who had been busy lately, and distracted, because her aunt was sick, or so she said. Surely Leona had no reason to lie, not to Salomé, with whom she shared everything; all the more reason that lies would be difficult, awkward, poorly delivered, causing Leona to look away when speaking about the aunt and her long illness, staring at the iron gates beyond the lawn.

The long white gloves began to itch. Some secrets are told with ease, but others can combust if they are brought too close to words. And if I am a woman now, if it's true that these white frills can make me a real woman, that this Champagne and dance can strip my childhood, then I want to go inside, I want to see what Leona sees, I want to step into the hidden places that she may not know but that I think she knows now, places hot with danger I can neither name nor imagine but that surely are not for children, would never be for children, are only for men and also perhaps for women who can say they're a real woman and are unafraid to look their own fate in the eye.

It took two months. They were in the basement bathroom, a half-abandoned spot that stank of mossy rust. It was raining outside. Salomé had a letter from Artigas.

"Listen to this part. 'We're still recovering from Che's departure. Some people say he abandoned the Revolution. But I think he's gone to spread it, elsewhere in Latin America. Who knows where it will turn up next?' "

She looked up. Pearls of sweat glistened at Leona's temples.

"What do you think?"

Leona tapped the sink with her fingernails. She seemed preoccupied with something: an exam around the corner, a sharp pebble in her shoe. "What do **you** think?"

"I think it's true. I think it's spreading." Salomé took a breath of mildewed air. "I want to be part of it."

"How much do you want it?"

Her tone was jolting. "You know how much."

Leona stepped closer. Her face grew strident around the jaw. "With your whole being?"

"Yes."

Leona scanned her friend's face. Her hair was in a ponytail; a few wayward coils formed a frizzy halo. She softened; her gaze grew almost tender. "Would you give your life?"

Salomé wasn't breathing. No windows graced the basement bathroom; the only light slunk out of a weak, bare bulb. It hung just above them, so that their foreheads were lit, while their chins were half-lost in the dark. Two schoolgirls gossip in a bathroom. Two young women define their lives. She heard the rain falling in distant thuds against the building. Her world was full of rain and teeth and nightsticks to knock out those teeth, and here she was, schoolgirl, woman, thrilled and alive and afraid, staring at her friend, listening to slick hungers in her body, to the promise she'd made with suspended breath when she was still a child, thinking she'd be strong enough one day, but am I strong enough? how strong is enough? some steps are final, you can't go back, you can't know whether you're ready or even see the road ahead, you can only look into the dark with its dim glints and far explosions and sharp turns and weigh—starkly, rapidly—the cost.

"Yes," she said.

Leona searched her face, smiled. She took paper from her backpack, wrote against the wall, pushed the page into Salomé's hand, and left the room.

Salomé read the note. **Meet me outside El Chivito Sabroso tomorrow at ten minutes to six**

o'clock sharp. Make absolutely sure you're alone. Destroy this note immediately.

The next day, after school, Salomé hurried through her homework. No time to change; the uniform would have to do.

"I'm going out," she told her mother as she headed to the door.

Mamá looked up from her book. "Where to?"

"To see a friend."

Mamá raised a sculpted eyebrow. "Which one?"

Salomé thought fast. **Hasta la Victoria.** "Victoria."

"Victoria. She's at Crandon?"

"Yes."

"You've finished your homework?"

"Yes."

Mami softened, and Salomé felt a pang for lying. She pushed it away, remembering the night Che Guevara came to speak. Her mother also lied about destinations.

"Will you be back for dinner?"

She had no idea. "No."

"Have fun. Don't come back too late."

At twelve minutes to six o'clock, Salomé stood outside El Chivito Sabroso. The rain had halted; dusk began to stroke the bricks and stones. She tried not to think about the hours before her, gaping and white, blinding, unknowable. Through the window of the restaurant, she watched three melancholy men share a pitcher of beer. A lone woman dove into her

chivito sandwich, its insides—steak, fried egg, ham, bacon, cheese—collapsing from the bottom when she bit. A waiter stood indifferent watch. Across the street, two policemen paused at the corner. A bus rattled by, bursting with worn workers. One officer grasped the pistol at his hip, unnecessarily, as they strode away.

Leona came around the corner. Salomé raised her hand to greet her, but she walked past as if they were strangers. She slowed without turning. Salomé followed, keeping an easy distance. They walked to the end of the block, then to the right, then two more blocks and to the right again. They were on a quiet side street, dimly lit, flanked by tired buildings. Leona stopped in front of a laundromat. Its lights were off. The sign in the window said CLOSED. She knocked on the door; it opened; she stepped through quickly. Salomé stood alone on the empty street. It smelled of gutters alive with rain. She approached the door and it opened before she could knock. Leona rushed her in and led her through the blackness, past rows of unseen washing machines, into the back of the store. They arrived at the far wall; reaching out to touch it, Salomé felt the handles of mops and brooms. Leona knocked on the left end. It opened and she pulled Salomé by the wrist through the invisible door.

They entered a cramped dark room with no windows. Four people sat inside: Leona's sister, Anna, with her long face and gold-rimmed glasses; a young man in a starched collar; another man in his late twenties with a square face and bushy beard; and a broad, large **muchacho** with hair that wisped into his face, who looked older than Salomé, about seventeen. He looked familiar, but she couldn't place him, couldn't think, because they all were staring at her.

Leona motioned for her to sit down. Salomé arranged herself carefully on the freezing floor, regretting that she'd rushed out in her knee-length school skirt. She tasted the mingled breaths of six people and two oil lamps.

Bushy Beard nodded toward Leona, who closed the door.

"So," Bushy said, "you're Salomé."

She nodded. All eyes were still on her.

"She can really be trusted?"

Leona's nod was decisive.

Bushy stared at Salomé. His eyes were dark green, shaded by a ledge of brow. "What do you know about the Tupamaros?"

She cleared her throat. So here it was. "They plan to liberate Uruguay."

"Where did you hear that?"

"In the papers—"

"The papers are much less favorable."

"And my family talking."

The wisp-haired boy grinned and now she placed him, the grandson of Cacho Cassella, the magician from Abuelo's youth. Tinto Cassella. He winked at her in the low light.

Bushy continued. "What do **you** think about the Tupamaros?"

She had rolled that question through her mind all day. "That they're important. And brave."

"What would you say to a Tupamaro if you met one?"

She saw Leona in her peripheral vision, lifting her chin, leaning forward, and Salomé could almost smell the eucalyptus, feel the stippled light of their lawn. " 'I admire what you're doing and I want to be part of it.' "

Bushy Beard was impassive. "What if that Tupa told you that liberation is only achieved by action— including force, when necessary?"

That was when she saw the guns. They almost blended into the dark walls: rifles in the corner, a pistol at Anna's knee. She'd seen guns before, on policemen, in soldiers' hands, in photos of the Cuban Revolution—but never so close, and not in the lap of a university girl, not within reach of a man giving her a test. Her body felt like a cup full of crushed ice, so tight and cold. But guns, of course, were necessary, weren't they? A dirty need that you don't want but can't ignore, like defecation. She thought of Che, luminous Che, embracing a sleek rifle in his sleep. The air hung thick, unventilated, pressing.

"I'd agree."

Bushy Beard leaned closer. "How old are you?"

"Fifteen."

"You understand what's being asked?"

"Yes."

"You don't think you're too young?"

"No."

He stroked his beard. He glanced around the room. "Any comments?"

Tinto raised his hand. "I know her. Our grandparents are friends. She's a good person, reliable."

Leona added, "I would trust her with my life."

"That's good," Bushy Beard said. "You may have to. Any concerns?"

The room was silent.

"All in favor?"

All the members raised their hands. Leona hugged her tightly. "Welcome, friend."

Each Tupamaro rose and kissed Salomé. Tinto's cheek felt smooth and taut; Bushy Beard's, quite gentle. His name was Orlando. He introduced the others—Tinto, Anna, and Guillermo, the man with the starched collar. Orlando was the head of their cell, he said; Anna would explain. Anna pushed up her glasses and turned tightly toward Salomé. The Tupamaros, she said, were also called the National Liberation Movement. Everything from now on had to be held in strictest secrecy. She paused. Salomé nodded. Anna went on. The movement was organized into cells. This was her new cell. Only one person in each cell knew any other Tupamaros. Orlando met with others and brought back information. If they were ever captured on assignment, they couldn't release more than a few identities, even if investigative pressure—she said these two words slowly, tasting each syllable—were applied. There was a knifelike quality about Anna, in her thin poise, her sharpened words. As if she wouldn't hesitate to cut the world in two. "Do you understand?"

Salomé nodded.

"Very well," Orlando said. "Let's continue."

She sat in silence for the remainder of the meeting. It was orderly, polite, almost banal; it reminded her of a study group assessing its homework, talking of research—who works in the top office of the Federal Bank? what does he do on weekends?—and craft projects—forty sets of homemade handcuffs needed by next week—and plans—next meeting is in Guillermo's uncle's basement. It was difficult to believe this was real. She pictured herself leaping to her feet, running to the alley, shouting **I am a Tupa!** to the shuttered windows and crushed-velvet sky. The meeting was adjourned. Tinto approached.

"Salomé. What a surprise."

She scrambled up from her awkward splay on the floor.

"A nice one, of course."

His burliness shocked her. He'd been a lanky child. They called him Tinto because his neck was long and thin like a bottle of red wine. Now there was nothing lithe about him, though his neck did seem to be craning. Eager. The oil lamps dimmed, and she was glad, because she had begun to flush. "How's your abuelo?"

"Still working. He says if he can't put food on the

table, he may as well be dead." He wiped a frond of hair from his eyes. It fell back immediately. "How about yours?"

"He's all right."

They looked at each other.

Leona tugged her arm. "We leave one by one. Your turn."

Tinto kissed her quickly. "See you next time."

"See you then," she said, and turned to the hall. She hesitated for an instant at the threshold; she couldn't see anything; outside, night had long fallen. She had never walked into so much darkness in her life. She would have liked a flashlight or a candle, but knew better than to ask, so she reached her arms in front of her and walked forward, into the pitch-black room with its hidden gauntlet of machines.

STEEL RABBITS AND
SONGS THAT MELT SNOW

They were preparing the revolution. There was plenty to do. Funds to gather, and weapons, and members; banks and gun clubs to raid for supplies; copper wire to coil into a shape that holds without hurting. Salomé tried on every pair of handcuffs she made. She pulled her wrists against the wires, and if they left red slashes she kept adjusting to make them gentler. Of course, they could always twist out of shape in some faceless Tupamaro's satchel or pocket or purse, but still, she did her best. The wearers might be guards, bank workers, customers, receptionists, the very people the Movement was for. The last thing we'd do is hurt these people, she thought, shaping circles slowly, massaging her good wishes into wire. Tupamaros were always kind and courteous during operations. Courtesy was an essential Movement rule.

There were many rules to learn. They seeped into her world and mind. Rule One: Be impeccable, don't attract attention. She could do that, she was a natural, she'd been preparing all her life. Rule Two: Be devoted. Yes. She was not too young, she could work, could be trusted, could give herself to something fierce and noble, she'd show them who she was. Rule Three: You're sworn to secrecy. She could do this too, though occasionally strange temptations took her by surprise. Her new identity roared and bubbled and frothed. She could have shouted at the bus driver, I'm going to save your country! She almost whispered at the nun in the back row, I understand, yes, yes, I've also made a vow. And the hoary man across the aisle, gaping at her legs: Watch out, she didn't say, you don't know who I am, you haven't seen the guns under my bed.

She hid them dutifully, as instructed. The trick was to store them under your mattress, and then to keep your bed so deftly made, your sheets so clean, that no one in your family thought to touch them. The day Salomé brought home her first cache—two pistols and one rifle—she fluffed her pillow for twenty-seven minutes, and adjusted her blue and green quilt for a full hour. It looked tidy, pristine, smooth, of course it did, a little to the left, a stretch to the right, was that a wrinkle, no, it was just the subtle pleat between the triangles, now the pillow has a hollow, now it's convex, now the blanket, how's the bottom, it seems fine, all things neat, all things tidy, this is an innocent bed.

"Salomé." Mamá knocked on her door. "Dinner's ready."

At the table, the voices of her family sounded distant, as though caught inside a seashell, or as though she were curled in a seashell and they were far off on the beach. She saw them rise and run to her bedroom, first Abuela, then Abuelo, then Roberto, then Mamá, eight hands hurling up her mattress, but there was only boisterous eating, unrushed laughter, the taste of fried **buñuelos,** the pour of Coca-Cola into glass.

Salomé learned to sleep—and to not-sleep—with hard hillocks against her back. All spring and summer she shifted in the dark, trying to find a position where she wouldn't feel them, but it was no use. Sharp protrusions stalked her hip bone. Long barrels lay from shoulder blade to waist. Some nights she lay in a restive state, half dozing, half awake, gazing through the window at a shard of moon or at the lack of moon. Other nights she'd catch enough sleep to dream, and then she'd find herself in a wilderness, in some unknown part of the world, waiting for other guerrillas to join her, curled up on a heap of weapons, surrounded by knotted trees and piercing birdcalls. As she lay, the pile grew, a rising mound of guns, higher and higher until she broke above the forest cover, and the sun poured down on her with hot and copious radiance, glistening on treetops and the pistols at her knees. She dripped with sweat beneath that sun. Then she'd wake (sweaty, on guns), and make her bed immediately. She'd shower and don her uniform, tucking the blouse carefully into the skirt. Then came breakfast—how did you sleep, Salomé? fine, Mamá—and then the bus to school.

It was difficult to concentrate on classes. They seemed so far removed from the new apex of her mind. But she was strong, she'd prove her strength, she would be impeccable: she wrote exhaustive essays, deciphered the laws of physics, polished her pronunciation of English words. Model students don't arouse suspicion. No one could know that she was not the same, except Leona, who knew everything, who also daydreamed of revolutionary splendors, who also slept with steel against her back, and who sat primly in class, taking notes, responding to Salomé's glances with a faint lift of the shoulder or an even fainter smile. Leona, sister in spirit, sister in crime, the wildest woman ever to seem so restrained. Their closeness had deepened into a feeling of shared mind. They each knew how the other lived, in a double life, a layered life, one life over the other, one in the sun and another teeming with movement underground.

She had to become larger to make room for so much life.

Meetings were punctual and cramped and efficient. Orlando delivered updates on recent operations—bank holdups, arms acquisition, delivery of food to a **cantegril.** Her role was limited to hearing the reports, storing a few guns, making the occasional handcuffs. Tinto distracted her with his enormous hands, the dark hairs curled above the top button of his shirt, wiry curls that surely led to more dark curls along his chest and how exactly did they lie between cotton and skin? He was the kind of **joven** old ladies fantasize about for help crossing the street, kind and large and just a little goofy. He had grown very quickly, judging from his stance, the slight stoop of his shoulders, an awkwardness with all that sudden bulk. Salomé liked this about him, both the bulk and awkwardness; sweet heft to pull down on a woman; what a thought, what a thought—where did that come from?

After meetings, in stolen moments, Tinto approached her with shreds of things to say.

"You know, my grandmother made your abuelos' wedding bed."

An odd conversation starter.

"You did know."

"Yes."

"Ah."

"My abuelo raves about your abuelo's singing."

He looked dubious.

"No, really. Apparently he was better than Gardel."

He laughed. His Adam's apple shuddered as he laughed. He looked at her. She felt the other Tupas, studiously averting their gazes.

"My turn to go," she said.

"Right. See you next time."

She thought about their brief exchange for days. She rolled each word through the thirsty expanse of her mind. He hadn't seen how plain she was, how dull-faced, in the dim light of hidden, cavelike rooms. He had seen but didn't care what she looked like. Or he did care and he liked what he saw. That couldn't be, but anyway it didn't matter, she didn't care, it wasn't what she went to meetings for and he was probably just being polite.

After the next meeting, Tinto approached and picked up the conversation as if they'd just put it down. "How did your parents meet?"

"In Argentina. In a hospital."

"Interesting."

She shrugged.

"You don't think so?"

"How did your parents meet?"

"It's a long story."

"So?"

"Your turn to go," he said.

September. Spring lifted its head and shook its warm, loose hair. Tinto slipped her a note before he slipped from the laundromat.

Would you like the long story? How about to-morrow night, Parque Rodó, at nine o'clock?

The next night, in the park, Salomé searched the darkness—path and trees and fountain, wrapped in night—for Tinto. She found him on a bench with **mate** and thermos. She sat down next to him. They passed the slow gourd back and forth. Their silence was as supple as the darkness. Behind them, the fountain sang its low, rippling chant.

"I still want the story," she said.

"Oh. Of course."

He told her that his papá, Joaco Cassella, was born on a stretch of road somewhere in the province of Rocha, on a carnival wagon surrounded by costume trunks. His mother filled several velvet curtains with her blood while giving birth. They settled in Montevideo, where Tinto's grandfather folded his magician's clothes, became a full-time carpenter, and faced the strange frontier of urban life. Tinto's mamá, on the other hand, had a lineage that linked her to the city for six generations. Her name was Magda. Her father was a tailor who had once made suits for President Batlle y Ordóñez himself. She met Joaco in the neighborhood bakery. She was sixteen, and she was struck by the way he stroked his coins before relinquishing them to the baker. They were soft strokes, intimate and assured. Joaco looked at her in a manner that made her leave the bakery without bread. The second time, she was on her way out with loaves in her arms and she looked down and didn't see him touch anything at all. The third time, she walked in to find him caressing a single coin. Their eyes met. He approached her.

"I can make this peso appear wherever you want it to."

"Excuse me?"

"In my sleeve. On the counter. In your hand."

She laughed. "I'm not stupid."

"Don't believe me?" Joaco leaned closer, and in his

version of the story he knew as soon as he smelled her hair. "Watch. If I succeed, you let me walk you home. Agreed?"

"Agreed."

Years later, Magda would claim he cheated by not revealing his paternity.

Tinto paused; a couple approached on the wooded path, nuzzling, taking their time. He waited until their silhouettes had blended into trees.

Joaco and Magda's walk was quiet and electric all the way to Quiroga's Tailor Shop. He asked who her father was. The tailor, Don Quiroga? Yes, she said, we live upstairs. She slipped inside, and he hovered on the street, staring at the exquisite door and proud brass sign. "I've met my future wife," he told his mother that night, "but to court her I need a suit fit for Batlle." His mother, Consuelo, Mistress of Disguises, dusted off her sewing machine and told her son to save up for fine cloth. It took two months for every coin and stitch to fall in place. Joaco shone his shoes and splashed on cologne and went to Quiroga's Tailor Shop. Its owner looked exactly like a bulldog.

"Don Quiroga. I've come to ask your blessing. I'd like to court your daughter."

Don Quiroga knew his daughter was beautiful and he had plans for her, marriage to a mayor or a bureaucrat at least, excellent wine, trips abroad, years of front-row seats at Teatro Solís. This young man came with no credentials. But his lapels were flawless, his cuffs classic, his face determined. He could not deny him outright.

"I'll leave it up to her."

They were married two years later. Tinto was born in a bedroom littered with woodchips. He'd built four tables by his seventh birthday.

"And now?" said Salomé.

Now his father worked longer hours for dropped prices. His mother found new ways, each day, to stretch the food and fill each mouth. His abuela Consuelo, Mistress of Disguises, was dying of cancer in the front room. Tinto brought her **mate** in the mornings, soup and crackers at midday. Pain or age made her crotchety and forgetful. At her insistence he had taken their only hanging from the wall, a watercolor of the Montevideo port, and nailed her old pink leotard in its place. She stared at it for hours, sometimes with horror, sometimes as if sighting a frayed angel.

Salomé could have listened to Tinto until the sun came up. "I should go."

"I should too."

Neither of them moved.

"Perhaps," Tinto said, "we could meet again."

The bench became their private lair. They always met at night. One night, he asked how she'd Become, and she told him about Leona, the eucalyptus shade, the cryptic invitation in the bathroom. Another night he told her how he'd Become, how he'd joined the Socialist party after a leaflet was pushed into his hand in the street, at a strike of sugarcane workers who'd marched from the northern fields to Montevideo, and he'd stood there on the sidewalk, damp from the heat, holding the half-crushed leaflet with both hands, thinking of his abuelo Cacho, also from the country, perhaps a very distant cousin to these men, hammering with arthritic hands. He went to the meeting described on the flyer. A man called Orlando watched him for a year before saying, You, Tinto, let's go for a drink. She told him stories too, sprawling ones, about a Venetian man's arrival in the city, when both he and the city were young, when so much promise filled them both; and about a baby girl who disappeared from a home that did not want her, that had not given her a name, and who survived mysteriously until she was discovered, wild, birdlike, alone, in the crown of a tree, and soared from there, or fell, depending on whom you asked and when you asked them. And she told of this girl's childhood in the **campo** when there still was unfenced land, and the knowledge of plants and their powers that began, perhaps, in rebirth from a tree, and that lasted all her life, became enough to feed her family through hard times, and filled her kitchen with jars and pots of herbs that seemed to whisper to her in the silence underneath the sounds of her family. She told him about another woman who, legend had it, met her future husband while she was his patient, in a wheelchair and a dull hospital gown, seducing him with her sheer intensity of spirit. Salomé had always imagined this encounter as a physical collision in the corridor, a hazardous accident of fate, the poet careening down the long hall on loose wheels, the doctor crisp and helpless in his starched white coat, her wheels aimed at his knees, her head rushing toward the space below his heart. She told about the love or need or complicated lust that drove them into marriage, and the opulent Buenos Aires house she was born into but could not remember seeing with her own eyes. The house, she said, was now filled with a life she did not belong to, a doctor with a new wife who sent cash for Christmas gifts, but never sweaters that might fit or books she might enjoy, except the year he published his volume on neurology, and sent two copies, one for each child, signed by the author. One copy, Salomé's, gathered indifferent dust under her bed, but the other stood on Roberto's highest shelf with its cover facing out so it could shine like a far-away star. She described all of this, and also her mother's book, **The Widest River in the World,** which fascinated her, each line of words uniquely shaped, like keys to her mother's inscrutable interior life, keys she fingered with her mind but could not use because the locks were intricately folded into the ever-shifting fabric of the woman who had penned the lines. A woman who kept writing, and who somehow found the time to teach poetry classes in various living rooms throughout Montevideo, an endeavor that brought virtually no money but after which she came home shimmering and triumphant. In Salomé's tales, her mother, to her surprise, became an icon of inspiration, beauty, glamour, all the qualities that seemed so slippery and foreign in her own hands. It surprised her, all this talking, all his listen-ing, all the stories that moved and breathed within her like creatures with limbs of their own. The air conspired with them, giving them darkness, enfold-ing them in lush and humid nights. One evening his hand landed on hers, a palm over her knuckles, broad, strong, tentative. She didn't move. Heat stung her arm. Beyond the trees, the fountain poured out its wet song.

"Tell me something," he said.

"Like what?"

"About you."

"I already have."

"Something more."

The hand, all she could think of was that big warm hand. "Nothing comes to mind."

"Nothing?"

"Nothing."

"You're beautiful."

She had seen herself in the mirror that day; she knew nothing had changed. "Liar."

"How dare you." She thought he was angry until he laughed. She liked the gravel in his laugh. A film of sweat had formed between their hands: her sweat, or his, or both of theirs. Everything surged, electri-cally, the trees, the heavy air, the skin of her hand and everything inside it. She wanted to shout. There was nothing in the world more powerful than this, a hand, a voice, the urge to shout. Tinto kissed her, briefly, firmly, a silent question that she answered with her fingers just above his top button, brushing curls, their texture silkier than she'd imagined.

"It's official." Eva pulled the newspaper taut between her hands. "The Tupamaros have declared themselves to the public."

Abuelo Ignazio snapped up a discarded jack. "Echh. Some news."

Salomé studied her poker hand. Across the living room, in the rocking chair, Abuela's knitting needles thrummed against each other. Rain speckled the window.

Eva did not seem rankled. "The communiqué is published, word for word. Listen to this: 'We have placed ourselves outside the law. This is the only honest action when the law is not equal for all; when even those who have created it place themselves outside it, with impunity. Today no one can take the sacred right of rebellion away from us.' "

Her mother, the orator. At meetings, the words had been dissected and discussed, reduced to their pedestrian essence; here, in the living room, intoned by Mamá, they renewed themselves, gleaming, virile, numinous. She wondered whether her mother's students ever felt this way, hearing their poems echoed in Eva's voice. If that was what happened in a poetry class; she had no idea what actually took place.

"They should all be shot," Abuelo said. "What's sacred about holding up a bank?"

Salomé fanned four queens on the table.

"Eh! You win!" He pushed seashells toward her, chipped from decades of betting. The scent of roasting beef swelled from the kitchen. Down the hall, in his room, Roberto turned on the radio. **One day,** the Beatles sang, **you'll look, to see I've gone.**

"The motive," Eva said. "That's what."

"It wasn't really a question."

"I still answered it. And besides," Eva said, "they never hurt anyone."

"How do you think the bank owners feel?"

"Like their money is going to the revolution. Which it is. What do you think, **hija?**"

But tomorrow may rain so, I'll follow the sun.

"I haven't really thought about it," Salomé said.

Eva eyed her. "Really?"

She nodded. Heat stung her face.

"And you?" Eva said, looking at Pajarita.

Abuela Pajarita kept on knitting, knitting. Salomé wondered how many stitches she had made in her lifetime. Hundreds of thousands for her alone. "I think I wouldn't want to be in the bank while they're robbing it."

Eva stretched lazily. The paper crumpled in her lap. "It sounds like they're quite polite."

Abuelo grimaced at his newly dealt cards (he was bluffing). "Sometimes, **hija,** you sound like one of them."

"If I were, you wouldn't know it, would you?"

"If you were I wouldn't let you in the house."

Salomé stood, too quickly. "I'm going to check on the roast."

"We just started a hand," Abuelo said.

"The roast is fine," Abuela said.

"I'll be right back."

In the kitchen, she forced herself to breathe. She had to be more calm, more careful. She opened the oven and imagined what her mother would say if she found out: **All those lies,** perhaps, or **You should have asked permission,** or **Tesoro, my treasure, I never guessed you had such strength.** Abuelo was wrong; Mamá was not a Tupamara. Salomé knew because she'd checked under her mattress, and found nothing but pages and pages of unfinished poems. There were days when Mamá left the house without making her bed at all. She was flagrant: she marched alongside unions, she read outraged poems in cafés, she published verses that made music out of words like **liberación,** leaflets poked unabashedly from her purse. Meanwhile—clearest of clues—she hadn't checked her daughter's mattress for guns. No, thought Salomé, she is not with me, I am alone. No one in this house knows the city I know, a city of doors, so many of them, tall and low, baroque and plain, bright and dark, peeled and fresh, and among those doors there are the ones that lead down passageways that lead to unseen doors only some can enter, only those who give each waking moment to their country and each sleeping moment to the guns.

They bred down there. Strange steel rabbits. Six

pistols and four rifles now. She had learned, from sheer necessity, to sleep on their hard bodies, alert and dreaming all at once. The piles still turned to mountains in the middle of her mind.

Salomé closed the oven door and turned up the heat.

Che Guevara died. It was the spring of '67. The news reached them on a sweet-sky sort of day, a rare blue above that made you want to taste it. He'd been living with guerrillas in Bolivia. He was shot in the chest many times over. According to **El País,** he fell in the midst of fighting. According to Orlando, soldiers captured and then killed him, **bolivianos** trained by U.S. agents. According to Orlando they had cut off both his hands.

They were silent, all eight of them, in a cement grotto under the floorboards of a restaurant. The air was scarce and smelled of overused grease. Salomé closed her eyes and saw two enormous severed hands, pressed together as if in prayer, saw herself clambering up them, toward heaven, blood sticking to her heels. She opened her eyes. Tinto was crying, without moving, without making a sound. Leona's eyes were shut. Anna looked stern, as usual.

Orlando coughed. "The best way to honor Che is to keep on." He looked much younger without his beard. He was working undercover at the police station, where employees were required to shave. "We always knew the risks."

And this was true, she'd known the risks, she was too smart not to be conscious of the risks; she knew about the chance of death, arrest, La Máquina with its rumored electric hell; the leap she'd taken could end in flight or fall or territories she could not or would not imagine. All of this was already true when Che was still alive, hopeful, grinning, hands attached. She shouldn't be shocked, nor should she be afraid, but she couldn't help it—it reared up in her, a wave of fear, and she hoped no one could smell its brackish presence.

Orlando leaned forward. She couldn't picture him at a police station. She couldn't picture him anywhere except in dark and airless rooms. "We cannot be distracted from our purpose. It's up to us to keep Che alive."

"Hasta la victoria siempre," Anna said.

Salomé repeated the words, along with everyone.

Spring expanded. Daisies raised delicate heads in Parque Rodó. In the dark, she couldn't see them, but she knew they were there, facing the black sky while she and Tinto murmured, drank **mate,** pressed together. She learned the curve of his neck, the hollow of his collar, hard bone along his jaw, back down to his collar, catching curls of chest hair on her tongue. She traced that path many times, up and down, back up again, hungry, hungry, never filled, while his hand ate her body, hair, neck, breast, waist, hip, breast. She hushed him when he tried to talk. She didn't want to hear his words, his thoughts, promises he could or could not keep. Words are an extravagance, you cannot eat a poem, she was not an ordinary girl who could sustain herself on sweets; give me the root-food of your skin, mouth, palms, nourishment I carry through the rigor of my days. During classes and exams and family dinners she pulled out morsels— his hand on her blouse, the taste of his tongue, the desperate restraint of his breath—and let herself taste them again. Good girl. Guerrilla girl. She had to steel herself to play both parts. Lust and fear and pleasure had to stay beneath the surface, stirring, gnawing, silent.

Even when the letter of acceptance arrived from the university and her mother shrieked with pleasure, jumping up and down like a drunk child, Salomé guarded her joy.

"History," Mamá said.

"Yes."

"You still want to be a historian?"

"Yes." She felt the pull of it, books piled in decadent mounds, halls littered with leaflets, forays into the struggles of the past, and herself, years down the line, a new kind of scholar for a new Uruguay.

"**Mija,** that's wonderful. At your age, I was already waiting tables. I don't want that for you." She wiped her eyes and held the letter of acceptance close so that it crinkled against her breasts. "Come, sit down, **mi amor.**"

They sat down on the sofa and Mamá put her arm around Salomé and began to speak, **I worked at a shoe store, at first, but it wasn't a good place, and**

things were better once I escaped to La Diablita, I was thirteen and those were golden days, the days when I found other poets, found the poet within me, and then I went to Argentina, I wanted to change the world, I wanted to see everything, taste everything, write everything, and certainly I've had my life but if I'd gone to university I could have—

Her words continued to roll, and Salomé half listened but she was preoccupied with something her mother had said at the beginning. Finally, her mother paused in the midst of retelling the story about the young man beaten to a pulp by the Buenos Aires police, and Salomé said, "What do you mean by 'escape'?"

"What escape?"

"You said you escaped to La Diablita."

"Yes."

"Why did you have to—"

"It wasn't an escape," she said tightly. "It was just a new job."

They were silent. The evening sun lengthened the shadows.

"In any case," Mamá said, "we'll celebrate tonight. I'll go out for some Champagne." She rose and picked up her purse, and the aperture between them was gone. Salomé watched her mother leave, and then she was alone on the couch with her letter of acceptance. She picked it up and examined its fresh creases, its formal words, the gathering dark that seemed to make the paper hum. She held it parallel to the ground, and imagined herself shrinking to a size where she could sit on the page and ride it, a magic carpet, into untried realms. She could almost pretend that it was possible—she felt that buoyant, that easy to hold aloft.

The feeling lasted a week, until, one evening, in the back room of an abandoned factory, Orlando said, "Salomé. You have an assignment."

Salomé sat up quickly. She was not used to being an agenda item. She felt the burn of eyes on her.

"There's a job open at the U.S. Embassy. They need a secretarial assistant: one who can type, translate documents, and speak excellent English. The employee will have access to many files. It's a full-time deployment." Orlando opened his palms. "We think you could get it."

She wanted to ask who the **we** was, what faceless men had declared along with Orlando that she could get, should get, would get this job. It was a deeply inappropriate question. She could have slapped herself for thinking it.

"Salomé." Orlando bent forward. His face was gentle in the oil lamp's glow. "The Movement has enough students."

In the corner of her vision she saw Anna, razor-thin, watching for a telling twitch or tightness.

"Of course," Salomé said.

Two weeks later, she had the job. The process involved a typing test, an English test, and a brief interview with Viviana, the head secretary, a woman in horn-rimmed glasses who had not yet mastered the English **th.** She was two weeks from graduating high school. Might they wait? Yes, certainly, Miss Santos. We'll be glad to wait.

She graduated, dutifully, a shell of a girl smiling for cameras and Champagne toasts and teary mothers and grandmothers. The next morning, she lay in bed with her eyes open until Mamá knocked and entered, bearing a tray with toast and **mate** and a single yellow rose, craning its thin neck out of a vase.

"For my new graduate!"

Salomé sat up.

"What's wrong?"

"I have some news." She felt small in the bed, a child who played with buttons and didn't braid her own hair. She put her feet on the floor. "I got a job."

Mamá looked at her blankly.

Salomé took the tray from her, placed it on the bed, tried to sound bright. "It's a great job. As a secretary. At the U.S. Embassy."

Her mother hovered in the middle of the room. Her purple bathrobe was inside out; the seams were splayed and tattered. She spoke slowly, as if her thoughts were laborious to gather. "What about the university?"

"I'm not going."

"But you want to study!"

Salomé stared at the red lamp shade on the bedside table. It was old and worn and should have been replaced years ago. "Not really."

"Since when?"

"Besides, we need the money."

"You can't quit school for the family!"

Salomé stood. "So I should go to school for family? For you?"

Mami's mouth hung open; she stared at her daughter; she let out a sound that was almost a bark. "All those years of perfect grades." She swayed. "What about your future?"

But Salomé couldn't speak about the future, couldn't tell her mother about the handful of the future she was carrying, the rifles in her mattress, the blueprint in her mind, the action she took daily, hotly, secretly, for the future, for the people, at the negligible cost of one girl's selfish urge to study, for surely they were right and it was negligible once you factored in the revolution and factored out her longing to run out of here in her pajamas and not stop until she reached the university and broke into its library and barricaded herself in with books that she would read and make a bed out of and wield against anyone who came for her. "Look, Mamá, it's an excellent job. Why aren't you proud of me?"

Eva bared her teeth like a cougar; for the first time in Salomé's life, she feared her mother's attack. "How can you say I'm not proud?"

"Not of this job."

"You're not taking this job."

"I am."

"You're sixteen, Salomé. I'm your mother, and I say you're going to school."

Salomé panicked, imagining herself dragged to class by the hair, Mamá stalking outside lecture halls, the job at the embassy lost, her reputation ruined in the eyes of Tinto, Leona, Orlando, Anna, faceless Tupamaros, the ghost of Che. "You're just mad because you never studied."

She instantly regretted saying it, or at least regretted having to see the thing that happened to Mamá, the stiffening, the draining out of any trace of cougar, trace of heat, leaving a shocked and empty woman in a bathrobe with all the seams exposed. Eva did not sway. She did not blink. She did not look at Salomé. The silence was so thick it left no room for breathing until her mother left.

Eva stayed in bed for three days. Salomé avoided her. Once, and only once, Abuela Pajarita broached the topic. "This job. It's what you want?"

"Sí," Salomé said, scrubbing the counter.

"You're sure?"

"Sí."

"Because you know you could study. We'd manage."

Salomé wrung the dishrag fiercely. "Why doesn't anyone trust me?"

"You're changing the subject," Pajarita said sadly. Salomé said nothing and Abuela Pajarita watched her hang up the rag and leave the room.

On her first day, Salomé rose at 5 a.m. to perfect her bun, her blouse, her panty hose. The embassy was a maze of wide, glossy halls. Mr. Frank Richards, her new boss, offered her a crushing handshake. He had long sideburns and a rapid smile; a triangular sign above his desk read BOSTON RED SOX.

"So, you're Salomé." He led her to a bare desk and motioned for her to sit. "You Uruguayans finish high school so early. I never woulda known what to do at sixteen." He took out a cigarette and a silver lighter. "Not that I know now." His eyes squinted as he laughed.

She smiled pleasantly. This wouldn't be too hard.

Mr. Richards brought her files to organize, files to translate, files to type into clean copies (**Here you are, Salomé,** she imagined him saying, **get that to the rebels at once**). There were banal letters full of pleasantries and promises, requests for help from U.S. nationals, official declarations with little to say. On Salomé's seventh day, President Gestido died and left Vice President Pacheco in power. Memos from Pacheco's aides poured into the embassy. She snooped in Viviana's files to read them. Pacheco vowed to be amenable to the United States' concerns. Their friendship would be strengthened. Lyndon Johnson need not worry: the plague of socialism would be thoroughly addressed.

"Commendable," Orlando said, receiving her report. It was stacked and tidy, full of well-organized recriminations. Leona beamed at her from across the room, in her banker's uniform. Salomé had thought deployment would devastate Leona, but she'd only said **there'll be time to study later, after the revolution.** Her faith in that coming era was unshakable.

At home, Mamá said nothing. She eyed Salomé's tight bun and panty hose with suspicion. She treated her daughter like a sudden houseguest, deserving of civility but foreign to her house, whose proclivities and moods could not be gauged. A strange guest who worked for the **yanquis** and dressed like a drone and did not seem incensed by this man who now called himself president, who had already shut down newspapers, outlawed meetings, outlawed leftist parties, railed about the need for strict force in Uruguay. Mamá, she wanted to shout, I'm not what you think—shut up about the censorship, shut up about the laws, I'm doing more about it than you could possibly imagine, and in fact, when we get out of this mess, if we ever get out of it, you'll see my sacrifice and you'll have me to thank. But she said nothing. She swallowed the picture of herself as an office girl, indifferent, eating her spaghetti without taking down her bun, while Mamá made futile complaints about the state of affairs, knowing just how the ritual would go: Abuelo would mutter something about security, Roberto would complain of disruptions at school, Salomé would shuffle food around on her plate, and Abuela Pajarita would make a tired but sincere comment about survival—**We'll get through this,** for example—and encourage everyone to have seconds, to eat more, there was enough.

She found a haven for her lunch hour, on a bench in a nearby plaza. A stone general claimed the center, sword raised high, covered with pigeons and their droppings. She'd never read the general's plaque and

didn't know who he was. How many people—how
many thousands—fought and died for their country
without having statues made of them? Who would
grace the city's plazas once the revolution won? I
don't want to be a statue, she thought, I just want to
know that I was part of it. That I did something
to help the change as it was coming, and can say so
to my grandchildren: I knew the change was coming, I gave myself to it, I did everything I could;
they'll look into my face in wonder and be proud.
Tell us again, they'll say. Tell us all about it. I was
fighting for you, so you could have a happy Uruguay,
where everybody has enough to eat. They'll be puzzled at the crazy past, where not everyone could eat,
and they'll grow up and grow old and tell their
grandchildren. Salomé took another bite of her sandwich. I am fighting for you, she said in her mind,
speaking to the city: you, Montevideo, flat and slow
and unassuming, the only place I know, with all your
hungry mouths and unsung charms, capital of a
small land at the far end of the earth, where light falls
on fractured pavement, where look, look, two old
ladies now walk arm in arm toward a bench carrying
purses that match their hats, and beneath those hats
who knows what memories lie fallow. She finished
her sandwich. The ladies were still walking. Their
steps were infinitesimal, they looked as though they'd
never hurried in their lives, the journey to the bench
could take all day. The wind rustled the leaves and
Salomé's collar and the skirts of the old ladies. An-

other day, another plaza, in this sweetsad city. The general bore his pigeon shit in silence. The park bench held nothing but sun.

Six minutes left of her lunch hour. She threw crumbs at the agitated birds.

President Pacheco ruled by decree. He routinely overrode the constitution. He proclaimed union strikers to be subject to the draft, which enabled soldiers to open fire on them, force them back to work, and take them into custody in martial jails. Reporters wrote obliquely, burying hints of unrest in careful columns. Jobs were slashed, including Abuelo Ignazio's, leaving him home each day, slumped on the sofa, staring out the window at the pale walls of the prison, which filled with political prisoners, from socialists to laborers to Tupamaros. His pension was paltry but the family could go on: Mamá still brought home cash from waiting tables, Abuela Pajarita still offered herbs and teas and listening ears in the back of Coco's butcher shop, and Salomé, of course, brought home a decent salary. Roberto, now a star in the biology department, did not need to leave the university in order to bring home wages, nor did the family have to join the bread lines that coiled around blocks throughout the city.

Her days were soft and hard, soft and hard, the soft hot lips of Tinto, the hard slopes of guns (twenty of them, newer kinds, including M16s just like the ones being used against Vietnam), the soft wind she read instinctively for signs of danger, the hard heels of her pumps against the office floor, the soft voice of Abuelo as he told and retold stories of an older mystic sepia Uruguay, the hard doors that closed for secret meetings to begin.

The Movement gathered momentum. Membership swelled. Her cell now had eleven members, more elbows and less oxygen. It was 1968 and the world heaved and gasped and coruscated with uprisings, you could read all about it, they were everywhere, all over their continent and also in Mexico City, Czechoslovakia, London, Paris, Vietnam, Warsaw, Berlin, Chicago, Australia, Japan, places she had never seen or touched but could connect to, was linked to already, one fleck in a gargantuan glittering web that spanned the globe, surrounded it, entangled it in sticky threads of change. Uprising threads. There was no escaping them. In her little peripheral country—she could feel it, sometimes, looking down a dusky street—she fingered the subtle reins of the world and it was true, wasn't it, the ride to revolution, the slant into a gallop. The time had come for headlong hurtles that would never be forgotten, that historians of the future would write of in grand terms: **that's where liberation began.** It called for intensity, concealment, sacrifice. Others sacrificed far more than she, like Orlando, for example, whose name had appeared on a list of people wanted for sedition and who now was in hiding. Tupas were wanted. They were notorious. Their name was banned from the press. Reporters could only use the words "criminal" or "terrorist." One paper called them "The Nameless Ones," and the office burned to the ground (buildings burn, thought Salomé, over our name!)—but the term stuck. She heard it on bus rides, in plazas, at kiosks downtown, over Coco's glass cases of meat.

The Nameless Ones are at it again—they've just robbed a casino.

They're just like Robin Hood.

They're going to save us from this mess.

The Nameless Ones, they caused this mess, what are you talking about, idiot, they're the problem.

They're the cockroaches of Uruguay.

More like the heroes.

More like the caca.

They're going to liberate this nation.

Pacheco won't let them.

The Nameless Ones are smarter than him.

That's for sure.

They care more about us too.

I hate them.

I applaud them.

Careful, don't clap too loudly.

Why not? You see? We're not free anymore!

The Nameless Ones are free.

How do you know?

It's obvious.

Nothing about them is obvious.

You should ask them.

Ha!

I fear them, if you've got to know the truth.

I wish I had the balls to be one.

I wish that I could meet one because, let me assure you, I've got a load of things to say.

Even children heard the whispers, as Tía Xhana recounted one night.

"Señora Durán, she teaches third grade next door to me. She's no sympathizer, I can tell you that." Xhana poured wine into Ignazio's glass. "But last week, she asked her students to write down a word, any word, that starts with 'T.' Nineteen of them— nineteen!—wrote 'Tupamaro.' So what did Señora Durán do? She tried to remove all the Robin Hood books from the school library. But guess what?"

A thick pause settled over the table.

"What?" Mamá said.

"She was too late. They were all checked out. Even kids know what's going on."

"As well they should," said Mamá.

Abuelo Ignazio looked as if the potatoes had soured in his mouth. "How can The Nameless be a good lesson for children?"

"How can repression?" Mamá swung her hair, which she wore today in a loose and supple mane. "People need all the hope they can get."

Abuelo rolled his eyes. Salomé pictured herself pouring hope—a viscous liquid stored in secret vats, now pouring onto streets, under cars, into gutters, over cobbles, right through walls, like the porridge in that story of the pot that wouldn't stop. Wine swirled sharply against her tongue.

In December 1968, Roberto crossed the river to visit his father in Argentina for the summer. He packed his bag fastidiously and wandered the house with buoyant steps. He assured his girlfriend, Flor, on the phone, **Of course I'll miss you, don't be silly,** leaning absently against the wall. Salomé was invited too, but did not go. She was needed at her embassy deployment. Times were brutal, times were bright; even the Beatles had written a song called "Revolution." The world sped at full tilt. There was work to do. And in any case, even though he'd offered, her father didn't want to see her as much as he wanted to see Roberto, a reality made clear by the discrepancy between the conversations they had on the phone. With Salomé, their father was awkward, sometimes monosyllabic. With his son, he seemed to become animated, keeping him on the line for many minutes, with long stretches in which Roberto the younger listened avidly, nodding slowly, then finally responding with a comment related to his studies, or their father's accomplishments, or a singular biological phenomenon that, of course, yes of course, he should know about, or how wonderful it would be to meet the scientists his father mentioned, eminent men, his father's friends. Men Roberto the younger looked up to the way his peers looked up to John Lennon. She, Salomé, would be a nuisance on this trip, an afterthought at best, the girl who dropped out after high school, a mere secretary—what would they talk about? When she searched herself for feelings about her father, in the candid dark of sleepless nights, she found not love or hate or rage or even longing, but a hollow absence of emotion, a cavity so old it had no desire to be filled. She lacked the words to explain this to her mother, but fortunately, she didn't need to. To Salomé's surprise, Eva responded to her decision with an acceptance that bordered on relief. Her son seemed to cause her far more worry, with his obvious enthusiasm, his distraction during dinner, his preoccupation with what to take and what to leave behind, all of which Eva bore with a tense smile, as though the ride across the river were a ride away from her, as though the pull he felt toward his father might capture him, mothlike, and never fully deliver him home. On the day he left, Salomé stood at the ferry station between Eva and Pajarita, who waved and waved as he walked down the ramp, even though his back was to them. Finally he paused and turned and they not only waved but called, **Adiós, adiós, llámanos.** They could have set a fire with the energy they generated, calling and waving and rising to their toes, and Salomé felt a sting of envy, not for the voyage, but for the ferocious love revealed in the goodbye.

She met with Tinto in the park later that night.

"I don't care," she murmured into his chest.

"How can that be? He's your fa—" He trailed off, her hand was on his trousers, on his fly, not opening, not ever, but speaking to his hard sex with her fingers. Wind kissed the treetops.

"Everything," he breathed later, "in its time."

The plans for Pando unfolded on a cool August night. Orlando outlined the operation with rare enthusiasm. It would take place on October 9, 1969, two years exactly after Che's assassination. They were going to seize the whole town for an afternoon. They would gather funds and weapons and show the world the strength of Uruguay's resistance.

"We're talking about a major military takeover." He stroked his beard, which had grown back darker than before. "All the most experienced members will be needed. Tinto. Anna. Leona. Guillermo. Salomé."

For all her steel-rabbit nights and devoted espionage, Salomé had never been on an operation. She had not held a gun in public, nor robbed a bank or casino or gun club. She felt exhilarated and slightly unsteady. She glanced over at Tinto, who winked at her through semidarkness.

In the days leading up to Pando—as she rode the bus and typed and washed the dishes—she strained to keep the thrill and fear of it contained. One day Pando could be remembered as the Moncada Barracks of the Uruguayan revolution, the watershed, the start of a new era. A plaza shone in her mind's eye, with a fountain or a statue at its center, and all of them were there, Tinto, Leona, Orlando, Anna, Guillermo, and dozens of unknown Tupamaros, raising rifles in the air, out in the open, not to shoot but to show their triumph, and the people felt the transformation of their town as a shimmer through the air and fell to their knees at the sight of guns so she called out **rise, rise, don't be afraid,** and then they rose and wept and danced and shouted incoherent words.

On the appointed day, she rose early to pack and unpack and repack her bag. Pistols, leaflets, one white handkerchief, one nice blouse, thirty copper handcuffs, secretarial files arranged across the top. She dressed in black, as directed. Her fingers shook. She tried to calm herself. She recited the instructions in her mind. Arrive promptly at the funeral home. Remember you're in mourning. Be convincing. Try to cry. Water, she thought. She needed water. And at least some toast for breakfast.

In the kitchen, Abuela Pajarita had already prepared the **mate.**

"Good morning," she said, and extended the gourd.

Salomé took it without removing the bag from her shoulder. The bitter drink soothed and woke her throat. This kitchen was not guaranteed, nor was her return to it. The light. The jars. The potted plants. The roots laid in a baking dish to dry, dark and twisted, destined to soothe an old lady's aching joints or heart or conscience. The stove at which three generations had cooked. All of it could disappear, and she could disappear from it, even though that seemed impossible, and yet it was always possible; contingency was obvious, a fact of life, and today even more so since a single bullet could do the trick, keep her from coming back, from ever learning the names of all the plants in all those pots; the names themselves were fragile, living as they did in Abuela's solitary mind, and who knew what would happen (to the bundles, the jars, the stool in Coco's shop) when she died, which seemed more impossible than anything, Abuela dying—surely this house would crumble or explode if Abuela ever died.

Abuela glanced at her with unnerving clarity. "Do you have time for toast?"

"Just enough time."

"I'll make it for you."

"That's all ri—"

"It's no problem." She had already placed two slices of bread on the griddle. Her braid poured down her back in a silver stream. Salomé wanted to clasp on to it. She wanted to shout that she was eighteen, a guerrilla, about to seize a town, able to make her own toast. She wanted to eat Abuela's toast forever, and this shamed her: that with the day's great battle waiting, she should want to stay here, safe, with her grandmother, surrounded by green smells and languorous light. Abuela buttered the toast and watched her granddaughter take big bites. "You won't sit down?"

"I have to get to work."

"**Ta.** We'll see you for dinner?"

"Of course," Salomé said, already facing the door.

By the time she arrived at the funeral parlor, two dozen mourners had gathered. They were young, somber, dressed in sharp black clothes. They approached her one by one and kissed her cheek. There was no exchange of names. They were supposed to be extended cousins, intimate already, mourning the death of their tío Antuñez, taking him, in a procession of cars, to his hometown for burial. Tupas. Tupas. Their cheeks were smooth as balm against hers; she fought the urge to clasp them in two hands so she could stare at and memorize their features.

Orlando and Leona approached her, along with a round man with fine white hair. "My name is Tiburcio," the man said. "I'm the undertaker. I'm sorry for your loss."

Salomé nodded. She searched for something adequate to say.

"I understand," he added. "It seems that everybody loved him very much."

"It's true," Leona said. She smelled like jasmine oil. "He was so generous. Always gave to the poor."

Tiburcio knit his face into a practiced empathy. "Yes. Yes."

The funeral was brisk and simple, and afterward the crowd of cousins headed outside. In the driveway, nine black funeral cars glistened in the sun. The hearse stood in front, its back doors open. Six pallbearers carried a coffin toward it. Garlands lay on top of it and guns lay inside. It was too much, the hot spring air, the polished coffin, the uncle who had given but not given to the poor, a funeral with no dead man, a coffin with no remains, no remains but guns, guns for bones, guns for flesh, only guns remain, and all of them standing in a strange and secret family, a family of Nameless Ones, a family of masks, a family mourning the death of—who? what?—and she longed to know them, these anonymous cousins, these **jóvenes** dressed in black, not their names or favorite foods but what they saw inside that coffin, what had sent them looking, what they mourned and treasured in the darkest corners of their bodies. Do you love what I love, do you know why you do it, and what for God's sake do you do with all the fear? Their faces were so lovely in the sunlight, fresh and stern and full of bones that could quite easily be broken. She wanted to shield their cheeks and all the brittle bodies of this country, their country, her country, but she could only carry out orders and begin to weep. She wept so well that the undertaker placed a hand on her back. She leaned into him; the hearse slammed shut. Tiburcio's eyes were wet.

"It'll be all right," he said.

They piled into the cars, a pallbearer at each steering wheel. Salomé rode in the car Tiburcio drove, with Orlando and two other Tupamaros. The highway grew sparse as they left Montevideo, city streets giving way to square huts and lone fruit stands. The sky expanded like a huge blue tent. They passed a **cantegril,** with its tin-and-cardboard shacks and a stench that muscled through the windows. Finally the road lay bare and flat before them, an incision between green fields. Tiburcio let his small talk trickle into silence. Orlando was impassive. They drove on.

The cars in front of them pulled over. It happened fast. The undertaker peered through the windshield. "Why is he—?"

"Just pull over, please," Orlando said.

The car stopped on the shoulder of the road. Orlando pulled out his pistol with celerity. "Sir, please exit the car."

Salomé could not see Tiburcio's face; she only heard a sharp intake of air, followed by the car door and the shuffle of feet on gravel. Orlando got out. Ahead of them, the other cars engaged in the same dance; a driver is startled into standing up and offering his wrists behind his back for wire handcuffs; he submits to the backseat; a well-dressed mourner takes the steering wheel and peels onto the highway, sun flashing against tinted windows.

Orlando drove. Tiburcio sat next to Salomé in the back, eyes wide and deerlike. Salomé held her pistol in her lap.

For a minute, there was no sound except the low rush of the road.

"What the hell is going on?" Tiburcio said.

"We're Tupamaros," Orlando said, eyes fixed on the road. "We've seized these cars for an operation."

"Tupamaros?"

"That's right."

"Really?"

"Yes."

"Where are you taking me?"

"To Pando."

Tiburcio chewed the inside of his cheek. "And your uncle?"

"Not real."

Salomé fished out a leaflet, one hand still on her gun. " 'The regime's sole aim is to humiliate the workers,' " she read. "We're workers, just like you. We want to stop injustice, and set things right for everyone."

The undertaker looked at her. His irises were gray, tight, verging on transparent. She felt ashamed of her earlier false tears. "**Pues,** that doesn't sound too bad."

"Don't be scared," she added. "We won't hurt you."

"Scared? Of you?" His laugh was sharp and tinny. "You look like my grandchildren."

Half an hour later they arrived in Pando, with its gentle watercolor streets. They drove up to the dappled plaza and stopped the car. Salomé, Orlando, and the two other Tupas tied white handkerchiefs around their arms. Her heart beat aggressively in her chest. Almost one o'clock. In the plaza, on a bench, a young couple ate sandwiches in the sun. They also wore white kerchiefs on their arms. Somewhere, a few streets away, a crew was poised to lay siege to the police. Tinto and others lay in wait at the fire station. Salomé's target, El Banco República, sat in full view across the plaza, with its stone walls and tall brass doors, an impenetrable-looking building that she was about to storm. Her whole body felt tight, as if composed of wire. Tiburcio leaned against her, chin on his chest, damp and fleshy and relaxed. His lips moved slightly. She slid her arm through his. "You're going to stick with me," she whispered. He nodded without looking up.

Three more black funeral cars pulled up to the plaza, one by one. The woman on the bench turned toward their car. She spied Salomé's kerchief; they smiled.

A motorcycle roared up and circled the edge of the plaza. Its rider waved a white handkerchief in the air. They sprang from the car, all four Tupamaros and Tiburcio in his handcuffs. They crossed the hot plaza; halfway across, two mourners joined them with five rifles. They swept into the bank.

"Everyone stay calm," Orlando called, raising a rifle into the air.

The lunchtime line of customers turned. A teller howled.

"You're safe," Orlando said. "Don't worry, we're Tupamaros, please line up against the wall."

Salomé helped shepherd people, one hand holding the pistol, the other arm threaded through Tiburcio's. She surged with a hot current of energy. The undertaker shuffled beside her, his sweaty bulk resigned and unimpeding. A chair appeared for a pregnant woman. Orlando left for the vault. The room was a thick sea of sweat and breath and unasked questions.

"Don't be afraid," Salomé urged their backs. "We're seizing the town on behalf of the people. No one will get hurt."

She moved down the row, holding Tiburcio close, passing out leaflets. Customers twisted in place to read the communiqué. "Keep your hands on the wall, please."

"But I want to read this."

"Good. But keep your hands on the wall."

"How can I do that and read at the same time?"

"Just try," Salomé said, as sternly as she could. She felt like a schoolteacher with smart, unruly students. She moved on to a bespectacled man in a plaid shirt.

"Gracias," he said, taking the leaflet.

"De nada."

"Tupamaros?"

"Right."

"Really?"

"Yes."

He brightened, pinned the leaflet to the wall, and lost himself in reading.

Through the half-open door, she heard an old woman arguing with a Tupamaro.

"I'm here to collect my pension."

"**Ta, Señora,** but you can't today."

"What's that, son?"

Louder: "You can't collect today. The bank is taken over by Tu-pamaros."

"Tupa—**¿qué?**"

"That's right. You have to come inside now; it's dangerous on the streets."

"Will they give me my pension tomorrow?"

"Ye—I don't know. Please, come **inside.**"

He entered, escorting the reluctant lady by the elbow. Her chin was high, her face austere. "Why should I come in," she grumbled, to no one in particular, "if they won't pay me?"

Salomé handed the lady a leaflet, which she folded into precise quarters and tucked into her purse. She examined Salomé accusingly; Salomé moved on, quickly, down the row, passing out paper, jostling the undertaker's shoulder. She wondered how it was going in the vault, on the street, at the firehouse. Stop thinking. Focus.

A woman burst through the door, her hair a long cape around her. "The Bank of Pando's being held up!"

She gaped at the row of captives, the empty counters, Salomé's pointed gun. "What? Here too?"

Salomé nodded; the woman laughed. Salomé motioned for her to turn around, and she did so, placing her hands against the wall, still laughing, hair shaking like fine black silk. Salomé handed her a leaflet, wishing the paper could somehow shut her up. It was good, yes, if citizens did not cower in fear, but she was a guerrilla, a warrior, armed and serious, how dare they laugh?

"Look," the woman said, "I can't read like this. What does it say?"

"It describes our aims. Why we're here."

"Well? Why are you here?"

"Read the leaflet," Plaid Man called out. "It's good."

"Why should I, when I can hear it from her?"

"She wants to set things right," Tiburcio said, cocking his head at Salomé.

"Really? That's why she's got you cuffed?"

Tiburcio shrugged.

The door flew open. Salomé turned, gun cocked for laughers or old ladies or anyone at all. It was Tinto, flushed, fresh from the fire station, hair falling in mad fronds over his eyes.

"It's official," he shouted. "The Tupamaros have taken Pando!"

He leaped onto the counter and broke into a speech, garbled, impassioned. "Liberation, see, it's in the air, we're breathing it, it's filling up this spectacular country, Uruguay, a forgotten gem on a lost continent—but no more—we're going to shine, nothing can stop us—**uruguayos,** dear citizens, brothers, sisters, you are the revolution, and you will be free—all of Latin America will be free. Che is here with us, cheering—can you hear him?" He talked on. Plaid Man's eyes grew moist behind his glasses. The old lady with the pension pursed her lips, out of annoyance or to keep from smiling. A few stayed wooden, but others nodded, cheered, hooted, their hands still on the wall, their bodies twisting to see Tinto over their shoulders, a large young man with open palms, awkward, damp-faced, bright-voiced, hair flung in several directions, arms wide on his sudden stage.

Orlando emerged from the vault, hauling sacks. "Let's go."

Tinto leaped down. They headed toward the door. Shots rang outside. More shots. The room fell silent.

"I'll look," a pale Tupamaro said. He came back quickly. "There's a cop outside. He's exchanging shots with two of ours."

Orlando's face was a wall of calm. "We'll wait inside."

They waited. Shots punctured the quiet of the room. Someone whimpered at the wall. The shots stopped and they walked outside and sun stabbed Salomé's eyes. Three funeral cars were parked across the street, the last one riddled with bullet holes. Its tires were shredded. A policeman lay behind it, young, black-haired, his pant leg soaked and shining. A red pool spread slowly from his leg.

"Shit," Orlando said. "We've lost a car. We'll have to double up. Pile in!"

Salomé ran to a car and pushed Tiburcio, the undertaker, into the backseat, then pressed in after him, Orlando after her. Through the rear window, she glimpsed Tinto crammed into the car behind them.

She threw the rest of her leaflets out the window as they peeled off, and they fell like huge confetti onto the street, blanketing the asphalt, absorbing, she hoped, some trickle of the officer's blood. They turned a corner. The avenue was thronged with people: on the sidewalks, perched in doorways, swarming in the middle of the street, waving white kerchiefs from balconies, lunging for their car.

"Will you be back?"

"When's the revolution?"

"Enroll me!"

"Take me!"

"Take my brother—"

"Hey!"

"Long live Che Guevara!"

The driver honked and yelled out of the window. "Clear the way! Please, clear the way!" He swore under his breath.

There were nine of them, jammed into the car: Orlando, Tiburcio, Salomé, and six others, three of them in Pando police uniforms. Flesh and sweat and thick air pressed on every side. The crowds abated. They pulled over at the edge of town, in front of cemetery gates.

"Let's drop him here," the driver said.

Salomé removed Tiburcio's cuffs with rapid tenderness. The feel of him had become familiar, almost second nature. "Thank you."

The undertaker squeezed her arm with his. "Listen, you be careful."

She didn't look at him. "I'm fine."

The car door opened. He stood alone on the gravel driveway, blinking in the sun, a round man with fine white hair just waking from a dream. She wanted to say more to him, but the door closed and they pulled away. She waved through the back window. He waved back, ornate iron gates looming behind him, his gesture smaller and smaller in the distance.

The highway opened its long arms to them. She was starving; she could have eaten the upholstery, the pistols, the sky's bright cloth. The boys in police uniforms were giddy, disheveled, recounting their stories from the front.

"You should have seen the looks on their faces. Those cops."

"I found one in the bathroom, taking a piss; a huge guy; he laughed at me until I poked him with my gun."

"No kidding?"

"No kidding."

"On our street we snarled the traffic, throwing leaflets, shouting, 'Long live the revolution!' "

She felt their charge: electric, untamable. It shot through her skin. They had done it, they had triumphed, they had come out unscathed.

Orlando leaned toward the driver. "Is this the fastest you can go?"

"I'm flooring it, **compañero.** It's the extra weight."

"Of course."

"They won't catch us. We're ahead. By the time

the Montevideo police get word, we'll all be safe at our—wherevers."

Orlando touched the driver's shoulder. He was really a gentle man. "Just go as fast as you can."

They reached the edge of Montevideo. A police car lurked on the side of the road. They fell silent. The officers—the real ones—sat up at the sight of the long black car, gunned their engine, then spied the uniforms in the backseat and slumped, no, those couldn't be the Tupas. She felt sick. They were hunted already. She said a silent, clumsy, half-forgotten Hail Mary, Full of Grace, Blessed Are You, isn't that how it goes, in any case protect us, here in this car, and also Tinto, wherever he is, and Leona, and Anna, and Guillermo, and all the Tupas who kissed me at the funeral this morning, all the Tupas still making their escapes; and Tiburcio as he finds his way home; and the officer with his wet leg; please see our hearts, Holy Mary Mother of, forgive us the wet leg; pray for us sinners, now and in the hour of, again for Tinto. Tinto. Tinto. They kept on, into the folds of the city. The car pulled into a quiet street and parked behind a blue Ford. A young woman with a white kerchief on her arm emerged from the Ford, approached their car, and opened the trunk without a word. The driver began to transfer bags of guns and cash from the black car to the blue. Orlando climbed into the backseat of the Ford and lay down, invisible to the street. She wondered where he would sleep tonight, where he had been sleeping this past year, where his wife imagined that he was. The rest of them scattered in four directions, without good-byes. Salomé stopped to buy empanadas in a bakery, six of them wrapped in crisp white paper. More than she could eat but she was famished. Her bus pulled up; she sat in the back with her surreptitious lunch and watched Montevideo's streets turn larger, louder, squat dwellings rising into tall apartment buildings, cobbles giving way to asphalt streets. Montevideo, city of urban guerrillas with smooth cheeks. City of pigeons and their shit and possibility. City of damp soft undertakers, hidden guns, stolen copper wires.

She arrived at the embassy building and headed to the bathroom. She freshened her lipstick, changed her blouse, pressed her searing thoughts into a ball where nobody could see them, and checked her hair in the mirror. It was 2:56 p.m.: and here she was, Good and Quiet Salomé, back from the dental appointment she'd dutifully requested time for weeks ago, ready to work, punctual as always. She slipped behind her desk and started typing the letter at the top of her stack. Mr. Richards came to her station.

"Salomé. How was the dentist?"

"Okay; not too painful after all." She cradled her cheek to nurse her invented ache.

He dropped his voice. "I'm not sure I believe you."

Breath trapped in her lungs.

He leaned closer, with his Marlboro scent. "The dentist is always painful."

She laughed, too sharply. He grinned and saun-
tered to his office.

Half an hour later, Viviana, the head secretary,
rushed into the room. Her eyes glittered behind her
glasses. "The Nameless! Have you heard?"

"No." Salomé looked up, careful to veil her face.

"Well, they did this crazy thing at Pando—"

"Oh?"

"Yes, it's terrible, but anyway, the police got them
on the way back."

"Got them?"

"There was a shootout at Toledo Chico."

Salomé couldn't speak. Viviana leered in satisfaction. "I know. They thought they were so invinci-
ble."

She forced a smile. "Well, look at that."

"Some of them are dead."

"What?"

"That's what the radio said."

Salomé stared at her typewriter. "And they de-
served it."

"Exactly what I say."

Viviana left. Salomé ran to the bathroom and
vomited up four and a half empanadas. The rest of
the afternoon was a dull haze. After work, she went
directly to her cell meeting. She could have torn her
skin off. Tinto wasn't there.

Anna gave the report. She had been in Toledo
Chico. Her words were flat; she spoke them to the oil
lamp. The police had surrounded two cars. Three

Tupas tried to surrender. Anna watched them raise their arms high and walk slowly toward the police through knee-high grass. They were shot down, and when they fell officers ran up and filled their bodies with more bullets, then kicking, then more bullets into corpses. One carload, with Anna in it, managed to escape; the other was captured. Tinto's car. Nothing to do but wait and hope for news.

Salomé couldn't vomit, her intestines were empty, completely stark, as if she'd never eaten and would never eat again. At the close of the meeting, Leona approached, arms open.

"Salomé."

"I have to go."

"Salomé."

"Leave me alone."

She stumbled out before her turn.

That night, at dinner, Salomé couldn't touch her food. Her family's voices meshed and blurred and rose around her. They were talking about Pando, how shocking it all was, how this side or that side had gone too far, the Tupa deaths were a tragedy, the Tupa deaths were a relief, shut up, shut up, and now Abuelo Ignazio was talking to her, **Eat, Salomé,** Mamá was eyeing her too keenly, **What's wrong, what's the matter,** Roberto at his (far, far) end of the table, **she looks sick,** Abuelita reaching over, **Perhaps you've got a fever,** her hand on Salomé's forehead, then shoulder, **Tomorrow you should stay home.**

She stayed in bed for four days. Fever shook and

pressed and stretched her and hung bits of Tinto in her vision, wide mouth, bent knee, torn hand, broken face. She was breaking every rule in the unwritten Tupa handbook, she should rise and show a calm and healthy face, but she either didn't care or couldn't help it anymore. Bad guerrilla, look at you, what shameful cracks in your self-discipline. Shut up, go to hell, where is he now, where is he? She didn't want to eat or drink, but Abuela came each mealtime with a bowl of soup and deep brown tea. Mamá slept on the floor beside her bed. This forced her to pretend to sleep, until she heard her mother's breathing grow audible and slow.

"What happened?"

Don't ask.

"Salomé."

Stop it.

"Is it a young man?"

You can't, Mamá.

"You can tell me."

"No. It's not."

"Then what?"

"It's just the fever."

"It seems like more."

"I just don't feel well. I don't know why."

"Just tell me what I can do."

You can shut up.

You can give me Tinto.

You can spit on me and call me a horrible daughter.

Each day, Abuelo Ignazio came in and sang her

lullabies, old ones he'd learned when he was a Venetian boy. He meandered, off-key. The songs were in Italian, a language she rarely heard and that made her think of glistening water and errant angels.

"My mother sang these songs to me."

"Oh."

"They cured my nightmares."

Nightmares? What did you dream about?

"Maybe they'll cure yours."

They kept coming and coming, with their teas and words and songs, and she was not a girl but a monster in girl's clothing for treating them this way, drinking tea and listening to songs and feigning sleep on a mattress full of secret steel. And there was part of her that wished things could be as they had been, long before, when she was small and didn't know how to stash parts of herself so far down she ran the risk of losing them, when wanting good things for the world was still a sweetsafe thing to do, and when Abuelo and Abuela and Mamá could be turned to for a warm embrace and sound advice on tricky homework or any other problem she might face. She was not that girl to them, not anymore, not even slightly. She was a thief who'd stolen their girl and left a false copy in her place.

Leona phoned on the fourth day. "I found your book."

Salomé leaned against the wall. She didn't want to buckle. "Where?"

"Oh, around. There's a hole in my bookshelf now." She paused. "It wasn't too cold today, was it?"

Hole. Pocitos. Guillermo's uncle's house was in Pocitos; their cell had met in the basement. The basement had a trapdoor that led into a tunnel, and Salomé had never gone down it but she knew it led to a **ratonera.** A rat's nest. A hiding place. Its code words: **cold today.**

"No, it was nice and warm."

"Well, I'll see you later."

"Okay. **Adiós.**"

Salomé grabbed her coat and darted out of the house before anyone could stop her. She walked to Pocitos and knocked on the uncle's door. Guillermo appeared, led her to the basement, and handed her a flashlight. She sank through the trapdoor and down a ladder through a fetid passage. When she landed, she saw a low tunnel in front of her. She bent over and walked down it; he was there, at the end, in a dank cave of a room.

He was a spectre of himself, hunched beside a bucket of his own shit and piss. He squinted in the beam of her flashlight as if it bruised him. She turned it downward; the room dimmed; but she had already seen the burns, welts, a face folded on itself like a sealed letter.

"You shouldn't have come."

She reached for the bucket. "I'll be right back."

Down the tunnel, up the ladder, carefully, don't spill, empty the bucket, rinse it out as if anything could be done about the smell, then trapdoor ladder tunnel and back again. She sat down next to him. They were silent for some time, breathing scarce air.

"I didn't want you to see me this way."

"I just wanted to see you."

"But like this?"

"You. I wanted to see you."

He recrossed his legs, trying not to grimace. "They don't know your name. Not from me."

She touched his hand. He flinched. She began to pull away.

"No," he said. "Stay."

They were quiet. His bottom lip shook. She looked away. More time passed.

"Salomé. Salomé."

She bent to the crook of his elbow, to a cigarette burn on which she placed an extremely gentle kiss. She kissed his wounds, slowly, one by one. She followed them beneath his clothes to all the tender hidden places that La Máquina had visited before her. They made love in that dark hole for the first time. Virginity melted like ice thrown into flames. After all the pomp and warnings, the loss of virginity was such a simple thing. You just raise your arms and hurl it. The rest is ready, waiting, beating hotly under skin. That is what she learned, that is how she did it, pressing in, against the bruised parts, the burned parts, everything. It was clear that he hurt everywhere but he wouldn't let her go. They took their time. She wrapped her legs around his body like two bandages; together they pushed through pain into intolerable ecstasies beyond it. Afterward, they stayed tangled, sweaty, charred, exhausted, in an airless room, with nothing but each other's breaths to breathe. With moth-soft fingers she stroked the swollen skin, its colors hidden in the dark although she knew them, red burns, white blisters, blue and tender bruises.

"We'll get them," she whispered, and only in that moment did Tinto Cassella weep.

The nation was at war. Everybody knew it. The president declared a long state of emergency. All **montevideanos** had to be home by nine o'clock. Soldiers rang their boot-songs out on stone streets, on boulevards, on lanes where they woke old couples in their beds, **Where is your son?** Orlando was among the captured. Salomé stole moments at the window, staring at the prison across the street. Orlando was inside, along with others, one hundred faceless Tupamaros; she tried to picture them, within those walls, her new neighbors, distant yet close. Facing what Tinto had faced. It seemed like a bad dream, that kind of pain across the street from her house, this house Abuelo Ignazio had built with his own hands so long ago. Hard to believe, even harder to stop thinking about. Was it possible that it could slide in through the window and mingle with their wine and breath and thoughts? She closed the curtains every day, and bickered with Mamá, who wanted them open. The light, she said, don't you want to let the light in? Salomé didn't. With the curtains open she couldn't take her eyes off the prison.

Its walls were as pale and elegant as always. They revealed nothing. She saw them frequently, as her mother kept battling for the light. Mamá liked to sit in the corner by the window and write. She wrote and wrote and didn't seem to care about the prison outside, as long as the sun cascaded down around it, through the window, to the page. She wrote every day, no matter how many hours she'd worked, or how tired she seemed. Some poems ended up published in journals, or performed at salons across the city, but many of them seemed to disappear into hidden hoards in her room. She wrote so much that Salomé imagined caches all over her mother's bedroom, like the one she had found under the mattress— surely the drawers and closets and dusty slits between furniture and wall now exploded with stashed words. Yet they still were not enough for Mamá to stop: she kept writing, writing, tilting her page toward the light.

Anna became the new head of their cell. She was exacting. Her words were clear and crisp and she demanded the same of others. Guillermo left their cell to head his own. Their numbers soared. The day at Pando had ignited the city's youth and sent them searching for Tupas in their urban lairs. Student groups across the globe had rhapsodized about the bold, clever guerrillas of Uruguay, as underground reports informed them. Fidel Castro himself had commended their victory and praised the Tupamaros: **Revolution is alive and strong in Uruguay.** Salomé felt the new members' excitement, the fresh sweat of their thoughts: **we're part of something. Robin Hood. People are hearing about us everywhere. Castro even said.** She wanted to shake them, wanted to shake her country, little country, forgotten country, wide-eyed for all its cleverness, so easily taken by a scrap of glamour. She was being unfair. They'd come for other reasons, surely, and were smart enough to know the risks. Still, they hummed with hope and purpose, while she felt old, worn, full of opaque layers that she herself could not see through. Autumn hurtled into Montevideo. She took part in the swift and seamless robbery of a casino, transferred stockpiles of guns and cash and uniforms, and helped arrange a jailbreak from the women's prison, which released a few dozen bodies back to work.

"It's a shame." Mr. Richards shook his head. The cigarette between his lips scattered ash. "You had yourselves a nice little country."

Salomé typed on.

"Sir." Viviana slapped the file cabinet. "With all due respect, it's far from over. The rebels don't stand a chance against the Measures."

Mr. Richards looked at Viviana's stalwart chin. She made his coffee and hung up his coat every morning. She was not a woman to offend. "You're right. You must be right. Still . . . I gotta say . . . those are some mighty smart guerrillas."

Salomé buried the impulse to smile. She had to focus, she had a mission: to find all the files she could about a man called Dan Mitrione.

It took her two weeks. He was hard to find. He

was not in the drawer with all the other U.S. nationals in Uruguay. He was in the top-secret drawer, the one Mr. Richards sealed with his own key, which Salomé stole one day and pressed into a bar of soap. Dan Mitrione, the file said, was an aid official, a minor one, sent by the Alliance for Progress. He was here to advise the police force. He had worked as a police chief in the state of Indiana, and since then had been an adviser in Brazil and the Dominican Republic. He had a wife and nine children, six of whom currently lived in Uruguay. He had an address in Malvín. He specialized in communications. There were some handwritten notes. Communications, the notes suggested, was an art form. It required nuance and practice and precision. Training was going well.

"Well done," Anna said at their next meeting. "This corroborates the other reports."

She briefed them on Mitrione. He gave lessons in a fully equipped studio in the basement of his house. The basement was soundproof. The police were the protégés. Trainings were conducted on "samples," beggars, prostitutes, **cantegrileros,** taken by force, never seen again. Salomé glanced at Tinto. He was staring at the flame of a candle. There were no oil lamps tonight, only two naked wicks, with their slow burn. She tried to catch his eye but he would not look up.

"So what are we going to do?" Leona said.

Anna brushed her hair back. She was beautiful, in a brutal sort of way. "Put him on trial."

Three weeks later, Mitrione disappeared. He was kidnapped, said President Pacheco and President Nixon and Mr. Richards and Abuelo Ignazio and all the newspapers still in print. No, the Tupamaros said in a communiqué, he was not kidnapped; he was arrested, held at the People's Prison, for crimes against the Uruguayan people.

It was August 1970, a bite-cold winter, the People's Prison a freezing basement. The defendant was offered a coat and coffee. He was brought meals by guards who kept their faces hooded at all times. He went on trial each morning—can you explain these memos from the Montevideo police? to the U.S. Embassy? these photos from Santo Domingo? what are they? again, sir, what are they?—and all his answers were elliptical, measured, cool. Salomé heard them from her post in the next room. She was on guard duty for the day. Just a day. She could do it. She had shivered from the cold as soon as she'd come in. The room was lit by one bare bulb and smelled of mold and sweat. She wore a burlap hood with eyeholes, held her rifle upright. The walls were plastered with newspaper, top to bottom, a cell with words for bars, words everywhere, crowing headlines, hemming their captive in. Finally the questions trailed off. The captive had reduced himself to monosyllables. She heard the shuffle of a blindfold being retied, and then two masked Tupas led him into the room. They sat him down, bound him to his chair, nodded to her, and left.

She sat across from the blindfolded man. Her hands were clammy in their leather gloves. He was tall, a little paunchy, his dark hair graying at the temples. He looked small through her eyeholes. A pocket of flesh hung under his chin. Stubby hairs grew on his jawline. His body was soft, mortal, made of flesh that drooped and bulged and sprouted hairs, and it was monstrous, untenable, that he should be man and not a monster, Dan to some, Dad to others, some other name—what name? what name?—to people on his table, made of flesh also, just as pliable and alive. He used water and electroshock together. He probed the tender darkness of the body. He taught the most recondite tools of pain. She couldn't fathom it, couldn't reconcile her thoughts with the plain man slouched against a battered wooden chair, but it seemed crucial to do so or else she'd never see the world with lucid eyes. Her eyes hurt. She closed them behind her mask. Here you are, the enemy, vulnerable and blind, and I can't even look at you. What kind of warrior does that make me? Who are you and what are you, how did you become Dan Mitrione, and how did we become these two cold people in a basement facing each other without looking? She saw him standing, unfettered, over Tinto, naked Tinto, writhing, mouth wide open, and then he turned into Mitrione, wide open, writhing, and it was she who stood over him and watched and bent in close to whisper, Do you understand yet? do you? do you?

Mitrione shifted. "Is there water?"

She poured a glass of water from a jug. She held it to his thin, pale lips.

He drank. "Thanks."

"De nada."

He raised his eyebrows. "A woman?"

She said nothing.

His mouth smirked. "You sound so young."

"The young have power too."

"So they think."

"What do you know?" she said, and regretted it immediately.

"What do I?" His voice was almost sweet.

Salomé looked down into his face. The blindfold was incongruous, a paisley bandanna stolen from Tinto's abuelo's drawer. El Mago Milagroso's bandanna. She thought of Tinto, the gentle muscle of him. She thought of Abuela too, with her panoply of plants; Mamá with her unslakable pen; the children of Dan Mitrione, in quiet beds, sharing a house with their father's machinations, the calibrated whispers, the patient escalation, the glazed eyes of officers acquiring a new craft.

"Not enough."

"What is that supposed to mean?"

"Not what matters." She walked back to her post.

"Oh, Christ," he said in a bored voice.

Silence spread into the dim, damp room. They sat across from each other, breathing the same air. Finally he slumped and seemed to doze. She relaxed her hands around her rifle. Two hours passed, walled in by written words. Her thoughts roamed to Tinto. His wide hands. Right now they might be sawing wood, or nailing hard, or cradling a gourd of **mate.** Tonight, at midnight, when they met in his uncle's car, she would peel the gloves off them despite the cold. She would slide them under her sweater to keep them warm, to bring them to the furnace. And maybe one day, after all, this lurching revolution would be done (was it still possible? where were they headed? toward the shining prize or off the road into dark gullies too deep to claw out of, no, don't think about that) and they could marry in broad daylight in a rain of uncooked rice. A liberated nation and a honeymoon. And then a quiet life of carpentry, babies perhaps, new lives for a new Uruguay. And Mamá wouldn't prod her anymore, the way she did now, disbelieving that her daughter, at nineteen, would have no suitors. Surely there's someone, she'd say, waxing on about Salomé's supposed beauty, calm disposition, brilliant mind. The only way to stop her was to say, Well, Mamá, what about you? Mamá would laugh—what, her, ha!—but it kept her from persisting. At first Salomé had done it in her own defense, no thought of answers, but something in the laugh, a glint of brass in it, had made her wonder, though of course it was impossible, it meant nothing, that glint of brass, that flush of Mamá's sometimes after seeing her hairdresser, a woman, and all those chic styles in hard times, impossible of course, but what had Tío Artigas said before he left for Cuba? **I don't judge you, Eva. Really.** He could have meant

her itch for luxury: or something else, the unthinkable, the unimaginable, a secret in her mother as
unimaginable as her own. People do not suspect
what they cannot imagine. If such a thing was true,
no one would suspect Eva, except perhaps the daughter who also knows about hiding the unthinkable.

Mitrione was awake. "Is it still you?"

"Yes."

"I'd like more water."

She rose and held the glass to his lips. He made
slurping noises. He dribbled water on his chin, like
a baby. She didn't need to clean him—it wasn't in her
duties—but she raised the edge of her shirt to his
face, and wiped. He drew back. She finished wiping,
wondering why she did it. She felt his stubble
through the cloth. When she finished, he nodded, as
if dismissing her from a mission he'd assigned. She
returned to her post. They sat.

"You Tupamaros," he said. "You're not what I expected."

"What did you expect? Vicious terrorists?"

"Of course."

Salomé settled the rifle on her lap. "How ironic."

Mitrione sighed, the long, slow sigh of a burdened
man.

They sat for another hour. She was hungry. Outside, the sun had surely swept its light off the streets.
She wondered whether there was any moon.

When he spoke again, Mitrione was hushed. "Are
you . . . they . . . planning to kill me?"

"We don't want to."

He cocked his head, as if cracking a code. A detective in a paisley blindfold. "The demands are still on the table?"

They were: the release of over a hundred Tupamaros, Orlando among them, in exchange for the life of Mitrione.

"I can't answer that."

"Ah." He paused. He looked as though he'd eaten something sour. "Can I have a cigarette?"

Salomé returned to his side, slipped a cigarette between his lips, and lit it. He sucked deeply; the tiny tip blazed orange.

"They'll never do it," he said. "I wouldn't either."

The thread between them—thin and sticky like a spider's—was too much. "All right," she said sharply, "no more talking."

His prediction proved right. Pacheco declared that he would not negotiate with terrorists, and no criminals would be released from prison. Soldiers pounded the streets, Montevideo was a drum, shaking with the rhythms of their boots, marching, percussive, continuous, kicking down the doors of people's homes, suspected Tupamaros dragged out of bed, **we will crush the terrorists,** and in a major coup they even captured the founder, long in hiding, Raúl Sendic, imprisoned to great fanfare and a flurry of photos in **El País.** Salomé couldn't sleep, because if she did she'd surely wake to the barrels of a dozen guns pointing through the dark at her full-of-steel bed, and—worse—be dragged out in plain sight of

Abuelo and Abuela and Roberto and Mamá, who would hover in the hall in their helpless pajamas, and she would not be able to bear, above all, the looks on their four faces.

The curfew tightened to six o'clock. Their cell met at dawn. They huddled in a supply closet, where mops and tubs of cleaning fluid stood around them like stern sentinels.

"It's time to vote." Anna looked haggard, but her makeup was crisp and perfect, ready for work. "Remember, this is not a sentimental choice. It never was for him. Think politically." She scanned them. "Well?"

Héctor, a new member, a soldier in full uniform, spoke first. "If we execute, the press will talk about his children, his poor wife. How violent and cruel we are. It gives them an excuse to come after us."

"But if we do nothing?" Leona asked. "It sends the message that we can't follow through on our word." She looked so poised, Salomé thought, no trace of child. "The whole world is looking at us."

"That's true," Carla, a schoolteacher, said. "If we look weak, that could cripple movements globally."

"Either way, they'll use this to try and crush us."

"Which they're trying to do anyway."

"So how do we decide?"

The debate kept on. Words lost their meanings in Salomé's ears, they slipped and slid in melted aural eddies. She tried to focus but something clamped her lungs, a tightening fist; she couldn't breathe; perhaps it was the air, the lack of oxygen, sleepless nights and dawns that stank of bleach; a mouth, her own, preparing for a simple yes or no; she felt light-headed, her mind spun, the debate was a sea of sound from which there rose, in her mind's eye, a stubbled chin, a drooling chin, heaving and enormous, like a whale.

"Salomé?" Tinto's voice cut through the rest. "Are you all right?"

She nodded. The room came back into focus.

"Your turn," Anna said tersely. Time was scarce. "Yes or no?"

She wanted to say no.

Anna frowned. "Salomé."

She looked around the room. Twelve faces turned to her in the paltry light. Moments from now, they would leave this cave and start their proper isolated days, each carrying, inside, a shard of the dream.

"Yes," she said.

She was stirring tomato sauce for dinner—she would never forget its lush, sweet-basil steam—when the phone rang. She raced to pick it up.

"**¿Hola?**"

"Salomé."

She didn't recognize the voice. "Yes."

"Cold today, wasn't it?"

Her knees her legs she couldn't feel them. Stop it, she thought, you know better.

"Yes," she said. "I have to wear my warmest coat."

"Good idea."

She listened to the hollow line.

"Bueno. Adiós."

"Adiós," she said, and hung up. The hall smelled of simmering tomatoes. She longed to taste one final spoonful, but there was no time. She thought quickly: her grandparents were napping, Roberto in his room, Mamá in the living room right by the front door. Perhaps she could run past her? No. Her purse was there, she might need it, she'd have to get it, she'd have to say good-bye.

She packed a small hasty bag of clothes, with files on top, and entered the living room. Mamá sat on the sofa, reading **Don Quixote** yet again. Gardel crooned from the record player, some old song about Buenos Aires. Behind her mother, in the window, an oak reached bare branches into black sky.

"Mamá," she said, marching toward her purse, "I brought the wrong files home. I'm going to the office to exchange them."

Mamá put her hand over the purse. "What?"

Salomé met her eyes, reluctantly. Mamá was still beautiful, sharp-featured, elegant, with her black hair and red lips. She glowed, gently, a tapered candle in the dark. "The translation is due by morning."

"But the curfew." Mamá waved her hand toward the city past the window. "The troops. The madness. You can't."

Salomé glanced down at the purse. Mamá's fingers

dug into it like claws. She pictured the two of them wrestling over it, thrashing on the floor. "I have to."

"Salomé. Anything could happen on a night like this."

"But it's for work."

"Who cares?" Mamá sprang to her feet. "Your safety is more important."

She stared at Salomé, and Salomé loved the long black lashes, angry eyes, mouth through which so many words (balms, sparks, razors) could emerge. For an instant she thought she might crumble into pieces and stay, after all, a pile of rubble at her mother's feet. But the purse was unattended; it was her chance. She lunged and grabbed it and raced to the door. "I'll be fine," she lied as it swung open.

Mamá clasped her wrist. "Stay!"

Salomé turned; their faces were just centimeters apart. She smelled the sweet-almond essence of Mamá's hair. Mamá probed her eyes, plumbed them, seeking an answer to a not-yet-spoken question, diving in search of secrets that could make the puzzle fit, yes, piece with broken piece.

"Hija—"

Salomé wrenched away. "Watch the stove for me," she said, and began to run.

She ran directly to the **ratonera** where she and Tinto had first made love. Through the trapdoor, down the ladder, down the tunnel, into the cave. Tinto was there, and Leona, and Héctor the soldier. They nodded to one another. No one spoke. She

curled up next to Tinto; he wrapped her in his arms.
She was shaking, his arms made her aware of it. He
gripped her fiercely, crushed her into him and she
crushed back. The bucket reeked already but she burrowed close until she caught his musk.

They slept fitfully on the floor.

The next morning, an unknown Tupamara
brought them bread, cheese, cigarettes, water, and
news: Mitrione's body had been found by the police.
Civilians had been urged to stay at home, the banks
were closed, the schools were closed, countless homes
had been turned on their heads. A national day of
mourning had been declared for Mitrione. Anna had
been taken, and many others. They had to stay in
hiding. The Tupa exchanged the full bucket for an
empty one, and rushed away. Their leader, Anna,
hung in the thick air like a ghost. Leona looked like
a statue of herself. Salomé broke the loaf of bread
into pieces. "Leona," she said, "I'm sorry."

Leona's eyebrows rose, a little, to show that she had
heard. Salomé handed her bread and cheese. Leona
shook her head.

"You have to eat," Salomé said. "We all do."

Leona ate. They all ate, in silence, in their dim circle lit by a single flashlight. Salomé tried not to think
about her house, the boots of soldiers, her guilty mattress, broken lamps, her family, her family, her family. The silence was as cloying as the smell.

"**Che,** Leona," she said.

"Yes?"

"Tell us a story."

"About what?"

"About your family. Russia. Anything."

Leona looked incredulous. She adjusted her glasses. She looked at Tinto, who nodded, and at Héctor, who shrugged. She began to speak. She told the story of Irina, her great-grandmother, who'd been known throughout Pereyaslav for the inimitable sound of her voice. When she sang, lovers ended quarrels, the ill found health, and dry brown plants returned to life. She could melt snow with a one-hour ballad. Then, one year, her husband and six of her eight children were killed in a pogrom. She stopped singing. Crops faltered; elders died. Townspeople left baskets of fruit at her door and begged her to sing again; she never did. But her daughter grew up with the gift, and spent her life crooning and wailing in the village square, and she and her children had enough to eat even in the longest winters. She was Leona's grandmother. In Leona's earliest memories, she curled in her arms, listening to old songs.

When Leona finished, they kept going. Stories spun, one after the other, from each of them in turn. The stories wove into a mantle that could cloak them from their now-just-past and their soon-to-be, enfolding them in something larger and brighter than anything they could see from where they sat, crouched, fidgeting. Tinto told about his grandparents' magic show, his parents' bakery encounters, his great-

great-grandmother from Paysandú whose empanadas were so good that **argentinos** used to swim across the Río Uruguay to taste them—sixteen horses had been drowned in their masters' quest for pastries, it was true, even today in Paysandú it was known to be true. And in any case, where they now sat, veracity was irrelevant; all that mattered was the texture of the story. Salomé told of the gauchos her abuela Pajarita was born from, and the ceibo tree she was reborn from soon thereafter; how it was said that she, Salomé herself, was the bastard great-great-great-granddaughter of José Gervasio Artigas; how her mother pursued poetry during the Second World War, and afterward, across the river, to **peronismo** and the mimeograph that sent her into exile; how her father, the eminent scientist, brought his patient out of a wheelchair and fell in love with her, all at once, defying his family to marry an immigrant poet (and she felt a raw, sudden affection for him as she told); Tío Artigas' adventures across the continent, Brazil, the Andes, Cuba. Another day went by, and a second, and a third; they filled them with their stories, with their mantle of stories, softening that hole full of their shit; sweat; breaths. Héctor, the soldier, finally joined in: he told them that his mother was the daughter of a wealthy **estanciero** who owned hundreds of acres of land. When she was very young, she fell in love with a cowhand and got pregnant with his bastard child. Her family disowned her, so she fled south through Argentina with her beloved.

She gave birth at the edge of a Patagonian glacier after ten days without food, and fainted from the exertion; when she awoke, a muscular puma was licking her newborn baby. She screamed; the puma lifted its sleek head to look into her eyes. She later told her son that, right then, she felt a strange and sudden kinship with this creature and knew it was an angel of God. In the days and months that followed, the puma hunted for them, helping them survive the stark terrain. Autumn approached. The puma led them north, back toward Uruguay. They followed, back through the villages and pampas and forests and hills, until they reached the Río Uruguay, where their nation of origin began. At that lush and gurgling shore, the puma stopped. The young soldier's mother wept and begged her friend to stay, to cross with them, but the creature's silhouette was already disappearing among the trees.

Such tales. They wrapped them, held them, kept them sane and even safe—until, on the fourth evening, as the sun sank in a faraway sky, they were found by soldiers with heavy boots.

Ocho

KEENS, HOWLS, HUNGER
FOR THE SUN

The days bled together. Her blood bled together. She could no longer tell which body parts had leaked which stains on the cement floor. She could no longer tell whether it was day or night, hell or death, blood or spit wetting her blindfold, three men or thirty in the room, the same man shouting or another, the same man crooning or another, whether the next thing would be blows or long long rapes or a journey to the room with the wet mattress, with peelyourskin electric shocks, the room with the full palette of imported arts, top of the line, state of the art, the art of state, oh my country, oh my country, you are not so backwoods after all, look what you bought, look what you have, just look at how you wield it. How seamless you are. You stop at nothing.

At first she wouldn't speak, I won't tell you anything, I will hold on and hold on, but time dragged on without the shaping force of days, she couldn't think, she was too cold, she was too wet, she was hungry and naked except for the hood, and sleep belonged to that other, distant world where the sun still rose and set; this can't be, can't be happening, not again, not again, and finally she knew her mouth was opening to beg; she was disgusting, filthy, bare, begging, she had so little she could tell them, really, almost nothing, and betrayal came and went without satisfying them. With nothing left to hide in the soft casing of her body, she broke freely. More breaking than she'd ever thought a person could survive. Sometimes she could hate them with a white-hot hate that burned her like La Máquina itself; could hate Salomé; could hate something else too, something that controlled the men around her like marionettes on strings—wasn't it there? wasn't it true?—a something the size of fifty buildings, so much larger than any single human being, looming over them all, drooling slime, teeth like spears, greedy for the writhe of breaker against broken, for the blood of the captive and the soul of the captor. But those were only moments, sharp and fleeting. Time was endless and her body had no edges, it was opened, opened, opened. Can't be happening. She prayed for death. She almost died one day, or perhaps it was one night, no way to know, in any case that time she felt it hovering, death, death so sweet, she almost grasped its wings except the words surged forward: Mamá's words: a line of poetry, of all fucking things, cutting through the voices and the low electric hum. **You, my fire, are all I have. Naked I still come to you.** The line arose and thickened and became a rope of words: **you my fire; you my fire you my fire my fire**

my fire my fire my fire my fire you my a rope of
words to hold, to grasp, to coil around the body, to
chant inside the ghost towns of the mind.

She had admitted, it seemed, to a list of crimes. The
hood was removed so she could sign the confession.
The light cut into her eyes, and she winced, but
hands dragged her back over the table. The docu-
ment was many pages long, but she saw only the last
page, where her hand was guided to the empty line
that waited for her name. She glimpsed the date
below it. Nine months had passed.

She was moved into the Women's Prison, an edifice
on the outskirts of the city. She had heard about it in
cell meetings, but whether it looked anything like
the men's facility in Punta Carretas, she couldn't say,
as she saw nothing until she was deep inside. When
the hood came off, she was in a cell: three gray walls,
one wall of bars, the room just large enough for its
single bed. She was wearing a rough cotton dress that
reached to her calves. She was not wearing under-
wear. Her feet were bare on the cement floor. The
guard closed the iron door, bars slamming against
bars. The limp hood swung in his hand. "No talking," he said, mechanically. There were sounds down
the hallway, women's sounds, murmurs and steps and
one shrill, aborted laugh.

She had eyes again. She could see, though day

brought only the suggestion of light, a charcoal creep from somewhere down the hall. The cell was icy cold. It was May already, winter was fast approaching. May, she thought, it is now May, I missed the rest of it, October breezes, hot January, heavy February, gentle March. There was no gentle where I was, wherever I was, except the gentle that was worse than the rest of it. The underworld. The not-world. And aren't I still there? Now I can see, and I have some things, today at least—a dress, a bowl, a pillow. It seemed shocking, almost profane, that there should be a pillow in the underworld.

She could sit or stand or lie down, whatever she felt like doing. The freedom was overwhelming. She sat on the bed. The mattress was thin and sharp with springs. She didn't move. She couldn't think. Her first meal came, cornmeal porridge in a bowl. She began to reach for the bowl on her floor, thinking the food would be transferred there.

"Want to eat out of your shit-bowl, do you?"

She pulled her hand back.

"You're disgusting."

She sat alone with the bowl in her lap. She didn't want to eat. She couldn't feel her body and was grateful for it. Hunger can't touch me, nothing can touch me, not this minute and maybe not the next one. The cornmeal looked thin and pale, but still, there was something shocking about the yellow. Strange, to see your food before you eat it. You start the eating with your eyes. I am almost full, almost sick from looking. She put the bowl down on the floor. Down the hall, she heard a woman raise her voice, saying, Álvaro, Álvaro. Salomé didn't want to think about Álvaro, whoever he was, or about anybody else who had a name and lived outside these walls, had lived the spring and summer in rhythms she'd missed, slow normal rhythms that belonged to the other world, the sunworld, and who now had thoughts about her, who knew what thoughts, no, she couldn't let them in, not any of them, stay out there, I am alone, I want to be alone. I can't exist for you. Don't want to exist, perhaps I'll die in here, just stop eating, just fade off, I'm halfway there already and wouldn't that be better? Like pulling the scab all the way from the skin. Better, better. Let the skin be smooth without it.

A rat entered through the bars and scurried to the cornmeal. It sniffed the food and began to eat.

"No," said Salomé, before she could stop herself.

The rat looked up. Its eyes were bright and alert.

"Hijo de puta."

She took the bowl from the floor. The rat, unafraid, followed her toward the bed. "No," she said again, and suddenly she felt that she could kill the rat with her bare hands or feet to keep what was hers. She kicked at the rat, hard, so hard that it should have bitten back, but instead it backed away and left as if it simply wasn't worth it, the food not good enough or too much of a bother.

She looked down into the cornmeal. She'd fought

for it, now she had to eat it. It was tepid and tasteless, but she ate it all, slowly, dutifully, thinking, mine, little bastard, mine.

After eating, sensation began a slow return into her body. Against her will she became, again, a brittle receptor of cold and pain. She lay awake that night, taking stock of the aches in her body. Body. I have one still, and if this body is to live I need to feed it, close its eyes for sleep, squat to let the piss out, lie it down and stand it up, I don't want to, I'm exhausted just thinking about it. She could not recall a reason to stay living, could not find one in the searches of her mind. The world outside, with all its streets and doors and voices, seemed unreal to her, irrelevant, unreachable. The past was hazy, shattered, a train demolished in the fog. And yet, if she were ready to die, if she really wanted to let go, why couldn't she let the rat eat? Where did it come from, the will to crush its body with her naked soles? Cold, my hands are cold, my feet. The coarse sheet gave no warmth. She bent her knees so she could press her hands to the warm flesh and thaw their frost. The will to live, she thought, is a strange thing, a beast itself, with its own teeth and mysteries, living inside us with such grace and quiet that we don't even notice it until it flees, goes, leaves you an empty hull, or so you think until you find its footprints somewhere inside you where you least expected them, indentations on your soul, I longed to live once, it was here, right here, the longing, this was where it nested, until dontsayit drove it away, but didn't I see its teeth glint today, couldn't it be roaming somewhere close, or even far, but not so far that it could not return?

She slept. In her sleep, large men stood over her, pressed in, too many.

Five days came and went in which she managed to eat, squat, open her eyes and close them. On the sixth day, guards came to take the women to the yard. The women formed a line in the hall. A woman in front of her started to walk too soon.

"Stop," a guard said, unnecessarily since the broad side of his rifle had already swung against her.

The woman moaned strangely and returned to the line.

"Now walk. Heads down."

Salomé kept her head down, but she was an expert at looking while seeming not to look, and as she walked she glimpsed other women's bunks in the corners of her vision, cells for two, cells for four, even for six.

They reached the outside. The ground was wet with recent rain, the sky gray and thick with rain to come. Still, to be outside, to feel the weight of sunlight, however distant and filtered through clouds—sun, you still exist, you're on my skin again, my skin was parched for you and I didn't even know it, greedy skin, it was too much and she squinted, whether from the glare of light, or to keep from weeping, she couldn't tell. Scores of women's bodies walked slowly in a circle, heads bent down, as directed. Those who walked too fast or slow were beaten with a rifle, but there was very little beating, really, they were experts at the pace, the speed, the collective shuffle. In their hour of exercise they became one body, one great ring of flesh, each woman just a muscle in the whole, see, move like this, pace yourselves, there you go, step in time, if we do it perfectly the guards won't care about a slight raise of the glance, a furtive gaze at the gray dresses and gray faces, look at the faces, women, women, faces shut, revealing nothing, closely holding whatever is inside, that's the trick, there you go, hold it in, that one too, and that one my God I know her, across the circle, Anna's face, Anna Volkova, tall and gaunt, jaw tense with dignity, and the outside world blasted into Salomé before she had a chance to steel herself against it—memories rose, images exploded in and she saw oil lamps, cramped rooms, Tinto's chest, the sweat at his temples, the growl of cars, closed doors, open windows, plates of food, a rocking chair, her mother's eyes. She looked down again, at the gray hem in front of her. The hem was not a prisoner's hem; it was her mother's hem, Mamá in front of her, in slow motion, in arm's reach, back turned to her. No. Stop. Gray hem, prison hem, Mamá would never wear that; it was not her dress, not her spurning back. But Anna, that was Anna— she hadn't imagined it, she was not alone in this place.

After the yard came showers, in groups of four, no heat, no soap. The water woke her skin and made it sing in silence. The guards watched.

That night, she lay in bed with her eyes open. It was dark, but dim light crept in from a bulb somewhere down the hall. She wondered where Anna was sleeping, and what other Tupamaras were here too. Tupas. I am a Tupa, now, still, here on the inside, I must think of my sisters, my brothers, the others who have given what I gave, lost what I lost, been where I was. Not alone. The thought roused and scared her. Leona. Tinto. Guillermo. Orlando. She didn't want to know, she had to know. She had to find Leona, if she was here, and talk to Anna also, somewhere, somehow. To link back up, to hear any news, perhaps even to find a way out. Impossible. But hadn't Tupas done many things that seemed impossible? Hadn't they arranged a jailbreak from this very prison? She remembered, she'd helped make the plans. But that was a long time ago, when the police were only amateurs, torturing haphazardly, unschooled, ambivalent. She couldn't know what was outside now, but things seemed different. Nine months. Things had changed, Uruguay had changed, who knew what kind of nation was out there now. She couldn't fathom what lay beyond the concrete walls, and didn't want to, couldn't let in the existence of a certain sand-colored house where too much was known and where the doors and windows might be closed, closed, closed. Instead she thought of Leona, obstinate, rich-haired, a serious child behind her glasses; God what if they took your glasses, Leona, I've got to find you.

She found her on the seventh trip to the yard. She

was five gray dresses ahead. Neither of them raised her eyes, but Salomé knew they'd seen each other, greeted with the same keen silence they had shared at school. She looked thin, numb, as if she'd gathered all her spirit into some hidden net. She had glasses and she was alive.

Two friends nearby. It gave her the courage to wake up further. That day, she noticed things she hadn't before. The guards, for example: that they were men, just men, full of shouts and beatings but men regardless, with their restless moments and distractions, the urge to be lazy, to chat with fellow guards, since they were, after all, just human beings, trying to do their duty and bring pesos home at night. They seemed to grow weary of their own thick skin. So if you played your part and walked your pace and kept your head down, you could not only obey but also coax them to relax, lean back, don't worry, the bitches are behaving, did you watch the game? The yard was the best place for it; guards also feel the sun. If given enough impetus, and if in the right mood, they turned away and let the ring of women be. Then it was possible to adjust the shuffle subtly, more sluggish, more clipped, just a little difference, but enough to move toward a particular woman, and the other women would make way and hide your different pace with the sway of their dresses, because you did it for them too, because every time the rain and guards let up there was someone shuffling quietly toward someone else.

Salomé reached Leona's side when the walk was almost over. She didn't speak so much as shape her breath around a word. **"Amiga."**

Leona heard it. **"Amiga."**

"You all right?"

It was a stupid question. Leona took three incremental steps. "Yes. You?"

"Alive."

They walked a few more paces. The guards stood upright, reluctantly; it was time to go in. The next day, Salomé approached Leona again, and they inched in silence. After that it rained for five weeks, there was no yard, there was only the inside, and on the inside, deep in the night, Salomé heard her body speak what she least wanted to hear.

When the ground dried and they were out again, Leona reached her early in the walk.

"We have news." Leona slowed down for a gray dress trying to overtake her. "Tinto is alive."

Salomé breathed a gulp of the white sky. There was so much inside her, clamoring to be said, to be carried, to be named, but if she started she feared she'd never stop.

"I'm four cells over," Leona whispered. "Listen for me."

Salomé listened, every night, and on the third night she heard the taps against the wall. It was not the rats; the taps had a pattern. They came in groupings, taps, pause, taps, pause, and when she counted them the code became clear. It was simple, one tap for each letter of the alphabet. Twelve taps spells L.

Five taps spells E. Fifteen spells O. L-E-O-F-O-R-S-A-L-O-M-E

Y-E-S-I-T-S-M-E, she tapped back, and waited while the woman in the cell next door moved to the other wall, to relay Y-E-S-I-T-S-M-E. Her neighbor was a woman whose face spoke of hard liquor, who never failed to groan at night. Salomé thanked her silently, in her mind, along with the two other women beyond her, faceless, tapping patiently, sending her message down the row.

She waited against the wall, hands resting on her belly. The taps began. P-L-A-N-N-I-N-G-E-S-C-A-P-E

She tapped back. H-O-W

She waited. Her fingers itched to tap and tap. The answer came. T-H-R-O-U-G-H-S-E-W-E-R

Salomé thought of her body pushing through an airless tunnel, swimming through shit, attempting to slither on her belly, the way her belly would be weeks from now. C-A-N-T-G-O

W-H-Y-N-O-T

Salomé tapped out what clamored to be said. I-M-P-R-E-G-N—her meaning was clear now, she could have stopped, but her fingers kept tapping until she'd fully said it, even though her neighbor had perhaps already left to relay through the other wall.

The silence lasted so long that Salomé wondered whether Leona, or someone between them, had fallen asleep. Then the taps returned. W-A-N-T-A-K-N-I-T-T-I-N-G-N-E-E-D-L-E

She knew what knitting needles did, how they could reach inside and puncture out a pregnancy, how women could survive it if they found a way to stop the flow of blood. She touched her belly. She could do it and should do it, perhaps, except the thing inside her already had an insect strength, scraping her with tiny appendages, humming with hunger for the sun. N-O

The taps went down the row, then returned. O-K

She would live. She had to live. She was not an empty hull.

In fact, just the opposite: she was fuller than she'd ever been in her life, fuller even than her early days as a Tupa when she almost let her secret burst out fresh and raw on the bus. Now she had a secret that made her cling to life, made her eat every drop of the sad soups, made her greedy for food, motion, rest, cushions, more food, and perhaps the hungers weren't hers but rather came from something deeper; in any case the source didn't matter, not the source of the hunger nor the horrifying source of the child. She turned her mind from sources, over and over. What mattered was that she was hungry and that made her more alive, she wanted real flesh on her bones again, she could have killed a man for a bowl of ice cream, dismembered him for a plate of **milanesas,** fresh from the pan, still sizzling, oil and beef and crushed-up bread she needed it, she wanted it, and even though she couldn't have it there was power—fierce, unfettered—in the sheer appetite. The other Tupamaras were on their way to freedom, making plans, guiding those outside as they dug a tunnel from the sewer. She would not be with them. Her future held unknowable unshaped things she couldn't see and didn't want to see. She didn't look at it, looked only at the brimming-over present. In the yard, Leona seemed sorrowful, pitying almost, Salomé the trapped, Salomé the burdened, and if they could have sat down together under their eucalyptus tree, she'd have said, Leona, stop it, I am full. Full of fullness. It made no sense, she made no sense, she was a crazy woman all the more insane for being willing to succumb to her own madness. She let her mind roam free. It roamed to her mother. Mamá, I want to see you, I'm so fucking sorry, I put myself at risk but never meant for this to happen and least of all to do this to you, whatever it is my absence is now doing, and now the most obvious fact in the world strikes me like a slap, that you carried me inside you, long ago in Argentina, and you felt things and I was born and you held my head up when I couldn't and I wonder what you thought when you were doing it. Whether you thought about your own mother and what she thought and felt when she carried you inside and then gave birth and held your head up for the first time in that very house we all lived in together. It's strange to think of the

woman who carried you inside her when you yourself are carrying a child, a child-almost, a child-
becoming. No words to explain—not in this language, we'd need expanded language—the feeling of
stark air, the sudden consciousness of womb not surrounding you, the exposure and aloneness you've
been living with since birth. The warmth, gone. The
warmth, remembered. Remembered or reinvented by
history repeating itself inside.

Winter approached. Even the rat shit froze. The
walks grew less frequent with the rain. Salomé grew
bigger. When her belly showed through her loose
dress, the guards avoided it with their rifle butts and
with their roving hands. There was one baby in the
prison, as far as she knew. It lived in its mother's cell
for two months, and cried when its mother was
beaten. It died in the growing cold.

She wanted what she couldn't have—to surround
her child forever. Starkness would come all too soon.

Salomé tapped: L-E-O-L-A-T-E-R-C-O-M-E-F-
O-R-B-A-B-Y

O-K

T-A-K-E-F-A-R-A-W-A-Y

O-K

Y-O-U-S-W-E-A-R

I-S-W-E-A-R

They escaped at the end of July. She lay awake all
night, in the dark, following the women with her

mind, through sewer tunnels, sludge and slips and sloshing, urging them on, go, go, soon there will be oxygen, don't stop, don't give up, just think of what you'll have on the other end. She saw Leona and Anna and thirty-six other Tupamaras, covered in feces, crawling through the fetid river. Without her. The child-almost inside her kicked and clawed.

The next morning, she woke to the roaring of the guards. They found one empty bed after another. Hair on pillows did not lead to women; it had been cut off with smuggled knives. As they pulled the sheets back, they found nothing but hair, laid out like amputated limbs.

"La puta madre," one guard said, down the hall. "The director's going to want our balls."

Another guard grunted agreement. "He's going to string them up like fucking Christmas lights."

"I'm in no rush to announce this."

"Mierda. Let's have a **mate."**

The first guard laughed.

"No, I mean it. Here, drink, collect yourself."

She listened to them drink and talk with shakier voices than she'd ever heard them use. She felt proud and victorious and immensely alone without Leona and the others, but how could she think that, she was not alone, inside she was constantly accompanied by a hungry little creature who was stronger ever day, whose feet and elbows danced to jagged music Salomé couldn't hear, wet music, womb music, a song free of gravity.

In September, when the men escaped, the guards were still so unsettled that they discussed the details right in the hall, and Salomé stayed quiet so she could hear them: it's amazing, absurd, the whole city is aflame with it, one hundred and six men got out through the sewers of Punta Carretas. There were distractions for the police last night: a flood of emergency calls, a knife fight on the other side of town. The symphony in the church beside the prison played abnormally loud. The tunnel surfaced at the floorboards of a butcher shop across the street—and this news made Salomé laugh, before she could stop herself, and the guard called out Shut up in there, but only halfheartedly; she was the crazy pregnant woman after all. There was only one butcher shop across from that prison. Its worn old sign glowed in her mind, vivid, peeling, nailed up by hand. She could see just how it happened: Coco and Gregorio, gray-haired, stooped, in matching bathrobes, shuffled downstairs to gape at the floor as it cracked open. Every tile on that floor was familiar, was scuffed from Mamá's childhood games, from Abuela's stool, from the shoes of women seeking verdant cures. She could smell the floor perfectly, as if she were there, the smell of meat and knives and the cycles of animal life, except of course it must have smelled quite different that night, when the tiles burst upward and the sewer burst too and the Tupamaros, Tinto among them, there you are my Tinto, rose from underground, spurting up, one after another, one hundred and six of them, filling that room of flanks and meat hooks, rising under the gaze of an old couple, returning to the map of the living, covered in shit, surging toward light.

Five days later, during birth, that same image returned to her: the bursting floor, the surge from filth, the surge toward light.

The baby was a girl: Victoria. She was too light and too fragile and cried all the time. There was not enough heat. There was not enough milk. There was cloth for diapers but she had to trade for it, in front of the baby, and more was always needed.

Still, those were her best three weeks in prison. Different from being pregnant—now she could hold and see and touch and smell and hear the girl, and every sensation amazed her. Victoria's skin was nectar against her body. Her voice the music before music. Her every scent incredible and perfect, even the sour ones, especially the sour ones, because they were so strong. **Be strong.** For the first time in years, she sang: softly, under her breath, wandering tunes, **Viqui, little one, dearest treasure, live, live, live.** The baby was so frail, so delicate, her fingers splayed, her eyes squeezed shut, her eyes would forget this place, forget this woman making a cradle out of her arms. No. No. Yes, for the best. Salomé memorized each moment, each toenail, each clumsy-perfect gesture, praying for Leona to keep her promise, for Leona to forget her, for her to succeed, for her to fail.

When Victoria was three weeks old, a guard came for her. He was an older man, and not unkind. He'd never touched her.

"The baby is going on a little trip," he said. "For a proper baptism."

Salomé tightened her arms around her daughter, instinctively, but the door opened, hands reached in, and she loosened her hold.

"Her name's Victoria," she called as the bars slammed shut.

The next morning, she woke to the sound of two guards' conversation down the hall.

"You hear about the baby?"

"No."

"Goddamn Tupas stole it. Right out of its grandmother's arms."

Seasons turned, heavily, exhausted as soon as they arrived. At first, she hoped they'd come for her. Arrange another escape, building on their record of thirty-eight women and one baby. Or perhaps they'd hold something or someone for ransom and the president would cave this time, or even go to court for her and argue that she'd had no trial, she'd done her time, wasn't it enough yet? and if not how much longer? and if it happened, if they saved her, she would go outside and feel the sun and see her baby while there still was baby to see.

But the flow of women seemed to run in the opposite direction: into, not out of, the prison. The population swelled with each month. There were women everywhere, new cots in every room, nobody had a solitary cell anymore. There were young ones, like her, just coughed up from La Máquina: Salomé could tell from their low chins, their flinching shoulders, the midnight screams cut off by slaps. She saw them in their slow walk in the yard, in the weekly showers, in the kitchen and laundry duties that she was now allowed and compelled to leave her cell for. She had to know what was happening out there, in the other world, the sunworld beyond the walls, to send so many women behind bars. She found a guard willing to trade for old newspapers; his name was Raúl, he had cigarettes too, it wasn't so bad, he might have taken it anyway but he preferred it sweet, and her body didn't seem to mind, didn't even flinch. The newspapers announced that the Tupamaros were weakened, then crushed, then gone. Pulled out by the roots like weeds that had infested the city. They used those words, **weeds, roots, infested.** The military was to be thanked for stepping in, for doing the job right, fixing what the police and president couldn't manage. They had cleaned things up and now they ran the streets. The streets relied on them for normalcy and order. She looked for a long time at a photograph of nine generals standing in a stiff circle around the president. President Bordaberry sat below them, shoulders hunched, slouched forward, smiling the smile of a gambler caught in a bluff. The generals weren't smiling. They stood as close together as you could without touching. The papers always came to her two weeks old; by the time she found out about the coup, she and everyone else in Uruguay already lived under a dictatorship. It was a small step, a formality, and so she couldn't be surprised. The paper, when it came, read June 28, 1973. Yesterday, it said, the president closed Parliament, locked the building, and surrounded it with soldiers. Or the soldiers locked the building and surrounded it and the president announced that, yes, he was behind this, the soldiers were sent by him. In any case, the senators could all go home, there was nothing left for them to do. A new military junta would be formed. She studied the firm press of his lips in the photograph. **Necessary,** he said, **as is the case elsewhere in the world.** It was bloodless. It was civil. It was done.

Salomé leaned back against the wall. The woman in the other cot slept or pretended to be asleep. She had only been here a few weeks. She was young and seemed disoriented, as if caught in a bad film she'd missed the start of. Why had they brought her here? Was she a criminal, a Tupa, a voice of dissent, or just a person in the wrong place at the wrong time? What would happen to her and to all of them now, in this new Uruguay? If only, she thought, I had the strength of ancient women who tore their hair out by the roots in mourning, wailing out with love and grief for what had died. Surely the nation deserves to have us all stripping our scalps, bleeding for it, for what has proven breakable which is everything, a nation, a woman, a collective dream. If I had the strength of the ancients, and the freedom, I'd dress in black and tear my hair and scale a mountain in my mourning, I'd scale El Cerro, our humble pretense of a mountain, and all the way up I'd howl and keen for what cannot be forgotten. But I am neither free nor ancient, and I need my howls and keens to stay inside. They are a fuel that keeps me going. Long ago when I was still a girl but thought I was a woman, and when I thought I was a warrior but didn't know how much I was, I learned to curl my shouting thoughts into a ball and hold them deep inside where nobody could hear or touch or take them. Keens, howls, elegies. I won't let them go.

She sat, watching her cell mate sleep or pretend to sleep, until the guards came to take the women out. The winter rains had paused, and they would catch a glimpse of sky. She listened to the cell doors as they opened and shut. The opening sound was a low click-and-rumble, quick to dissolve, but the shutting slammed and seemed to echo, over and over, down the hall.

Things were scarce—food, water, warmth, space, air, light. She was lucky, she had Raúl, he brought her extra water when he was in a good mood, and she shared it with the other women in her cell. Three of them now. There was barely room to move. Salomé slept on a thin pallet on the concrete floor. Their names were Paz and Olga and Marisol. Olga and Marisol rarely spoke. Paz was a reporter's wife, arrested for the crime of being married to a reporter. She was in her forties, and was not afraid to look guards in the eye. She learned to place her urine on the floor, in a thin arm of sun that reached through a metal grating. She moved it as the sun moved, until the salts settled and it became a drink that could be swallowed.

"Try it, Salomé. It's not so bad."

Salomé shook her head.

"Then try your own. It's easier with your own."

A week later, she admitted that Paz was right.

It took months for the women's stories to leak out, slow and hushed, in the circle on the yard, in the laundry room, in the showers, in whispers across the cell, in the taps that had become nightly percussion on the walls: they were union members, university students, university professors, socialists, communists, **batllistas,** artists, journalists, or they were the sisters or daughters or mothers or girlfriends or wives or friends of the same. They'd been pulled from the street, from their beds, from the doors of cafés. In the new Uruguay, every citizen was under surveillance. Every citizen was classified according to his or her level of threat to social order. A or B or C. Only A's were safe from losing jobs, family, the outside world. The regime had its hands full. Many, the women whispered, had fled the country.

With some people fleeing and so many behind

bars, what was left in the city? Salomé tried to imagine it. Surely life went on, it had to, there were still some people after all, and buildings and asphalt and cobblestones, and the river pressing up against its edge, a living breathing city with its ordinary moments. Surely no military junta could empty the whole river or remove all the ordinary moments from the world. It carried on, it must, it had to be better out there than in here; somewhere Abuela was still boiling roots and frying pastries, cars hummed and honked, the church bells rang, Coco was cutting meat (red, bloody, delicious) in a room with repaired floorboards, Mamá was smoking a cigarette as a poem took shape in her mind, Abuelo playing poker with his ghosts, Tinto sanding wood into smooth curves and maybe missing her, maybe, maybe, Roberto staring through his microscope at God knows what he sees and talking on the phone with their father **how are you** and **all is well** and **let me tell you about our last experiment,** Xhana rocking to her César's drums and César's hands moving like rapid birds, Leona doing whatever she would do without a revolution on its way, girls and boys studying out of new gutted history books, babies shrieking and clapping and learning to walk and say **Mamá** (and learning whom to look at as they said it), and thousands of men making their **mate** in the morning, under surveillance but still waking up and rising for each day; surely there were still microscopes and cigarettes and church bells and drums, and even if the taste of fear now tainted the morning **mate** it was still there, still passed from hand to hand. Unless they'd gone into exile. Leona, Tinto, Orlando, Anna might have fled. And her family, they might have stayed, she wanted to think of them as safe and sound in Punta Carretas, but she could not be sure they all had A status. Per-haps their blood relation to a Tupamara placed them in danger; or, perhaps it helped in bureaucratic halls that their daughter-sister-niece-granddaughter was long broken. Perhaps they didn't know their status, and were afraid, and hated her for endangering them, Salomé the family traitor.

Some nights, she dreamed of babies, floating on the water, she was in the water, swimming, swim-ming, looking for just one.

On other nights, lying on her pallet, unable to sleep, she conjured up her childhood quilt, the one made by Abuela Pajarita's hands. She evoked each tri-angle, each little patch of green and blue and flower and stripe, until she felt it with precision and was warmed by its heft, its supple body, its grainy hint of leaf and seed and shredded stem. Then she raised it with her mind's fist and hurled it through the wall, toward the city, a quilt spreading its wings in the night air, a dark bird, hovering, testing the wind for its way home.

Raúl was gone. There were new guards in her quar-ters, she was nobody's favorite, nobody wanted her for himself. They shared. They broke the skin. There were no newspapers.

Years sped by.

Years moved slowly, slowly, time was a snail, inching forward, there was a surfeit of it, other things were scarce but she had time. Constant, endless, unrelenting. Shuffling forward, past gray cloth, around and around the yard.

She had been in prison now for eight years, in which time stretched and pushed like air in an accordion, endless and contracted all at once. You learn to live like that, a speck trapped in a current shaped by forces you cannot see, expecting nothing, surprised by nothing, riding the dark unmapped trajectories of each day, shrinking in the face of pressure, barely affected, a speck after all, too small to bear scars or sink or stand in anyone's way, no bother to anyone, no threat to anyone, suspended alone in the shiver of the hour. You attract no attention and the world forgets you're there. You yourself forget it. You shock yourself with moments of existence.

One day, in 1978, a miracle was smuggled in along with her cigarettes. The pack was dropped into her apron pocket, in the laundry room, as usual. Steam pushed from the machines, filling the air, and her forehead dripped with sweat. The guards, equally hot, had stepped into the hall for reprieve. She opened the case and saw a piece of paper folded and tucked between the cigarettes. She pulled it out immediately.

It was a drawing. It was a tree. The trunk was dutifully brown, but the froth of leaves was gold and crimson and violet, all meshed together in the looping strokes of a child's hand. At the bottom of the page there was an autograph: VICTORIA.

Salomé traced the **V** with her fingers, traced the tree's thick trunk, ran her fingertip along the loops of color. She was wide awake. She could have crawled into the picture, climbed into the leaves, curled there like some mangy forest animal; she felt the press and warmth of all its colors around her body; she longed to eat the picture, sleep in it, trace it back to where it came from, to the hand that—existing somewhere out there in the world—had chosen this crayon, that one, that one too.

She crawled in, climbed up, curled there every night.

Two years later, the guards removed the metal gratings from the windows, under orders, and painted the panes to keep the sun from entering. Cells darkened. At night, Salomé lifted Paz onto her shoulders, so she could scratch the black paint with her fingernails. **Ktchh, ktchh,** a hole formed, and the next day light leaked in, pale, sweet, contraband.

In that thin light, the loops of foliage kept their colors: violet was violet, crimson still crimson, gold a fading but discernible streak of gold. Each slash of color gave her sustenance, fed her every time she looked. There was no more potent antidote to the world's poisons than a curve of crayon. She could drink it, dream it, rock in it. Think about the hand itself, the one that drew, envision its shape and softness.

A new decade had begun: an empty slate of time. Outside there was a city, still, and a wide world beyond it. The first news from outside Uruguay leaked through the nation's borders and the prison's stubborn walls. Far away, in other countries, the sun still rose, and Uruguayan exiles had been speaking. Human rights groups had paid attention. They had done studies. Uruguay had broken a world record: more political prisoners per capita than any other nation. This record was not reported within the country, of course, but outside, across borders and seas, where a sad record-breaker from a tiny country did not reach the headlines but managed, at least, to occupy a bottom corner of some international pages. It was enough to make the junta nervous. They drafted a new constitution, one that would allow night raids on civilian homes, give the military more formal power, and eradicate unions, strikes, and certain political parties. The prison walls tapped and pulsed and whispered. At night, in code, in long percussive dispatches, she learned that they were putting it to a vote.

Why? she asked the stone.

Why allow a vote?

Conjecture drummed into the night.

Because it worked for Pinochet in Chile.

Because of the scrutiny.

To seem legitimate.

To show the world that people backed them.

Because the people are too intimidated, classified, cleansed of dissenters to defeat it.

But they were wrong. The vote came and went and two weeks later the walls rang euphoric. V-O-T-E-W-A-S-N-O.

Salomé pictured **montevideanos,** walking haunted streets, crouching in their homes, hearing the collective **no** they'd cast a vote for but not discussed with neighbors or coworkers or family or anyone at all, now trying to understand their world with this new **no** in it, not just their own but made of many voices, surreptitious, unidentified, shocked at their own resonance.

A crack in the fortress. It gave her hope. Slippery hope that you could glide or skid on.

She turned thirty, in utter privacy. She planned her celebration for weeks. She saved a bowl of water and a dozen smuggled matches. On the night of her birthday, she waited until her cell mates were asleep. The bowl was cold and smooth in her hands. She placed it gently on the cot in front of her. No drop spilled. She lit a match and bent over the bowl. In the flare of light, she saw the surface of the water, a black circle bearing her reflection. She stared at the

woman in the water, who stared back, eyes un-
flinching in their sunken caves of flesh. The match
went out; she lit another. The woman in the water
was still there. She looked at the gaunt cheeks, thin
hair, mouth pursed tightly out of habit, eyes, eyes,
eyes. She wanted to know the woman, or at least to
see her clearly, this face she never looked at but
looked out of all the time, that held the stories in but
also told them with its lines. Her face. Thirty, she
thought, and it didn't feel possible, didn't feel like a
number so much as a presence, a thing that hung
around her like a scent. Salomé, she mouthed at the
water, and the mouth in the water said it back. The
match went out, and with the next one and the next
she held the gaze of water-eyes, watched the mouth
move in silence, searched and searched for eyes and
mouth inside the water, saying and not saying Salomé, Salomé.

Two months later, a visitor was authorized to see
her. She was escorted to the room in hood and handcuffs. When her eyes were bared again, there was
Mamá, beyond a glass wall, phone to her ear, gray-
haired all of a sudden, though of course it was not
sudden, it had been more than a decade. The hair
was shorter than before, falling in delicate layers
around her face. She looked tired and alert. She wore
red lipstick, today as always. Salomé looked for blame
or hate in her mother's face and could not find it.

She picked up the phone on her side. "Mamá."

Mamá touched the glass. **"Hija—"**

"Keep your hands on your side."

Mamá pulled back. "**Sí,** Señor, of course." An automatic response to authority, without arguing that the rule was ridiculous, a woman could not reach through a glass wall. Responding, Salomé thought, like a prisoner. Mamá stared at her face, hair, neck, ears, eyes, as if looking for her daughter in what she saw. Her mouth twisted. Salomé looked down.

"It's been so long," Mamá said.

"Yes."

"I've been trying to come. It took time."

"Thank you." She wanted to say **I'm sorry you have to see me this way,** but there was no other way Mamá could see her. "I'm sorry."

Mamá brushed the words away. "You're all right?"

"Yes."

Mamá looked relieved, even though the lie was obvious. "We're all right."

"Abuela?"

"She is well."

"Abuelo?"

"Well."

"Roberto?"

"Very well. He's in the United States."

Salomé stared. She hadn't thought he'd need to flee.

"He got a job in California, back in '71."

"I see."

"He's a professor. Flor is well, too, and so's their daughter."

"They have a daughter?"

Mamá nodded, and said, slowly, "Their daughter draws trees."

The room was hot, unventilated, Salomé was breaking into sweat. "With green leaves?"

Mamá glanced at the guard, who looked apathetic. "No. With red, purple, yellow, all sorts of colors."

Salomé could not breathe.

"Your niece seems happy."

Salomé could not breathe.

"She has everything she needs."

"Oh."

Mamá stared through the glass, lips open, hands on the metal desk in front of her. Her eyelashes were striking, and Salomé found this intensely comforting: that no matter how the world rent and warped, or how age took them both, her mother still painted her lashes in the morning, still made them dark and long so she could look and blink with force.

"One more minute," the guard said.

Mamá's hands shut into fists. She turned to the guard, then to Salomé. "I'll return. I'm authorized for once a month."

She did return, each month, for precious minutes in the visitors' room. Salomé stored up a trove of questions between visits—about the streets out there, the way things tasted, how people were, the where and what and how of California. There was never enough time, and of course there was always a guard or two, keeping watch, and so the answers came in fragments, indirect, cryptic, gradual. She learned that Abuelo and Abuela had reached their eighties in astonishingly good health. That Tía Xhana and Tío César had left, to live, in Mamá's words, **where Xhana's father is.** That Abuela Pajarita had been giving remedies from her kitchen, covertly, since Coco's death, while Abuelo spent long hours by the window, looking out at the prison and the oaks. That they always had enough to eat, thanks, in part, to envelopes that came from the United States. That the city in the U.S. was San Francisco, a city with a bridge that was called golden though in fact it was red. That the school was called Stanford, the research on the topic of eclosion, the thing, Mamá explained, that moths did to get out of their cocoons, which involved unique secretions, sharpened wings, and lots of thrashing. The house was blue and pretty and had two telephones, which were used once a year to call Uruguay for Christmas. The girl was an only child, a lively child, with crayons and roller skates and more dolls than she could count. Mamá brought a picture that the guards let her hold up, on her side of the transparent wall: a girl, brown-haired, brown-eyed, well fed, painfully pretty, two yellow bows in her hair, grinning in the arms of a gargantuan Mickey Mouse. A blue fairy-tale castle loomed behind them.

That spring, Victoria, the niece, the roller skater, turned ten years old, saying **please** and **wish** and **birthday cake** and **mother my mother is** in a faraway language, in a faraway place.

The guards were under orders to remove the paint from windows, and replace it with green acrylic screens. There was no scratching them away. In the cell, the women's faces were bathed in a dim green glow. They looked diseased, or like creatures from another planet, interlopers in the heavy atmosphere of earth.

News trickled in. More hairline cracks in the fortress. An exiled politician had returned. A protest—a true and actual protest—had occurred on the street. One night, at eight o'clock, the homes of Montevideo had turned off their lights, and at eight-fifteen the kitchen pots had banged and banged, throughout the city, in the dark. The word **elections** made its way into rumors, buzzed in the air, in the laundry room, across the yard, through the walls of cells. Salomé thought of the junta, aging generals around a table, in their beds, on the beach in Punta del Este, vexed by the hassle of ruling a country, vexed by signs of their own fragility, dreaming of rest and cash and cadres of topless dancers, dreaming of laying their burdens down, of an end to the bother of ruling an ungrateful people in a world that did not like you. And if they did allow elections. Then. Then.

She stored up for the visits from Mamá—stored questions, stored the flicker of herself. On some visits, they spoke so greedily that their voices overlapped with each other, quick, hushed, both listening, both talking, too hungry to slow down. On other visits they sat quietly, for minutes on end, hands close to the glass, close to touching, each looking at her own point in space. But even in the silence she was there. Her mother, in the flesh, breathing and alive, proof of the continued existence of another world.

If, thought Salomé, lying in her cell. If, in fact, it could be true that her whole life would not drag out here in this prison, that she would not die between these thick gray walls, that the regime could change and she could walk the streets again—then what? Here she was in her dark box of a room, the heavy breaths of women around her, here on this pallet where she not so much slept as collapsed, each night, let her pieces fall away from one another in quiet crashes, muscles free to twitch in any direction at all, mind purging itself, over and over, of dull hours pierced by intermittent spines; she was alive still, this she knew, she breathed, she walked, she counted the hours until visits from Mamá, she followed the instructions of the guards, she imagined her own hands tying yellow ribbons into brown hair, or plunging her knife into hot rare steak, or holding a book in her old living room, she could feel the ribbons, the knife, the book, she was alive, but how much, that was the question; the hours and years had rubbed off on her, she herself had dulled, she was absent from her body most of the day, a small speck, floating elsewhere, it was only here, late at night, in the dark, when her pieces freely fell and she could feel herself, the pit inside, dark, seething, half of herself had fallen in, she'd changed in these slow years, what had she become? Who would she be if she stepped outside the fence? What awaited her out there? Freedom would mean fencelessness and sun and hot fresh food and people she once knew for whom time had also passed and scores of small decisions, thrust back into her hands. She wondered how she'd bear it. She wondered what it tasted like out there.

The next year, 1984, was different. It stretched like the long body of a cat shaking off sleep. A year stretching and rising, looking around itself, waking in chaos, arching its back. Elections were set for November, the first ones in thirteen years.

It came. November came.

The junta lost; the winner's name was Sanguinetti. He smiled for many cameras, said the word **democracy,** shook hands with men in uniform. It was bloodless. It was civil. It was done. It was hard to believe, she didn't want to believe it and start to hope and then regret it; hope is dangerous, it lifts you and gives you farther to fall, anything could happen, they could change their minds and kill him and his family so don't hope, and yet she couldn't help it—everything was different, the soup was hotter, the cornmeal porridge thicker, the women's steps louder on concrete, guards slouched more wantonly, Mamá glistened across the glass from Salomé as if to say without speaking, **He will, he'll let you out, you'll see we'll get you out of here,** and she wanted to believe it, everyone around her seemed to believe it, the women in gray dresses with their higher-held-than-ever heads, she herself was not the same, a keen electric rush moved through her body, images of freedom rushed in uninvited, streets that could be walked, sky that could be tasted, bread that could be eaten in large bites. They haunted her. They wouldn't let her sleep.

Sanguinetti took his oath in March, still real and unassassinated. A week later, two guards came to unlock cells in the morning, too early for the yard.

"You. You. You four. You."

Salomé and the majority of her neighbors formed their customary line down the hall. They waited. Salomé stared at Paz' back.

The guard coughed. "The president signed a law yesterday."

Nobody made a sound.

"It grants amnesty to all political prisoners."

Paz' shoulders flinched.

"You'll be released in half an hour."

Paz heaved. A woman near the back moaned. She was not told to shut up.

There was almost nothing to pack. Salomé had her body and the dress she wore and a single faded drawing of a tree. She slipped it into her panties and stood against the wall of her cell, trying to see it, actually see it, now that she was in a dream in which the cell was about to become a memory. Olga was crying, Marisol was watching, Paz was holding their hands and talking in a buoyant tone Salomé had never heard her use. She herself felt light, as if she might float out of her body and through the bars and into the sky where she would rise into the blue and higher still until she fell and fell and fell back to the city and landed on something green, or white, or any other color but not gray. Anything but gray. The guards came back and led them down the hall in a line that came apart into rebellious clumps of women, they didn't care about being punished and they weren't anyway because there was no point anymore, down more halls with rows of bars and long blank concrete walls, to a drab gray lobby Salomé had never seen. The horde of women filled it and signed papers, pressed together, quiet, whispering, then talking louder, eyeing the door, walking to it, pausing in a frozen group, then pushing, out, out, out into the sunshine. The light stabbed Salomé's skin. The day was crisp; it was autumn, it was fall, and it was falling, the sun, over Montevideo, from a vast un-yielding sky.

She walked toward the prison gate. A throng pressed at it from the street, bodies and faces and open arms. She looked and looked until she saw them, standing, waiting, jostled, **mate** in hand: Abuela and Mamá.

SOFT TONGUES BY THE MILLIONS

Monte. Vide. Eu. I see a mountain, some man said, eons ago, and so a city started to invent itself. Now the city had to invent itself again: rising, clearing its throat, rubbing nightmares from its eyes. Salomé sat at the window in the living room, staring at a small slice of the city: oak trees, women on church steps, cars slowing for the stubborn cobbles, their radios blaring some English singer's heartbreak, he had guilty feet and would not dance again. The women on the church steps were gray-haired and mournful and glared at the rock-and-roll cars. The leaves rustled, high up in their oaks.

She spent long days at the window. She didn't leave the house. She could do so if she wanted, she was free, but free was too large a space for her to occupy. The great unfettered air filled her with terror, she couldn't breathe in so much open air, and anyway, there was no need to go out, there was more than enough for her inside. It took weeks to grow accustomed to doorknobs and light switches—oh, remember, that's how it's done, anytime you want to you just turn it, flip it, change the light, change the room, almost too much. Memories surged from the walls, streaming around her, some her own and some much older, some real, some reimagined. They pulsed from every piece of furniture, every corner with its cradle of dust. The memories clothed her. Every object—fork and photo, mirror and tray—spun stories. A spoon sang of entering countless mouths of relatives. I stood watch, the mahogany table said, when your mother was born. I know, crooned the lamp shade, precisely what was whispered every time this room was dim. Remember, said the corner, you were five once, and then, and then. She sat for hours, quiet, rocking, surrounded by the murmurs of the room, which gave her solace from the murmurs within her, the **shut up** of a guard, the nightwail of a woman, the voice inside that said you don't belong here in this city, not anymore, you're like that man in the legend who fell asleep under a tree and woke up years later to a world that had changed without him, leaving him lost in his own skin. But I'm not lost, she told herself, over and over. I know this place, it knows me, I'm home.

"Don't worry about money," Mamá insisted. "Take some time. We're doing fine."

They were doing fine. They had enough. There were Roberto's envelopes, Mamá's tips from two weekly shifts at the café, and, also, the neighborly invasions. Pajarita had tried to put away her basket seven years ago, when Coco died of cancer, but the women came rapping on her door, skirting curfews, sneaking past the soldiers in the shadows, looking for her, requesting cures, presenting pains, creaking joints, lost memory, sharp memory, strange aches below the hip, heartache for children who'd disappeared or flown away, yearning for the husband in prison, fear of prison, stiff hands, strange twitches, bitten lips, misplaced keys or grievances, night sweats, dark lusts, blind panics, rages where the husband had to dodge the kitchen pots. Abuela Pajarita did not turn anyone away. She brought them to her kitchen, listened quietly, then reached for her glass jars. Her citizen status fell from A to B, due to these illicit visits, or perhaps due to her granddaughter's sedition, or her daughter's written words. She didn't mind. That's what she said. She was eighty-six years old. Her fingers shook but did not err. Eva helped her in order to alleviate the toll, becoming her mother's hands. Salomé watched them sometimes, mother and daughter, both gray-haired, tending to a tear-faced or stone-faced woman. But most of the time she hid from these guests, in her bedroom, or in the living room, with Abuelo Ignazio, who occupied the sofa like a throne. He was ninety-one, wizened, surprisingly strong; his mind shifted from agile to foggy to sharp again, in the span of a single conversation. He rambled for hours about yellow scarves, the heft of them, their texture and brightness, his wife's insistence on hiding them from view.

He thought that Salomé had been away in the mountains. Eva had warned her of this on the bus ride home from prison. "At first," she'd said, "he wouldn't talk about you. Don't be upset. I have to tell you. He'd skirt over your name as if he hadn't heard it. Then, in '81, I think that's when it was, he started talking about some mountain. How tall it was, how steep, full of clean snow. How Salomé must like it there, since she still hadn't come back. I don't know whether he believes it, or just wants to. Mamá, which is it?"

Pajarita looked down into her lap, where her hand clasped Salomé's hand, two sets of lean fingers shaking with the movement of the bus. "Both."

"It's best to go along with it," said Eva.

Salomé had gone along, which wasn't hard. Abuelo Ignazio had risen when she walked into the house. She was struck by how briskly he rose.

"Salomé. You're back!"

She nodded and smiled for him.

"How did you like the Alps?"

She wasn't sure how to answer. She embraced him, awkwardly. He smelled of soap and vinegar and just a little sweat.

"Was it cold there?"

"Yes."

"Lots of snow?"

"Yes."

"Very pretty?"

Salomé felt his hand stroke her back, up, down,

up, down. The house smelled of roast beef and oven
heat and herbs she could not distinguish, a meal prepared for her arrival home, the smell of heaven, better even, heaven with the best of carnal life mixed in.
"I'll tell you the truth, Abuelo." She heard her
mother clinking plates, already, in the kitchen. "I like
it better here."

Abuelo seemed suspicious. Salomé felt exhaustion
fall on her shoulders in chunks of lead.

They were too good to her, really, all of them,
Abuela, Abuelo, and Mamá. Too kind, too careful.
They laid out meals before she knew she was hungry. They chased her from the kitchen when she tried
to clean. They straightened out the quilt on her bed
when she wasn't looking. They never woke her, no
matter how late she slept, or how her naps stretched
on, unless it was the middle of the night and she was
screaming. Then she would wake from the sound of
herself or maybe from the touch of Mamá, her hands
in the dark, arms cradling her head, perfume exud-
ing from her breasts, and all she would say was **shhh,
shhhhhh,** gently, rocking, cradling, as though Salomé were four, not thirty-four, humiliating, horrible, all the more so because of how she craved it. She
pretended to be asleep, pretended not to remember
in the morning. In the daylight, she and Mamá spent
a lot of time not looking at each other. They smoked
together, sat together, read at each other's side. They
spoke only about the now of things: the heat or wind
or drizzle, the marinating meat, the water boiling for

mate, the customer knocking at the door. There were teas for her, of course, deep bitter things prepared three times a day, and Salomé drank them without a word. It was a relief that no one made her talk. She had little to say, except what gathered in her throat, unsaid, unsayable. Her mother was a labyrinth, winding, folded, indecipherable, a sixty-year-old woman who still left the house with sudden, vague excuses, going somewhere secret, hers alone. In prison, secrecy developed like second skin. Salomé wondered how the dictatorship had felt, here on the outside, the nation itself perhaps a kind of jail, Mamá perhaps adapting the way others adapted behind bars. She wondered whether Mamá had ever thought to leave, perhaps to follow her son to the north of the north, and if so, what had kept her in Uruguay. Or who. Surely her family, her mother, father, brothers, daughter behind bars, and perhaps there was more, a further, hidden reason to stay. She reached for her mother, in private, in the pages of a book: **The Widest River in the World,** by Eva Firielli Santos. There were a few poems in there, erotic poems, that Salomé did not think could be inspired by her father. **I was born to touch you, my life for this, my hand along your skin.** She devoured verse after verse. She entered them. She wanted to do more than read: she wanted to shrink and crawl into its words, move between its letters, dig for secrets in the attic of an **A,** climb a **Y** into its branches and listen to its dreams, slide along an **S** toward its hot and hidden source, enter an **O** and taste the mad brightness or bright madness at its core, touch her mother's essence—as it breathed when Salomé was still a child, small, open, and kept breathing somewhere in the white between black letters.

Winter came. Rain cloaked Montevideo. She still did not go out, and it made sense, didn't it, it was so wet and cold. She helped Abuela Pajarita make soup and **puchero** and bread. As they cooked, they listened to the radio, to newly imported rock songs and optimistic news, about rebuilding, exiles' impending return, new jobs to come, unemployment, tortures revealed, whispered, wailed, still uncounted, speeches about moving into the future. Salomé thought of generals and guards and troops she didn't want to think about. She thought of airplanes coming back into the country, carrying, perhaps, Leona, Tinto, the others, Tinto, Tinto. Years had passed. Fifteen of them. Surely, wherever he was, he'd grown a life of his own, and there was no reason to think, now, of his face, his smell, his muscular hands, his huge body with her in the dark. But he reared into her mind and she was with him, frozen in time, reaching for his young body with young hands, supple, reckless, able to trust and bend and open out of joy. She could not be that girl again, even if he walked in today and miraculously hadn't aged a bit. And yet the thought persisted. She couldn't stop. While she was cooking with Pajarita, in the calm aura of her presence, thoughts surged like a stubborn spring escaping pressure underground. She also thought incessantly of the phone in the next room, of the call she wasn't making, the call that would cost a fortune, was worth a fortune, to a blue and pretty house in California. Victoria's voice, enclosed in static, Victoria, Victoria, far girl, lost girl, grown-insanely-fast girl, what is the sound of you, I dream it but it slips away and shifts into new timbres, I dread and also long for the sound of your real voice. But first there would be Roberto and Flor and what the hell to say to them? Better to wait. They'll call at Christmas. Wait.

The radio warbled on about the long road of rebuilding.

In September, when spring dried the sidewalks, Salomé left the house for the first time. She took a long walk through the city. Montevideo. Monte. Vide. Eu. City of echoes. City of worn shoes and worn faces. City of clear sun on crumbling stoops. They hurt her, all those streets, with their familiarity, their hushed alleys, their sweet cobbles, and also with their change, the peeling paint, boarded windows, shut-down stores, moldering buildings, cracks in the ground, faded street signs, hopeful bowls of flowers up on balconies, vanquished flowers shriveling on sills, the fragrance of chorizo charring, slow and rich and futile, in empty cafés. She had never seen her city so empty. The few people she passed looked like ghosts just returning from the dead. She walked through Barrio Sur, past Tía Xhana's old home, toward the river. At the shore, the city seemed to loosen its belt and breathe. She sat on the ledge over-looking rocks and water, brown water, silty, rippling, reaching all the way to the horizon, to the end of Uruguay, where the rest of the world began. She roved it with her gaze. The breeze roved her skin. A man walked by behind her, slowed, and came to a stop a few paces away. Without turning her head she knew without a doubt that he too had met La Máquina. She could tell from his tremor, motionless, invisible, as though haunted by an earthquake that no one else had felt. She glanced over; he leaned against the ledge, staring at the water. He wore broken glasses, held together with masking tape. She wondered whether she looked that way to people, exposed, skinless, a giant nerve walking on two legs. She thought of running to him with open arms to wrap him like a small boy, oh look you've scraped yourself, come here, what in God's name happened to your glasses; she thought of running the other way, escap-ing him, I don't know you, you don't know me, nothing here to say. She didn't move. He didn't either. They stood, the two of them, silent, apart, breathing each other's presence, watching the river catch the broken light.

She returned many times after that, to stand alone and stare at the river. As she stared, she tried to fathom everything she'd lost, the way she'd lost it, the sheer voracious power of water, how much can sink below the surface, never to be seen again. Even ripples disappear after some time. You start to wonder

whether what was lost ever existed. You start to wonder why you're still upright on dry ground. You marvel, above all, at that very fact—the river, and you
beside it instead of under it, lungs full not of mud
but of air, breathing in spite of everything, here to
stare at the river one more day; the river is still and
wide and reveals nothing, nothing, nothing, but it
runs, it breathes, it pulses, like you it kept on pulsing all these years, and perhaps the river didn't steal
what you are looking for, perhaps you're searching in
the wrong place, the river after all survived the same
years you did, pushed and pulsed, innocent, rebellious, but no, that's not right, no one who rebelled retained their innocence, surely the only innocents are
the dead.

She always walked to the west. Only west. The
shores of Parque Rodó, Palermo, Barrio Sur, La Ciudad Vieja, these could be walked freely. Eastward lay
another part of city and river, and if she walked too
long she could end up in Malvín, where Dan Mitrione had lived and where his protégés might live also,
and beyond that, Punta Gorda, Carrasco, large
houses with lawns and fences in between, with their
swimming pools and beautiful china and men of impunity, completely free, able to rise in the morning
and shake off whatever they had dreamed and kiss
their wives and put on plainclothes now that uniforms were out of fashion, able to say, Querida, **I'm
going to walk the dog,** or **I'm going to take some
air,** and go walk and breathe and stretch their legs at

the eastern edges of the Rambla. Breathing public air. And so she kept to the west, turning right in Punta Carretas and stalking the pressed-together parts of La Rambla, its older parts, lined with edifices older than the century itself, shameless as matriarchs in their quaint adornment, settled in themselves, unafraid to speak to the river or let a passing woman imagine that they spoke. Better not to think about the east. She had her hands full with the west and the water and herself. She was an animal, voracious, hunting for something she couldn't name, prowling the city in silence, listening for a sign of it, following inscrutable tracks. On her good days, her hunger was enormous, primal, it had burned through her blood before she was born, had run through the blood of all her family, an ancestral hunger that had made generations sweat and have sex and survive, had urged her grandparents forward and hundreds before them, could urge her forward now. Not every day. Some days she was too fragile—I can't get up, the day's an empty palm, begins to close around me, and everything is too heavy, my arms, my feet, what's in my chest, the images I can't keep from my mind, the hot air of my first summer out, I cannot move but I must move, there are teeth to brush, they don't always get brushed. But she kept trying. Lighter days arrived. On those days she rose to see the river and expose it to her thoughts, and the day held her gently in its palm.

That year, at Christmas, Roberto called. The

phone was passed around the living room. Every instant was expensive.

"Hello?"

"Salomé?" Her brother's voice was tinny, far, reaching through static.

"Yes. How are you?"

"Fine. **Ay,** Salomé, it's good to hear your voice."

"Yours too."

"Flor's also on the line."

"Hello, Salomé," Flor said, also tinny, also far.

"Merry Christmas," Roberto said.

"Thanks. You too."

"You are . . . all right?"

"Yes."

The pause stung with static.

"Would you like to say hello to Victoria?"

"Oh," Salomé said, trying to sound casual, "yes."

"Viqui," her brother called, in the distance, "Salomé's on the phone." Then, further from the receiver, "Your aunt."

Shuffling. A girl's voice. "Hello?"

"Victoria?"

"**Sí. Hola,** Tía Salomé."

Her Spanish was tenuous, lilted toward English. Her voice was not two, or three, or six years old. She was fourteen, a little sullen, but her voice was a clear thing, even in static, a sweet clear crystal that Salomé would not ever want to break.

"Are you having a nice Christmas?"

"Yes."

"What did you get?"

"A stereo."

"Wow!"

"I wanted a motorcycle."

"Aren't you too young for that?"

Victoria, nonplussed, said, "Yeah."

In a matter of seconds, Salomé thought, she had managed to become the prudish aunt. She tried for a recovery. "Well, I hope you get everything you want. In life, I mean, not just today," she added, feebly. She heard only static. "Are you still there?"

"Yeah." More static. "Thanks."

Salomé paused. Already, it had been so long, more than a minute. Abuelo Ignazio was waiting beside her, next in line. "Well, I know this is expensive. I'll pass you to your great-grandfather, okay?"

"Okay."

"I love you," Salomé said, and quickly passed the phone.

Crystal. Sullen crystal. It echoed in her for weeks.

One day, near the end of summer, Orlando called. He'd just returned to Uruguay. It was the first time she'd ever heard his voice on the phone.

"Salomé?"

"Yes?"

"Thank God. It's me—Orlando."

She thought of a thick beard, calm eyes, dim rooms, shit in a bucket. "Where have you been?"

"Spain. I just got back."

"To Montevideo?"

"**Sí.** I'm at my mother's. Listen, I heard that you—"

"Thanks for calling," she interrupted, prepared to hang up.

"Salomé. Wait. Can we meet for **mate?**"

She paused for a moment. From the kitchen, she heard the radio's muffled voice. "When?"

"Whenever. Thursday."

They met in Parque Rodó, on a bench by the murmuring fountain. The tiles on the ground were still the same, painted with pomegranates, dragons, dancing fish, all in blue, an old mythical world beneath their feet. He was in his forties now. His beard was tended carefully around the edges, and sprinkled with gray. His face was rugged in a manner that suggested years of sun, or labor, or labor in the sun. He'd developed a potbelly—too many barbecues, he said, on the beach at 2 a.m. Laughing as he said it.

"So you liked Spain?"

"I did. But I missed Uruguay. I wanted to come home."

Salomé passed him the **mate** gourd.

"It's good to see you, Salomé."

She knew she looked as old as he did, and maybe older, even though, when they met, he was a man and she was just a schoolgirl. She knew the inside years were written on her skin. She kept her mouth closed when she smiled, to hide the missing teeth.

"Really, Salomé. I mean it. Your spirit has survived."

She shrugged.

"I worried about you," he said. "We all did."

The wind played with the trees' green hair. "Who's we?"

"Me, and Tinto, Anna, Leona."

Salomé's throat shut as if a string had pulled around it. "You're in touch with them."

"Yes."

"Where are they?"

"Mexico City. Since '73."

"Ah." It rose in her, against her will: the thought of Tinto's hair, chest, hands, which had grown more than perfect in her mind. Between her feet, the dragon in the tile seemed to be smiling. "You think they might come back now?"

"I don't think so. They seem settled." He poured hot water into the gourd.

"Oh."

"Salomé," Orlando said gently, "Tinto and Anna are married."

She waited for him to say **but not to each other.**

"They have three children."

The tile dragon sneered; she stepped on it.

"And Leona teaches at a university."

She should be happy for Leona, happy for everyone, all these people who had kept their sun and teeth and time and babies, who likely looked the age they really were, who'd seen other countries, married, studied, taught, gone to parties on the beach. Anna was so severe, too much for Tinto, like a knife that woman, surely her touch had sliced him into pieces. Unless she'd changed. Unless everyone and everything had changed.

"Salomé?"

"What?"

Orlando extended the **mate.** Salomé took it. She stared at it for a moment before she drank.

"I didn't know how to tell you."

"I guess you found a way."

"I thought you'd want to know."

"Maybe I did."

They sat in silence again. The wind was still playful, still rustling the leaves, with their superficial flecks of sun. The fountain wept copiously.

"Let's keep doing this," Orlando said.

"Why?"

"Why not?"

"I don't need pity."

"Good. I wasn't planning on any."

She looked at him. He was turning the cap of his thermos back and forth. "I've been gone a long time. My wife stayed in Barcelona; she's not my wife anymore. I could use an old friend."

They drank **mate** together twice a week. They sat in silence for long minutes at a time. Orlando was easy to be silent with. He leaned fully into quiet, the kind of quiet that holds your thoughts up like buoys in water. He never pried. His smile was genuine and seemed to belong to a much older man. Sometimes they sat in the park, and other times they walked La Rambla, watching the sun bend its orange head toward the water and the rocks. When winter came, they met at cafés or at each other's houses. His mother was a kind, square widow whose apron was always smeared with flour. At Salomé's house, Orlando listened generously to Abuelo Ignazio's meanderings, and discussed plants with Abuela Pajarita, who had never met a man with so much botanical knowledge. He shrugged modestly, I gardened a bit in Spain, I don't know much, what do you use this bark for? Salomé had always kept him so separate from her home life, part of her clandestine second world, that it was strange now to have him in the open, laughing and sniffing jars with her grandmother, but then again, in this new Uruguay, anything could happen—things could touch and mix that never could before. He discussed politics with Eva, over afternoon **mate** in the living room, the state of the new democracy: The president has increased exports, did you hear his speech, Oh yes, so proud of the dip in unemployment rates, but that dip didn't come because of more export in goods, but from export of people, **uruguayos** emigrating in search of work, Yes, yes, you're right, And exiles failing to return—one fifth of the population is still flung across the world. Eva nodded raptly. Why don't they come back like you did? Come back to what? I was lucky—my mother's still here—but look at our country. Knots of children begging on boulevards. Oh, yes, I know—I've seen those run-down horse carts prowling the city at dusk, picking through

garbage to take back to the **cantegril.** Everybody's
seen them, it's a disgrace. You're right, it is, and so is
all the grown men out on the street selling old clothes
and lottery tickets, pretending they aren't doctors or
lawyers or engineers now desperate for a peso. I've
seen them too. We all have, yes? No matter how the
president tries to pull the wool over our eyes. Eva
filled the gourd for him. You're right, **sí,** you're right.
What is going to happen to this country? She was
mournful, elegiac, riveted. Salomé had not managed
to talk about politics with her mother since returning home. The topic was too close to untold portions
of the past. Orlando's presence opened a new ease
between them, a neutral state of dialogue where beggars and pesos and presidents could be themselves
without toppling the conversation into cells that no
one wanted to return to.

In the spring, Orlando started writing for a leftist
newspaper. By December he'd gotten Salomé to work
there. The office was in the attic of a former Tupa's
house, with a desk, a chair, a great deal of shelving,
and a broken sofa. It was a small job, part-time and for
no pay, but it was good work for her, fact-checking,
copy editing, translating from foreign sources. There
were investigative articles, interviews, opinions,
analyses, requiems for the revolution. The most heat
surged around the topic of human rights, on the
swells of new confessions, new evidence, disappear-
ances of **uruguayos** in Argentina, where a commission documented all the crimes, but no commission

here, not in Uruguay, no call to justice, no call even to memory; the president called for amnesty for military men, urged the people to press forward from the past, but he was pushing against the public tide, which swirled with emotion and debate. Salomé could not have brought herself to write about these things. She lacked the stridency. But she could correct the grammar, could pare down exclamation points, could add commas and periods where the authors had dropped them in the fierce push of their pens. It soothed her to bring order to brash text.

The day after Christmas, after another awkward call with Roberto and Flor and Victoria, Salomé received an envelope from Mexico City. The return address said LA FAMILIA CASSELLA Y VOLKOVA. It was thick enough to hold a letter, perhaps a photograph or two. She left it on her dresser, unopened, for a week. Each morning she woke up enraged at its existence, at the fact that she would see it when she opened her eyes. She hated herself for her own rage. She battled. She opened her eyes facing the wall, the door, the ceiling, shredded by her own thoughts by the time she was out of bed. Finally, at New Year's, she threw the letter away.

But perhaps she wouldn't stay this way. The thought unfolded slowly, carefully, a shocking missive written on torn paper. Perhaps there was another way to open her eyes in bed. The seasons turned. Her sleep grew calmer after two years of brown teas brewed by Abuela Pajarita's creased old hands. She woke in sweats but did not scream, and this was good, although she missed (she'd never say this) her mother's secret visits, her **shhh, shhhh,** her perfumed body in the dark. There were things to wake for; the world held more than pain. She told herself this, at first, to trick her way out of her covers: there is more out there than pain, wake up, wake up, at least live long enough to brush your teeth. She had some teeth left, after all—she saw this in the bathroom mirror as she brushed, and since she wasn't dead or toothless what excuse did she have not to sink them into something? Sink them into the soft flesh of days: afternoons of cards and **mate** with Abuelo and Mamá; mornings in the kitchen with Abuela, trimming plants, braiding her hair, the radio chattering between them, Abuela with her tender forceful silence, her radiant unspoken stores of memory. Abuela still sank teeth into her life. And look at Mamá—she did too, leaving for card games that surely were not card games, writing poems while the onions fried and occasionally burned.

"Salomé," she said one night, scraping blackened remains from a pan, "it's never too late to start over."

"Yes," she said, too quickly. "Don't worry, I'll chop."

"I really mean it."

She turned away, to the cutting board. "I know."

Three days a week, she climbed the stairs to an

attic office and sat beside Orlando, fixing text, on a sagging sofa that tilted them both toward the middle. They traveled to different neighborhoods together, gathering signatures for a referendum against the new law of impu-nity, knocking on bruised doors, looking into the faces of Uruguay: Hello, good sir, we are here to ask, I stayed alive today so I could meet you. Some evenings, Orlando persuaded her to stay out.

"Just for a drink," he'd say.

She knew as well as he did that Just a Drink, in Uruguayan, means as long as you please, means at 3 a.m. the night is young, however short life seems to be the nights will still be young.

"Just one," she'd say, and stay.

They went to bars with round tables and many candles. La Diablita was her favorite, thanks to its piano that sounded like it hadn't been tuned in her lifetime, but still did its best. They met with Orlando's friends—our friends, he said—who were old communists and socialists and Tupas, no longer different camps, now part of one broad and ostensibly united left. Some had been in exile, some in prison, some in both, all adherents to an old defeated dream, disciples after the crucifixion, toasting to the days when suppers had not seen their last. They talked and smoked and drank too much wine, just enough wine to let the past fall on the table like so many poker chips.

I was here.

I was there.
I was not there, I want to know. Tell me.
No.
Oh, come on.
It was like this—
I always wondered.
One time I.
And I.
Now that you say it.
And what about.
And also—
Don't get me started.
You already have.
That's true.
Another time I.
And I.
I never told, never.
Tell it tonight.
Tonight—
She came home late and lay awake, swimming with their stories and her own, imagining the dizzying routes that **uruguayos** had taken through the years, imagining a house in Spain, an Australian bar, a certain family in Mexico, a certain girl on a California beach, in a California car, until she slept and dreamed of dark lakes, oceans, Victoria on a raft that Salomé was swimming after. In other dreams she was alone in a dark room, and suddenly Victoria was present, she could make out the shape of her but could not see her face, and Salomé would say, **Turn**

on the light so I can see you, but when Victoria did, she disappeared, the room disappeared, and all around her on the walls were the shadows of the past, shifting, dark, expansive, demanding witness, demanding space, demanding light.

And there was this city. Montevideo. She lived and rose each day to see it. It was the only city she'd known, and not the flashiest, but surely like none other, so it was said by those who'd returned from Paris, New York, Caracas, Sydney, Salerno. Anyway, it didn't matter what they said. It was her city and she roamed it, at 3 p.m., at 3 a.m., skulking the streets, touching windowpanes, inhaling the scent of other people's cooking, turning left or right according to her impulse. She was free. She could walk anywhere. Usually, though, she found her way, over and over, to the water. She walked along La Rambla, watching moonlight wink along the wide river. There were always other people, day or night, **mate** thermos under one arm, ambling slowly, talking, laughing, never rushed; perhaps most of their relatives were gone overseas; perhaps their jobs had evaporated; perhaps their lovers were haunted by La Máquina; perhaps they wished they were living in the United States; but here they were. Many had gone. The years had been centrifugal, distending her known world, scattering **uruguayos** across the globe. But look, some clung on, insisting, Uruguay still exists within its own borders, even though it's not the same, will never be the same, the idyllic country

Batlle shaped is gone forever. But we have this one. This Uruguay: less innocent, smaller somehow, dwarfed by the looming world, more wounded, bleeding people out through its wounds, mourning the lost blood of the exiled and the dead and also those who simply shrugged and flew away, but also stronger for its wounds, mature, tenacious, wiser about what it can withstand, with a heart that beats and people who pulse through its pathways. She watched the people walk by. She made eye contact and struck up conversations. La Rambla opened its curved path to everyone, echoed all their feet, caught their gazes in the glitter of the river.

One night, Orlando kissed her at the shore, gently, his tongue like water.

"Come home with me," he whispered.

Phhh, said the waves on the rocks.

Salomé leaned into him. He smelled of musk and wool. "I don't have much to give you."

"So don't give anything. To hell with giving. Just come home."

That night she touched him like a feral cat, all claws and hunger.

Victoria had grown up. She was a young woman. Salomé heard it in her voice on Christmas Eve of '88. It shouldn't have shocked her—it was normal, inescapable, it happened to everybody after all—but still she could have crushed the receiver in her hand.

"Victoria? That's really you?"

"**Sí,** Tía."

"You finished high school."

"Yes. I'm in college."

"You like it?"

"Mostly. It's cold in New York."

"You must be glad to be back home."

"Yes."

"What are you studying?"

"I don't know yet." Static. "How are things in Uruguay?"

"Fine. Maybe you'll come visit us one day."

"I'd like that."

The force of Victoria's response surprised her. "Me too." She'd been terribly greedy. It was a costly call, she should stop, she should pass the phone. "There's always a place for you here."

"Really?"

"Really," Salomé said. More static. "Okay, I'd better pass you to your great-grandmother, before I get in trouble. You know how threatening she can get."

Victoria laughed. "Okay. Merry Christmas."

"Merry Christmas."

Salomé gave the phone to Pajarita and slipped into her bedroom. Victoria's voice echoed from the bare walls. **Really?** She couldn't discern the tone of the question, and with each unheard echo it shape-shifted from pleasure to longing, from longing to surprise, from surprise to mere familial courtesy. She a girl with remote origins in a small and remote country, a place she'd never been to, or at least not since she was old enough to retain memory. Perhaps she'd been raised with bits and pieces: inflected Spanish, an amethyst doorstop, occasional empanadas, branded leather images of gauchos on the walls, photos of her parents' childhood homes, selective tales of how things used to be, an annual call. Perhaps she hadn't. Perhaps she felt like a plant cut at the root. She might crave this place—to know it, to imbibe it—or she might not care at all. Maybe Roberto and Flor were experts at forgetting, and raised Victoria not to care. But girls don't become exactly what they're shaped to be, I of all people should know that. All this forgetting, it was exhausting, it required intricate invisible convolutions of the mind, and what was served by it? What would she do if she were not a coward? She was a terrible, terrible coward. The room was quiet. The sealed envelope leered at her from the bedside, another annual card from Mexico, unopened, as always. She looked at it for a long time. She picked it up and traced its edges with her fingertip. **No, I can't.** She put it down and picked it up four times before tearing the flap open. The front of the card held an image of Frida Kahlo, bleeding, heart exposed. Inside, she read:

Dear Salomé,
 We hope that you are well. We are well here, the three of us and the children— Cacho is 10 now, Ernesto is 7, and Salomé

has just turned 6 years old. We are grateful for our health, our humble house, and the carpentry business. This year, Leona became a full professor of history. We celebrated with a Uruguayan-style asado, **which our Mexican friends enjoyed!**

We think of you often. The offer of flying you out still stands. We hope that one day you'll accept it and come visit us, here in México D.F.

With lots of love,

Leona, Tinto, Anna, Cacho, Ernesto, and Salomé

She reread the card several times. Her hands shook. She closed it, looked at the picture on the front, put it back in the torn envelope, took it out, looked at the picture, put it away and took it out and read it again and again and again. **We hope that you. The offer of. Salomé has just turned.** She felt sick. She felt like laughing. She felt like throwing everything in sight. She felt as though she were in a glass box and the world beyond it breathed a different air. She wanted to break every pane around her. She wanted to cling to the staleness inside, but no, you can't, you won't, not this time, there is too much waiting on the other side. She rose and walked to the hall. From the living room, she heard Abuelo telling some exaggerated tale about a man staying up all night to build a boat. He was making his wife laugh, well into his nineties—miraculous, really, their good health. The door to her mother's bedroom was ajar. She went in without thinking. She was alone. She opened Mamá's closet with hands that seemed to know before her mind what she was doing, and reached up to the shelf that she now accessed with no trouble, pulling down the heavy box that was still there. She unfolded the flaps and pulled them out, her childhood shoes, Roberto's shoes, the Mary Janes and oxfords and worn tennies, red galoshes, white leather that must have been her first communion, white patent baptisms even deeper down, all with three eucalyptus leaves hanging from their mouths like tongues; somewhere one was broken—she had broken it—but which one, she didn't know, couldn't remember, it was too late to find it, too late to fix it, the shoes spread across the floor like an army. She stared at them. They didn't charge. They stuck their leafy tongues out at her.

She heard steps and looked up. Mamá stood in the doorway. They stared at each other. Mamá made a sound that could have been the first part of a word.

"I've always wondered," Salomé said, "what these were for."

Mamá hovered for another moment. She was wearing a red silk blouse for the occasion; it matched her lipstick. Her hair was swept up with two silver combs. She sank down on the floor beside her daughter. "Me too."

"I failed you."

"No."

"Of course I did."

"Stop it."

"I thought things would go differently."

"I know."

"You must have hated me."

Mamá looked immensely sad. "No."

"How can that be?"

Mamá leaned forward. She smelled of rose perfume. "Salomé. Salomé."

Salomé looked away, at the crowd of child-shoes. Her mother gripped her, wide awake, right there in the lamplight, and wept without making a sound. Years of unsaid words shook out in her mother's convulsions, shook out the way dust shakes from a beaten rug, and Salomé felt that it was true—she somehow knew it—her mother had no hate for her, had never hated, and this shamed her but made her feel something else also, something nameless and sharp and hollowing; I can't ever be the same woman I was or would have been, and if I am to live then I must kill her—now, here, sitting on this floor—must kill the woman I could have been and cannot be. Because there is another woman waiting that I can still be, but am not yet, am just now becoming. She held her mother tightly and let her sob. Over her shoulder, she watched the oxfords, galoshes, tennies, Mary Janes hold their leaves and do nothing.

Mamá finally subsided. They leaned into each other. Time passed.

"Mamá."

"Yes."

"I'm tired."

"You could rest—"

"I'm tired of secrets."

"You can tell me anything."

"I want to meet Zolá."

Mamá stiffened. "To get your hair done?"

Salomé touched her mother's gray locks. "You must love her very much."

Mamá was silent.

"I hope she's good to you."

Very softly, almost inaudibly, Mamá said, "She is."

Salomé traced slow arcs along her mother's scalp.

Zolá was a graceful lady in her sixties. Her hair was sleek and white. Her apartment was a tableau of peach marble, mirrors, gold. She received Salomé with **mate** and a platter of **bizcochos.** Salomé sat down on a velvet sofa by a floor-to-ceiling window, where the eye could roam out over buildings to the river to the sky. She had never been so high up in her life.

"Thank you for coming to visit an old lady like me." Zolá smiled. She wore pearls, bold makeup, and a periwinkle dress. "Go ahead. Ask me."

"Ask what?"

"Whatever you like."

"How did you meet my mother?"

"She didn't tell you?"

"No."

"Long ago, when we were children. We met again when she returned from Buenos Aires."

"How long have you been . . . ?"

"Thirty-three years."

Salomé watched her hostess fill the gourd. "And do you lo—"

"Immensely."

"Ah."

"Who wouldn't?"

Salomé smiled, almost parting her lips, almost forgetting her lost teeth. "I can't imagine."

Zolá handed her the **mate.** "I'm glad to meet you."

Salomé drank.

"I'm glad to see you in one piece."

She sucked until the gourd was empty, gurgling at the bottom of its leaves. She imagined her mother coming here over the years, while her daughter was imprisoned, to weep or kiss or rage at heavens that were a few flights closer to this space. Zolá's home, the sanctuary. The brightest secret. Outside, the sun was shattering in its slow fall toward the water, shards of it catching on the waves. A gull rose from a rooftop and slanted into flight. "Am I in one piece?"

"You're asking me?"

She handed the gourd back. "Why not?"

Zolá refilled the **mate** and drank. She lowered the gourd. She looked at Salomé. Her eyes were dark, almost painfully awake. For all the powder on this woman's face, there was nothing masked about her eyes. "Would you let me wash your hair?"

In the basin, Salomé slowly surrendered her own weight. She was submerged in the scent of her mother, that sharpsweet emanation of hers, rose and almond, opulent, mysterious to her when she was a child. Two hands entered the water and touched her, lightly, sinuously, like fish. Like fish they dove through hair and reached her scalp, which was so naked and so pale, it was unbearable, this touch, it hurt, it was sweet, hurt sweetly, she loathed it, cringed from it, but when the fingers backed away she heard her own voice say **No, come back please,** and they did. She didn't know what fell from her, into that water, what unseen crusts broke off and turned to foam or filth or barnacles, but she was naked with torn skin and a man laughed as he raped her; no, not true, she was not there, she was in Zolá's home, and a voice came through the water, **Breathe, Salomé, breathe.** Such gentle hands. Now they rocked her head as if she were a baby who couldn't lift it for herself. Roses. Almonds. They seeped into her scalp.

When it was over, Zolá wrapped her in a fresh, warm towel. "Don't get up. Just relax."

She lost track of time. When she opened her eyes, Zolá was reading on the sofa. The sun had fallen farther, and stared straight into the room.

Zolá looked up. "How are you?"

"I didn't mean to intrude."

"On the contrary. Why don't you stay for dinner?"

"I have to be somewhere," she lied.

"Are you sure you're all right?"

"More than all right. I have no way to thank you."

Zolá smiled. "That's easy. Just come back."

Salomé descended fifteen floors and walked to La Rambla. There was gold in the light on the sidewalk, fleeting gold, the kind that would be swallowed by the dusk any moment. She traced it with broad steps.

She went back to Zolá the following week. She wanted to be cut. Zolá received her with open arms, a warm basin, and ready scissors. Snip, snip, the tufts of her, worn ones, split ones, fell to the floor. After her first cut, she went to Orlando's house and wept for seven hours (he didn't ask her anything, he dried her face with his palm, his shirt, his towel, he enfolded her, he smelled of forest floor). She woke up the following afternoon, at 4 p.m., exhausted, thick-limbed, rearing slowly out of a deep fog.

She went to her second cut with pen and paper ready in her purse. Afterward, she went to the bench at Parque Rodó she used to share with Tinto, but could not sit there because a young couple sat entwined. Their thrill at each other's touch was palpable. She kept her distance, resisting the urge to run up to them and say, We did that too, we did, but not in full view of the sun, we did it under the cover of night, we had so many things to hide, I'm sorry, am I interrupting? Of course she'd be interrupting. They were young, they could not imagine and did not want to imagine a couple who had found refuge on that same bench over twenty years ago. Instead, she went to the fountain and sat down facing it. The water rose and fell and whispered in a liquid language she could not interpret. She stared at the green crowns of the trees. Pen and paper sat still in her hands for a long time, until finally she wrote to La Familia Cassella y Volkova: **Thank you, so good to hear, I'd love to accept your invitation, perhaps next year.**

After the third cut, she drank a whole bottle of red wine, alone in her room, watching the oak outside her window cradle the cold moon. At two in the morning, when she was sure everybody was asleep, she went to the hall and picked up the phone. She dialed. The rings were long and foreign.

Her brother picked up first. "Hello?"

"Roberto. It's Salomé."

"What?" He sounded alarmed, across the distance. "What time is it over there?"

"I hope I didn't wake you."

"Of course not. We just finished dinner."

"Good."

"Everything's fine?"

"Yes. I'm sorry. No deaths in the family."

"Oh. Good."

"I want to talk to you about Victoria."

Crackling silence.

"I want to tell her."

More silence.

"Roberto?"

"I'm here. This is expensive. Let me call you right back."

She hung up. She waited. The hall was full of shadows; through her bedroom door she saw her window and, through that, farther away, the oak. She saw herself, in bed, at seven years old, gazing at that oak, deciding to break her first rule. The phone screeched. She picked up quickly. "Roberto."

"Yes. Flor's on the line too."

"**Hola,** Salomé," Flor said, shortly, or perhaps it was the static, hard to tell.

"**Hola,** Flor. How are you?"

"Fine."

"So," Roberto said, "you've thought about this?"

"Obviously."

"Look, I'm just—"

"Sorry, Roberto, sorry. Don't hang up."

"I won't. Don't be ridiculous."

Salomé tried to picture them, in their pretty house, the dinner dishes stacked up in the sink, ready to wash, now poised on separate phones, on tasteful chairs, casting glances at each other across the room. She saw her brother in his old Donald Duck pajamas.

He asked, "Why now?"

Salomé closed her eyes. "Because she's old enough. Because I owe it to her. Because I finally can." They were quiet. She waited. "Are you still there?"

"We're here," Flor said.

Salomé bit her lip.

"It's not like we haven't thought about this," Flor said.

"Ah."

"Only we wanted to tell her."

Salomé waited for her to add, **because we're her parents.**

"Give us a moment," Roberto said.

"Of course," said Salomé. She heard the rustle of phones being put down. Somewhere, thousands of miles away, a married couple walked off to the kitchen or the back porch or the hall, to whisper, to deliberate, to think. The phone line crackled into her ear. Her sweat slicked the receiver. She marveled at the realities of distance, the way her brother's voice could reach her while her brother himself stood in a house far away, in a place she couldn't fathom but that he'd claimed as his and where he'd raised his daughter, her daughter, what a twisted family tree, spliced and splayed all over the world. She stared out, through her bedroom, through the window, at the oak tree, with its branches curving upward, just a few leaves left.

Five minutes passed. Six. Seven. She thought of hanging up. She thought of the cost of each second of silence. Then rustle, rustle, and they both were back.

Roberto spoke first. "Salomé?"

"Yes?"

"Thanks for waiting."

"Yes."

"Look," he said, "don't do it in a phone call."

"Please," Flor said. "The connections are horrible. You sound like you're in an electric generator."

Roberto said, "We're wondering whether you'd write her a letter. Write whatever you want in it. We'll be there when she reads it. It's the closest thing to telling her together."

Salomé leaned against the wall. It was cool against her back.

"Salomé?" Roberto said. "Are you there?"

"Yes."

"Is that all right?"

"Yes. It's great. **Gracias.**"

"**De nada.**"

"It might take me a while. To write it."

"Fine," her brother said.

"That's fine," Flor said.

The three of them listened to the static.

"It's late for you," Roberto said. "Maybe you should go to bed."

"Okay, **hermano.** Good night, Flor."

"Good night, Salomé."

"Good night, Roberto."

"Good night."

The letter was much harder to write than she'd imagined. One wrong word, it seemed, could ruin the whole endeavor. The right words, however, could perhaps perform a miracle—close a circle that was torn open years ago; perhaps could even close deeper, older circles, ones she herself had barely glimpsed. She started the letter dozens of times, over and over, seeking its tone, its opening, its voice. At times she forgot who she was writing for.

Dear Victoria, she wrote, **I hope you can forgive me.**

No. That wasn't right.

Dear Victoria, here's the terrible truth.

Dear Victoria, here's the shocking truth.

Dear Victoria, here's the truth.

Dear Victoria, what is truth? And who decides what's shocking? Some days I'm shocked to be alive. But that's not what I wanted to tell you, so

Dear Victoria, you must wonder who I am.

Dear Victoria, I'm your mother, it sounds strange—let me explain.

Dear Victoria, I love you God I love you, I know you're going to hate me. I've already spent far too much time hating myself—it gets me nowhere—and it gets too heavy to carry and so, sometimes, I just put it down—I actually do it— it sounds insanely simple, but it's not—but wait, wait, that's not for this letter—

Dear Victoria, your conception was not pretty but you still deserve to know.

Dear Victoria, I'm sorry. Your conception was a distended brutal nightmare that still shakes me to the core. But you're the best thing that ever came

out of me—isn't that a paradox? Will you know the word "paradox" in Spanish? Are you using a dictionary to read this? You'll never read this, I won't let you, this draft is a disaster.

Dear Victoria, please read this whole letter, please don't throw it away.

Dear Victoria, I'm writing in case roots matter to you.

Dear Victoria, roots are essential. We begin long before we're born.

Dear Victoria, don't let the lies about roots get to you. People have a great deal to say on the subject, but your roots don't define who you are. Don't let anyone ever tell you what to think. Jesus, now there I went, telling you what to think.

Dear Victoria, look, I stayed in prison thirteen years so I could bear you.

Dear Victoria, your violet tree kept me alive—do you remember it? Why would you? It was perfect, marvelous, so full of colors. I dreamed and breathed and swayed inside your colors.

Dear Victoria, I have something to say, I don't know how to say it.

Dear Victoria, please believe me, I'm not writing this to wreck your life—I've done enough wrecking and I'm ready to do something else—I really am—like build, hope, make things, listen, wander, wonder, see—above all, see.

Dear Victoria, what's your favorite color? Did you ever get that motorcycle?

Dear Victoria, I'm sorry I've let so much time pass. Deeply sorry.

Dear Victoria, I want to get to know you, I'm not sure how to do that. I wonder what it means to know another person. I wonder what it means to know yourself. Here I am, approaching forty, with no idea what it means to know yourself, something you'd think would be so simple, Socrates was concise about it long ago, yet here we are, modern humans, circling like lost dogs, unable to find what's inside us. Maybe not you. Maybe you know yourself, and I want to know you, Victoria, more than anything.

Dear Victoria, I wish I'd known you as a child.

Dear Victoria, couldn't you be five years old again? Just for a day?

Dear Victoria, what is happening to me with these letters? What are you doing to me, for me? I find words I didn't know I'd written. I find pages between my sheets in the mornings, crumpled by my sleep. When I write, I get tangled in thoughts of you. There are so many of them, thoughts, thoughts, they all cry out and rush toward the page, a mob that roars with every sound you can imagine, stampeding all at once. I fear that you won't hear them clearly. I fear that you won't understand.

Dear Victoria, at your age I was sleeping on rifles. I hope you're not.

Dear Victoria, I wouldn't blame you for burning this letter. I hope you don't.

Dear Victoria,
Dear Victoria,
Dear Victoria.
Through winter, through spring, all the way to hot December, the pages filled box after box.

That spring, Tío Artigas died in Havana. Xhana sent a letter with a photo of a mound of earth and a headstone engraved with a drum. He had lived, she wrote, to the formidable age of ninety-four. On receiving this news, Pajarita loosened her mooring to the world. She stopped tending her plants; they withered in their pots; counter space appeared for the first time in sixty years. She would not rise from her rocking chair, not for meals, not for the door; the family brought her lunch and dinner on trays, and ate nearby on the sofa, taking turns feeding her, bite by bite. She was not sad, or sick, exactly; just absent, ambivalent, open to the drifts beyond the world. She barely spoke. Eva entreated her to eat, just one bite more, just one. Ignazio sat near her in a panic, staring, muttering in Italian, shaking her arm.

"Papá, don't shake her. Let her rest."

"Rest? She's just staring out of the window."

"Then let her do it."

Ignazio shook his wife, who neither resisted nor broke her gaze.

"Papá."

"All right. All right."

Salomé watched her grandmother stare across the

street, at the prison. The oaks cast shadows on its
ivory walls. She had grown up across from it, as had
Mamá, and it was hard to believe that it would
change, that construction would begin in as little as
a year. That it would be a shopping mall, the largest
in Uruguay, modeled after **yanqui** malls, with shiny
imported products in shiny stores. The outer wall
around the courtyard, with its attractive fortress trim,
would be retained. Shoppers would walk through the
same gates that had held prisoners. But the edifice
beyond those gates, the prison itself, would be demolished and yield to a new building, whose condi-
tioned air and hidden pipes would supposedly hold
no imprint of the past, no haunting trace, nothing
but the clean gleam of the future. She had been editing scathing commentaries, **a new kind of prison
for a new era; this is madness; what we should
really do is, the fault lies with. It is painful to remember but more painful to forget.** Abuela Pajarita seemed to do neither anymore, or else she had
blended both into a single mental gesture. She
watched the prison wall as though everything else
were superfluous, as though it held the whole story,
told in the idioms of sun and shadow.

When the doctor came, Pajarita moved politely for
his stethoscope. Her pulse was faint, he said. She
should be careful, she was quite old, but she seemed
generally in good health. He prescribed some pills
and rest.

In December, Pajarita abandoned the rocking
chair and window and stayed in bed. The days grew

long and humid. Salomé sponged the sweat from her fragile body. She cleaned her slowly, gently, wiping the damp furrows between flesh, Abuela, Abuela, so this is your body, here are your private folds, your aging stores of darkness. Abuela kept her eyes closed. Her body ceded gently to the motion of her granddaughter's hands. Her skin felt like paper, the very thin kind, through which one sees the shadow of one's hand. Salomé wondered whether she would live to see her own skin grow so loose and soft and delicate. She wanted to. She realized this while soaping her grandmother's hips: I want to stay here in this world until my hips are brittle and sore and covered in wrinkles and even smell of urine until someone cleans me, even so, I don't care, I want to be alive.

By the third week, extended family poured into the house, day after day, all of Salomé's tíos (Bruno, Marco, Tomás) and tías (Mirna, Raquel, Carlota) and her cousins (Elena, Raúl, Javier, Félix, all the ones who hadn't left) and their spouses and their children, worried, crowding the hall, wanting to see her, wanting to help, and Salomé ran back and forth to keep up with the flowers needing vases, the dishes stacking up. On Christmas Eve there were so many people to pass the phone to that she didn't greet Roberto, Flor, or Victoria, which was all right in any case, she wasn't ready. Pajarita lay on a throne of pillows, staring at the throng around her, closing her eyes for long stretches of time. When her eyes closed, voices fell to whispers, so she could sleep.

Three days after Christmas, Javier's daughter Clara

brought Pajarita her last meal. It was a single beef empanada. She had made it herself, the way Pajarita had taught her, with the small innovation of a pinch of cinnamon, a trick she'd learned from her Lebanese great-grandmother, María Chamoun. Clara cut a piece with very little crust, and pierced it onto a fork. Pajarita took the bite. She chewed very slowly. The room hushed. From the threshold, Salomé watched her gaze, clear-eyed, around the room at each member of the great sprawl of her family, at Mamá, at Abuelo Ignazio with his jaw slack like an abandoned puppy, at Mamá again, at Salomé herself with an expression of unsettling intensity in which Salomé could have sworn she saw not only Pajarita the old woman but Pajarita the young woman and Pajarita the girl and even Pajarita the strange and legendary baby, all awake in those dark brown eyes, staring around the room in astonishment.

"Ah," Pajarita said, and closed her eyes.

Her heart stopped beating in her sleep.

Ignazio insisted on a gondola. For a real Venetian funeral, he said. His sons tried to dissuade him with every reason they could think of: it was impractical, there were no gondolas around, there was nowhere for a boat to take a coffin, his wife wasn't from Venice anyway. Ignazio had an answer for each reason. She wasn't Venetian but he owed her a bit of Venice. It didn't have to take her anywhere; they could put it on the beach, gather around it, talk, cry, then carry her coffin to the cemetery. They didn't need to buy a gondola, he had one in his mind; they would build it; he'd tell them how.

It was insane, everyone knew it, and they would have pressed the point but he was red-eyed, stricken, a fragile old man with who knew how many days left on the earth. When days are scarce, what better way to spend them than in a bout of madness? And anyway, Salomé thought, grief needs a place to pour to. The grief in her was rising in a cold, enormous sea-salt wave, expanding and expanding, larger than her, than the house, than the city, wet and ancient, rushing around her, submerging her completely, a cleansing force that seemed capable of washing the whole world, and she would not drown if she could move her hands, make something, hammer, carry, saw. She couldn't stop. The gondola took shape in Tío Bruno's garage. It took three days and three nights. There were planks to gather, meals to serve, nails to hammer, tears to wipe, wood to cut, wood to sand, wood to carve, instructions to absorb from Ignazio, on his rocking chair, arthritic hands poised in his lap. Sawdust entered everything: Salomé's clothes, her breath, her fingernails, the scent of all her cousins as they worked. Mamá prepared a lining of fine yellow silk, and as she sewed she did not weep but seemed transported, transfixed, a woman stitching the fabric of sorrow or passion or time. The boat's inner anatomy unfolded, and then its body, long and sinuous.

"There has to be an oar," Ignazio said.

"Why?"

"Let's not."

"We won't be rowing."

Ignazio scowled. "It's not a gondola without an oar."

They made an oar. They carved the sides of the gondola with images: leaves, crosses, curling vines, fish, moons, knives, rough-hewn angels, even rougher sylphs (at Abuelo's insistence) engaged in coitus, **V**'s with their arms extended like birds in flight.

On New Year's Day, 1990, the family hauled the gondola and the coffin to the shore. They went at dawn, for privacy, twenty-six of them, all in black. The early sun was pale on the stairs down to the sand. Behind them, the city was still dancing or asleep, dreaming at the lip of a new decade.

The gondola landed at the edge of the water. Salomé helped her uncles place the coffin in its hull. The crowd circled around it. They stood still. Someone coughed.

"Bueno," said Abuelo. "Who wants to start?"

Tío Marco told the first story about his mother, her strong will, her wrath the time her little sons were taken to a bar. Tía Mirna spoke of Pajarita's patience. She explained things with such grace, such a calm presence, she taught me how to be a mother. Clara told the story of the Final Empanada, which everybody knew, having been there, but savored anyway.

Eva read a poem she had written years ago, in Argentina, a poem about a woman who has a vision of her mother in an ethereal tree, and the woman is sick, and the vision saves her life. Salomé stopped listening. The words became sounds that blended together and told her as much as words themselves. She looked past the black-clad bodies, at the water. It had been another sleepless night and soon she would lie down again, but for now her exhaustion was a sword, a sharp lucidity, cutting through the air to peel away the layers of time, so that she saw beyond her own longing and pain into the whole of it, the huge span of the river, and she could swear the long brown water surged with people—they were all here, they rode the waves: the young man in his boat from Italy; the poet-girl escaping a bright city; Artigas; Pajarita; the dead and the past spectres of the living, sighing on the surface of the water, listening to voices from the land, shifting, floating, staring, sparking, dimming, reaching, pressing toward the shore—and it seemed as though they'd always pressed the water, as though the water would not be itself without them, as though they would press on past time and death and sadness, without ever arriving, some dark exquisite secret in the pressing. Finally the speeches trailed to silence. The mourners shifted awkwardly. The breeze tickled their necks.

Ignazio surveyed them. He looked like a paper version of himself. "I need a moment with her. Alone."

They hesitated.

"Go all the way back to the stairs, so you can't hear us."

Reluctantly, they walked away, a cloud of black cloth moving across the sand. They gathered at the steps. Tío Bruno pulled out his **mate.** Salomé sat down on the steps and closed her eyes. Behind her lids she still saw the crowded river, and saw herself at the shore, a stone's throw from the spectres. We are still here, their faces said, and she said back without speaking, So am I. She met their eyes and they stared back at her, faces awash with blue-green light.

She opened her eyes to the sound of her uncles shouting. She could not understand their words, but then she saw them, her uncles, running toward the water, flapping their arms like clumsy ravens. The gondola was gone—no, not gone: it had pushed out onto the river, it was mov-ing away, and Abuelo was in it with the coffin, his back turned toward the shore. He was rowing, fiercely, with shocking strength, bent into motion, ninety-five years old, intent on getting away with his stolen goods, a pirate with his coffin-treasure, his children and grandchildren and great-grandchildren yelling at the water's edge, plunging into the water fully clothed, swimming in pursuit, but who knew where that old man was getting his strength, what a bastard, what a madman, there was no one like him in the world, he just rowed farther and farther, into the river, he would row to Argentina, he would row to the Atlantic, he would row on back to Venice for all she knew, or he would drown with his arms around a coffin; and Salomé ran to the edge of the water, kicked her shoes off and ran in. The water was cold and soothing, it soaked her skirt, white foam gathered in a wreath around her knees, **wsshhh,** white tongues of foam and rush of current underneath, soft tongues but by the millions they could carve a shoreline into rock. The black cloth of her skirt rose around her, wet and floating, and she shouted along with the others but inside she shouted **Row,** for Ignazio, for his madness, for the woman in the coffin, for the apparitions on the river, for all of them left living on the shore, for the city itself, her city, Montevideo, the flattest city that ever dared to take the name of a mountain. The water was alive with morning sun. Its glitter hurt her eyes. Ignazio was becoming a black spot on the water. Her toes were in wet sand, her eyes on the horizon. She was ravenous—but before she ate today, before she slept, before her skirt had had a chance to dry, she'd pick up pen and paper and compose a letter, because she finally had the opening words. **Victoria,** she would write, **my dearest treasure, it's been so long.**

ACKNOWLEDGMENTS

Although this book is a work of fiction, much of it is based on actual historical events. I consulted a range of texts and sources in my extensive research. I am particularly indebted to **The Tupamaros**, by María Ester Gilio, and to the photographic archive at Montevideo City Hall. I am also indebted to Evelyn Rinderknecht Alaga, who sent me home from Uruguay with a stack of dog-eared books that contributed gems to my research.

One of my most important resources was my own family. In Uruguay, my cousins Andrea Canil and Oscar Martínez offered me a warm welcome, a place in their home, and long nights of discussing Uruguayan history and culture over **mate** or **grappa miel.** Tía Mary Marazzi read a draft, and demonstrated her belief in me long ago by carrying one of my childhood essays in her purse for years. Germán Martínez strengthened my hopes and desires for Uruguay's future. And many members of my family in Argentina, the United States, and France have held and nourished me in the long years of writing, and each of them has my heart: Cuti, Guadalupe, and Mónica López Ocón; Daniel, Claudio, and Diego Batlla; Ceci, Alex, and Megan De Robertis; Cristina De Robertis; and—last but never ever least—Margo Edwards and Thomas Frierson, Jr.

My gratitude goes to my extraordinary agent, Victoria Sanders, for her vision, acumen, and dedication, as well as to Benee Knauer for her in-sights and support. I am thankful to Carole Baron at Knopf for her skill, passion, and editorial finesse. My British editor, Susan Watt, also contributed insights for which I am deeply grateful.

I also thank Shanna Lo Presti, without whose encouragement and friendship I might never have finished; Carlos and Yvette Aldama, for their wisdom and for opening the most wondrous doors; Micheline Aharonian Marcom, for the way to the well; Daniel Alarcón, for his consistent generosity; Joyce Thompson, for the right words at the right time; and Jill Nagle, for sharing her savvy. Many more people read versions or ex-cerpts of this book at various stages, whether in writing groups or as friends, and I am grateful to each one for their time, attention, and feedback—particularly to Natalia Bernal, Ilana Gerjuoy, Denise Mewbourne, and Luis Vera. I am also thankful to the incomparable faculty and staff at Mills College, as well as to the gifted fellow students I met there, for the fuel, growth, and discoveries.

This book would simply not exist as it now does

without my wife, Pamela Harris, who has infused the words **faith** and **support** with new, incandescent meaning. No one has believed in this book more than you, nor brought more joy and adventure into my life. **The Invisible Mountain** is yours as much as it is mine, or anyone's.

Finally, I thank my ancestors for their lives and stories. There is no more precious inheritance in this world.

ABOUT THE AUTHOR

CAROLINA DE ROBERTIS was raised in England, Switzerland, and California by her Uruguayan parents. Her fiction literary translations have appeared in **Color-Lines, The Virginia Quarterly Review,** and **Zoetrope: All-Story,** among others. She is the recipient of a 2008 Hedgebrook Residency for Women Authoring Change and the translator of the Childean novella **Bonsái** by Alejandro Zambra. She lives in Oakland, California.

www.carolinaderobertis.com